Penguin Crime Fiction
Editor: Julian Symons
The Ninth Simenon Omn

Georges Simenon was born at Liège in Belgium in
1903. At sixteen he began work as a journalist
on the *Gazette de Liège*. He has published over
180 novels in his own name, sixty-seven of which
belong to the Inspector Maigret series, and his
work has been published in thirty-two languages.
He has had a great influence upon French cinema,
and more than forty of his novels have been filmed.

Simenon's novels are largely psychological. He
describes hidden fears, tensions and alliances
beneath the surface of life's ordinary routine
which suddenly explode into violence and crime.
André Gide wrote to him: 'You are living on a
false reputation – just like Baudelaire or Chopin.
But nothing is more difficult than making the
public go back on a too hasty first impression. You
are still the slave of your first successes and the
reader's idleness would like to put a stop to your
triumphs there . . . You are much more important
than is commonly supposed', and François
Mauriac wrote, 'I am afraid I may not have the
courage to descend right to the depths of this
nightmare which Simenon describes with such
unendurable art.'

Simenon has travelled a great deal and once lived
on a cutter, making long journeys of exploration
round the coasts of Northern Europe. He is
married and has four children, and lives near
Lausanne in Switzerland. He enjoys riding,
fishing and golf.

Georges Simenon

The Ninth
Simenon Omnibus

Penguin Books

Penguin Books Ltd,
Harmondsworth, Middlesex, England
Penguin Books Australia Ltd,
Ringwood, Victoria, Australia
Penguin Books (N.Z.) Ltd,
182–190 Wairau Road, Auckland 10, New Zealand

Maigret et Monsieur Charles first published in France, 1972
Copyright © Georges Simenon, 1972
Translation published in Great Britain by Hamish Hamilton, 1973
Translation copyright © Georges Simenon, 1973

La Disparation d'Odile first published in France, 1971
Copyright © Georges Simenon, 1971
Translation published in Great Britain by Hamish Hamilton, 1972
Translation copyright © Georges Simenon, 1972

Le Chat first published in France, 1967
Copyright © Georges Simenon, 1967
Translation published in Great Britain by Hamish Hamilton ,1972
Translation copyright © Georges Simenon, 1972

Published in Penguin Books 1976

Made and printed in Great Britain by
Hunt Barnard Printing Ltd, Aylesbury, Bucks
Set in Monotype Times

Contents

Maigret and Monsieur Charles

Translated by Marianne Alexandre Sinclair

Chapter One

Maigret was playing in the tepid rays of a March sun. It was not with his childhood bricks he was playing but with his pipes.

He kept five or six pipes on his desk and he invariably selected with care the one which suited his mood.

His gaze was vacant and he was slumped in his chair. He had just made a decision which would affect the remaining years of his career. He had no regrets, but even so he could not help feeling a touch of melancholy.

Mechanically and with great solemnity, he rearranged the pipes on his blotting paper in more or less geometric patterns, or else into shapes that reminded him of various animals.

His morning's post lay in a pile on the right-hand side of his desk and he did not feel like dealing with it.

On his arrival at the Police Judiciaire just before nine o'clock, he had found a summons from the chief of police. This in itself was unusual and as he went to the Rue du Palais he wondered what it could mean.

The chief of police saw him immediately and was extremely affable and well-disposed.

'Can you guess why I wanted to see you?'

'I must admit I can't.'

'Do sit down and light your pipe.'

The chief of police was a youngish man, hardly more than forty. The product of a good university, he was a stylish dresser, perhaps a little too much so.

'You know that the head of the Police Judiciaire is retiring next month after twelve years in office . . . I discussed the question of his successor with the Minister of the Interior yesterday and we both agreed to offer you the post.'

The chief of police undoubtedly expected Maigret's face to

light up with joy. Instead of which the latter's expression grew sombre.

'Is it an order?' he asked, almost abruptly.

'No, of course it isn't. But as you know it's an important promotion; there's no higher position in the Police Judiciaire . . .'

'I know that. Yet I'd still prefer to remain at the head of the Criminal Division. Please don't be offended at my reaction. I've had forty years of active police service. It would be hard for me to spend my days cooped up in an office, looking through files and occupying myself with administration . . .'

The chief of police could not conceal his astonishment.

'Shouldn't you think it over for a few days before giving me your answer? Perhaps you'd like to talk it over with Madame Maigret?'

'She would understand how I feel.'

'So do I and I don't want to insist . . .'

Nevertheless, his expression was one of slight annoyance. He understood without understanding. Maigret needed the human contact which he got from his investigations. People had often disapproved of his not directing his inquiries from his office and of his becoming actively involved, carrying out routine tasks usually considered the duty of ordinary inspectors.

Maigret was playing, his mind a blank. He had now arranged his pipes in a pattern which reminded him of a crane.

The sun poured in through the window. The chief of police had accompanied him to the door and had shaken hands in a friendly way. Yet Maigret knew that his decision would be resented in high places.

Slowly, he lit one of his pipes and began to smoke it, taking short puffs.

It had taken him a few minutes to decide about a future which of itself would not be very long, since he would retire in three years' time. Good God, they could at least allow him to spend those three remaining years as he wished!

He needed to escape from his office, to be out and about in all weathers, to discover a whole new world with each inquiry. He needed those long hours spent waiting at the counter of some *bistrot*, drinking calvados or beer depending on the circumstances. He needed the long, patient struggle in his office with a suspect who, after refusing to say anything for several hours, would often break down and make a dramatic confession.

He was uneasy. What he feared was that they would reconsider and somehow oblige him to accept the promotion. And he did not want that at any price, even though it was as good as a field-marshal's baton.

He continued to rearrange his pipes, occasionally moving one like a chess piece. A discreet knock made him jump, on the door which communicated with the inspectors' duty room.

Before he could reply, Lapointe walked in.

'Sorry to disturb you, *patron* . . . '

'You're not disturbing me in the least . . . '

It was now almost ten years since Lapointe had joined the Police Judiciaire, and he had been known as 'little Lapointe'. In those days, he had been tall and lanky. He had since grown stouter. He had got married and had two children. Yet he was still known as 'little Lapointe', and some would have added: 'Maigret's pet'.

'There's a woman in my office who insists on seeing you personally. She won't tell me anything. She's sitting bolt upright on her chair and is very much determined to have her way.'

That often happened. People would read about Maigret in newspaper articles and would insist on seeing him in person. It was often difficult to make them change their minds. Some of them even managed, God knows how, to discover his home address and would come and ring his doorbell in the Boulevard Richard-Lenoir.

'Did she give you her name?'

'Here's her card':

> *Madame Sabin-Levesque*
> *207 bis Boulevard Saint-Germain*

'She seems peculiar to me,' Lapointe added. 'She stares right at you and she's got a sort of nervous twitch that makes the right-hand side of her mouth droop. She hasn't taken her gloves off, but you can see that her fingers never stop clenching.'

'Ask her to come in, and stay with us. Bring your short-hand pad just in case.'

Maigret looked at his pipes with a sigh of regret. His little break was over.

He stood up when the woman came into the room.

'Please sit down, Madame ...'

She was staring at him.

'Are you really Superintendent Maigret?'

'I am.'

'I imagined you fatter.'

She was wearing a fur coat with a matching hat. Was it mink? Maigret had no idea; the wife of a divisional superintendent usually had to make do with rabbit fur or, at best, musquash and racoon.

Madame Sabin-Levesque's gaze travelled slowly round the office, as though making an inventory. When Lapointe sat down at one end of the desk with his pencil and pad, she asked:

'Is this young man going to stay here?'

'Yes, he is.'

'He's going to take down our conversation?'

'It's the regulations.'

She frowned and her fingers clasped her crocodile handbag more firmly.

'I thought I could speak to you in private.'

Maigret did not answer. He was watching her and he had to agree with Lapointe that there was something extremely odd about her. At some moments, her stare was so intense as to be embarrassing, while at others she seemed far away.

'I suppose you know who I am?'

'I've read the name on your card.'

'Do you know who my husband is?'

'I expect he has the same name as you.'

'He's one of the best-known solicitors in Paris.'

The corners of her lips twitched constantly. She seemed to find it difficult to keep calm.

'Please go on.'

'He's disappeared.'

'In that case, you shouldn't have come to me. There's a special department which concerns itself with missing persons.'

She gave a sad, ironic smile and did not bother to answer.

It was difficult to decide how old she was. Probably in her early forties, at most forty-five; but her face was lined and there were bags under her eyes.

'Had you been drinking before you came here?' Maigret suddenly asked her.

'Do you really want to know?'

'Yes, I do. It was you who insisted on coming to see me, wasn't it? You must expect me to ask questions you might consider indiscreet.'

'I expected you to be different, more understanding.'

'It's precisely because I'm trying to understand that I must know certain things.'

'I had two glasses of cognac, to give me courage.'

'Only two?'

She looked at him without replying.

'When did your husband disappear?'

'Over a month ago. On February 18th. It's now the 21st of March . . .'

'Did he tell you he was going off on a journey?'

'He didn't tell me anything.'

'And you've waited until now to tell us that he's disappeared?'

'I'm used to it.'

'To what?'

'To his going away for several days at a time.'

'How long has this been going on?'

'For years. It began shortly after our marriage, fifteen years ago.'

'Doesn't he give you any explanation when he goes away?'

'I don't think he does go away.'

'I don't understand.'

'He stays in Paris or in the suburbs.'

'How do you know?'

'Because in the beginning I had him followed by a private detective. Then I stopped it, because it was always the same thing.'

She spoke with some difficulty; she had certainly drunk more than two glasses of cognac. And it wasn't simply to give herself courage that she had drunk them, for it was obvious from her raddled face and from the effort she had to make to keep her composure that she often got drunk.

'I'm waiting for you to tell me the details.'

'My husband's like that.'

'Like what?'

'He has these fancies all of a sudden. He meets a woman he likes and he feels the need to live with her for a few days. So far, his longest romance, if you could call it that, has lasted two weeks.'

'Do you mean to tell me that he picks up these women in the street?'

'Almost. He usually finds them in nightclubs.'

'Does he go out by himself?'

'Always, yes.'

'He never took you with him?'

'We have meant nothing to each other for years.'

'Yet you're worried.'

'I am, for his sake.'

'Not for your own sake?'

She gave him a hard, defiant look.

'No.'

'You don't love him any more?'

'No.'

'Does he love you?'

'Even less so.'

'But you still live together.'

'We have a big flat. We keep different hours, so we don't meet often.'

With astonishment across his face, Lapointe continued to take his shorthand notes.

'Why did you come here?'

'So that you'd find him.'

'This is the first time you've been worried?'

'A month is a long time. He didn't take anything with him, not even a small suitcase, no spare clothes, nothing. He didn't even take one of the cars.'

'Have you several cars?'

'Two. A Bentley, which he usually takes, and a Fiat, which I normally use.'

'Do you drive?'

'Our chauffeur, Vittorio, drives me when I go out.'

'Do you get out a lot?'

14

'Nearly every afternoon.'

'Do you go and see friends?'

'I don't have any friends . . .'

Maigret had seldom met such a bitter, disconcerting woman before.

'Do you go shopping?'

'I loathe going into shops.'

'Do you go for walks in the Bois de Boulogne, or anywhere else?'

'I go to the cinema.'

'Every day?'

'Almost every day. When I don't feel too tired.'

As with all addicts, the moment had come when she needed a drink to give herself a lift. Maigret could see that she would have given anything for a brandy, but he did not intend to offer her one, even though he kept a bottle in his cupboard for special occasions. He felt slightly sorry for her.

'I'm trying to understand, Madame Sabin.'

'Madame Sabin-Levesque,' she said, correcting him.

'As you wish. And so your husband disappears regularly?'

'Never for as long as a month.'

'So you've told me already.'

'I have a foreboding.'

'What kind of foreboding?'

'I'm afraid something may have happened to him . . .'

'Do you have any reasons for supposing that?'

'No. You don't need a reason to have a foreboding.'

'According to you, your husband is a prominent solicitor.'

'Let's say that he has one of the most successful practices in Paris.'

'How does he manage to go away so regularly?'

'Gérard isn't at all like the usual solicitor. He inherited his father's firm, but it's the head clerk who handles everything . . .'

'You seem tired . . .'

'I'm always tired. My health isn't good.'

'What about your husband's health?'

'He's forty-eight, but he's as fit as a young man.'

'From what you tell me, we'd be most likely to pick up his trail around the nightclubs . . .'

'That right.'

Maigret was thoughtful. He felt that he was on the wrong track and that her answers were not getting them anywhere.

He wondered for a moment if the woman were mad, or at least unbalanced. Quite a few of that sort had sat in his office and he was always at a loss to know how to deal with them.

Her actual words made sense and sounded normal enough, but at the same time one could sense a divorce between her and reality.

'Do you know if he had a lot of money on him?'

'As far as I know, he mostly used his cheque-book.'

'Have you discussed this with the head clerk?'

'We're not on speaking terms.'

'Why not?'

'Because about three years ago my husband forbade me to go down to the office.'

'Why was that?'

'I don't know.'

'You must know the head clerk, even if you're not on good terms with him.'

'His name is Lecureur; he's never liked me much.'

'Did he work in the firm before your father-in-law died?'

'He's been there since he was twenty-two.'

'He may know more about your husband's whereabouts.'

'Perhaps. But if I went to ask him he wouldn't tell me anything . . .'

Maigret was beginning to find that twitch of hers exasperating. He realized that the interview was becoming more and more of an ordeal for her, but in that case why had she come?

'Was there a marriage contract between you?'

'No.'

'Have you any money of your own?'

'No.'

'Does your husband give you all the money you need?'

'Yes, he does. He's not at all mean. I couldn't swear to it, but I think he is very rich.'

Maigret was questioning her in no particular order. He had investigated a number of avenues at random and, so far, he had got nowhere.

16

'Listen, you're tired. That's understandable. If you don't mind, I'll come and see you at your flat this afternoon . . . '

'As you wish.'

She did not get up, but still fidgeted with her handbag.

'What do you think of me?' she finally asked him, in a lower voice.

'I don't think anything yet.'

'You find me complicated, don't you?'

'Not necessarily.'

'The girls at school used to find me complicated and I've never really had any friends.'

'Yet you're very intelligent.'

'Do you think so?'

She smiled, her lips quivering as she did so.

'It hasn't done me any good.'

'Have you ever been happy?'

'Never. I don't know the meaning of the word.'

She pointed to Lapointe, who was still taking notes in shorthand.

'Does this conversation really have to be recorded? It's difficult to talk freely when someone's writing down every word you say.'

'If there's something confidential you want to tell me, we'll stop taking notes.'

'I have nothing more to say just now . . . '

She got up with some effort. Her shoulders drooped, her back was slightly hunched, and she was hollow-chested.

'Does he have to come with you this afternoon?'

Maigret hesitated, wanting to give her a chance.

'I'll come alone.'

'What time?'

'The time which suits you best.'

'I usually have a nap. What about four o'clock?'

'Fine.'

'It's on the first floor. You take the right-hand door under the arch.'

Without offering her hand, she walked stiffly to the door, as if afraid of losing her balance.

'Thank you all the same for agreeing to see me,' she said, in a remote voice.

17

And, throwing Maigret one last glance, she made her way towards the large staircase.

The two men stared at each other, as though to postpone the moment when both would open their mouths to begin asking questions. The difference was that Lapointe seemed dumbfounded, while the chief superintendent's expression still remained solemn, although there was a malicious gleam in his eye.

He went over to open the window and began to fill a heavy pipe which he had chosen. Lapointe could no longer contain himself.

'What do you think, *patron*?'

Those who worked with him rarely ventured to ask such a question, since he usually replied by grunting, in a now familiar way:

'I don't think.'

Instead, it was now he who asked a question:

'About this vanished husband story?'

'About her particularly . . . '

Maigret was lighting his pipe as he stood by the window, contemplating the *quais*. He gave a sigh.

'She's a strange woman . . . '

Nothing more. He did not try to analyse his impressions, still less put them into words. Lapointe could see that he was troubled and regretted having thoughtlessly asked the question. Nevertheless, he murmured:

'Perhaps she's mad?'

The chief superintendent looked at him searchingly, without speaking. He remained a long while by the window, then asked:

'Will you have lunch with me?'

'Certainly, *patron*, especially since my wife's gone to see her sister at Saint-Cloud.'

'Shall we say in fifteen minutes?'

When Lapointe had left, Maigret picked up the phone and rang the Boulevard Richard-Lenoir.

'Is that you?' his wife's voice asked, even before he had opened his mouth.

'It's me.'

'I bet you're going to tell me you're not coming home for lunch.'

'You win your bet.'

'At the Brasserie Dauphine?'

'With Lapointe.'

'A new case?'

His last important case had ended three weeks earlier; this wish of his to have lunch at the Place Dauphine was, in fact, his way of celebrating his return to active duty. It was also partly his way of cocking a snook at the chief of police and the Minister of the Interior, who had wanted to lock him up in a luxurious office.

'Yes.'

'I haven't read anything in the papers.'

'The papers haven't mentioned it yet; perhaps they never will.'

'Have a good lunch – I only had grilled herrings for you.'

He remained in thought for a few minutes, then picked up the phone again, staring at the armchair where his visitor had sat. He could almost picture her sitting there again, so edgy, with those staring eyes and nervous tic.

'May I speak to Maître Demaison, please?'

He knew that Maître Demaison would be at home at this hour.

'Maigret speaking.'

'How are you? Got some poor old murderer you want me to defend?'

'Not yet. I only want some information. Do you know a solicitor on the Boulevard Saint-Germain by the name of Sabin-Levesque?'

'Gérard? I'll say I do! We read law together.'

'What do you think of him?'

'Has he gone off again?'

'You know about that?'

'All his friends know. He falls for a pretty woman now and then and vanishes for the night, or for a few days. He's got a taste for what you might call semi-professionals, such as strippers or nightclub hostesses.'

'Does this happen often?'

'As far as I know, about ten times a year . . . '

'What's he like as a solicitor?'

'He inherited one of the best practices in Paris, practically the whole of the Faubourg Saint-Germain, but he's nothing like the

19

conventional type of solicitor. He wears light-coloured suits and sometimes check tweed jackets.

'He's a very cheerful, easygoing fellow who looks on the bright side of life, but that doesn't prevent him from managing his clients' affairs very astutely . . .

'I've known several men and women who are clients of his; they think the world of him . . .'

'Do you know his wife?'

There was a pause.

'Yes.'

'Well?'

'She's an odd woman. *I* wouldn't like to live with her, and I dare say Gérard feels the same way, since he makes a point of avoiding her.'

'Does she ever go out with him?'

'Not as far as I know.'

'Does she have any men or woman friends?'

'I don't know of any.'

'Any lovers?'

'I've never heard any gossip about her. Most people think she's either neurotic or mad. She's a heavy drinker.'

'I've noticed that.'

'I've told you all I know.'

'It seems the husband disappeared a month ago.'

'And no one's heard from him?'

'Apparently not. She was worried and so she came to see me this morning.'

'Why you and not the Bureau of Missing Persons?'

'I pointed that out to her. She didn't answer.'

'Usually, when he's away for several days, he keeps in touch by phone with his head clerk, whose name I've forgotten . . . Have you spoken to him?'

'I'll probably be seeing him this afternoon.'

A few minutes later, Maigret opened the door of the inspectors' duty room and motioned to Lapointe. The latter darted forward with a clumsiness he could not conceal in Maigret's presence. For Maigret was his god.

'We don't need our overcoats,' the chief superintendent said in a low voice. 'We're not going far.'

That morning he had only taken a light overcoat, which he had found hanging up on a hook.

The pavement echoed under their footsteps. It was good to be in the atmosphere of the Brasserie Dauphine again, with its mingled smells of cooking and drink. At the bar there were several police officers, to whom Maigret waved.

They went straight into the cosy dining-room, which overlooked the Seine.

The proprietor shook hands with them.

'A little glass of *pastis* to greet the Spring?'

Maigret hesitated, then finally agreed, and so did Lapointe. The proprietor brought the drinks.

'An inquiry?'

'Probably.'

'Mind you, I'm not asking any questions . . . We're discretion personified here and our lips are sealed . . . How would you like some sweetbreads with mushrooms?'

Maigret sipped his *pastis*, his first for a long time. The *hors d'oeuvres* was set out before them.

'I wonder if she'll be more talkative this afternoon when I'm not there.'

'I wonder too . . .'

They took their time over the meal, and the proprietress insisted on their trying her home-made almond cake with which, after wiping her hands on her apron, she now served them.

It was not quite two o'clock when the two men climbed the vast staircase of the Police Judiciaire.

'They've modernized the buildings but it never occurred to them to put in a lift,' Maigret grumbled, out of breath.

He went into his office, lit a pipe and began to sort through his mail in a desultory fashion. It consisted mainly of administrative forms which needed filling out and reports to be countersigned. The time passed slowly. Occasionally, he would look out of the window and let his mind wander far away from the office.

For once, Spring was on time. The air was crystal-clear, the sky a delicate blue, and the buds on the trees were already swelling. In a few days, the first leaves would begin to show their pale green shoots.

As he passed the door of the inspectors' duty room, he called out:

'I don't know when I'll be back.'

He had decided to walk to the Boulevard Saint-Germain, but he soon regretted the idea, for it seemed a long way to number 207 *bis*, and he had to mop his forehead several times during the journey.

The huge stone building, which had turned grey with age, looked like most of the other houses along the Boulevard. He went in through a highly-polished oak door and found himself in the vaulted entrance, at the end of which he could see a paved courtyard with old stables which had been converted into garages.

On the left-hand door there was a solicitor's gilded escutcheon and a brass plaque which stated:

Maître G. Sabin-Levesque
Solicitor

Across the way, to the right of the other entrance, a man was peering at him through the window of the concierge's lodge.

Madame Sabin-Levesque had told him that the flat was on the first floor. On the same side, there was another brass plaque which read:

Professor Arthur Rollin
Paediatrician
Third Floor – By appointment only

That doctor's fees must have been high. The lift was vast. Since the flat was only on the first floor, Maigret decided to walk up the elegant staircase, with its thickly-carpeted steps.

When he reached the first floor, he rang the bell. Almost instantly, an attractive young maid opened the door and took his hat.

'Will you please come in? Madame is expecting you . . . '

He found himself in a panelled hallway. The large drawing-room into which he was next ushered was also panelled, with nineteenth-century portraits hung on the walls.

He did not sit down. The furniture was massive, mostly in the Louis-Philippe style, and though the total effect was of luxury and comfort, all gaiety was absent.

'Madame is waiting for you in her boudoir. I'll take you there . . . '

They went through two or three more rooms, which Maigret did not have time to take in, until they at last came to the boudoir, hung with blue silk, where Madame Sabin-Levesque lay reclining on a chaise-longue. She was wearing a *peignoir* of darker blue and held out a hand loaded with rings to Maigret, who, not knowing whether to kiss or to shake it, merely touched it with his finger-tips.

'Please sit down. I'm sorry to be receiving you in this fashion, but I'm not feeling well and I think I'll go back to bed after our talk.'

'I'll try not to keep you long.'

'What's your impression of me?'

'I told you this morning that you're a very intelligent person.'

'You're wrong about that. I only follow my instincts, nothing more.'

'First of all, let me ask you a question. Before you came to tell me your husband had disappeared, did you check with the head clerk to find out if he had any news of him?'

'I rang him several times during the last month . . . There's a private line between the flat and the office . . . I ought to tell you that my husband owns this building. He inherited it from his father . . . '

'Monsieur Lecureur . . . that's his name, isn't it? . . . Monsieur Lecureur hasn't heard from him either?'

'Not once.'

'Did he on previous occasions?'

'I didn't ask him. I think I told you that I'm not on very good terms with him.'

She hesitated.

'Would you care for a brandy or anything else to drink?'

'No, thank you.'

'I'm going to have a brandy. You see, I'm not ashamed to drink in front of you . . . Anyway, everyone will tell you I'm an alcoholic, which is true . . . They'll probably also tell you I'm mad . . . '

She rang a bell and the butler arrived a few moments later.

'Bring me the brandy and a glass, Honoré . . . '

'Only one glass, Madame?'

'Yes, just one. Superintendent Maigret doesn't want a drink . . .'

Her manner had become rather aggressive. She stared at him defiantly, a smile hovering painfully on her bitter lips.

'Did you share a bedroom with your husband?'

'We did for about three months, immediately after we were married. Now the rooms on this side of the main drawing-room are mine. My husband's domain is those on the other side.'

'Do you usually have your meals together?'

'You've asked me that already . . . Yes, we do, once in a while, but we don't keep the same hours and we have different tastes . . .'

'What do you do during the holidays?'

'We have . . . Sorry, I mean Gérard was left a big villa near Cannes . . . We go there . . . He bought a yacht recently and I see even less of him than I do in Paris.'

'Does he have any enemies that you know of?'

'None that I can think of . . . except for me . . .'

'Do you hate him?'

'Not really. I don't even resent him. It's just his character.'

'Are you his heir?'

'Yes, his sole heir.'

'Is he very wealthy?'

'Enough to make quite a few women wish they were in my place. But, you see, it so happens that I'm not interested in money, and I'd be happier living in a garret . . .'

'Why don't you ask for a divorce?'

'Too lazy. Or too indifferent. There comes a time when one doesn't feel like anything any more; one just goes on repeating the same gestures, day after day, without thinking . . .'

She picked up her glass with a shaking hand.

'Cheers . . .'

She emptied it to the last drop.

'There, you see? I suppose I ought to blush with shame . . .'

'Who said you ought to? Your husband?'

'Yes, when I began drinking. That was many years ago . . .'

'And now?'

'He doesn't care.'

'Would you be relieved to discover he was dead?'

'Not really. He means so little to me, alive or dead.'

'You think some misfortune's happened to him, don't you?'

'I think it may have; that's why I came to see you.'

'What do you think could have happened?'

'He usually picks up his ... shall we call them his girlfriends? ... in nightclubs, where one meets all sorts of people ...'

'Do you know any of these clubs?'

'I know of about two or three, from finding some matchboxes with the names printed on them ...'

'What were they?'

'The *Chat Botté* ... the *Belle Hélène* ... let me see ... the *Cric-Crac* ...'

'Have you ever felt tempted to go and see one of them for yourself?'

'I'm not curious ...'

'So I see ...'

She was helping herself to more brandy and her lips had begun to twitch again. Her gaze was blank and unseeing; Maigret had the feeling that at any moment she might look up and demand to know what he was doing there.

'In other words, you think there may have been a crime?'

'Don't you?'

'Couldn't he have fallen ill?'

'He's as strong as a horse.'

'An accident ...?'

'I'd have seen it in the papers ...'

'Did you ring up the hospitals?'

'I did, yesterday.'

If she was capable of doing that, then despite appearances she was keeping her wits about her. There was a photograph in a silver frame on the white marble mantelpiece, and Maigret got up to have a closer look at it. It was a posed portrait of Madame Sabin-Levesque when much younger, probably before her marriage. She had been very pretty in those days, with something rather waif-like about her face.

'Yes, it's me ... I've changed, haven't I?'

'Was this photograph taken before or after your wedding?'

'A few weeks after. Gérard insisted on having it done, by a well-known photographer in the Boulevard Haussman ...'

'He must have been in love with you in those days . . . '

'I don't know. He seemed to be.'

'Did you grow apart suddenly?'

'No. The first time, he went off for twenty-four hours and I didn't say anything. He told me he'd gone to see one of his clients in the provinces . . . Later on, he began to do more or less as he pleased. He stopped telling me in advance. He'd go out after dinner and I'd never know when he'd be back.'

'What sort of man is he?'

'Everyone will tell you that he was a very cheerful person, who got on well with everybody and who was always ready to do others a favour. Some people found him rather childish . . . '

'And you?'

'I can't really complain. Either I simply didn't know how to handle him, or else he was mistaken about me . . . '

'In what way?'

'He took me for a different kind of person than I am . . . '

'What did you do before you met him?'

'I was a secretary in a law firm . . . Maître Bernard d'Argens, Rue de Rivoli . . . Gérard knew my boss . . . he came to his office several times . . . and then one day he asked me to go out with him . . . '

'Were you born in Paris?'

'No. In Quimper . . . '

'What makes you think he's been murdered?'

'Because there's no other explanation . . . '

'Is your mother still alive?'

'Yes. My father's dead. His name was Louis Frassier. He was an accountant. My mother's maiden name was Countess Outchevka . . . '

'Do you send her any money?'

'Of course I do. Gérard doesn't care about money. He used to give me as much as I wanted, with no questions asked . . . '

She emptied her glass and raised her handkerchief to her lips.

'Will you allow me to look around the flat?'

'I'll come with you . . . '

She got up from her chaise-longue and, walking carefully, made for the door.

Chapter Two

There was an atmosphere of wealth, the grand families of the last century, austerity even, about the apartment, which occupied a whole floor of the building. Madame Sabin-Levesque, still unsteady on her feet, began by showing Maigret round her rooms.

The boudoir gave on to a vast bedroom, also lined in blue silk, which seemed to be her favourite colour. The bed was unmade, though she did not seem bothered at giving Maigret this intimate glimpse of her life. The furniture was white. There was a half-empty bottle of brandy on the chest-of-drawers.

'What's your first name?' Maigret asked her.

'Nathalie. I suppose because of my Russian blood.'

The bathroom walls and floor were covered with grey-blue marble; it was as untidy as the bedroom.

There was another room, completely lined with cupboards, and a kind of small sitting-room not unlike the boudoir.

'This is where I take my meals when I don't wish to eat in the dining-room.' Her manner was detached, like that of a museum guide.

'Now we're going into the servants quarters.'

They first entered a very large room containing glass cabinets full of silverware, then a small white-painted dining-room, and finally into the kitchen with its old-fashioned stove and copper saucepans. There was an old woman at work in the kitchen.

'That's Marie Jalon. She was already here when my father-in-law was still alive.'

'When did he die?'

'Ten years ago.'

'So you lived here with him?'

'For five years ... '

'Did you get along well with him?'

'He was completely indifferent to me. I used to eat in the

27

dining-room in those days and I could easily count the number of times he spoke to me.'

'How did he get on with his son?'

'At nine o'clock, Gérard would go down to the office, where he had a room of his own. I don't really know what he did there.'

'Was he already in the habit of disappearing in those days?'

'Yes, for two or three days at a time.'

'What did his father say?'

'He'd pretend not to notice anything . . .'

Maigret felt as though he had stumbled on a different world, a decayed world, turned in upon itself.

They must have given balls and soirées here in the last century, or the beginning of this one, for there were not one but two drawing-rooms, of which the second was nearly as enormous as the first.

The panelling which covered the walls had grown dark with age.

The pictures hanging everywhere, portraits of gentlemen with side-whiskers and very high starched collars, also spoke of a bygone era.

It was as though at a given moment time had stopped.

'We're going into my husband's domain now . . .'

They went into a book-lined study. There were walnut library steps to get to the higher shelves, which reached the ceiling. The desk, placed at an angle near the window, was topped in brown leather, with leather accessories. Everything was tidy, as though no one lived there.

'Does he stay here in the evening?'

'When he's at home.'

'I see he has a television.'

'So do I, but I never watch it.'

'Have you ever spent an evening in this room?'

'Yes, just after we were married.'

She spoke with some difficulty and seemed totally indifferent to what words she was uttering. Those once more down-turned lips of hers gave her face a bitter expression.

'His bedroom . . .'

Maigret had had just enough time to establish that the drawers of the desk were locked. What did they contain?

The ceilings everywhere in the flat were extremely high. The windows were also high, though the dark red velvet curtains prevented much light from coming in.

The walls of the bedroom were not panelled but lined with light brown leather. It contained a double bed and some armchairs which showed signs of wear.

'Did you ever sleep here?'

'A few times during the first three months . . .'

He wondered if he could detect any hatred in her voice or her face.

She went on showing him round like a museum guide.

'His bathroom . . .'

He observed the toothbrush, the razor, the hairbrush and the comb.

'He never took anything with him?'

'Not as far as I know.'

A room lined with cupboards, like the one in Nathalie's suite, then an exercise room.

'Did he use it?'

'Hardly ever. He's grown rather plump; not exactly fat, but overweight . . .'

She was opening a door.

'Here's the library . . .'

It contained thousands of books, mostly old ones, with very few modern works.

'Did he read a great deal?'

'I didn't come to check on what he did in the evenings. We've reached the far side of the building, so these stairs will take you straight down to the office. Do you still need me?'

She was going off to her bottle again.

'I suppose you're going down to the office now?'

'As a matter of fact, I'd like to ask Monsieur Lecureur a few questions. I'm sorry to have disturbed you . . .'

She left him. Maigret felt sorry for her, but also found her irritating. He began filling his pipe as he went downstairs, for he had refrained from smoking in the flat.

When he entered the large office, where six typists were working busily, they looked up at him in surprise.

'Monsieur Lecureur, please.'

In the filing cabinet were hundreds of green-backed dossiers, of the type used by civil servants and most solicitors. A small dark-haired woman led him through a room which was quite bare except for one long table and a large old-fashioned safe.

'This way . . . '

In the next room, an elderly man sat alone, poring over a huge ledger. He glanced up without curiosity as Maigret went through, into the next room where five more people were working.

'Is Monsieur Lecureur alone?'

'Yes, I think so.'

'Will you please ring through and ask him if Chief Superintendent Maigret can see him?'

They stood waiting for a moment, then a padded door opened.

'Come in, please . . . I must admit I'm rather glad you've come . . . '

Lecureur was younger than Maigret had imagined, after hearing that he had worked for Monsieur Sabin-Levesque's father; he did not seem more than fifty. He was dark, with a small moustache, and wore a very dark grey suit, which seemed almost black.

'Please sit down.'

More panelling. The firm's founder must have had an exaggerated passion for walls covered in dark wood.

'I imagine you've been notified by Madame Sabin-Levesque?'

'Yes. In fact, she came to see me in my office this morning.'

The mahogany furniture was in the Empire style.

'I assume you take over Monsieur Sabin-Levesque's work when he's away?'

'It's my duty, as his head clerk. However, there are certain deeds I can't sign, so it's rather awkward.'

He was a self-assured man and, like many men who constantly deal with important people, there was something not exactly servile but perhaps slightly deferential about his manner.

'Was he in the habit of warning you when he went off like that?'

'No. It was never planned in advance. Of course, I know nothing about his private life . . . I'm only guessing. He often went out in the evening . . . almost every evening, in fact . . . '

'Just a moment. Did he play an active role in the running of this practice?'

'He spent most of the day in his office and he saw nearly all the clients personally. He never gave the impression of being a busy man and yet he worked harder than I did . . . Especially at anything which concerned the handling of private fortunes or buying and selling country houses and estates . . . He was incredibly shrewd and I couldn't have done the same in his place . . .'

'Is his office next to yours?'

Lecureur went over to a door and opened it.

'Here it is . . . You see, it's just like this one except that it's got three more armchairs.'

The spotlessly tidy office overlooked the Boulevard Saint-Germain and the monotonous rumbling of the traffic could be heard outside.

The two men went back into Monsieur Lecureur's office.

'I gather he usually appeared again after two or three days . . .'

'There have been times recently when he stayed away for as long as a week.'

'But he kept in touch with you?'

'He nearly always rang me up to find out if he was needed . . .'

'Do you know where he rang you from?'

'No.'

'Do you have any idea if he had another flat in Paris?'

'I've thought about that possibility. He never had much money on him and he paid for nearly everything by cheque . . . I saw the cheque stubs before they went to the accountant . . .'

He stopped talking and frowned.

'I wonder if I have the right to go into these matters. I am still bound by professional etiquette.'

'Not if, say, he's been murdered . . .'

'Do you really think something like that may have happened?'

'His wife seems to think so.'

Monsieur Lecureur shrugged, as if to imply that anything she said was of no account.

'To tell you the truth, the idea's crossed my mind too. It's the first time he's been away for so long and hasn't telephoned me. He had an appointment here more than a week ago with one of our clients, one of the largest, if not the largest landowner in France.

'He knew about it . . . he may have seemed absent-minded or rather frivolous, but in point of fact he never forgot anything and he was if anything over-conscientious as far as his professional life was concerned . . .'

'What did you do?'

'I postponed the appointment and pretended he was ill.'

'Why didn't you warn the police if you were worried?'

'It was up to his wife, not me, to do that . . .'

'She tells me she never comes down here.'

'That's true . . . She came in once or twice, years ago, but she didn't stay for long . . .'

'Did she get a chilly reception?'

'No one was exactly delighted to see her, not even her husband.'

'How come?'

Once again, Lecureur stopped, even more embarrassed this time than previously.

'Please excuse me, Monsieur Maigret, but you're placing me in an awkward position. My employer's relations with his wife are no business of mine . . .'

'Not even if a crime's been committed?'

'Naturally, that would be a different matter . . . We all love Monsieur Gérard . . . I call him that because I've known him almost since his student days . . . Everyone who works for him admires him . . . They don't presume to judge his private life . . .'

'I gather they don't feel the same way about his wife.'

'It's as though she were a discordant element in the house. I'm not saying she's mad, but the fact is that she gets under everyone's skin.'

'Because of her drinking?'

'There's that, too.'

'Was your employer unhappy with her?'

'He never complained. Over the years, he's made another life for himself . . .'

'A moment ago you spoke about those cheque stubs that would pass through your hands. I imagine some of those cheques were made out to the women he stayed with now and again . . .'

'I suppose so, but there's nothing to prove it . . . the cheques weren't made out to specific people but to the bearer . . . Some of them were for five thousand francs, anything up to twenty thousand . . . '

'Were any of the cheques made out for the same sum every month?'

'No. Which is why I don't think he did rent another flat.'

The two men looked at each other in silence. Eventually, the head clerk continued, with a sigh:

'Some of our employees saw him now and again going into a nightclub . . . On those occasions, he nearly always vanished for a time . . . '

'Do you believe something's happened to him?'

'I'm afraid so. What do you think, Superintendent?'

'Judging by the little I know so far, I think something may have happened to him, too . . . Did he ever receive calls from women in his office? . . . I'm assuming all incoming calls go through a switchboard . . . '

'I've asked our operator about that, of course . . . There's no record of any calls of that kind . . . '

'Which leads on to suppose that he took an assumed name whenever he disappeared like that . . . '

'I think I ought to mention one thing . . . I began to get worried two weeks ago . . . I rang up Madame Sabin-Levesque to tell her so and advised her to get in touch with the police . . . '

'What did she say?'

'That there was nothing to worry about yet and that she would take care of the matter in due course . . . '

'Didn't she ask you to come upstairs or else come down here herself to talk it over with you?'

'No.'

'I haven't any more questions to ask you for the time being. If you have anything new to tell me, will you please ring me up at the Police Judiciaire? Oh yes, I just wanted to know one more thing . . . Do the servants upstairs feel the same way about Madame Sabin-Levesque as the staff do down here?'

'Yes, they do. Particularly the cook, Marie Jalon, who's been there for forty years and who knew Monsieur Gérard when he was a child. She absolutely loathes her.'

'What about the others?'

'They just put up with her. Only the maid, Claire Marelle, is devoted to her. It's she who undresses her and puts her to bed when she collapses on the floor ... '

'Thank you.'

'Are you going to open an inquiry?'

'Yes, though I haven't much to go on. I'll keep in touch.'

Maigret left the building and went into a café next to the Métro Solferino. He did not order a brandy, for Madame Sabin-Levesque had put him off that drink for some time; instead he had a big glass of ice-cold beer.

'I want a *jeton* for the telephone.'

He went into the phone-booth and looked up the number of the lawyer Nathalie claimed to have worked for before her marriage. The name Bernard d'Argens was not in the directory.

He drank his beer and then took a taxi, asking the driver to take him to the Rue de Rivoli.

'Wait for me. I shan't be long.'

He went to the concierge's lodge, which was like a little parlour. The concierge was not a woman but a white-haired man.

'Where can I find Maître d'Argens, please?'

'He's been dead for over ten years.'

'Were you here in those days?'

'I've been here for thirty years.'

'Who took over his practice?'

'No one. There's an architect there now.'

'Is all his staff gone too?'

'Maître d'Argens only had one old secretary, who retired to the country.'

'You don't remember someone called Mademoiselle Frassier?'

'A very lively, pretty brunette? ... She worked for Maître d'Argens over twenty years ago ... She only stayed for a year because the job didn't suit her. I don't know what became of her ... '

Maigret went back to his taxi, his brow clouded over. Of course, the inquiry had only just been opened, but it had got off to a bad start. There was almost nothing to go on, and they would also have to be very discreet, just in case the solicitor turned up suddenly without warning.

The sun had vanished behind the houses and it had grown

cooler. Maigret was sorry to have left his overcoat at the office.

He felt like another beer, so he asked the taxi to stop at the corner of the Quai des Orfèvres and the Rue du Palais.

He kept on thinking of Nathalie, that strange Madame Sabin-Levesque, and he had a feeling she knew a great deal more than she was giving away.

He went back to his office, filled one of his pipes, then walked over to the door of the inspectors' duty room. Lapointe was typing and Janvier was looking out of the window. Lucas was on the phone.

'Janvier . . . Lapointe . . . Will you both come into my office? . . .'

Janvier was not getting any younger either; he now had a promising pot-belly.

'Are you free, Janvier?'

'Nothing important right now. I've finished with the young car-thief . . .'

'Can you face spending the night out?'

'Why not?'

'I'd like you to go to the Boulevard Saint-Germain as soon as you can, to keep a watch on number 207 *bis* . . . I'll give you the particulars of a woman . . . If she leaves the house, you're to follow her . . . You'd better have a car handy . . .

'She's rather tall, dark and extremely thin, with staring eyes and a nervous twitch. If she goes out, she'll probably be walking, but she does have a chauffeur and two cars . . . A Bentley and a Fiat . . .

'Ask Lourtie to come and take over from you tomorrow morning and tell him what I've told you . . .'

'What is she wearing?'

'When she came here, she had a fur coat on, mink I think.'

'O.K., *patron.*'

Janvier went out and Maigret turned to Lapointe.

'How about you? Anything new?'

Lapointe blushed and stammered without looking at Maigret:

'Yes . . . a few minutes ago . . . There was a call . . .'

'Who from?'

'The woman this morning.'

'What did she want?'

'First she asked if you were there ... I told her you weren't. She sounded dead drunk.

' "Who is it speaking then?" she asked.

' "Inspector Lapointe."

' "What, the young nincompoop who was writing down everything I said this morning?"

' "That's right."

' "Well, could you kindly tell your boss from me to go to hell ... and the same goes for you, too ... " '

Lapointe, still embarrassed, went on:

'Then it sounded as if she were struggling with someone.

' "Leave me alone, for Christ's sake! ..."

'Then someone must have snatched the phone out of her hand because the line went dead.'

Just before he left the Police Judiciaire, Maigret said to Lapointe:

'Could you please come and collect me at my flat in one of the cars at eleven o'clock?'

'Tomorrow morning?'

'Tonight. I feel like going to take a look at a few nightclubs.'

Madame Maigret had kept the herrings for him, since it was one of his favourite dishes. He ate while watching the news on television in an absent-minded way. Madame Maigret could guess, just by looking at her husband, that his new case was a rather unusual one and that he was taking a special interest in it, almost treating it as if it concerned him personally.

And indeed, this was true. On that mild, clear first day of Spring, Maigret had been plunged into a world which was foreign to him; moreover, he had met a type of woman quite disconcertingly unlike any he had ever come across before.

'Will you get a dark suit out for me? My best one.'

'What's happening?'

'Lapointe is coming to fetch me at eleven. We're going to visit a few nightclubs.'

'That'll make a change for you, won't it?'

'If only it can help me to clear up a few problems ...'

He dozed in his armchair in front of the television set. At ten-thirty, his wife brought him a cup of coffee.

'You'll be staying up late . . . '

He lit a pipe, then started to sip the coffee; for him, a pipe always went well with coffee.

He had a wash in the bathroom and changed his clothes. Not that it mattered what he wore, but he belonged to a generation which had always changed into tails to go to the opera and into a dinner jacket for going out to a nightclub.

At five minutes to eleven, he thought he heard a car stopping outside. He opened the window and saw the small black police car drawn up at the kerb below, with a tall silhouette standing next to it.

He gave Madame Maigret a kiss and walked across to the door, grumbling, but at bottom delighted not to be the head of the Police Judiciaire.

'Now you're not to wait up for me . . . '

'I won't, don't worry. I'm sleepy.'

It was not too cold outside and the moon was rising over the roof-tops. Many windows were still lit up and some of them were open.

'Where are we going, *patron*?'

He took out an old envelope from his pocket. On it he had jotted down the addresses which he had found in the phone-book.

'Do you know the *Chat Botté*?'

'No.'

'It's in the Rue du Colisée . . . '

They went down the Champs-Elysées, with its double stream of car headlamps and its neon signs blazing on either side. A doorman stood in front of the nightclub entrance. He was wearing as much gold braid as an admiral and he gave them a military salute as he opened the swing doors for them. They went through a heavy red curtain and left their hats and coats in the cloakroom.

The pianist was allowing his fingers to wander the keyboard at random, while the guitarist was tuning his instrument. There was also a double-bass, but the musician who played it had not yet arrived.

The room was entirely decorated in red. The walls, the ceiling, the seats, everything was red, a rather orangey red which seemed cheerful rather than garish. The bar, by way of contrast, was of stark white stucco. Behind it, the barman was wiping glasses and putting them away.

The *maître d'hôtel* came up to them, without much enthusiasm. He had perhaps recognized Maigret, or else it was just that the two men did not look like serious customers.

Maigret shook his head and went towards the bar. Three women sat at separate tables and, at another table, a couple seemed to be arguing. It was still too early; the club would not come to life until midnight.

'Good evening, gentlemen . . What can I get you?'

The barman had white hair and looked distinguished. He was watching them with a show of unconcern.

'I don't suppose you serve beer?'

'No, Monsieur Maigret.'

'Give us whatever you like . . . '

'Dry Martini?'

'That'll do.'

One of the women came over to sit at the bar, but the white-haired barman made a slight gesture in her direction and she went back to her table.

When he had filled their glasses, he asked:

'Well?'

Maigret smiled.

'You're right, he admitted. 'We're not just here to have a good time. We're not here to make trouble for you either . . . I need some information . . . '

'If I can help, it'll be a pleasure . . . '

A kind of complicity had been established between the two men. Maigret found it hard, however, to describe someone he had never seen.

'Medium height, if anything a little on the short side. Between forty and forty-five years old . . . Plumpish . . . A pot-belly already . . . Fair hair which is thinning . . . a chubby face . . . He dresses very smartly, usually wears beige . . . '

'Are you looking for him?'

'I'd like to know where he is.'

'Has he disappeared?'

'Yes.'

'Has he committed any crime?'

38

'None.'

'It could be Monsieur Charles ... '

'Does the description fit?'

'More or less ... A very jolly sort, wasn't he? ... Always in a good mood? ... '

'I think so.'

'Haven't you met him?'

'No.'

'He comes here from time to time and sits at the bar. He orders a bottle of champagne ... then he takes a look around the room and goes over each hostess one by one ... When he finds one to his liking, he has her sent over ... '

'Does he stay late?'

'It depends ... Sometimes he leaves with the girl ... At other times he just slips her five hundred francs and goes away ... Probably to go and look elsewhere ... '

'When did you last see him?'

'Quite a long time ago ... Let me see, about six weeks ... perhaps two months ... '

'When he went off with one of the girls, did she stay away for a few days?'

'Not so loud. The proprietor doesn't like that kind of thing. There he is, over by those tables ... '

A man in a dinner jacket was watching them from a distance. He looked like an Italian, with brilliantined hair and a small moustache. He too had probably recognized the chief superintendent.

'In theory, the hostesses aren't allowed to leave before we shut ... '

'I know ... I also know that, in practice, the rule isn't too strictly enforced. Have any of the young women here ever gone out with him? ... '

'I think Martine has ... You'd better go to her table if you want to speak to her ... I'll have a bottle sent over ... '

The young woman, whose long hair fell loosely down over her shoulders, was looking at them, intrigued.

A few customers had arrived, some with their wives, and the trio was now playing a blues.

'Did you order something to drink?' she asked.

39

'The barman ordered it for us,' Maigret grunted, wondering how he would manage to charge this to expenses.

'Have you ever been here before?'

'No.'

'Would you like me to call one of my friends over?'

The proprietor, who was standing near the table, said to her: 'Watch out, Martine, they're cops.'

'Is that true?' she asked Maigret.

'Yes, it is.'

'Why do you want to talk to me in particular?'

'Because you've been out with Monsieur Charles.'

'What's wrong with that?'

She did not ask the question defiantly. Her voice remained gentle and friendly and she seemed amused by the whole incident.

'Nothing, but it so happens that Monsieur Charles disappeared a month ago. On February 18th, to be precise. Have you seen him since that date?'

'I wondered why he wasn't coming here any more. I mentioned it to some friends of mine ...'

'What do you think of him?'

'I'm sure his real name isn't Charles. He must be an important man who has to conceal his identity when he wants a bit of fun. He's very well-groomed and neat. I told him he had hands like a woman, they were so beautifully manicured ...'

'Where did you go with him?'

'I thought we'd go to a hotel, but he asked me to take him back to my place ... I've got a nice little flat on the Avenue de la Grande-Armée ... I don't usually take anyone there ... Mind you, I hardly ever go out with clients ... Some people think that's what hostesses are there for, but it isn't true ...'

The champagne had been poured out and she raised her glass.

'Here's to Monsieur Charles then, as it's thanks to him you're here. I do hope nothing's happened to him.'

'We have no idea. He just disappeared ...'

'Did that crazy wife of his get worried?'

'He told you about her?'

'We spent four days together ... He was funny; you know, he insisted on helping me do the cooking and the washing up ... Sometimes he spoke about himself in a vague sort of way ...

'I won't ask you who he is . . .'

'An important man . . . as you guessed . . .'

'Does he live in Paris?'

'Yes.'

'I suppose he has a little fling from time to time?'

'That's right . . . Four or five days, maybe a week . . .'

'I rang my boss, Monsieur Mazotti, and told him I was ill, but I don't suppose he believed me . . . He gave me a dirty look when I came back to the *Chat Botté* . . .'

'When did all this happen?'

'About two months ago. Perhaps a bit longer . . .'

'Was it the first time he had come to this nightclub?'

'I'd seen him here a few times before, sitting at the bar . . . I suppose he didn't find what he was looking for, because he left by himself . . .'

'Did he go to other nightclubs?'

'He didn't tell me, but I'm sure he must have done.'

'Did he have a car?'

'No. We walked back to my place, arm in arm. He was in such a good mood . . .'

'Had he drunk a lot?'

'Not what you'd call a lot; just enough to be feeling merry . . .'

'Did he say anything about having a bachelor flat in town?'

'Why, did he have one?'

'I don't know.'

'No. He wanted to come back to my flat . . . We were like a couple of newlyweds during those four days . . . He would watch me having a bath or getting dressed . . . He'd lean out of the window to see me leave when I went out shopping . . . Then, when I'd return, I'd find the table laid . . .'

'Can you think of anything else which would help me to find him?'

'No. I'm trying to think . . . We went for a walk in the Bois de Boulogne but it looked like rain, so we came home again quite soon . . . He was very . . .'

She stopped, grown suddenly shy.

'Go on.'

'You're going to laugh at me . . . He was very affectionate and considerate, just like a real sweetheart . . . When he left, he slipped a cheque in my hand . . . You're going already?'

Mazotti, the proprietor, was waiting for them by the red curtain which hung in front of the entrance.

'Did you find out what you wanted to know, Superintendent?'

'Martine will tell you. Goodnight . . . '

Maigret was beginning to get a clearer picture of Gérard Sabin-Levesque's character. He had just learned more about the solicitor than either Madame Sabin-Levesque or the head clerk had been able to tell him.

'Shall we go on?' he asked Lapointe.

'Why not, while we're at it? . . . *La Belle Helène*, Rue de Castiglione . . . '

The atmosphere of this nightclub was more genteel. Pastel shades everywhere and violins playing a slow waltz. Once again Maigret walked up to the bar, followed by Lapointe. He frowned when he saw the barman.

'Have they released you?' he asked.

'I'm on parole for good conduct . . . '

It was Maurice Mocco, a Corsican criminal who had a long record.

'What will you have to drink, Superintendent? . . . And what about you, young fellow? . . . Is this your son, Monsieur Maigret?'

'One of my inspectors.'

'I hope it's not me you're after?'

'No.'

'What will you have to drink?'

'Two beers . . . '

'I'm afraid we don't serve beer . . . '

'Then some water . . . '

'You must be joking!'

'No, I'm not. Do you know Monsieur Charles?'

'Which one? We've got at least two. The first one is completely bald and must be at least seventy. He's from Bordeaux; he comes to Paris once a week on business, then on to us for pleasure . . . The other one doesn't come so regularly . . . He's on the small side, very well-dressed, extremely friendly, always wears light colours . . . '

'Rather plump?'

42

'I suppose you could say that . . .'

'Has he ever gone off with one of the hostesses?'

'He usually leaves alone, but there was one girl who caught his eye once. Her name was Leila and she's been gone a long time . . . This happened last summer . . . They were sitting over at that table, having a chat . . . Leila kept on shaking her head and he kept on insisting . . . After he left, I called her over . . .

' "What sort of guy is he?" she asked me.

' "A real gent . . ."

' "He asked me to go to a country hotel with him for a few days . . . the simple life . . . fresh air . . . all that jazz!"

' "How much was he offering you?"

' "Ten thousand to start with . . . Then, when I refused, he put the price up to fifteen, then twenty thousand . . . He just couldn't believe it when I still refused . . .

' "The country, my eye! . . . With all the perverts you meet these days! . . ." '

'What became of Leila?'

'I think she got married to an engineer from Toulouse . . . She never came back here.'

Maigret needed fresh air himself, for it was terribly stuffy in the nightclubs and the perfume used by the women made him feel giddy. The two men walked down the deserted street.

'That old scoundrel, Mocco, gave us one precious piece of information, which is that Monsieur Charles sometimes took his conquests off to the country . . .'

'I think I know what you're getting at.'

'Those women come from every sort of background . . . I once met one who had a Ph.D. in sociology . . . some of them have lovers . . . and some of their lovers can be rather unsavoury characters . . .'

It was two in the morning, but Maigret felt wide-awake.

Ten minutes later, the two men got out of the car in the Rue Clément Marot, in front of the *Cric-Crac* nightclub, where pop music spilled out into the street. The exterior of the club was painted in rainbow colours, just like the interior, where couples were dancing on the tightly packed dance-floor.

Once again the two men headed for the bar. But this time the proprietor, a fair young man called Ziffer, went over to greet them instantly.

'What can I do for you, gentlemen?'

Maigret waved his badge under his nose.

'I beg your pardon, Superintendent ... I didn't recognize you ... It's so dark in here ...'

The room, which was quite small, had only one lamp, a slowly revolving globe entirely covered with tiny reflecting mirrors.

'You won't find anything irregular here, I assure you.'

'Do you know a Monsieur Charles?'

Ziffer frowned, like a man trying hard to remember something.

The barman, a very fat man with bushy eyebrows, called out:

'He always used to come and sit at the bar ...'

'When did you see him last?'

'Not for weeks ...'

'Did you see him on the 18th of February?'

'What day was that?'

'A Tuesday ...'

'I can't remember off-hand ... All I know is that he was sitting up at the bar with Zoé the last time he came here ...'

'Did she go off with him?'

'That isn't allowed, Superintendent,' the proprietor interrupted.

'I know ... I know ... Did she go off with him?'

'No. But he jotted down something in a little notebook; it must have been an address Zoé gave him ...'

'Is the girl here?'

'She's dancing just now ... The platinum blonde over there ... the one with the gorgeous breasts ...'

'I'll go and fetch her for you,' Ziffer offered eagerly.

And Maigret, mopping his forehead, once again asked the barman:

'I don't suppose you serve beer? ...'

Chapter Three

Zoé had big, innocent blue eyes just like a little girl. She fluttered her eyelashes and stared curiously at this unknown man, while the propretor whispered in her ear:

'It's Maigret, the famous Police Superintendent. You can be frank with him.'

She had obviously never heard of the superintendent, and she waited patiently for him to start asking her questions, like a schoolgirl in class.

'Do you know Monsieur Charles?'

'I know him by sight, of course. He comes here once in a while.'

'What do you mean by once in a while?'

'Nearly every week.'

'Does he go off with one of the hostesses every time?'

'Oh no! In fact, he practically never does. He takes a good look at us all and occasionally treats one of us to a bottle of champagne.'

'Does he dance?'

'Yes. He's a rotten dancer.'

'How long has it been since you saw him?'

She looked up at the ceiling, exactly like a schoolgirl answering her teacher.

'Let me see ... quite a long time ... Last time, we drank a bottle of champagne together ...'

'You don't happen to remember what date that was?'

'Yes I do ... It was the 18th of February ...'

'How can you remember that?'

'Because it was my birthday ... He even bought some flowers for me from Joséphine, the old flower-seller who comes in every night ...'

'Did he ask you to spend the night with him?'

'Yes he did ... I told him the truth, that I had a boy-friend

45

waiting for me at home and that made him sad ... I was sorry
because he's very nice ...'

'Did anything else happen?'

'I told him that if he wanted a nice girl I had a friend who
wasn't a hostess but who had men to visit her sometimes ... only
high-class ones, mind you ... I said I'd go and ring her up to find
out if she was free ... I spoke to Dorine ... She agreed to see
him ...'

'Did you give Monsieur Charles her address?'

'Yes, it's in the Avenue de Ternes ...'

'What time was it?'

'About one in the morning ...'

'Did he set off right away?'

'Yes.'

'Have you seen Dorine since?'

'I rang her up that same night at about three in the morning,
just to see if everything had gone well ... She told me Monsieur
Charles had not arrived yet and that she was still waiting for
him ... When I next saw her, she told me he never turned up ...'

'And since then what happened?'

'What do you mean?'

'Have you seen Monsieur Charles again?'

'No. Actually I'm surprised he's stayed away so long ...'

'Thank you, Zoé.'

'Is that all?'

'Yes, for the time being.'

He watched her return to her table; the proprietor came over
and asked:

'Are you satisfied?'

'Fairly.'

So far, Zoé was the last person to have seen the solicitor. He
had left at one o'clock in the morning to go to the Avenue de
Ternes and had never arrived there.

'Where now, chief?' Lapointe asked him, once again at the
wheel of the little car.

'Back home ... I've had enough for today and you must be
tired too ...'

'Funny kind of chap, wasn't he?'

'Yes, funny kind of chap. Either he had a soft spot for nightclub hostesses, or else it was just that he didn't want to complicate his life by having a regular mistress . . . '

When Maigret got home, he began to undress; Madame Maigret, who was in bed, asked him in a friendly voice:

'Did you enjoy yourself?'

'I think I've made a little discovery . . . we'll soon see if it's worth anything.'

'Not too tired?'

'I'm all right. Wake me up tomorrow at the usual time . . . '

He took a long time to fall asleep. He was feeling a bit edgy and his head still buzzed with the din of the nightclubs.

This did not stop him, however, from being in his office at nine o'clock on the following morning; the first person he saw in the inspectors' duty room was Janvier.

'Come in here . . . '

The sun was a little warmer than on the previous day; he had a slight headache, so he went to open the window.

'What sort of night did you have?'

'Quiet. Except for one odd incident.'

'Tell me about it . . . '

'I parked the car a hundred yards from the house . . . I was sitting at the wheel, watching number 207 *bis* . . . A few minutes after eleven, the door opened and I saw the woman coming out . . . '

'Madame Sabin-Levesque?'

'Yes. She was walking stiffly, as though she was finding it hard not to stagger . . . I let her go on a bit, then I started up the car . . . She didn't go far . . . Less than two hundred yards . . . She went into a phone-box . . . '

Maigret frowned.

'She put a coin in but she probably couldn't get through because she hung up again almost at once . . . She did the same thing a second time . . . The third time, she got through . . . She spoke for a long time and she twice had to put more money in . . . '

'Strange she didn't call from her own flat . . . I suppose she thought her line was being tapped . . . '

'I imagine so . . . When she came out of the phone-box, her coat fell open for a second and I could see she was only wearing a nightdress underneath ... She went straight back to 207 *bis*, rang the bell, and the door opened immediately ... Nothing else happened all night ... I passed on your instructions to Lourtie and Bonfils will take over from him at about midday ...'

'Get her phone tapped as soon as possible ...'

Janvier was about to leave the room.

'Ask them to tap the office phones too ... After that you can go to bed ...'

'Thanks, *patron*.'

Maigret rapidly glanced at his mail, signed a few forms and went in to tell the director of his progress.

'Are you going back there?'

'Yes. I don't think you'll see me at the office much during the next few days.'

Did the director know that Maigret had been offered his job? He did not mention it, but Maigret had the feeling that he was being unusually courteous today.

Lapointe had arrived, looking rather frail. He drove Maigret to the Boulevard Saint-Germain.

'Shall I come up with you?'

'Do. You may have to take some notes.'

'I've brought my notebook.'

Maigret almost stopped on the ground floor, but then he changed his mind and went up to the flat. Claire Marelle, the young maid, opened the door; she seemed far from delighted to see them.

'If it's Madame you've come to see, I can tell you straight away she's asleep ...'

This information did not stop Maigret from walking into the flat, with Lapointe at his heels.

'Sit down,' he said to the young woman, pointing to a chair.

'I'm not supposed to sit down in here ...'

'You're supposed to do as I tell you ...'

She finally sat down on the very edge of a leather-covered chair.

Some people disapproved of Maigret's methods. A police officer of his rank was supposed to summon witnesses to his office, and he should have sent an inspector on that tour around the nightclubs.

Maigret lit his pipe. Claire Marelle watched him disapprovingly; she obviously found his behaviour uncouth.

'What time did your mistress come home last night?'

'She would have had to leave before she could return.'

'All right, let's put it this way, what time did she go out?'

'I don't know.'

'Were you asleep?'

'I told you, she didn't go out.'

'I'm sure you're much too devoted to her not to stay up until you can put her to bed, considering the state she's usually in . . .'

The maid was quite pretty, but the sullen look she always wore did not suit her. She looked at Maigret, pretending to be indifferent.

'So what?'

'I can tell you that she came back around eleven-thirty.'

'She has the right to go for a breath of fresh air, doesn't she?'

'Didn't you feel worried when you saw her going out? She could barely stand on her feet . . .'

'You saw her?'

'One of my inspectors saw her. And do you know why she was going out at that time of night?'

'No.'

'To make a call from a public phone-box . . . Whom did she call up usually?'

'No one . . . Her hairdresser . . . Tradesmen . . .'

'I mean private calls . . . You don't ring up a hairdresser at eleven in the evening, or a dressmaker, or a shoemaker . . .'

'I don't know anything.'

'Do you feel sorry for her?'

'Yes.'

'Why?'

'Because she's been pretty unlucky with her husband . . . She ought to be leading the kind of life to which she's entitled . . . society, parties, friends . . .'

'Does her husband prevent her?'

'He never pays any attention to her. Besides, he goes off for whole weeks on end. This time he's been away for over a month . . .'

'Where do you think he is?'

'With some woman or other ... He only fancies the women he picks up God knows where ...'

'Has he ever asked you to go to bed with him?'

'I'd like to see him try ...'

'Very well. Could you go and fetch the cook? While I'm talking to her, wake your mistress up and tell her I want to see her for just a few minutes ...'

She obeyed him reluctantly, darting him angry looks as she left the room; Maigret winked at Lapointe.

Marie Jalon, the cook, was a short, stocky woman; she stared curiously at the chief superintendent and seemed delighted to be meeting him in the flesh.

'Please sit down, Madame. I already know you've been in this household a long time ...'

'Forty years ... I used to work for Monsieur's father ...'

'Has anything changed since those days?'

She gave a deep sigh.

'Everything's changed, sir ... Ever since that woman came here, I just don't know where to turn ... No regular hours any more ... Meals served when she decides she's hungry ... Sometimes she doesn't eat a thing all day, then I hear a noise in the kitchen in the middle of the night and I find her raiding the fridge ...'

'Do you think your employer is unhappy about the situation?'

'I most certainly do ... He doesn't say so ... I've never heard him complain ... He's not the complaining sort ... I've known him since he was a little boy, forever playing about my feet ... He was shy then ...'

'Do you find him shy?'

'And how! You can't imagine what dreadful scenes he puts up with without ever daring to raise a finger to her ...'

'Aren't you worried about his absence?'

'I wasn't to start with ... We're used to it ... He has to have his little treat now and again ...'

Maigret smiled to hear her use that expression.

'I'm wondering who could have warned you ... Would it be Monsieur Lecureur? ...'

'No. It was Madame Sabin-Levesque who came and told us she was worried ...'

'Worried? Her?... I see you don't know her... She wouldn't lift her little finger if he fell dead at her feet...'

'Do you think she's mad?'

'Drunk, more likely. She starts on the bottle the moment she's had her morning coffee...'

'Have you seen your employer since the 18th of February?'

'No.'

'Have you had any news of him?'

'None... I must say, I'm worried about it...'

Madame Sabin-Levesque was standing motionless in the doorway. She was wearing the same dressing-gown as on the previous day and had not even bothered to comb her hair.

'Was it to me or to my cook you wanted to speak?'

'To you both of...'

'Whenever you wish...'

She led the two men to the boudoir where she had first received Maigret. There was a bottle of brandy and a glass on a silver tray.

'I don't suppose you'd care for one?'

Maigret shook his head.

'What do you want this time?'

'First of all to ask you one question. Where did you go last night?'

'Yes, my maid told me you were having me watched. It'll save me telling you a lie. I didn't feel well so I went out to get a breath of fresh air. I saw a phone-box and all of a sudden I felt like calling up one of my girl-friends...'

'Do you have any girlfriends?'

'Does it surprise you? Yes, I do...'

'May I know the name of the friend you rang up?'

'It's none of your business, so I won't tell you.'

'Your friend was out?'

'How did you know?'

'You had to dial three different numbers...'

She did not answer but swallowed her drink. She was not feeling well and it was obvious that she always woke with a hangover, for which liquor was the only cure. Her face was swollen and this made her nose look longer and more pointed.

'Right, then I'll ask you another question. The drawers of your husband's desk are locked. Can you tell me where the keys are?'

'They must be in his pocket. I didn't search his rooms.'

'Who was his best friend?'

'In the early days of our marriage, a lawyer called Auboineau and his wife often used to come here for dinner . . . They went to law-school together . . .'

'Do they still see each other?'

'I don't know . . . All I know is that Auboineau doesn't come here any more . . . I never liked him . . . He's very pompous and never stops talking as though he were pleading in court . . . As for his wife . . .'

'What about her?'

'Never mind . . . She's just so haughty because she's inherited her parent's château . . .'

She had another drink.

'Are you going to stay much longer?'

Maigret realized that she was exhausted and he felt sorry for her.

'I suppose you'll go on having me watched by one of your men?'

'Yes, I will. That's all for today . . .'

Maigret nodded to Lapointe, who got up to follow him.

'Goodbye, Madame . . .'

She did not answer; the maid was waiting in the drawing-room to show them to the door.

On the ground floor, Maigret went through the archway to the solicitor's office and asked to speak to Lecureur. The head clerk came to meet the two police officers and ushered them into his private office.

'Any news?' he asked.

'Not really what you'd call news. As far as I know, the very last person to see your employer was a nightclub hostess who works at the *Cric-Crac* in the Rue Clément Marot; when he left her, he was on his way to visit another young woman in the Avenue de Ternes, who was expecting him . . . This was in the middle of the night of February 18th . . . He never reached his destination . . .'

'Did he perhaps change his mind on the way there?'

'Perhaps . . . Are you quite sure he hasn't telephoned you even once during this last month?'

'Not once.'

'Whereas during all his previous absences he kept in touch with you by ringing up regularly?'

'That's right, every two or three days. He was extremely conscientious. Two years ago, he came rushing back on one occasion because we needed his signature . . . '

'What sort of terms were you on?'

'Very friendly . . . He had complete trust in me . . . '

'Did you know what he kept in the drawers in his desk upstairs?'

'No, I didn't know. I seldom went up there and I never saw those drawers open . . . '

'Have you seen his keys?'

'Many times. He had a set of keys which he always carried with him. One of the keys was for the big safe you probably saw in the typists' room . . . '

'What's in it?'

'Confidential documents concerning our clients' affairs, particularly their wills . . . '

'Have you also got a key to it?'

'Naturally.'

'Who else?'

'No one.'

'Did he ever deal personally with certain matters which he would not discuss with you?'

'Sometimes he saw a client privately in his office, but he nearly always took notes and, when the client was gone, he would give me a full account.'

'Who controls the financial side while your employer is away?'

'I do. I have power of attorney.'

'Is he very wealthy?'

'Yes, he's wealthy.'

'Has he increased his fortune since his father's death?'

'He certainly has.'

'And is his wife his sole heir?'

'One of the employees and I acted as witnesses when he signed his will, but I didn't read it. I assume he made quite a number of other large legacies.'

'What would happen to the practice?'

'That would depend entirely on Madame Sabin-Levesque.'

'Thank you.'

It suddenly occurred to Maigret that, ever since Nathalie's first visit to the Police Judiciaire, they all spoke of the solicitor both in the present tense and in the past.

Mostly in the past.

'If you wish to see me today, you'll have to come right away. I'm performing an operation at one o'clock.'

Maigret noticed that Doctor Florian, like most society doctors, affected a solemn tone of voice. He lived in the Avenue Foch, which presupposed a select clientele.

'I'll be there in a few minutes . . . '

Maigret and Lapointe had gone into a bar on the Boulevard Saint-Germain to have a beer and to make a phone call.

'He's waiting for us . . . the Avenue Foch . . . '

Soon afterwards, the small black car was making its way up the Champs-Elysées. Lapointe was silent, a trifle gloomy, as though something were troubling him.

'What's the matter?'

'That woman . . . I can't help feeling sorry for her . . . '

Maigret did not answer but he probably felt the same way as Lapointe; yet as they drove round the Arc de Triomphe, he muttered:

'We'll have to know her better before we can feel sorry for her . . . '

The doctor's house was luxurious and more modern than the one on the Boulevard Saint-Germain. They glided up to the sixth floor in a spacious lift and a butler in a striped waistcoat opened the door for them.

'This way . . . Professor Florian is expecting you . . . '

The butler took their hats and coats, then opened the swing doors to let them through. Two Greek statues in almost flawless condition stood on either side of the door.

The surgeon was tall, even taller and stouter than Maigret. He shook hands with the two men energetically.

'This is Inspector Lapointe . . . ' Maigret said, introducing his young colleague.

'Please forgive me for sounding so rushed, but I have a very busy schedule. I've been wondering why you want to see me ever since you rang fifteen minutes ago . . . '

His consulting room was huge, very luxurious and sunny. The french windows, which opened on to a terrace, were ajar and from time to time the curtains billowed in the breeze.

'Please sit down.'

His greying hair made him look older than his age; he was dressed severely in striped trousers and a black jacket.

'I believe you're a friend of Gérard Sabin-Levesque . . . '

'We're the same age and we were at university together. He studied law, I did medicine . . . He was the ringleader of a rather fast set to which I belonged.'

'Has he changed a lot?'

'I haven't seen much of him since his marriage . . . '

Doctor Florian frowned.

'I really must ask you for what reason you question me in this way. As a doctor, I'm bound by the Hippocratic oath, while as a friend, I naturally wish to be discreet . . . '

'I do understand. Sabin-Levesque has been missing for over a month . . . He didn't tell anyone he was going away, neither his wife nor his head clerk . . .

'He left the house one evening, the 18th of February, without taking any luggage. We now know that on the evening, or rather the night, of the 18th, he went to a nightclub called the *Cric-Crac* in the Rue Clément Marot. He left the club alone, to go to an address in the Avenue de Ternes which he had been given, but he never reached his destination . . . '

'What does his wife have to say?'

'Do you know her?'

'I used to go and visit them sometimes in the early days of their marriage.'

'In those early days, was he already going off on those – what shall we call them – escapades?'

'You know about those? He was always attracted to women and to the atmosphere of nightclubs, even in his student days . . . He never outgrew the attraction, but there's nothing abnormal about it and I don't think the term "escapade" is appropriate.'

'I'm only using it for lack of a better word . . . '

'He never actually told me so when I went for dinner there, but

55

I had the feeling he never really stopped leading a bachelor life, if I may put it that way ... '

'How well did you know his wife?'

'I met her perhaps a dozen times ... '

'Do you know how they met?'

'He's always kept rather quiet about that ... I have the feeling she doesn't come from his sort of background ... I seem to remember that, at one time, she worked as a secretary for a lawyer ... At least I think so ... '

'That's correct. What impression did she make on you?'

'She seldom spoke to me. During those dinners, she was either morose or aggressive; at times she would leave the table, mumbling some excuse ... '

'Would you say she was unbalanced?'

'I couldn't tell you. I'm a surgeon, not a psychiatrist. I think the main problem was her drinking ... '

'She's drinking more than ever. She was drunk when she came to the Quai des Orfèvres to tell us that her husband was missing ... '

'When was that?'

'The day before yesterday.'

'And he's been missing since February?'

'Yes. She waited for over a month. After the first week, the head clerk told her she ought to tell the police but she told him it was none of his business ... '

'Strange ... '

'And worrying too.'

The doctor lit a cigarette with a gold lighter. He said to Maigret:

'Go ahead, please light your pipe ... I'm disturbed by what you tell me. All I can say is that Gérard was, and I am sure still is, an extremely brilliant man. When I knew him, he was what you would call a playboy. He loved sports-cars and amusing places. I gather that he often didn't turn up at lectures, but that didn't stop him from passing exams with the greatest of ease.

'I don't know if he's changed ... '

'Your account fits in with what we've been told already by others. I imagine he got married on the spur of the moment and that he soon realized it was a mistake ... '

56

'I would think so . . . His friends stopped seeing him because of his wife . . . She was always humiliating him in front of them . . . I never heard him answer back . . . He would carry on with the conversation as if nothing had happened . . .

'Later, he still went on living with her but he completely ignored her existence . . . '

'Do you think he was unhappy about the situation?'

'It's hard to tell with someone who is always joking . . . It wasn't a normal life, of course . . . I understand why he had to have those flings . . . But his going away like this for a whole month is a more serious matter . . . Hasn't he even been in touch with his office?'

'No, though he usually kept in touch. This time he hasn't bothered to find out if they needed him at his work . . . '

'You seem very interested in the wife . . . '

'She lived in the same apartment as him and they were presumably fond of each other once . . . '

'Poor old Gérard . . . '

The doctor got up.

'Please excuse me but duty calls . . . Come to think of it, we had a mutual friend who is a psychiatrist; he works at Sainte-Anne . . . He's called Doctor Amadieu and lives in the Latin Quarter . . . He attended some of those dinners at the Boulevard Saint-Germain . . . '

He escorted them to the door. The butler was waiting with their hats and coats.

'Ten past twelve . . . ' Maigret said when they got into the little car. 'Let's try and find out if Doctor Amadieu goes home for lunch . . . '

Ringing up the psychiatrist gave him an excuse to go into a café and drink an aperitif; this time, he chose a *pastis*.

'I'll have the same,' Lapointe said.

Amadieu was at home. This week he would not be on duty at Sainte-Anne until two in the afternoon.

'I suppose it's urgent?'

'Yes, I think it could be described as urgent.'

The psychiatrist lived in a rather untidy flat; he was probably a bachelor, for he was eating alone at table. A maid was clearing up the dishes. Amadieu had bushy red hair and freckles; his

57

rumpled tweed suit looked as though it had been slept in.

Maigret found out later that Amadieu was one of the most eminent psychiatrists in France, if not the whole of Europe.

'Do sit down. Light your pipe and tell me what you'd like to drink.'

'Nothing for the moment. I know your time is valuable. You used to be on close terms with Sabin-Levesque . . . '

'Yes, I think you could say that, after all those nights on the town we had when we were students together . . . Don't tell me he's in trouble with the law? . . . '

'He vanished over a month ago . . . '

'Without telling anyone?'

'No one. He used to go away, but never for more than a week, and he would always keep in touch with his head clerk. This time, he hasn't . . . '

'I wonder what's happened to him?' Amadieu muttered to himself.

Then he added, puzzled:

'But how can I help you?'

'I'm looking for a man I've never met, whom I knew nothing about until yesterday; I'm trying to get some kind of picture of him.'

'I see.'

'I've just been to see your friend, Doctor Florian. He's the one who gave me your address. He says that Sabin-Levesque was actually a very reliable sort of person.'

'I agree with that.'

'Do you think the sort of life he's been leading all these years could have driven him to suicide?'

'It wouldn't be like him. Besides, his life had its consolations . . . '

'I know about that. I've met several of his girlfriends . . . '

'I had dinner at the Boulevard Saint-Germain quite a few times soon after his marriage . . . '

'Just as a friend?'

'I think I can tell you the truth, despite professional etiquette . . . Gérard asked me to come and observe his wife . . . He wondered if she was quite sane . . . I found her extremely intelligent; she seemed to see right through me from the very first . . . She would look at me coolly, as though challenging me . . . and she would deliberately drink like a fish . . . '

'She still does . . . '

'I know, but when I was present she drank twice as much. She would glance at me every time she poured herself another drink.

' "It's a disease, isn't it, doctor?" she would say to me . . . "I'm what you call an incurable alcoholic . . . "

' "Practically no disease is uncurable," I would reply, "if the patient really wants to be cured . . . "

' "How can I want to be cured when I can't face life? . . . I'm all alone in the world; my husband despises me and doesn't give a damn about me . . . "

' "I'm sure you're mistaken. I know Gérard. If he didn't love you, he wouldn't have married you . . . "

' "He thought he loved me once . . . I never was in love with him but I thought I might be in time . . . He's the most selfish and cynical human being I've ever met . . . " '

Amadieu relit his pipe and blew a puff of smoke up towards the ceiling. The room in which they were sitting was a cross between a living room, a consulting room and a study, without quite being any of the three; books and magazines lay scattered everywhere.

'You can imagine what a spot I was in. Poor Gérard would just sit there and listen while all this went on, never saying a word.

'The sixth or seventh time I went there, she came up to me in the big drawing-room and, before I could even say hello, she announced in a slurred voice:

' "Please don't bother taking off your coat, Monsieur Amadieu. We won't be having dinner. From now on, you're *persona non grata* in this house. I'll choose my own psychiatrist when I need one . . . "

'And she turned her back on me and staggered off to her rooms.

'The next day, my friend Gérard came here to apologize. He told me she was becoming more impossible every day and that he now just did his best to avoid her. Incidentally, he added that she was trying just as hard to avoid him . . . '

'Why didn't your friend ask for a divorce?'

'Because he was a Catholic and, in spite of the life he led, he was

59

quite religious. Besides, those escapades of his would have been held against him in any divorce court . . .'

Maigret puffed on his pipe thoughtfully, gazing at the big red-headed man with the light blue eyes. He sighed and rose to his feet:

'In other words, you don't think she's mad?'

'Not at first sight. Mind you, I've only ever seen her when she was drunk. I'd have to study her case far more thoroughly before I could establish a diagnosis . . . I'm sorry I can't help you more . . .'

They shook hands and Amadieu watched the two men walk down the stairs; there was no lift in his house.

'The Brasserie Dauphine?'

'With pleasure, chief.'

'Pity we can't send her to Sainte-Anne to be looked after by a man like that . . .'

'There must be times when her husband finds it hellish to live with her, even though they don't see much of each other. Just to know she's there under the same roof and feeling as she does . . . I think I'd be frightened . . .'

Maigret looked at Lapointe, dead serious:

'Do you believe she'd be capable of . . .'

'I told you a while ago I felt sorry for her . . . I still do feel sorry for her, because she must be terribly unhappy, but even so she scares me . . .'

'Anyway, he's got to be somewhere, dead or alive . . .'

'More likely dead,' Lapointe sighed under his breath.

As soon as they reached the Brasserie Dauphine, Maigret went to the phone and rang up his wife.

'I know, you're not coming home for lunch,' Madame Maigret said before he could open his mouth. 'In fact, I was so sure you wouldn't that I only got a bit of ham and some salad for you.'

He would have liked another *pastis*, but he remembered his friend Pardon's advice and decided against it. Nor was he supposed to eat the *Tripes à la Mode de Cäen* which were on the menu, but he did anyway, enjoying them thoroughly.

'I can't decide whether or not to ask for a search warrant. I'd have trouble getting one anyway, since there's no proof of any crime . . .'

'What would you be looking for?'

'A weapon . . . Did the solicitor own a gun? . . . Did his wife? . . .'

'Do you think she would be capable of killing him?'

'She'd be capable of anything. She could just as well have killed him with a poker or a bottle . . .'

'And what would she have done with the body?'

'I know. I don't see her waiting to murder him outside the *Cric-Crac* either. No shots were heard, so she would have had to knock him out first and then get rid of the body . . .'

'Perhaps she had an accomplice . . .'

'Or else we're just on the wrong track and our man was mugged . . . It happens every night . . .'

'If he was mugged, why should the killer go to the trouble of getting rid of the body?'

'I know . . . I know . . . I can't make it out . . . One moment I think I'm near the answer, and the next moment I feel I'm going round in circles . . .'

Maigret gave a strained laugh.

'The big joke would be if our solicitor reappeared suddenly, fit and smiling, and demanding to know what we were up to . . .'

'What do you think of Lecureur?'

'The head clerk? I don't like him much, though I couldn't say why. He's a cold fish; nothing ever troubles him and he's always too self-controlled . . .'

'You spoke about what would happen to the practice if Sabin-Levesque turned out to be dead . . . Lecureur's been working there for over twenty years . . . He can't help but feel a little as though the business belonged to him . . .'

'The widow would have to agree to keep him on and I don't think that's very likely . . . There certainly doesn't seem to be much love lost between the two . . .'

'Well, naturally they wouldn't kiss in front of us . . .'

Maigret stared at Lapointe.

'Do you really think that might be so?'

'Yes I do, ever since this morning . . . I may well be wrong but . . .'

'Isn't that explanation too facile? They're both intelligent people. Nathalie is as cunning as they come . . . You heard what the psychiatrist said . . . It reminded me of some phrase I read recently: "Frenzied and utterly amoral . . . " '

'You think that description fits her?'

'It does when she's drunk. And since she drinks from morning to night that makes her a dangerous woman . . . '

'Dangerous enough to murder her husband?'

'Who knows? . . . She's got quite a temper . . . I'm going back there to see her, just to provoke her . . . '

'Perhaps she was frightened?'

'Of whom?'

'Of her husband . . . There must also have been times when he wished she was dead . . . He put up with her for fifteen years, I agree, but there can come a moment when a man just can't take any more . . . '

Maigret laughed uneasily.

'We must sound rather foolish, the two of us, constructing our fine theories around a subject we don't know the first thing about . . . '

He did not order a brandy with his coffee. He was sick of it and would be for a long time to come, having seen the solicitor's wife gulp it down like water.

Chapter Four

Maigret sat at his desk, with an apparently blank look in his eyes. He was watching the man who sat opposite him, who was wearing a smartly-cut chauffeur's uniform and twisting his cap round and round in obvious embarrassment.

As usual, Lapointe sat at one end of the desk with his shorthand pad. It was he who had gone to fetch the Sabin-Levesques' chauffeur at the Boulevard Saint-Germain, finding him in a room over the garages.

At first the chauffeur was too nervous to sit down and Maigret had to insist.

'Your name is Vittorio Petrini?'

'Yes, sir.'

He was so smart that Maigret expected him to salute when he replied.

'Where were you born?'

'In Patino, a small village south of Naples.'

'Are you married?'

'No, sir.'

'How long have you been in France?'

'Ten years, sir.'

'Have you been working for your present employer all that time?'

'No, sir. I worked for the Marquis d'Orcel for four years.'

'Why did you leave that job?'

'Because he died, sir.'

'Tell me about the work you do for Monsieur and Madame Sabin-Levesque.'

'I don't have much to do, sir. In the morning I go shopping for Mademoiselle Jalon . . .'

'Is that the cook?'

'Yes, sir. She has trouble getting around, as she's quite

old. Then I used to clean the car, unless Monsieur needed me.'

'You're talking in the past tense . . . '

'Excuse me, sir?'

'You talk as though it were in the past.'

'I haven't seen Monsieur for a long time.'

'Which car did he use?'

'Sometimes the Fiat, sometimes the Bentley, it all depended on which client he was going to see. Sometimes we drove as far as fifty, or even a hundred kilometres out of Paris. Many of Monsieur's clients are very old and don't come into town any more. Some of them live in beautiful châteaux . . . '

'Did your employer talk to you on those journeys?'

'Sometimes, sir. He's a very good employer, not at all stuck-up and nearly always in a good mood.'

'Did Madame ever go out in the mornings?'

'Practically never. Her maid, Claire, told me that she gets up very late. Sometimes even after lunch.'

'What about the afternoon?'

'Monsieur almost never needed me. He stayed in his office.'

'Didn't he drive himself?'

'Sometimes. But then he preferred to take the Fiat . . . '

'What about Madame?'

'She went out sometimes at about four or five o'clock. Without me or the car. It seems she would go to the cinema, usually to one of the local ones, and then she would take a taxi home.'

'Didn't you find it odd that she never asked you to take her there or to come and fetch her afterwards?'

'Yes, sir. But it's none of my business.'

'Does she ever go out in the car with you?'

'Yes, once or twice a week.'

'Where does she go?'

'Not far. To the Rue de Ponthieu. She goes to a little English pub and stays there quite a long time.'

'Do you know the name of the pub?'

'Yes, sir. It's called the Pickwick . . . '

'What state is she in when she comes out?'

The chauffeur hesitated, reluctant to answer the question.

'Is she drunk?' Maigret insisted.

'Sometimes I have to help her get into the car.'

'Does she go straight home?'

'Not always. Occasionally, she would ask me to take her to another bar, the one at the Hôtel George V.'

'Was she alone when she came out of there too?'

'Yes, sir.'

'Was she able to get back into the car?'

'I helped her, sir.'

'What about the evening?'

'She never went out in the evenings.'

'Did your employer?'

'He went out, but he didn't use the cars. I think he preferred to go by taxi.'

'Did he go out every night?'

'Oh no. Sometimes he didn't go out for eight or ten days.'

'And did he stay away for a few days sometimes without coming home?'

'Yes, sir.'

'Did you ever drive them anywhere together?'

'Never, sir. Except once, to a funeral. That was three or four years ago . . . '

He continued to play nervously with his cap, which had a leather peak. His blue uniform was impeccably cut and his shoes shone like mirrors.

'What do you think of your employer's wife?'

He gave a faint smile, obviously embarrassed.

'Do I have to tell you? It's not my business to discuss her . . . I'm only the chauffeur . . . '

'How did she behave towards you?'

'It varied. Sometimes she never said a word and she would purse her lips as if she were furious with me. at other times, she would call me her little Vito and chat the whole time . . . '

'What about?'

'It's hard to say. Maybe she'd say:

' "I wonder if I can bear this sort of life much longer . . . " '

'Or else, when she wanted me to drive her home, she would say:

' "Back to the prison, Vito . . . " ' '

'Is that what she called the flat in the Boulevard Saint-Germain?'

'Yes, when she'd been to a few bars.

' "You know, it's only because of this pig of a boss of yours that I drink the way I do. Any woman would do the same in my place ..."

'That sort of thing, you know ... I listened to her but I never said anything. I'm very fond of Monsieur ...'

'What about her?'

'I prefer not to answer that.'

'Do you remember the 18th of February?'

'No, sir.'

'That was the day your employer left the house for the last time.'

'He must have gone out by himself because he didn't ask for the car.'

'What do you do in the evenings?'

'I read or else I watch television. I try to get rid of my accent but I never manage to ...'

The telephone rang, interrupting the conversation. Maigret motioned to Lapointe to answer it.

'Yes ... He's here ... Just a moment ...'

Lapointe turned to Maigret:

'It's the Police Commissioner for the XVth *arrondisement* ...'

'Hello, Jadot ...'

Maigret knew him and liked him very much.

'I'm sorry to disturb you, Superintendent ... But I thought you'd be particularly interested in what I have to tell you ... A Belgian bargeman called Jef van Roeten was testing the motor of his boat at the Quai de Grenelle when the wash brought a body floating up to the surface. It gave him quite a shock ...'

'Did you identify the body?'

'His wallet was still in his trouser pocket ... Gérard Sabin-Levesque. Does the name mean anything to you?'

'I'll say it does! Are you on the spot?'

'Not yet. I wanted to tell you first. Who is he?'

'A Boulevard Saint-Germain solicitor. He's been missing for over a month. I'll see you there ... Thanks ...'

Maigret put a second pipe in his pocket and turned to the chauffeur.

'I won't be needing you any more for the time being. You can go. Thank you for your cooperation ...'

As soon as the chauffeur was gone, Maigret turned to Lapointe:

'He's dead all right.'

'Sabin-Levesque?'

'They've just fished his body out of the Seine at the Quai de Grenelle ... Come with me ... but tell the Criminal Identity Laboratory first ...'

The little car threaded its way through a traffic jam and got to the Pont de Grenelle in record time. Below street level was the river wharf with its barrels and piles of timber and brick. Two or three barges were being unloaded.

A crowd of fifty people jostled around an inert shape in the centre. A policeman was doing his best to keep them back.

Jadot had already arrived.

'The deputy officer will be along soon ...'

'Have you got the wallet?'

'Here it is ...'

He handed the wallet to Maigret; it was limp, slimy and water-logged, not surprisingly. There were three five-hundred franc notes and a few hundreds in it, an identity card and a driving licence. The ink had almost completely faded, but certain words were still legible.

'Anything else?'

'Yes. A cheque-book ...'

'In his name?'

'Yes.'

Maigret had been throwing a few covert glances at the sodden corpse lying stretched out on the ground. As always in such cases, he had to make a real effort of will to go any closer.

The corpse's belly was bloated, like a distended wine-skin. There was a gaping hole in the chest, leaving horrid whitish viscera exposed. The face had lost almost all human resemblance.

'Lapointe, go and ring up Lecureur. Tell him to come immediately ...'

He could not inflict such a sight on Nathalie.

'Where's the bargeman?'

Someone answered with a thick Flemish accent:

'I'm right here, Monsieur ...'

'How long ago did you moor your boat on this spot?'

'Almost two weeks. I only meant to stay for two days to unload my bricks, but my motor broke down. Some mechanics came to repair it and it was a long job. They only finished this morning . . . '

His flaxen-haired wife stood by his side, holding a blond baby in her arms; she did not seem to understand French and was looking anxiously at the two men while they spoke.

'At about three o'clock, I decided to try out the motor because I want to return to Belgium tomorrow morning when I've picked up a cargo of wine at Bercy . . . Something seemed to be obstructing the motor . . . then, when it started up, the body suddenly shot up to the surface . . . It must have got caught in the anchor or in the propeller, which explains why it's all cut open like that . . . Not my lucky day, sir . . . '

Oron, the deputy officer, couldn't have been more than thirty years old. He was very smartly dressed and distinguished-looking.

'Who is it?' he asked, after shaking hands with Maigret.

'Someone who disappeared over a month ago. Sabin-Levesque, a Boulevard Saint-Germain solicitor . . . '

'Had he swindled his clients?'

'It would seem not.'

'Did he have any reason for wanting to kill himself?'

'I don't think so. The last person to see him alive was a night-club hostess . . . '

'Murder then?'

'Very likely.'

'Committed right here?'

'I don't think he'd have let anyone bring him to the banks of the Seine alive. He was no fool . . . Hello, Grenier . . . I've some dirty work for you to do . . . '

'I've seen it . . . '

Doctor Grenier belonged to the new breed of forensic experts.

'I can't do anything here. Not much use in my giving a coroner's verdict of death, since it's fairly obvious . . . '

The Forensic Institute had sent a special van to collect the body, but it had to wait until the Criminal Identity photographers had done their work. Lecureur soon arrived and walked down the stone steps which led to the wharf.

Maigret pointed to the shapeless heap, which gave off a nauseating smell.

'Will you confirm that it really is him . . . ? '

The head clerk approached reluctantly. He walked stiffly, holding a handkerchief to his nose and mouth.

'It's him all right,' he said as soon as he came back.

'What makes you recognize him?'

'His face. It may be disfigured, but you can still tell it's him. Do you think he threw himself in?'

'Why should he have done that?'

Lecureur moved still further back, trying to get as far away from the corpse as possible.

'I don't know. A lot of people drown themselves . . . '

'I've got his wallet and his cheque-book . . . '

'That proves it then . . . It is him . . . '

'You'll be summoned to the Quai des Orfèvres tomorrow morning to make a sworn statement . . . '

'At what time?'

'Nine o'clock . . . Have you got a taxi waiting?'

'Vito had just returned . . . I asked him to bring me here . . . He's up there with the Fiat . . . '

'Then can you give me a lift? . . . Come on, Lapointe.'

He walked up to Grenier, who seemed to be the only one not to mind the presence of the corpse.

'Can you tell me by this evening whether he was murdered before he was thrown into the water?'

'I'll try to . . . It won't be too easy, because of the condition he's in . . . '

The three men made their way through the crowd of onlookers. Jef van Roeten ran after Maigret.

'You're the boss, aren't you?'

'Yes.'

'Can I leave tomorrow morning? I've told you everything I know . . . '

'You'll have to go to the police station first to make a statement and then sign it . . . '

'Which police station?'

'That gentleman over there will explain. The one with the little moustache and the black overcoat; he's the chief of police for this district and he'll tell you what to do ... '

They got into the small Fiat which Vito drove very smoothly, like all expert chauffeurs.

'Monsieur Maigret, will you excuse me,' the head clerk whispered, 'but if I don't stop at a bar and swallow some thing strong, I may vomit ... '

The three men got out again and went into a bar, empty except for two lightermen. Lecureur, who was white as a sheet, ordered a double brandy. Maigret asked for a beer, but Lapointe had a brandy also.

'I never thought they'd find him in the Seine.'

'Why not ?'

'I don't know. Sometimes I thought he might have gone off with a woman ... he could have gone to the Riviera or anywhere ... The only thing which really worried me, though, was that he didn't ring up ... '

They soon reached the Boulevard Saint-Germain.

'Will you please look up all recent transactions and get in touch with the bank ... ? '

'Perhaps you could give me the cheque-book so that I can look through the stubs ... '

Maigret gave it to him and went in by the right-hand door under the arch, while the head clerk went into the office on the left.

'What! You again!' the maid exclaimed when she opened the door. She seemed furious.

'Yes, mademoiselle, it's me again. And I'd be grateful if you would go and tell your mistress right away that I'm here, waiting for her ... '

He started walking towards the boudoir, keeping his pipe in his mouth just to annoy her.

Ten minutes later, Nathalie entered the room; she was not wearing a dressing-gown today but a very elegant suit.

'I was just going out.'

'Which bar were you going to ?'

'It's none of your business.'

'I've some important news for you. Your husband's been found.'

She did not ask if he was dead or alive.

'Where?' was her only question.

'In the Seine, by the Pont de Grenelle . . . '

'I knew something had happened to him . . . '

The corners of her lips twitched, but her gaze remained steady. She had been drinking, but she was in fairly good shape, for once.

'I suppose I must go and identify the body. Where is he? In the morgue?'

'We don't have morgues any longer. It's called the Forensic Institute now . . . '

'Will you take me there?'

'You won't have to identify him. Monsieur Lecureur has done so already. However, if you wish to see him . . . '

'Are you trying to insult me?'

'What do you mean?'

'Do you really think I'd be so morbid?'

'One can never tell with you . . . '

The precious bottle of brandy was on a small table, with some glasses. She helped herself to a drink, without offering one to her guests.

'Well, what now?'

'The press will know about it by tonight and they'll be sending reporters and photographers around to see you.'

'Can't you stop them?'

'You can refuse to let them in.'

'What will happen if I do?'

'They'll start ferreting around for other sources and they'll be pretty tough on you, you can be sure of that. They're a susceptible lot. They may well find out certain things . . . '

'I've got nothing to hide.'

'Do as you wish, but if I were you I'd see them and try to put up a good show. The first ones will be here in an hour, at the latest.'

This piece of information did not stop her from gulping down another glass of cognac.'

'They keep in touch with the police . . . '

'You enjoy speaking to me like this, don't you?'

'Believe me, I don't.'

'You hate me . . . '

'I hate no one ... '

'Is that all you had to say to me?'

'Yes, that's all. We'll be meeting again soon, I have no doubt.'

'It won't be a pleasure. I despise you, Monsieur Maigret. And now, push off ... Claire! Throw these characters out! ... '

Maigret wondered whether to call off the inspector who still stood on the pavement opposite 207 *bis*, waiting to tail Madame Sabin-Levesque. He finally decided to leave him there; after all, they had got nowhere so far by tapping the phones, which was not surprising as Nathalie had not hesitated to go out at night, wearing only a nightgown under her fur coat, just to find a public phone-box.

'What do you make of it all, Lapointe?' Maigret asked, getting into the car.

'If she behaves like that with the press, she's in for a real caning in the papers tomorrow ... '

'I've got nothing more to do at the office today. Drop me off at my flat ... '

Madame Maigret gave him a sly smile when he came in.

'Happy?'

'Why should I be happy?'

'You found your body, didn't you?'

'Did you hear about it on the radio?'

'Yes, in a news bulletin at six o'clock ... Are you hungry?'

'Not really. Not after the afternoon I've just spent.'

He went over to the drinks cabinet, wondering what he might drink to get rid of the queasy feeling in his stomach. He finally chose a small glass of gin, an unusual choice for him; the bottle had not been touched for a year.

'Want some?' he asked.

'No, thanks ... Sit down for a moment and read the papers. I'll make you something light ... '

The soup was ready. After that, she gave him some ham, salad and diced cold potatoes.

'You're worried, aren't you?' she asked him in an undertone, while they were eating.

'I don't understand certain things and I never like that.'

'Who are you working with?'

She knew that he always worked with one or another of his closest colleagues. Sometimes it was Janvier, or else Lucas, although the latter usually took over from him in his absence. This time, it happened to be Lapointe.

'Would you like me to turn on the television?'

'No, thanks. I'm feeling too lazy to watch it.'

He sat down in his armchair and began to look through the papers. But his thoughts were elsewhere, chiefly with Nathalie, who had turned them out of her house with such rude comments.

At nine o'clock he was dozing, and his wife was about to wake him up so that he could go to bed when the telephone rang and roused him with a start.

'Hello . . . Yes, it's me . . . Is it you, Grenier? . . . Did you find out anything? . . . '

'I'd like to ask you one question first. Did the gentleman usually wear a hat or not?'

Maigret thought it over.

'I never met him and I didn't think of asking his wife or his staff . . . Wait a moment . . . He was a smart dresser and liked wearing youthful-looking clothes . . . I imagine he went bare-headed . . . '

'Or else someone took his hat off before hitting him over the head . . . Not just one but I'd say at least a dozen very heavy blows . . . The skull is in little pieces, like a jig-saw puzzle.'

'No bullets?'

'None in the head or in the body either . . . I couldn't tell you exactly what the weapon was; a hammer, a spanner, a car-jack . . . Probably a car-jack . . . Two blows would have killed him, but the murderer was really determined to finish him off . . . '

'What about that hole in his chest?'

'That's more recent. The body was already in a state of decomposition when it must have got caught on an anchor or something of that sort . . .

'There's one detail which may interest you . . . His ankles have been bound very tightly, with wire probably. So tightly that one of the feet was almost severed . . . The wire must have been used to tie him to something heavy, like a block of stone or a weight of some kind . . . '

'How long would you say he's been in the water?'

'It's hard to tell ... Several weeks ...'

'Four or five weeks?'

'About that. By the way, I examined the clothes. There was a set of keys in one of his pockets ... I'll have them delivered to you first thing tomorrow morning ...'

'I'm eager to see them ...'

'Then send someone over for them ... You've more men than I have ...'

'Right. Leave them with the concierge ...'

'I'm going to take a nice warm bath now and eat a big dinner ... I wouldn't like to do this sort of work every day ... Goodnight, Maigret ...'

'Goodnight, Grenier ... And thanks ...'

He was at his office before nine o'clock on the following morning. The first thing he did was to send an inspector to fetch the keys from the Forensic Institute.

There was a knock on the door. It was Lapointe, who instantly guessed that Maigret had some fresh news.

'Grenier rang me ... Sabin-Levesque was murdered with a qlunt, or what the reports call a contusing, instrument. Ten or so very violent blows ... the murderer tied a stone or some sort of weight around his ankles before throwing him into the water ...

'Incidentally, Grenier found a set of keys in one of the dead man's pockets ...'

'Have you seen the papers?'

'Not yet.'

Lapointe went to fetch them from the inspectors' duty room and, when he brought them back to Maigret's office, there was a smile on his face.

'Look ...'

On the front page of one daily, Maigret read the headlines:

WELL-KNOWN SOLICITOR MURDERED

The photograph which illustrated the item would have astonished anyone who had seen Madame Sabin-Levesque about an hour before the picture was taken. She did not look in the least bit drunk and had gone to the trouble of changing into a black suit with a white blouse.

Her brown hair was meticulously groomed. Her face, which

seemed longer, wore a sad expression which was both appropriate and photogenic. She was holding a handkerchief in her hand, as though she had just been weeping and was afraid of breaking down again.

HIS GRIEF-STRUCK WIDOW CANNOT UNDERSTAND

There followed quite a long interview with Nathalie with all the questions and answers. She had received the reporters in the big drawing-room, not in her boudoir.

'When did your husband disappear?'
'About a month ago. At first, I didn't worry because he sometimes had to go and visit a client out of town.'
'Who was left in charge of the practice?'
'His head clerk. A most competent man. My husband trusted him implicitly and had given him power of attorney.'
'Did you go out a lot?'
'Not much. We saw a few friends at home, but we led a quiet life.'
'Was it you who warned the police?'
'I decided to go and see Superintendent Maigret and to let him know I was worried . . .'
'Why Maigret?'
'I don't know . . . I've read accounts of several inquiries he's conducted and it made me trust him . . .'

There was another, shorter interview with Jean Lecureur.

'I have nothing to tell you.'
'Did he leave you a message?'
'No. He never left messages, but he usually rang me every two or three days . . .'
'Did he do so this time?'
'No.'
'Weren't you worried?'
'I was after about ten days . . .'
'Why didn't you get in touch with the police?'
'I preferred to let Madame Sabin-Levesque know I was worried.'

Another paper carried a photograph of Nathalie sitting in the main drawing-room.

MYSTERIOUS DEATH OF A SOLICITOR

The text was more or less identical, but it stressed the fact that the police had not been warned initially. The article ended with the words:

'Apparently, Madame Sabin-Levesque was used to these mysterious absences.'

'What's incredible,' Lapointe said with grudging admiration, 'is the way she managed to pull herself together so quickly . . .'

An inspector came in with the set of keys. It contained half a dozen small keys and a safe key, most probably the key to the big safe in the office.

Bonfils brought in a list of all the Paris nightclubs and cabarets. Maigret was surprised to see how many there were: the list was three closely-typed pages long.

He slipped it into a drawer, got up and said with a sigh:

'Boulevard Saint-Germain . . .'

'Do you think she'll let us in?'

'I'm not going there to see her. I'll have to go up to the Magistrates' Court first . . .'

He found out that Coindet was the examining magistrate who had been put in charge of the case. Coindet was an affable, good-natured old soul; Maigret had known him ever since the beginning of his career. He went down the long corridor of examining magistrates' rooms until he came to Coindet's office.

Coindet shook hands with him.

'I was expecting you. Sit down . . .'

A clerk of the court was sitting at the typewriter; he was at least as old as Coindet.

'You didn't send me a report, so I only know what I've read in the newspapers . . .'

'I didn't because there's nothing to report,' Maigret replied, smiling. 'You forget we only found the body yesterday.'

'Yet I hear rumours that you've been investigating this case for three days . . .'

'Without results. I need a search warrant this morning . . .'

'For the Boulevard Saint-Germain?'

'Yes. I'm not very popular with Madame Sabin-Levesque . . .'

'That's not the impression she gives in the interviews . . .'

'What she tells the journalists is another matter . . . I want to go over the solicitor's flat thoroughly; I've only glanced at it so far . . .'

'You won't leave me without news for too long?'

Coindet was alluding to Maigret's reputation for conducting investigations in his own good time, without worrying too much about keeping the magistrates informed.

Twenty minutes later, Maigret and Lapointe were going into the by now familiar gateway on the Boulevard Saint-Germain. It suddenly occurred to Maigret to go and talk to the concierge, a dignified-looking old man.

'I was wondering when you'd come and see me, Superintendent . . . '

'I've been so busy . . . '

'I understand . . . I'm an ex-policeman myself; I used to walk the beat . . . I suppose you're particularly interested in the lady?'

'She's an unusual sort of woman.'

'And a pretty unusual pair they both are, or I should say were now that he's dead. They had two cars and a chauffeur, yet when they went out, they nearly always went on foot. I've never seen them leave the house together and I hear they even ate separately.'

'Nearly always.'

'She told the reporters they received friends but in fact they never had visitors. From time to time, the solicitor would go off, his hands in his pockets, whistling a little tune, just like a young man, never taking anything with him. I suppose he must have had another woman, or at least another flat somewhere . . . '

'I'll come back and see you when I have a moment. You seem like a man who keeps his eyes open . . . '

'Habit, you know . . . '

A moment later, Maigret was ringing the doorbell of the apartment. The maid glared at them with fury when she opened the door. She would probably have slammed it in their faces if Maigret had not thought of putting his foot inside first.

'Madame is . . . '

'Never mind Madame. If you know how to read, take a look at this. It's a search warrant, drawn up by an examining magistrate. Unless you wish to be arrested for obstructing the law . . . '

'What do you want to see?'

'I don't need your help. I know the flat . . . '

Maigret started to walk towards the solicitor's rooms, followed by Lapointe. He was particularly interested in the mahogany desk and the contents of its four drawers. It was the only piece of furniture in the flat which was locked.

'Why don't you open the window? It's stuffy in here . . .'

He tried three of the keys before he found the right one. There was nothing in the first drawer except for some writing paper with Sabin-Levesque's name printed on it, some envelopes and two fountain pens, one of them in solid gold.

The contents of the second drawer were more interesting. It contained several snapshots, most of them taken in the garden of a huge villa. It was Sabin-Levesque's house on the Riviera and looked as though it had been built at the turn of the century. The photographs were of Nathalie, who seemed about twenty years younger, and of the solicitor in his shirt-sleeves, looking like a student.

The words 'La Florentine' were written on the back; this was obviously the name of the villa.

In one of the pictures, there was a huge Alsatian standing close to Sabin-Levesque.

It occurred to Maigret, seeing the picture of the dog, that he had seen no pets anywhere in the apartment.

He was about to close the drawer when he noticed, right at the back, a small passport photograph taken in a Photomat. It was of Nathalie, looking even younger than in the Cannes pictures and also very different. In this photo, she had a mysterious expression and her smile was deliberately provocative.

One word was written on the back: Trika.

It was obviously an invented name and equally obvious that she had not adopted it just to go and work as a lawyer's secretary in the Rue de Rivoli.

When she had told Maigret about her past life, he had begun to get suspicious, especially after he discovered that her so-called employer had been dead for ten years.

When she had spoken to him, she had known the lawyer was dead, so that no one could contradict her story. She had probably never been a secretary, or a typist for that matter.

'Lapointe, look at this . . . What does it remind you of?'

'Of a high-class call-girl . . .'

'And we know where the solicitor looked for his lady friends.'

Maigret carefully slipped the photograph into his wallet. He now opened the two left-hand drawers. The top one contained some cheque-books, all unused, except for one in which every cheque stub had been made out to 'The Bearer'.

There were a few odds and ends in the last drawer: a platinum wristwatch, some gold-embossed cuff-links, rubber bands, stamps.

'Having fun?'

Nathalie had just come into the room. Claire must have woken her up. She had already drunk a good deal of brandy, for they could smell it on her breath three feet away.

'Hello, Trika . . .'

She had enough self-control not to seem too taken aback.

'I don't understand.'

'Never mind. Read this . . .'

He showed her the search warrant. She drew away.

'I know. My maid told me. Make yourselves at home. Do you want to search the pockets of my dressing-gown?'

Her expression was no longer the same as on the previous day. There had been a look of anxiety in her eyes before; now there was a look of barely disguised terror. Her lips were trembling even more than usual, as were her hands.

'I haven't finished searching this suite yet.'

'Am I disturbing you? . . . It's been such a long while since I came to this part of the house . . .'

Ignoring her, Maigret began to open and close other drawers and cupboards. There were at least thirty suits in the wardrobe, most of them light-coloured and all bearing the label of one of the best tailors in Paris.

'I see your husband didn't wear a hat?'

'How should I know? I never went out with him . . .'

'Congratulations for that act you put on with the reporters yesterday . . .'

She smiled, flattered in spite of her circumstances.

The bed was huge and very low; there was something very masculine about the whole bedroom, with its leather-covered walls.

The bathroom looked as though the solicitor had only just left it. The toothbrush was in its mug, the razor on a shelf with some shaving-soap and a pumice stone. The bath-tub, the basin, the floor and the walls were all made of white marble. The window overlooked a large garden which Maigret noticed for the first time.

'Is that your garden?' he asked.

'Why shouldn't it be?'

It was unusual to see such fine trees in a private garden right in the centre of Paris.

'Tell me, Trika, you were a hostess in which nightclub?'

'I know my rights. I don't have to answer you.'

'You'll have to answer the examining magistrate.'

'I'll have my lawyer with me then.'

'Have you got a lawyer?'

'I've had one for a long time.'

'The one in the Rue de Rivoli?' he asked ironically.

He did not know why he was so hard on her, but there was something about her manner which constantly irritated him.

'That's my business.'

'We'll go to your rooms now . . .'

On the way, he glanced at the titles of some of the books in the study. There were quite a few good modern authors, including some in English; Maigret assumed the solicitor had spoken the language fluently.

They went through the smaller drawing-room, then into the main one, finally reaching Nathalie's boudoir. She stood watching them while Maigret opened a few drawers, which contained only trinkets.

He went into her bedroom. Her bed was as large as her husband's, but it was white, like the rest of the furniture. In the drawers, Maigret found nothing but some very fine made-to-measure underwear.

The grey-blue marble bathroom was untidy, as though it had just been used in a hurry. There was a bottle of brandy and a glass on a small table.

In the wardrobe, Maigret found only dresses, coats, suits and at least thirty pairs of shoes on special racks.

'Do you know how your husband died?'

She looked at him, tight-lipped, without answering.

'Someone hit him on the head with a blunt instrument, probably a car-jack. He was hit not once but at least a dozen times, so that his skull is in little pieces . . . '

She remained quite still and went on staring at the chief superintendent. There was a glazed look in her eyes and anyone seeing her at that moment would have taken her for a mad-woman.

Chapter Five

Maigret paid another visit to the concierge in his lodge.

'Tell me, didn't the solicitor have a dog when he got married?

'Yes, a beautiful Alsatian; he was very fond of it and the dog was devoted to him.'

'Did it die?'

'No. They gave it away a few days after they came back from Cannes, where they had spent their honeymoon . . . '

'Didn't you think it odd?'

'I hear the dog would snarl at Madame Sabin-Levesque every time she came near. It almost bit her once and tore the hem of her dress. She was terrified of it and so she made her husband give it away . . . '

When he got back to his office, Maigret sent for the photographer who worked for the Criminal Identity Department. He produced the snapshot of the couple with the dog in Cannes.

'Can you enlarge this for me?'

'The result won't be perfect, but you'll be able to recognize the people in it . . . '

'What about this one?'

He took out the passport photograph.

'I'll do my best. When do you want them for?'

'Tomorrow morning . . . '

The photographer sighed. The chief superintendent always wanted things done in a hurry. He was used to it by now.

Madame Maigret looked at her husband a little anxiously, the way she always did when he was conducting a difficult investigation. She was used to his silences and his grumpy manner. He would wander about the flat, not knowing what to do with himself.

Sometimes, when he was eating in an absent-minded way, his wife would ask him, smiling:

'Are you there?'

In fact, his thoughts had wandered far away. His wife recalled a conversation between Pardon and her husband one evening, when they were having dinner at the doctor's home. Pardon had said:

'There's one thing I just can't understand. You're the exact opposite of most policemen; why, you seem to hate having to arrest a criminal.'

'Yes, that's sometimes true . . .'

'Yet you carry out your investigations as though the outcome affected you personally . . .'

Maigret had answered:

'That's because each case is a personal experience in which I become involved. When you go to visit an unknown patient, don't you get emotionally involved too? Don't you struggle with death as though the patient were someone dear to you?'

He was weary and in a bad mood. The sight of the corpse on the Quai de Grenelle had been enough to upset even a forensic doctor like Grenier.

Maigret was fond of Sabin-Levesque, even though he had never met him personally. At school, he had known a boy who was rather like the solicitor, light-hearted and unconcerned. This boy had been the most undisciplined pupil in the class, interrupting the teacher or drawing in his exercise books during lessons.

When the teacher sent him out of the room for an hour, he would look in through the window and make faces at the class.

In spite of this, the teachers did not bear him a grudge and they even ended up by laughing at his antics. But then of course, he was also one of the three top boys in his class at every exam.

After leading the life of a playboy, Sabin-Levesque had suddenly got married. Why? Had he fallen madly in love with Nathalie, alias Trika? Or had she cleverly manipulated his feelings for her?

What did she expect? A brilliant social life, a luxurious home, exotic holidays and fashionable resorts?

Then, about three months after the wedding, Sabin-Levesque had begun to go off on his own again.

Why?

Maigret kept on asking himself this question and could not find a satisfactory answer to it. Had she gradually revealed herself to be the way she was now? They were not getting along well together and then, at some point, they simply stopped being on speaking terms.

Yet neither of them had asked for a divorce.

Maigret finally fell asleep, still turning things over in his mind. When he woke up the next morning, he first drank the cup of coffee his wife had brought him in bed and then got up. It was raining a little outside.

'Are you going to have a busy day?'

'I don't know. I never know what's waiting for me.'

He took a taxi, which was significant, for he nearly always went by bus or métro.

He found the photographs lying on his desk; they were surprisingly clear. He took one copy of each and went to Peretti's office at the other end of the corridor. Peretti was head of the Vice Squad and he was the only police inspector to wear a diamond ring, as though something of the underworld had rubbed off on him.

A good-looking man with jet-black hair, he was still young and dressed in a rather flashy way.

'Hello there! Haven't seen you for a long time.'

It was true. The two men had their offices in the same corridor yet they hardly ever met and when they did it was usually at the Brasserie Dauphine.

'I don't suppose you know this lady?'

Peretti studied the enlargement of Nathalie's passport photograph, going over to the window to examine it more closely.

'Isn't it an old picture of that solicitor's wife, the one who was in the papers yesterday?'

'Yes, it's her, about fifteen years ago . . . Here's another one of her with her husband, taken a few weeks or maybe months later . . .'

Peretti studied the Cannes photograph as intently as he had done the other one.

'I can't place either one of them . . .'

'I didn't expect you to. But there's something else I'd like to know. My men have drawn up a list of all the nightclubs in Paris. Here's a copy of it. Do you see any clubs there which are still run by the same people as fifteen years ago? I'm particularly interested in clubs round the VIIIth *arrondissement*.'

Peretti looked at the list.

'Most of these clubs didn't exist fifteen years ago. Fashions change. At one time, the smart place for nightlife used to be Montmartre. Then it was Saint-Germain-des-Prés . . .

'Wait a moment . . . *Le Ciel de Lit*, Rue de Ponthieu . . . That used to be run by a nice old crook whom I've never been able to pin anything on; he still owns it . . . '

'Any others?'

'*Chez Mademoiselle*, Avenue de la Grande Armée. A very classy place run by a woman called Blanche Bonnard. She must be well over fifty by now, but she still looks pretty good. She has another club called *Le Doux Frisson* in Montmartre, Rue Fontaine; it's less genteel than the other one . . . '

'Do you know where she lives?'

'She's got a flat in the Avenue de Wagram; I gather she spent a small fortune doing it up . . . '

'I'll leave you the list. I've more copies of it. If you happen to think of any others . . .

'I forgot to ask you where the owner of *Le Ciel de Lit* lives . . . '

'Marcel Lenoir? In the same building as his club, on the third or fourth floor. I raided his place once, hoping to find some drugs . . .'

'Thanks, old chap.'

'How's your case getting on?'

'So-so . . . '

Maigret went back to his office. Then, as usual, he went to the office of the director for a briefing. During the briefing, he could not help recalling that he might have been sitting in his boss's place only a month hence.

'How are you getting on with your solicitor's case, Maigret?'

The superintendents of the other departments were all present, each carrying various files.

'I'm not getting anywhere. I'm just accumulating bits and pieces of information which may or may not come in useful later . . . '

He sent off the enlargement of Nathalie's photograph to the newspapers, with the caption: *Madame Sabin-Levesque, aged twenty.*

He then went upstairs to the police archives and looked up the names Trika and Nathalie Frassier. He found nothing. Nathalie did not have a police record and had never had any encounters with the law.

'Will you take me to the Rue de Ponthieu?'

Lapointe or Janvier drove Maigret everywhere; he had never sat behind the wheel of a car in his life. He had bought a car recently to go to his little house in Meung-sur-Loire on a Saturday evening or Sunday morning, but it was Madame Maigret who did all the driving.

'Anything new, chief?'

'We're going to see the proprietor of a nightclub. He's been running the same place for twenty years . . . '

The gates of the nightclub were shut, but they could see, through the grating, some large framed photographs of nearly-nude women.

They went in by the main doorway. The concierge sent them up to the third floor on the left. A rather grubby little maid opened the door for them.

'Monsieur Lenoir? . . . I don't know if he can see you . . . He's only just got up and he's eating his breakfast . . . '

'Tell him Superintendent Maigret wishes to see him . . . '

A moment later, Lenoir came out into the hall to greet his visitors. He was huge, very fat and not very clean-looking. He wore an old, wine-coloured dressing gown over faded pyjamas.

'To what do I owe the pleasure . . . ?'

'Pleasure has nothing to do with it. Please carry on with your breakfast . . . '

'I apologize for receiving you in this fashion . . . '

Lenoir was an old rogue who had run a brothel twenty-five years earlier. He was probably about sixty but he looked older; he was unshaven and his eyes were still heavy with sleep.

'Will you please come this way . . . '

The apartment was as untidy as its occupant, whose belongings lay strewn everywhere. They went into a small dining-room which had a window overlooking the street.

Lenoir had finished one boiled egg and was just opening a second.

'I need a good start in the morning . . . '

He was drinking black coffee. The ash-tray was full of cigarette ends.

'Well, what can I do for you?'

'I want to show you a photograph and you must tell me if it reminds you of anyone . . . '

Maigret showed him the enlargement of Nathalie's passport photograph.

'She looks vaguely familiar . . . What's her name?'

'In those days, about fifteen years ago, she used to call herself Trika . . . '

'They all love to choose the most idiotic names . . . Trika . . . '

'Do you recognize her?'

'No, I don't to tell you the truth . . . '

'Can you look up her name in your files?'

Lenoir was a messy eater; there was egg yolk on his chin and on the lapel of his dressing-gown.

'Do you imagine I keep a file on every girl who works in my nightclub? . . . Those women come and go . . . A lot of them get married and you'd be surprised how many of them make really good marriages . . . One of my girls became an English duchess . . . '

'Don't you even keep their photographs?'

'They nearly all take their photographs with them when they go . . . And if they leave them, I just tear them up and throw them away . . . '

'Thank you, Lenoir . . . '

'It's been a pleasure . . . '

He got up, his mouth still full, and accompanied them back to the door.

'31, Avenue de Wagram . . . '

Number 31 was the luxury apartment block where Blanche Bonnard lived, as well as a dentist, two doctors and a barrister.

'Whom shall I say is calling?' the maid asked. She was dressed like the classic housemaid in a French comedy.

'Maigret.'

'The inspector?'

'Yes.'

Blanche Bonnard was not eating her breakfast but she was talking on the phone. They could hear her from another room.

'Yes ... Yes ... My dear boy. I can't just commit myself like that ... I need more information, my architect will have to make a survey ... Yes ... No, I don't know how long it'll take ... I'll see you this evening at the club, all right? ... If you like ... Bye ... '

When she walked into the room, the sound of her footsteps was muffled by the brightly-coloured rugs which lay strewn everywhere on the carpet. She stared at Maigret for a long time, glancing only briefly at Lapointe.

'You're lucky not to find me in bed. I usually get up late but today I've got an appointment with my business manager ... Do come in ... '

The living-room was sumptuous, much too sumptuous for Maigret's liking. Blanche must have been in her late fifties but she was still a good-looking woman, even at this time in the morning. She was plump, but pleasantly so, and she had beautiful eyes.

'I suppose you've come because of the Sabin-Levesque affair? I was expecting you one of these days, but I had no idea you'd be so quick ... '

She lit a gold-tipped cigarette.

'Please smoke your pipe ... It won't disturb me, or my parrot for that matter ... When I saw that picture in the papers yesterday, I immediately thought I recognized her from somewhere. So I checked and of course I was right ... '

'Did you know Madame Sabin-Levesque in the days when she called herself Trika?'

'And how!'

She got up, went into another room and reappeared, carrying an enormous album.

'My memory isn't very good so I keep everything. I've got five albums like this one, all stuffed with photographs ... Look ... '

She opened the album and showed it to Maigret. There was a photograph on the right-hand page, of the kind taken by photographers in nightclubs.

It was of Nathalie, looking very young and demure. She was wearing a low-cut dress which showed her cleavage.

Sabin-Levesque was sitting by her side, bending slightly towards her ... There was a bottle of champagne in an ice-bucket on the table ...

88

'He met her here ... She'd been a hostess for about two months ...'

'Do you know where she had come from?'

'Yes. She had been working in a rather sleazy nightclub in Nice ...'

'Did she speak about her past to you?'

'Oh, they all do. Most of them live on their own and have no one to talk to ... So they come and tell Mama Blanche everything ... Can I offer you a drink? ... I don't drink much myself, but I have a glass of port about now.'

The port was exceptional; Maigret had never drunk a finer one.

'Her family name was Frassier. Her father died when she was about fifteen. He was an accountant or something of the sort ... Her mother was the daughter of a Russian count and she liked people to know it ... You see, I haven't got such a bad memory after all ...

'She always sat at the same table in my club. At first, the customers were a bit shy with her because she looked so young and innocent. They would hesitate before going up to her table; she would always smile and act friendly, but she was rather withdrawn ...

'She hardly ever went off with anyone. I don't think she did more than three times ...'

'Did she have a steady boyfriend?'

'No. She lived alone in a little hotel room not far from here, in the Rue Brey. I liked her, but I never could quite figure her out ...'

'One evening, Gérard Sabin-Lévesque came in ... I mean Monsieur Charles, because that was the name we knew him by ... He had been coming to the club for a long time ... He liked gentle and quiet women and he noticed Trika the moment he came in ... He went over to sit at her table ... He asked her to go off with him but she refused ...

'He came back every evening for a week before she finally agreed to leave with him ... She left me some of her belongings, a couple of dresses, some underwear and a few odds and ends ...

'She came back a few days later to fetch her things.

' "Madly in love?" I asked her.

'She looked at me without answering.

' "Is he setting you up?"

' "It's not definite yet . . . "

'Then she kissed me and thanked me and I never saw her again.

'Two months later, though, I saw a wedding picture of them in the *Figaro*. Trika was wearing a wedding-dress and her husband a tail-coat.

' "Monsieur Gérard Sabin-Levesque, well-known society solicitor, was married this morning to . . . " '

Maigret and Lapointe exchanged looks, wondering what to make of the story. The little girl from Quimper, the hostess who had worked in a sleazy Nice nightclub and after that in Blanche Bonnard's establishment, had become the wife of one of the richest and best-known solicitors in Paris.

Gérard's father was still alive in those days. He was a man of principles. What had been his reaction to his son's marriage? And how did the three of them get along when they were all living together in the same flat?

Was Nathalie already drinking in those days? And did she spend most of the time in her rooms, the way she did now?

The years had passed and she drank more than ever. The solicitor had given up hope of a real married life. Husband and wife had grown estranged, almost becoming enemies.

'She's free now . . . free and rich . . . Is that what's bothering you, Superintendent?'

'What the newspapers haven't said yet is that Sabin-Levesque was hit a dozen times over the head with a blunt instrument, which broke his skull into small fragments . . . '

'Would a woman be capable of doing that?'

'In certain circumstances, women can show as much strength as men, if not more . . . Let us suppose she did it . . . Where would she have committed the murder? . . . In their flat? . . . He lost a great deal of blood . . . It would have left stains and she's too clever not to realize that . . .

'Besides, how would she have got the body to the Seine? How would she have got it out of a car and into the river?'

'Of course . . . Perhaps he was murdered by some ruffian he met in a deserted street?'

'Nothing was removed from his wallet and there was over two thousand francs in it.'

'A revenge killing?'

'Why would anyone want to revenge themselves on him?'

'A lover . . . the lover of one of those women he picked up in the nightclubs . . .'

'That sort of lover isn't jealous of a paying customer . . . Unless perhaps one of them was trying to blackmail him . . .'

Maigret took another look at the photograph of the young couple drinking their champagne. He finished his port.

'Will you have another?'

'No thank you, though it's delicious . . .'

He had learned a few more details about Nathalie's past, but had it got him any further in his investigations?

Madame Maigret was surprised when her husband came home for lunch, but it obviously did not mean very much, for he was sullen and withdrawn as before.

He usually loved the *pot-au-feu* with *pauvre-homme* sauce which she had made for him, but today he hardly noticed what he was eating.

'Can I have a really large cup of coffee . . . ?'

She knew this meant one like his morning cup, which held a good third of a litre. He glanced at the papers: there were interviews with the concierge and with one of the employees from the practice. The reporters had also tried to interview Vito, but he had not been very forthcoming.

When Maigret got back to his office, he found a transcript of all the telephone calls made to and from the Sabin-Levesque flat.

Nathalie had not telephoned once since the police had started to tap her phone, but she had received an incoming call that morning. It had been very brief.

'Is that you?'

'Yes.'

'I must see you . . .'

Without waiting or saying anything, she had hung up. On the same line, but probably on another extension, the cook had ordered some veal from the butcher, which the chauffeur would collect later on.

The practice, however, had been flooded with incoming calls from clients. Many of them sounded worried. Lecureur had tried to reassure them and to answer their questions as best he could.

Maigret went up to see the examining magistrate, although he had nothing much to tell him. But Coindet was in no hurry. He sat at his desk, slowly sucking on an old pipe and looking through some files.

'Sit down, Maigret.'

'I've got practically nothing to tell you. You must have received the report of the autopsy . . . '

'Yes, I did, this morning . . . The murderer won't be able to claim that he didn't mean to kill his victim . . . Have you any idea where the crime was committed?'

'No, I haven't, not so far . . . The experts at the Criminal Identity Laboratory are examining his clothes and shoes down to the last little seam . . . But the body's been in the water for such a long time that it may well yield no results . . . '

Maigret filled his pipe, lit it and offered Coindet some tobacco from his pouch.

'I've had some successes in one area. Madame Sabin-Levesque claims she was working as a secretary for a lawyer in the Rue de Rivoli when she met her future husband. This lawyer turns out to have been dead for ten years, so he can't refute her story.

'I found some photographs in one of the solicitor's drawers. One of them was of Nathalie when she was much younger; there was a name written on the back of it: Trika.

'That's a false name, of course. I knew what sort of women the solicitor liked, so I did some investigating around the nightclubs. I learned that his wife used to be a hostess, not a secretary. I even know in what nightclub she met Sabin-Levesque . . . '

Coindet gazed thoughtfully at the smoke coming out of his pipe.

'Do you think she ever went back to her old haunts?' he asked in his mild voice.

'I shouldn't think so . . . After her marriage, she must have thoroughly despised that world; she had always felt it was unworthy of her . . .

'This morning, someone telephoned her. It was a man's voice but we didn't have time to find out where he was ringing from. He just said:

' "I must see you . . . "

'She hung up without answering. I still have the feeling that she knows far more than she's telling us; that's why I'm hounding her rather. I'll go back and see her, not for any reason in particular.'

The two men smoked their pipes in silence for a moment; then they shook hands and Maigret returned to his office.

He went into the adjoining room and asked Janvier:

'Who's on duty out there at the Boulevard Saint-Germain?'

'Inspector Baron . . . '

Lapointe was looking at him expectantly. Maigret turned to him and said:

'I'm going there alone . . . It's an experiment . . . She might be less wary and perhaps . . . '

He finished his sentence with a gesture, implying that he did not really believe there was much hope of it.

He took a taxi and when he got there he could see Inspector Baron across the street walking up and down; he went over to speak to him.

'Has she gone out?'

'No. I've nothing to report. The chauffeur went out in the Fiat this morning; I assume he only went to do the shopping because he came back soon afterwards . . . '

The concierge was such a nice fellow and so proud to shake hands with a police superintendent that Maigret went to pay him a brief visit.

'I gather she hasn't gone out?'

'No. All the people who've come in were for the doctor up on the third floor.'

'How many years have you been working here?'

'Sixteen years. My feet get sore easily, so it didn't suit me to be in the City Police force.'

'Did you know Sabin-Levesque when he was still a bachelor?'

'He was married six months after I came here.'

'Did he disappear for several days at a time even then?'

'Yes, except during the last two or three weeks before he got married.'

'And was his father still alive in those days?'

'Yes. He was a fine-looking man, the picture of a solicitor, with a youthful face and snow-white hair.'

'How did he get on with his son?'

'I don't think he was especially proud of him, but he had resigned himself . . . '

Maigret went up to the first floor and rang the bell.

The maid, Claire, opened the door and said with a sneer:

'Madame Sabin-Levesque has gone out.'

'Are you quite certain of that?'

'Yes.'

'What time did she leave the house?'

'About two o'clock . . . '

It was ten past three.

'Did she take one of the cars?'

'I don't think so.'

Maigret knew that Baron could not have missed Nathalie; and besides, the concierge would have seen her going out too.

He walked into the flat, closing the door behind him.

'What are you going to do?'

'Nothing. Pay no attention to me. If you're frightened I'll steal something, you can follow me around . . . '

He started searching the left-hand side of the apartment, which was Nathalie's section. He even peered into the wardrobes, which made Claire smile.

'Why do you think she would hide in a closet?'

'It's as good a hiding-place as any.'

'She has no reason to hide.'

'She has no reason not to go out by the main door, either . . . '

He walked around the drawing-room, studying the austere-looking portraits of Sabin-Levesque's ancestors; he thought of the life their descendant had led and wondered if they had carried on in the same fashion when they were not sitting for their portraits.

'Where's the other way out of the house?'

'I suppose I can tell you, since everyone else knows about it . . . '

'By the courtyard?'

'No. There's a little glass door next to the lift. You open it and walk down a few steps into the garden. You cross the garden and you come to a door in the wall. If you go out by there, you find yourself in the Rue Saint-Simon.'

'Isn't the door locked?'

'Yes, it is. But Monsieur and Madame Sabin-Levesque happen to be the owners, so they've got a key.'

'Where do they keep the key?'

'I don't know . . .'

It was an interesting point. Did Gérard or his wife keep the key? And if it was Gérard, when had she taken it from him?

He went into the solicitor's small study and sat down in a comfortable leather armchair.

'Are you planning to stay here for long?'

'Until your mistress comes back.'

'She won't be pleased.'

'Why not?'

'Because you're not supposed to be here while she's out.'

'You're very loyal to her, aren't you?'

'Why shouldn't I be?'

'Is she nice to you?'

'She can be extremely disagreeable sometimes, rude and unfair, but I don't hold it against her.'

'Do you feel she's not responsible for her actions?'

'Not at those moments . . .'

'Do you think of her as a sick woman?'

'It's not her fault if she only has drink to fall back on.'

'If she asked you to lie for her, to perjure yourself, would you do it?'

'Certainly.'

'It can't be very nice for you when she vomits in her bed at night . . .'

'Nurses have to cope with far worse things than that.'

Maigret thought he heard a sound in the hall, coming from the door. He did not stir and the maid did not seem to have heard.

'What would you do if I began to scream and then accused you of having tried to rape me?'

Maigret could not help laughing.

'Why don't you try? . . . It might be amusing . . .'

She shrugged and walked off through the main drawing-room in the direction of Nathalie's rooms. She did not return, but Nathalie soon came into the study from the drawing-room, very unsteady on her feet.

She was white as a sheet and there were dark circles around her eyes. The lipstick on her mouth looked like a gash. She almost fell as she came in and Maigret rose to help her.

'Please don't worry about me. I can still stand up by myself . . .'

She sank down into the armchair opposite the chief superintendent and stared at him with a dazed look in her eyes.

'Who told you . . .'

She shook her head as though to erase the words she had just spoken.

'Could you please ring that bell over by the door?'

Maigret rang the bell, which would summon one of the servants.

'It's hot . . .'

Without getting up, she took off her brown tweed jacket.

'Aren't you warm?'

'Not right now. You must have walked too fast.'

'What makes you think I've been walking?'

'Because you knew I would find your driver if you took a taxi and that I'd learn where you've just been that way . . .'

She stared at him, a look of shock in her eyes. She seemed incapable of pulling herself together.

'You're clever . . . But you're cruel . . .'

He had hardly ever seen anyone as acutely distressed and crushed as Nathalie was at that moment. Claire must have known why she had been called, for she came in carrying a tray with a bottle of brandy, a glass and a packet of cigarettes on it . . . She filled the glass herself and handed it to Nathalie, who almost dropped it . . .

'You won't have one, will you? You're not an alcoholic yet . . .'

She had trouble pronouncing the word alcoholic and had to repeat it.

'Hasn't your doctor ever suggested you should go to a hospital for treatment?'

'Oh yes! If he had his way I'd have been locked up in an asylum long ago . . . Which would have suited my husband perfectly . . . You see how odd life is . . .'

She stopped abruptly, as though she had lost her train of thought.

'Odd ... odd ...' she kept on repeating to herself, with a far-away look in her eyes ... 'Ah yes ... Life ... Now my husband's dead and I'm still alive ...'

She looked around the study, then glanced towards the drawing-room, and a rather satisfied expression came into her face. She took another gulp of brandy and said in a joyless tone:

'Everything's mine.'

He expected to see her collapse on the floor any minute and yet, in spite of her drunkenness, she retained some sense of reality.

'I never used to come in here ...'

She was now gazing at the walls of the study.

'He only came in here to read.'

'Do you remember the *Chez Mademoiselle* nightclub?'

She gave a start and her eyes grew hard again.

'What did you say?'

'Madame Blanche, the owner of *Chez Mademoiselle* ...'

'Who told you about it?'

'Never mind. I've got a very nice photograph of you and Gérard drinking a bottle of champagne together. This was before your marriage ...'

She did not stir; her manner had grown defensive again.

'You never were a secretary. You worked in a third-rate club in Nice where you were forced to go upstairs with the customers ...'

'You're a bastard, Superintendent.'

She swallowed the rest of her brandy in one gulp.

'I'm the wife of Monsieur Sabin-Levesque now ...'

She corrected herself.

'I mean the widow of Monsieur Sabin-Levesque ...'

She was panting slightly.

'I don't believe you killed your husband ... You're a very energetic woman but you wouldn't be physically capable of such a murder ... Unless an accomplice ...'

'I never even went out that evening ...'

'On the 18th of February?'

'Yes.'

'You remember the date?'

'You told me that was the date ...'

'Who rang you up this morning?'

'I don't know.'

'Someone was determined to see you and said it was absolutely necessary . . . '

'It must have been a wrong number.'

'You hung up, guessing that the phone was tapped, but by a strange coincidence you went out this afternoon . . . You did not leave by the main door but by the little door in the garden. By the way, was it your husband or you who kept that key?'

'It was me.'

'Why?'

'Because he never went into the garden and I did from time to time. I used to go and sit there in the summer. I hid the key in a crevice in the wall.'

'Did you ever use it?'

'Yes, to go and buy cigarettes across the way . . . Or maybe to go and have a drink . . . They'll tell you . . . I'm the local drunk, aren't I?'

'Where did you go this afternoon?'

'I went for a walk.'

'And where did you stop?'

'I don't know. In a bar, perhaps.'

She was swaying and he began to feel sorry for her.

He got up.

'I'll ring for your maid and she'll put you to bed . . . '

'I don't want to go to bed . . . '

The idea seemed to frighten her; she was living in a nightmare.

'I'll ring for her anyway.'

'No . . . Stay here . . . I'd rather even you were here . . . Do you know anything about medicine?'

'No . . . '

'Give me your hand . . . '

She put his hand on her chest; her heart was throbbing violently.

'Do you think I'm going to die?'

'No, I don't. What's your doctor's name?'

'I don't want to see him either . . . He'll have me locked up . . . He's a beastly man . . . One of Gérard's friends . . . '

Maigret looked up the doctor in the directory. He lived just around the corner, in the Rue de Lille.

'Hello ... Doctor Bloy? ... It's Superintendent Maigret speaking ... I'm at Madame Sabine-Levesque's house ... She isn't feeling at all well and I think she needs your help ...'

'Are you sure she isn't putting on an act?'

'Does she do that sometimes?'

'Yes. Unless she's dead drunk ...'

'I'd say that was the case today ...'

'I'll come over right away ...'

'He's going to give me an injection,' she was moaning. 'He always gives me an injection every time he comes ... He's a fool and he thinks he's smarter than anyone else ... Don't go ... Don't leave me alone with him ... He's a wicked man ... The world is full of wicked people and I'm all alone ... Do you realize that? ... All alone ...'

She began to weep; the tears rolled down her cheeks and her nose was running.

'Haven't you got a handkerchief?'

She shook her head and Maigret gave her his, as he would have done to a child.

'Whatever happens, don't let him send me to a hospital ... I can't bear the idea of going there ...'

There was no way of stopping her from drinking still more. She would suddenly grab her glass and empty it in a flash.

They heard the door-bell ring. A moment later, Claire ushered in a very tall, athletic-looking man. Maigret found out later that the doctor had once been a rugby player.

'Glad to meet you,' he said, shaking hands with Maigret.

He glanced at Nathalie with indifference; she did not stir but stared at him, terrorized.

'Well? Like on the previous occasions? Come into your room ...'

She tried to protest but he caught her by the hand, holding his medical bag in his other hand.

'Monsieur Maigret ... Don't let them send me ...'

Claire followed them out of the room. Maigret wondered what to do next and finally sat down in an armchair in the main drawing-room; he knew the doctor would have to cross the room on his way out.

The doctor reappeared much sooner than Maigret had expected. His expression remained as indifferent as before.

'It must be the hundredth time,' he said. 'She ought to be sent to a clinic and kept there for quite a while.'

'Was she like that already when Sabin-Levesque married her?'

'Yes, but not quite as bad. She was already a heavy drinker and she couldn't do without it even in those days. Then there was some story about her being scared out of her wits by a dog . . . Though I must admit the dog really did snarl at her every time she went near it or her husband . . . She made Gérard fire the chauffeur and get another at least two or three times in succession, just as she got rid of one maid after another . . .'

'Would you say she was mad?'

'Not in the clinical sense of the word. Let's just call her neurotic. Because of all her drinking . . .'

For some reason, the doctor changed the subject abruptly.

'Have you discovered who killed poor Gérard? . . . I've lived around the corner ever since I was a child and we used to play in the Luxembourg Gardens together . . . We went to the same school, then we were students at the same time . . . He was the nicest chap you can imagine . . .'

They went downstairs together and continued talking outside on the pavement for a while before they parted.

Chapter Six

Maigret walked along the *quais*, vaguely looking at the waters of the Seine. He kept his pipe clasped between his teeth and his hands in his pockets, and he seemed to be in a bad mood.

He could not help feeling rather guilty. He had been hard, almost ruthless, with Nathalie, yet he felt no animosity towards her.

He had been particularly tough today. She was helpless, incapable of acting her part, and then, suddenly, she had collapsed. He felt quite sure that her collapse had not been part of an act, that she really was at the end of her tether. But he had been doing his work and was only being conscientious in carrying out his duty; if he had been cruel, it was only because he felt it was necessary.

Besides, the doctor who had known her for a long time had been just as hard on her.

She must be fast asleep by now, thanks to the injection the doctor had given her; but what would happen when she woke up?

There was only one person in that huge apartment who cared about her and that was the maid, Claire Marelle. It had been like that for fifteen years.

Marie Jalon, the cook, who had been almost like a mother to Gérard Sabin-Levesque, always looked upon his wife as an intruder. The butler, Honoré, watched all those bottles of cognac vanish with disgust. There was also a cleaning-lady called Madame Ringuet, who came to the flat every morning. Maigret had only met her briefly, but he suspected that she too belonged to the husband's camp.

There had been something rather child-like about the solicitor, and this made people forgive him everything. He was basically selfish, like a child, and at the same time honest about it.

Shortly after his marriage he returned to the kind of life he had been leading as a bachelor. He was brilliant at his legal work and success came easily to him. And, whenever he wished, he would turn into Monsieur Charles again for the evening.

He was known in most of the nightclubs around the Champs-Elysées; that in itself was odd. He never went to clubs in Montmartre or Saint-Germain-des-Prés. He hunted his quarry, so to speak, only within a defined territory, in the most elegant and chic places.

When those doormen with their gold braid saw him arrive, they called out with a mixture of respect and familiarity:

'Good evening, Monsieur Charles . . .'

And he would remain Monsieur Charles for the whole of that evening, a young man who would never grow old, who smiled at everyone and gave generous tips.

The hostesses would eye him, wondering if it would be their turn tonight. Sometimes he only drank a bottle of champagne with one of them. Or else he took the girl away with him and the manager did not dare complain.

He had been a happy man with no problems. He did not mix with people from his own world; you never saw him at their parties. He liked the convenience of going out with professionals, and if he spent a few days with one of them, it amused him to help her with little household tasks.

He had certainly not intended to get married. He did not feel the least inclination towards matrimony.

Yet he had married Nathalie. Had she won him over by playing the gentle, docile and helpless little woman? It was likely. There was something touching about her in the passport photograph; in it, she looked like a vulnerable little girl.

She was asking for his protection, making him feel big and strong . . .

She was married in white, like a chaste young maiden. She had been dazzled by the house in the Boulevard Saint-Germain. And the big old-fashioned villa in Cannes must have seemed like paradise to her at first; she had put up with everything, even the presence of the strange dog which snarled at her.

What had gone wrong?

She was alone in the huge apartment for days on end. Her

husband and her father-in-law were working in their offices downstairs. Mealtimes were rather formal affairs. She did not have Claire with her yet but another maid, for whom she was merely the boss's wife.

She had gradually grown harder. She started by insisting that her husband got rid of the dog, which he did very reluctantly. They had nothing to say to each other in the evenings. She did not read books and did nothing except watch television.

They still slept together in the same bed, but they never really became intimate.

Then, one day, Gérard left without warning anyone, to go and play the part of Monsieur Charles again in the Étoile district.

This was his real nature, his child-like side. He was happy-go-lucky and cheerful; everyone welcomed him and was pleased to see him.

Nathalie had thought that she would be the centre of attraction; instead, she discovered that she was superfluous. Her husband tolerated her. He did not ask for a divorce, but they began to sleep in separate rooms and she would lie in bed, brooding over all her grievances.

It was a mild day. The sun was slowly sinking in the west and Maigret strolled along, without hurrying. Twice he bumped into a passerby coming from the opposite direction.

Nathalie was already drinking in her hostess days. She started to take to the bottle in earnest when she found herself all alone in the flat; she was trying to knock herself out.

Maigret wondered if it had all really happened the way he imagined. The more Nathalie drank, the more her husband grew away from her.

Then her father-in-law died. Gérard had to shoulder new responsibilities and as a result he needed to relax more than ever before.

They had both held out for fifteen years. This was what really astonished Maigret. For fifteen years, they had met without exchanging a word in those rooms where no one seemed to live. In the end, she could no longer even bear to sit and eat her meals with him.

She had become a stranger and her only good fortune was to have found someone like Claire, who was her ally.

Why didn't she leave? How could she bear to continue leading that stifling existence?

She went to the cinema in the afternoons. At least she claimed she did. She would ask the chauffeur to drive her to a bar in the Champs-Elysées district from time to time. There she would sit perched on a high stool at the bar and drink by herself.

The barmen would fill her glass the moment it was empty, without waiting for her to ask. She spoke to no one. No one spoke to her. She was known as 'the woman who drinks'.

Had she finally met a man who was prepared to look after her and to restore her shattered ego?

So far, Maigret had found nothing in his investigations to make him suppose such a thing had occurred. Vito claimed that she always left the various bars alone, staggering a little.

She was a widow now. The house, the practice and the money belonged to her, but wasn't it too late? She was drinking more than ever. She was frightened of something. She seemed to be fleeing from reality, from life itself.

Where did she go when she slipped out by the garden door? Who had telephoned her that morning?

It was hard to know when she was lying or when she was speaking the truth. She was a clever actress; within minutes, she had been able to transform herself into a high society lady for the benefit of those photographers and reporters.

Maigret went half-way across the Pont-Neuf and stopped at the Brasserie Dauphine.

'A *pastis* like the other day?'

'No, a brandy . . . '

It was a challenge. He would do the same as her. He would have a brandy. The first sip burned his throat. Yet he had a second brandy before he went back to the Police Judiciaire.

The file which he had shown to his colleague in the Vice Squad lay on his desk.

He picked it up and took it to the inspectors' duty room, which contained at that moment about twenty inspectors.

'I need ten of you, those who don't look too much like policemen . . . '

The men smiled, some of them a trifle sourly.

'Here's a list of all the nightclubs in Paris . . . Forget about the ones in Saint-Germain-des-Prés and Montmartre. Concentrate on the ones in the VIIIth *arrondissement* and thereabouts . . .'

He gave Lucas the list, with a dozen copies of the Cannes photograph.

'You don't have to hide your profession, but don't be too obvious about it either . . . Each one of you will be given a photograph and some addresses . . . You must go there at about midnight and question the barmen, the *patron* and the hostesses . . , Keep the date of the 18th of February in mind . . . Also the name Monsieur Charles . . . I forgot, also talk to the flower-sellers who go from one club to another . . . I know it'll be a miracle, but I want to find someone who saw Monsieur Charles on February 18th . . .'

He gave Lucas the whole file and returned to his office, still looking preoccupied.

It was probably a stab in the dark, but people did sometimes remember a date because of a birthday or because of some particular incident which happened that day.

Lapointe had followed him.

'May I come in, chief? . . . I wanted to tell you about a phone call which came through for you while you were out. I took the liberty of answering in your place.

'The municipal police rang . . . A police officer in Puteaux reported a black Citroën abandoned apparently quite a while ago on some waste ground.

'Apparently there are some bloodstains on the front passenger seat, especially on the back of the seat . . .'

'Who does the car belong to?'

'To a man called Dennery; he's a municipal engineer who lives in the Rue La-Boétie.'

'When was the car stolen?'

'On the 18th February, which is the interesting part . . . He reported the theft to his local police station . . . No one thought of looking for the car in that god-forsaken corner of Puteaux . . .'

'Were the number plates removed?'

'No, they weren't. That's what allowed them to trace the owner immediately . . .'

'Where's the car?'

'I asked the police commissioner of Puteaux to leave it where it was and to send a police officer to keep a watch on it . . . '

So they had one positive clue at last! It was not definite yet, but it might eventually lead them somewhere.

'Put me through to Doctor Grenier . . . '

Maigret hoped that the doctor was not busy with some other autopsy.

'Grenier? Maigret speaking. I need you . . . '

'Right away?'

'The sooner the better . . . '

'Another corpse?'

'No. But maybe the car which transported the corpse.'

'Where do I have to go?'

'Come over here. I don't know the exact location; we'll drop in at the Puteaux police station and they'll tell us.'

'All right. I'll be with you in fifteen minutes.'

He then rang up Moers at the Criminal Identity Department.

'I need those specialists who worked on the solicitor's case.'

'They're right here. Where do you want me to send them?'

'To the police station in Puteaux; they'll be told where to go from there.'

Maigret had almost forgotten how difficult the afternoon had been. They picked up Doctor Grenier and Lapointe drove them off to Puteaux, no easy job at that time of day.

'We don't often see you in these parts, Superintendent Maigret . . . '

'I'd like one of your men to take us to the car you've just found.'

'That's easily done.'

He gave instructions to a policeman, who just managed to squeeze into the small car with them.

'It's very near . . . Next to a demolition site . . . They're pulling down an old house to build a block of flats . . . '

The car was very dusty. The headlamps and the tyres had been stolen. A policeman was standing guard over it and a man of about fifty came rushing over to Maigret.

'Look at the state my car is in!'

'Are you the owner?'

'My name is Georges Dennery. I'm an engineer . . . '

'Where was your car stolen?'

'Right in front of my house. My wife and I had just finished dinner and we were going to drive to a cinema in the Latin Quarter . . . The car had disappeared . . . I dashed over to the police station . . . Who is going to pay for the repairs, the tyres and the headlamps?'

'You'll have to inquire at the appropriate department.'

'Which is the appropriate department?'

'I don't know,' Maigret had to admit, a little testily.

The grey material of the upholstery had absorbed the blood. Doctor Grenier took a small glass phial out of his medical kit and began his intricate task.

The men from the Criminal Identity Department were searching for fingerprints on the doors, the steering-wheel, the hand-brake and the gear-lever.

'Can you find any?'

'There are some beautiful ones on the steering-wheel. The other prints aren't so clear . . . Somebody was smoking Gitanes . . . the ashtray's full of them.'

'What's on the dead man's side?'

'Nothing except for the blood on the upholstery.'

'And bits of brain,' the doctor added. 'The traces here correspond exactly to those which would have been left by the corpse I examined . . .'

They went on working meticulously for another hour. A small crowd of curious people had gathered to watch them and two Puteaux policemen were keeping them at bay.

The car was parked in the middle of the building site, which seemed abandoned for the moment.

Monsieur Dennery nervously went from one police officer to the other, obsessed by the question of who would pay for the damage done to his car.

'Aren't you insured against theft?'

'Yes, but the insurance companies never pay the whole amount . . . And I don't want to have to fork out for the rest . . . This sort of thing wouldn't happen if the streets of Paris were better patrolled.'

'Had you left the keys in the car?'

'I never dreamt that someone might steal it. The seats will have to be replaced . . . I don't even know if my wife will want to ride in a car which has carried a corpse . . . '

The men from the Criminal Identity Department had found a few woollen threads which probably belonged to a tweed jacket.

'Boys, I'll let you get on with your work. Try to establish a preliminary report for me by tomorrow morning, even if it's incomplete.'

'We'll do our best, chief.'

'My job won't take long at all,' Doctor Grenier said. 'I only have to do a blood test. I'll ring you at your flat this evening . . . '

Lapointe dropped Maigret off at the Boulevard Richard-Lenoir. Madame Maigret came to the door to greet her husband. She took one look at him and frowned.

'Not too tired?'

'Very tired.'

'Are you getting somewhere?'

'Could be . . . '

He was still quite grumpy and did not seem to notice what she gave him for dinner. After the meal, he sank into an armchair, filled a pipe and watched television.

He was thinking of Nathalie.

Maigret was dozing in his armchair when the phone rang, rudely jolting him out of his little oasis of silence. Only one lamp was lit. They had turned the television off. Madame Maigret sat on a chair a few feet away, sewing.

She never sat down in an armchair, claiming that it made her feel imprisoned.

With heavy footsteps, he walked over to the phone.

'Superintendent Maigret?'

'Yes. Speaking.'

His voice must have been slurred, for his caller asked:

'Have I woken you up?'

'No. Who is it calling?'

He did not recognize the voice.

'Doctor Bloy. I'm at the Boulevard Saint-Germain. Madame Sabin-Levesque has just tried to commit suicide.'

'Is her condition serious?'

'No. I thought you might like to see her before I give her another stronger injection.'

'I'll come over right away ... Thank you for calling ... '

His wife was already helping him on with his jacket; she went to fetch his overcoat.

'I suppose you'll be away a long time?'

'Will you call a taxi ... ?'

While she rang for the taxi, he filled his pipe and poured himself a small glass of *prunelle*. Madame Maigret noticed how upset he was. Of course, he did not know any of the details, yet he felt partially to blame for what had happened.

'The taxi will be here in a minute ... '

He gave his wife a kiss. She followed him to the door and opened it for him. Leaning over the balustrade, she watched him going down the stairs, giving him a little wave of her hand.

The taxi arrived a couple of minutes later. Maigret was about to give the address when the taxi-driver asked him in a sly tone:

'To the Quai des Orfèvres?'

'No. Not this time. Boulevard Saint-Germain. Number 207 *bis* ... At the far end of the boulevard ... '

He noticed a street clock which said that it was twenty past ten. This meant that he must have been asleep for nearly two hours, without realizing it.

He paid the taxi driver and rang at the main door. The ex-policeman turned concierge came to open it for him.

'I don't know what's happened, but the doctor's up there.'

'He rang me a moment ago.'

Maigret raced up the stairs and Claire Marelle opened the door for him. Doctor Bloy was waiting for him in Gérard Sabin-Levesque's little study.

'Is her condition serious?'

'No. The maid happens to have worked for a doctor once and she immediately tied a tourniquet above her wrist, even before she phoned me ... '

'I thought the injection was supposed to knock her out until tomorrow morning, if not later ... '

'It ought to have done. I don't understand how she woke up or how she was able to get up and walk around ... The maid was sleeping in a camp bed in the boudoir so as not to leave her alone . . . She woke up suddenly and saw her mistress walking through the room like a ghost, as she put it, or a sleepwalker . . .

'She went across the main drawing-room and into the dining-room . . . Then she went into her husband's rooms . . . '

' "Madame, what are you doing? You must go back to bed . . . You know what the doctor said . . . " '

'She was smiling in a peculiar, twisted sort of way.

' "You're a good girl, Claire . . . " '

Here the doctor added:

'And don't forget that all the lights were out at that moment, except for the one in the boudoir. It must have been quite an awesome sight, but the maid kept her nerve.

' "Give me something to drink." '

' "I don't think I ought to." '

' "Then I'll go and fetch the bottle myself . . . " '

'Claire preferred to get it for her. She put her mistress to bed, then she telephoned me. I was playing bridge with some friends. I dashed over. It's a deep wound; I had to make three stitches . . .

'She didn't speak to me. She just stared at me without any expression on her face, except perhaps indifference.'

'Does she know you telephoned me?' Maigret asked.

'No. I called you from the study . . . I thought you might like to speak to her before I really knock her out with another injection.

'That woman is incredibly tough.'

'I'll go and see her.'

Once again, Maigret crossed the apartment and went into the boudoir; he could still see the imprint of Claire's body on the camp bed.

'You see what you've done?' Claire said to him; her voice was not angry but sorrowful.

'How is she?'

'She's lying without moving, and staring at the ceiling; she won't answer when I speak to her. All I ask is that you treat her humanely . . . '

Maigret felt awkward as he went into the bedroom. Nathalie lay with the sheet pulled up to her chin; only her bandaged arm was resting on top of the bedclothes.

'I had a feeling they'd get in touch with you . . . '

Her voice sounded weary.

'I really wanted to die ... It's the only solution, isn't it? ... '

'Why do you say that?'

'Because I've nothing left to live for.'

Maigret was startled to hear her say this, as it did not fit in with what he knew. She had not loved her husband. She had not even pretended to like him.

She could never have felt that Gérard was her reason for living.

'I know you were only doing your job, but you were cruel ... '

'Have you anything to tell me?'

She did not answer him immediately.

'Pass me the bottle .... It'll be too late once the doctor gives me another injection ... '

He hesitated, then took down the bottle from the chest of drawers.

'Don't bother about a glass. My hand is shaking too much; I'd spill it ... '

She drank straight from the bottle, a sorry sight to see in those luxurious surroundings.

She almost dropped the bottle on the bedspread and Maigret caught it just in time.

'What are you going to do with me?'

Was she in her right mind? Her words, spoken in a muffled voice, could be interpreted in several ways.

'What do you expect'

'Nothing. I don't expect anything any more. I don't want to be alone in this big house ... '

'It's yours now ... '

Her mouth grew twisted once again.

'Yes ... It's mine ... It's all mine ... '

Her voice was full of a melancholy irony.

'If they had told me such a thing in the days when I was just a little nightclub hostess ... '

Maigret did not reply and for once did not even feel his usual urge to take his pipe out of his pocket.

'I'm Madame Sabin-Levesque ... '

She tried to laugh, but only succeeded in producing a sob.

'You can leave me now. I promise you I won't try to kill myself again ... Go back to your wife ... Because at least you're not alone ... '

111

She turned her head slightly to one side and looked at him.

'You've chosen a dirty sort of job, but I suppose it's not your fault . . .'

'I hope you sleep well . . .'

'Don't worry. This time, Doctor Bloy will increase the dose and heaven knows when I'll wake up . . .'

'Goodnight . . .'

Maigret left the room on tiptoe, rather as he would have left a deathbed. Claire was waiting for him in the boudoir.

'Did she talk to you?'

'Yes.'

'Did she reveal anything to you?'

'No. Is the doctor still in the study?'

'I think so.'

Maigret went to find him.

'Your turn now . . . I'll wait for you here . . .'

He filled his pipe and sank down into an armchair. Claire came into the room a few seconds later. She seemed much less hostile to him now.

'Why are you so hard on her?'

'Because I'm convinced that she knows who killed her husband.'

'What proof have you got?'

'I haven't any proof. If I had, I would already have arrested her.'

Oddly enough, the young woman did not protest.

'She's an unhappy woman.'

'I know that.'

'Everyone in the house hates her except me.'

'I know that too.'

'It's as though she usurped someone else's place by marrying Monsieur Gérard.'

'Did you ever go out anywhere with her?'

'No.'

'Do you know where she went?'

'To the cinema.'

'Did you ever find any old cinema tickets in her handbag or in her pockets?'

'No,' Claire answered, after thinking over his question carefully.

'Did she spend a great deal of money?'

'Monsieur Gérard gave her all she wanted. She would ask me to prepare a handbag for her and to put a specific sum of money in it . . .'

'How much, for example?'

'Sometimes a few hundred francs, sometimes two or three thousand . . .'

She bit her lip.

'I shouldn't have told you that.'

'Why not?'

'You know as well as I do . . . She hardly ever went shopping . . . All the tradesmen came here to the flat . . . She never went anywhere personally except to the hairdresser . . .'

The doctor came into the study and said to the maid:

'This time I think you'll get a good night's rest. I've given her the dose used for sleeping cures . . . Don't worry if she doesn't wake up tomorrow morning . . . I'll drop in shortly before noon . . .'

'Thank you, Doctor . . .'

She left the room and the doctor sat down and crossed his legs.

'Did she say anything interesting? Sometimes, when they're in that kind of state, people are more outspoken than they mean to be . . .'

'One of the things she asked me was what I was planning to do with her.'

'She's just been asking me the same question.'

'I think she knows quite a lot about her husband's death.'

'In any case, she's certainly trying hard to hide something. That's what has reduced her to this condition. I'm surprised she hasn't had an actual breakdown yet . . .'

'She asked me for something to drink and she was so insistent that I gave her the bottle . . .'

'You were right . . . Practically nothing could make her worse at this stage.'

'What's going to happen to her medically speaking?'

'Her condition will continue to deteriorate.'

'Do you mean that she'll go mad?'

'I'm not a psychiatrist . . . And indeed, I'd like a psychiatrist to examine her in a day or two . . . Anyway, if she goes on drinking at this rate, she'll be finished soon . . . She can't stay here; I haven't got the sort of equipment I'd need to look after her . . . She'll have to go to a clinic . . . Not necessarily a psychiatric clinic . . . They'll dry her out and make her take the rest she needs . . .'

He sighed.

'I don't like dealing with this kind of patient . . . By the way, do you know when the funeral will take place?'

'I didn't dare bring up the subject with her . . .'

'Do you think she'll want a lying-in?'

'The head clerk will probably deal with it. She's in no condition to do so herself.'

'It'll be much better for her if there isn't too much upset in the flat itself. I can't imagine a catafalque lying in the hallway or in the drawing-room . . .'

The two men got up and said goodbye to each other in the street. Maigret went home to bed. He slept badly and had nightmares. When his wife woke him up by bringing him his morning coffee, he discovered that he was aching all over, as though he had performed strenuous physical feats.

'Lapointe?' he asked over the phone. 'Is he there yet?'

'He's just coming in.'

'Let me speak to him, Lucas.'

'I'm listening, chief,' he heard Lapointe say.

'Come and get me at my place. First make sure that nothing new has happened.'

He had a bath, shaved and got dressed; then he swallowed a couple of aspirins, since he had a bad headache. He hardly touched his breakfast.

'I'll be glad when this inquiry is over,' Madame Maigret said in a low voice. 'You're taking it so much to heart you'll end up by falling ill.'

He looked at her gloomily and forced himself to smile.

'How come the papers hardly mention it any more?'

'Because there's nothing to say for the time being . . .'

He found Lapointe sitting behind the wheel of the car and got in next to him.

'Anything on my desk?'

114

'A report by the experts . . . The woollen threads found in the car are of the same type as the material of the dead man's jacket . . .'

'What about the men I sent out to the nightclubs?'

'Almost all the clubs saw Monsieur Charles and they all thought highly of him . . .'

'What about the 18th?'

'Not a single barman, *maître d'hôtel* or hostess remembered that particular date. Jamin may be on to something, though. An old flower-seller who goes round the clubs in that district remembers the 18th of February because it's her daughter's birthday. She claims that Monsieur Charles, who always used to buy flowers from her, was at the *Cric-Crac* that evening, in the Rue Clément Marot.'

'Did she say anything else?'

'He was with Zoé and he gave her some red carnations . . .'

'Have we got her address?'

'Jamin wrote it down. She's longing to come and see you in person because she knew you long ago, when you used to be walking the beat . . .'

They were standing in front of the large oak door which Maigret knew so well by now.

'Shall I wait for you?'

'No. Come inside with me.'

He said hello to the concierge as he walked past the lodge, then went into the office. The receptionist let him go through and, crossing the solicitor's office, he went into Lecureur's room. The head clerk was dictating a letter to his secretary. He stopped, sent her away and got up to shake hands with Maigret.

'I gather she tried to commit suicide during the night and that the doctor had to come?'

'It was nothing serious. She's asleep now . . .'

'Why did she do it, do you think?'

'If I knew, the inquiry would soon be over. What have you arranged, professionally speaking?'

'The will is to be read out this afternoon at three o'clock. I know what's in it, more or less, because I was one of the witnesses who signed it. Madame Sabin-Levesque inherits the money, the Cannes villa and the profits of the practice . . . The Institute of

Solicitors will decide my position, since my employer expressed the wish that I should succeed him . . . '

'There's another urgent matter to be looked after: the funeral.'

'I know the family has a vault in the Montparnasse cemetery.'

'That's one point settled. I suppose it wouldn't do for the coffin to be fetched directly from the Forensic Institute to be taken to the cemetery. Madame Sabin-Levesque is in no condition to deal with the question. I don't imagine it will be possible to arrange a lying-in in the apartment.'

'Why not here in the office?'

'That's what I had in mind. Will you deal with it?'

'I'll ring up an undertakers right away. Should we send out announcements to all the clients?'

'Yes, I think so. And don't forget to put an announcement in the papers. Incidentally, aren't you besieged by reporters?'

'We've had at least ten who came along and asked me all sorts of indiscreet questions; I threw them out. Two of them even wanted to know how much Monsieur Sabin-Levesque had left . . . '

'Keep in touch with me concerning the funeral arrangements, but Madame Sabin-Levesque is not to be disturbed.'

'Won't she be going to the church?'

'I don't think so. It'll depend on the doctor.'

Maigret then went upstairs with Lapointe. Claire opened the door.

'I had business to do downstairs so I came up to find out how everything was going.'

'She's asleep.'

'Have there been any phone calls?'

'No. Only one from a journalist who wanted to see her and who got very angry when I told him it wasn't possible.'

She was obviously tired and had probably not slept much.

'Drive me to the Rue Clément Marot . . . '

He felt like taking a look. At night, the street must be almost deserted. The multi-coloured door of the nightclub stood ajar.

Two cleaning-ladies were sweeping the floor, which was covered with confetti and paper streamers. The walls were hung with gaudy-coloured cloth.

'What do you want? If you're looking for Monsieur Felix, he isn't here.'

'Who is Monsieur Felix?'

'The barman.'

A man came in, looking very self-possessed.

'Well, well! The chief superintendent in person . . . One of your inspectors came to see us yesterday evening . . .'

'Tell me what you think of Louisa.'

'She used to be a street-walker and she's never left the district. But she had to change jobs in the end, so now she sells flowers in nightclubs and restaurants . . .'

'Is she reliable?'

'In what way?'

'She won't let her imagination run away with her? Can I believe what she tells me?'

'Certainly. She also knows how to keep a secret. Most of our young ladies have secrets and she knows every single one.'

'Thanks.'

'Why are you interested in her?'

'Because she claims to have seen Monsieur Charles here with a hostess on the evening of February 18th.'

'How can she remember the date?'

'Because it's her daughter's birthday.'

'Then she's telling you the truth.'

The club was not far away from the banks of the Seine; there was a ramp which led to the water's edge.

Chapter Seven

Once again Maigret had lunch at the Brasserie Dauphine with Lapointe. He hardly said a word during the entire meal. Not that he was particularly depressed, but he was in a mood which Lapointe knew well: a solemn and introspective mood, in which he kept his thoughts very much to himself.

When they returned to the Quai des Orfèvres, they saw an old woman through the glass partition of the waiting-room. Maigret did not know who she was at first, but she instantly recognized him and smiled.

It was old Louisa, as they called her now. Maigret had known her when she was young and sexy, one of the best-looking prostitutes along the Champs-Elysées.

He asked her into his office and took off his hat and coat.

'Just think, Inspector, what a long time it's been since we last met! You were a young fellow in those days and once you arrested me I really thought for a moment that you were about to make a pass at me!'

'Please sit down, Louisa.'

'You've come a long way since then, haven't you? Mind you, I haven't done too badly myself. I had my daughter raised by some decent folk in the country and now she's the wife of a cashier at the Crédit Lyonnaise bank . . . She has three kids, which makes me a granny three times over . . . Her birthday's on the 18th of February, that is why I remembered the date . . .'

'What exactly did you see?'

'To start with, I saw a black car with a fellow in it, about a hundred yards from the *Cric-Crac*. Then, inside the club, I saw Monsieur Charles sitting at a table with Zoé, a nice little girl . . . When I left, the car was still there and the man was sitting in the driver's seat, smoking . . . I could see the little red glow of his cigarette end in the dark . . .'

'Can you describe the man to me?'

'It was too dark . . . I did my rounds . . . I have my routine and I know my customers . . . Then I came back at about three . . . The car had gone and so had Monsieur Charles . . . Zoé was now sitting with a strapping American fellow . . .'

'Is that all you can tell me?'

'Yes. I really came here because I wanted to see you again . . . Men are lucky . . . They don't age as fast as we do . . .'

The phone rang and Maigret picked it up.

'Yes . . . speaking . . . What? . . . A dead man in the Rue Jean-Goujon? . . . Five bullets through the chest? . . . I'll come over right away . . . Warn the Magistrates' Court and Coindet, the examining magistrate . . .'

He turned to the old flower-seller.

'Thanks for coming. I have to go now . . .'

'That's all right . . . I've seen you and that's what matters . . .'

She shyly held out her hand to Maigret before leaving the room.

'Lapointe! We're off again . . .'

The Rue Jean-Goujon was only two hundred yards from the Seine. The two policemen who were guarding the building saluted respectfully when they saw Maigret.

'It's on the top floor.'

They took the lift. The door was ajar and Maigret shook hands with the police commissioner, who was probably new as Maigret had not met him before.

'The concierge alerted us. She came up here to do the housework as usual . . . The tenant didn't answer so she used her passkey and found the body . . .'

The doctor was leaning over the corpse of a tall young man in his early thirties lying stretched out on the carpet.

It was not really an apartment but an artist's studio, for one entire wall, as well as part of the ceiling, was made of glass.

'Have you discovered who he is?'

'Joe Fazio . . . Came from Marseilles four or five years ago . . . Was a pimp before he got a job as barman in a rather sleazy little bar called the Paréo . . . He left about two years ago and we don't know how he's made a living since . . .'

The doctor stood up and shook hands with Maigret.

'It's odd . . . Someone shot him point blank, almost touching him, with a small-calibre gun. As far as I can tell, two bullets perforated the left lung and another one is lodged in the heart . . .'

There was a startled look on the dead man's face. As far as Maigret could tell, he had been handsome. He was wearing a very smart gabardine suit of a shiny, almost luminous brown.

'Has the weapon been found?'

'No.'

The men from the Criminal Identity Department had arrived with their various bulky instruments. Next came a rather elderly deputy who disliked the police commissioner but who shook hands with him all the same.

Coindet, the examining magistrate, was puzzled.

'Why did you ask to have me put in charge of this case? Do you think it has any connection with the solicitor's death?'

'It may well have. I was expecting something like this to happen. When Nathalie slipped out via the garden yesterday, she must have had a reason . . .'

He turned to Lapointe.

'Are you coming?'

There were too many people in the flat. He would come back when the experts and the magistrates were gone.

He went into the concierge's lodge with Lapointe. The concierge was a small, dark, energetic-looking woman.

'How long had this Fazio been living here?'

'For two years. He was a good tenant; he was quiet and he paid his rent regularly . . . He lived by himself and he had asked me to do his housework for him. I went up there every day around noon . . .'

'Was he at home when you went up there?'

'No, usually not, because he ate his meals at a restaurant. I didn't always see him going out. I'm very busy . . . The tenants come and go and I don't notice . . .'

'Did he have many visitors?'

'No. Just one lady . . .'

Her tone was full of respect as she mentioned the 'lady'.

'Every day?'

'Nearly every day.'

'At what time?'

'Around three in the afternoon.'

'Would he come back with her?'

'No. He'd be upstairs already.'

'Describe her to me.'

'She was a real lady, you could see that right away. She wore a fur coat in winter and she must have owned at least three different ones. She usually wore suits in summer. Those suits of hers came from top couturiers . . . I've got an eye for those things . . .'

'What about her face?'

'It's hard to say . . .'

An orange cat was rubbing its head against Maigret's legs.

'Was she young?'

'Not young, but not old either . . . She could have been attractive . . . She certainly must have been once . . . I'd say about forty, but her face was rather battered . . .'

'What do you mean, battered?'

'She nearly always had dark circles under her eyes and her features were very drawn. Her lips twitched in a funny way . . .'

'Did she speak to you?'

'No. She went straight upstairs.'

'How long would she stay?'

'She would leave at about five-thirty.'

'By car?'

'No. I noticed that she arrived by taxi, but she would get out at the street corner so that the driver wouldn't know where she was going.'

Maigret took the Cannes photograph out of his pocket and showed it to the concierge, who went to fetch her glasses from the other room.

'Do you recognize her?'

'I'm not sure. The one here is so young and she's got a different mouth . . . Yet the face is pretty much the same . . .'

The chief superintendent then showed her the passport photograph.

'What about this one?'

'Now that's more like it . . . At a distance of twenty years . . .'

'Would you say it was the same person?'

'I think so . . .'

The police commissioner was walking past the lodge. Maigret ran after him.

'Did the doctor extract the bullets?'

'That's the forensic doctor's job and he hasn't arrived yet . . . But I think they've found one which hit a rib and ricocheted . . .'

'Will you go and fetch it, Lapointe . . .?'

He thanked the police commissioner and went back to see the concierge.

'Did your tenant work?'

'I don't think so. He didn't keep regular hours except for meal-times.'

'Did he come home late at night?'

'Do I have to tell you everything?'

'You might as well, since you'll be summoned as a witness anyway.'

'Apart from the three o'clock lady, as I used to call her, he had another girlfriend who was much younger and prettier . . . She usually came here at about two or three in the morning, either with him or alone, and spent the rest of the night up there . . . I once overheard him calling her Géraldine . . .'

Maigret remained expressionless, as though he were not thinking at all.

'Do you know where she lives?'

'No, I don't. She probably works locally, since they always came back on foot . . .'

Lapointe had come down again with the bullet. Maigret thanked the concierge and walked out of the lodge.

'Where are we going now?'

'To Gastinne-Renette . . .'

Gastinne-Renette was the gunsmith who usually gave ballistic advice to the Police Judiciaire. When they got there, the shop assistant went to fetch his employer.

'Well, well! Maigret . . .'

The two men had known each other for twenty years.

The chief superintendent showed him the bullet.

'Can you tell me at a glance what sort of gun this bullet comes from?'

Like the concierge, Gastinne-Renette put on a pair of spectacles.

'This won't be a strictly accurate assessment; I'd need more time for that. It obviously comes from a small-calibre gun, like a Browning 65, for example. They make those models in Belgium; some of them have mother-of-pearl handles. I sold a gold-encrusted one to a client . . .'

'How lethal is it?'

'Not very, from a distance. The aim isn't accurate further than three yards away.'

'The doctor thinks the shots were fired point-blank . . .'

'In that case, of course . . . How many shots?'

'Three or four . . . One in the heart, two in the lungs.'

'The murderer must have meant business . . . Who was the victim?'

'A man by the name of Jöe Fazio . . . barman turned gigolo . . .'

'Nice to have seen you. Shall I keep the bullet?'

'I'll tell our forensic expert to send you the others . . .'

'Thanks. Happy hunting . . .'

Maigret did not laugh at the joke but mustered a strained smile.

Chapter Eight

On the ground floor, the undertakers were busy turning the solicitor's office into a mortuary chapel. They were draping the walls with black cloth; the coffin had been left in a corner, as though no one knew what to do with it.

'Is the body inside?'

'Of course . . . '

Jean Lecureur came out of his office.

'The funeral is tomorrow at eleven,' he said. 'The church is just across the way. We've sent off the announcements. Do you think Madame Sabin-Levesque will attend the funeral service?'

'I'm certain she won't.'

'That might be best. How is she? I don't know what's going on up there . . . '

'Doctor Bloy probably went to see her late this morning. I'll go up now . . . '

As they walked up the stairs, he said to Lapointe:

'You're to take down everything which is said.'

'All right, *patron*.'

The footman opened the door.

'Where's Claire?'

'In the boudoir, I think . . . '

But Claire was just coming forward to meet them.

'Is she asleep?' Maigret asked her.

'No. She's been sitting on the bed in her nightgown ever since the doctor left. She won't speak to me or take her bath or allow me to do her hair . . . '

'What did the doctor say to you?'

'Nothing much. Just to watch her.'

'Has she eaten anything?'

'No. She just shakes her head or nods at me instead of answering.'

'What about you? Have you been eating?'

'I just can't. I feel as though I were at someone's deathbed . . . What's going to happen, Superintendent? . . . I gather the coffin is downstairs . . . '

'Yes, it is . . . Before I go in and see her, I'd like you to put a dressing-gown on her if you can . . . '

'I don't mind trying . . . '

Claire was no longer hostile towards him. He could see that she was at a loss as to what to do. The two men waited in the drawing-room for a long time. Finally, after a quarter of an hour, the maid returned.

'She's in the boudoir. I had to give her the bottle.'

Maigret went in first. Nathalie was sitting in her usual easy-chair. She was holding the brandy bottle in one hand. Yet her eyes remained steady and her expression was almost calm.

'May we come in?'

She did not seem to have heard him. Maigret sat down opposite her. She was stroking the bottle as though it were her most precious possession.

'I've just come from the Rue Jean-Goujon,' he told her, his tone gentle, as though he did not want to frighten her.

When she finally opened her mouth, it was only to say a single word in an indifferent voice:

'Already!'

Having said this, she drank straight from the bottle as Maigret had seen her do once before. Her pale cheeks grew slightly flushed and her lips began to twitch again.

'I don't suppose it matters much any more, does it?'

'Were you afraid that he would denounce you as his accomplice if he was arrested?'

She shook her head.

'No . . . It was worse than that . . . He only wanted to see me yesterday to demand a very large sum of money, assuring me that he would leave me alone after that and go back to Marseilles . . . '

'Did you love him?'

She did not answer; there was a despairing look on her face.

'Why did you go there with the gun if you loved him?'

This question seemed to make her even more desperate.

'I've never had any illusions about him ... He was my last chance ... Don't you understand? ...'

She tried to light a cigarette but her hands were trembling too much. Maigret bent forward with a lighted match. She did not thank him.

'You've always been a proud person, haven't you?'

She corrected him in a dull voice.

'I am proud. I mean I was proud once ... Now ...'

She did not finish her sentence.

'You found it humiliating to work in a cabaret and you would have found it even more humiliating to work as a sales-girl in a department store ...'

She was listening to him, showing interest, as she always did whenever anyone spoke about her.

'Sabin-Levesque fell in love with you ... You soon found out Monsieur Charles' real identity ...'

She said nothing and listened tensely.

'You hoped to lead a dazzling, luxurious existence with cocktail parties, receptions, dinners ...'

'I soon found out that he was the most selfish man I had ever met.'

'Why? Because he refused to let you come before him?'

She seemed startled and Maigret went on:

'He was the king of this household and you counted for nothing.'

Her eyes grew hard.

'Everyone loathed me except Claire.'

'Why didn't you get a divorce?'

She looked around as though taking in the whole apartment, the house and the entire fortune of Sabin-Levesque.

'Because you were greedy ... You didn't care if he went off from time to time to go and look for a pretty girl ... You were Madame Sabin-Levesque ... and you intended to remain that, whatever happened ...'

She drank. The gesture had become automatic.

'You turned to drink. I suppose you must have had lovers too? ...'

'One-night stands ... Men I met in bars ...'

Now that the truth was out, she no longer cared to defend

126

herself. It was almost as though she got pleasure from baring her soul.

'Hotel rooms . . . Some of the men got the wrong idea and tried to give me money . . . '

Her lips were quivering.

'You met Joe Fazio two years ago . . . '

'That was different. I loved him . . . '

'He was a barman . . . '

'I rented a studio flat for him and kept him . . . '

She admitted this cynically, once again showing defiance.

'I couldn't expect him to love me for my sake alone . . . I'm too much of a wreck now . . . He pretended to love me and I pretended to believe him . . . '

'Whose idea was it to kill your husband?'

'I think we both thought about it.'

'Fazio found out which clubs Monsieur Charles went to . . . He followed him several times and waited for the right occasion . . . '

She shrugged. It was all so obvious!

'Your husband came out of the *Cric-Crac* one night and Joe Fazio took advantage of the fact that the street was deserted to kill him. He dragged him into a stolen car and carried him to the Seine. He then abandoned the car on a building-site at Puteaux . . . '

'I didn't go into any of the details . . . '

'Did he ring you up afterwards to tell you what he'd done?'

'Yes.'

'What sort of life would you have led with your ex-barman?'

'I never thought about it.'

'Admit it wasn't out of love for Joe Fazio that you let him kill your husband . . . '

'I don't know any more.'

'You just wanted to remain Madame Sabin-Levesque . . . You would then be undisputed mistress of the household . . . '

'You don't think much of me, do you?'

'No. But I also can't help feeling sorry for you because, although you're hard, you're vulnerable too . . . '

'Vulnerable?' She gave a harsh laugh.

'Yes, vulnerable,' Maigret repeated.

'I suppose you're taking me away with you?'

'Yes. It's my duty. Go and get dressed. Keep an eye on her, Lapointe. I don't want her to slip out again by another little door.'

Maigret slowly filled his pipe and began to pace up and down in the room. He waited for nearly half an hour. She came back with Claire, who was carrying a pigskin suitcase.

Nathalie took one last, seemingly endless swig from the bottle of brandy before she started walking towards the staircase.

'I don't suppose they'll let me have any there, will they?'

She would certainly be found guilty. But given the appalling state she was in, she would probably go straight into the prison hospital.

The door of the solicitor's office was open. The undertakers had finished hanging up their black drapery. She took a couple of steps forward and looked at the coffin.

Her face remained expressionless.

'Is he in there?'

'Yes. He's being buried tomorrow.'

'And I'm being buried today . . . '

They put her suitcase in the boot and Maigret sat down next to his prisoner. She gazed at the *quais*, the bridges, the people in the streets, the buses, the cars, as though they were all part of an already distant past.

When they got to the Palais, Lapointe carried the suitcase, which was too heavy for her. Maigret knocked on the examining magistrate's door.

'She's all yours . . . ' he said in a faltering voice.

He looked at her but she paid no attention to him. Before anyone asked her to, she sat down opposite Coindet; she seemed very much at her ease.

Epalinges, 11 February 1972

The Disappearance of Odile

Translated by Lyn Moir

Chapter One

Bob had got up at seven o'clock as usual. He had no need of an alarm clock. There were two of them in the household who organized their time like clockwork.

At that hour his father, who got up much earlier than he, had finished dressing and would be in the dining-room, drinking the enormous cup of coffee which was all he had for breakfast, before taking his morning walk.

When Bob opened the curtains the sun burst suddenly into the room, and the luminous disc, which changed place according to the seasons, quivered on the mirror.

It was the end of September, and since the beginning of the month not one drop of rain had fallen. The sky had not even been covered over, except for a few pale clouds which sailed slowly across the sky like boats on the sea.

He had shaved, then taken a quick shower. At half-past seven he went downstairs. There was no one in the dining-room. His place was set, as was his sister's, but Odile did not get up until much later. Still later than that, round about eleven o'clock, their mother would have her breakfast taken up.

He went into the kitchen.

'Will you make me two pieces of toast and marmalade, quickly, Mathilde?'

She had been part of the household years before he was born. Short-legged and squat, she had, in spite of her sixty-four years, a young, fresh face, and it was her custom to grumble away all alone in the kitchen.

She was the most solid member of the household, and when everything threatened to reach a state of total disorganization, she put each thing back in its proper place.

He opened the refrigerator mechanically, looking for a left-over of some kind to nibble.

'Tell me what you want, but don't start picking around in all the dishes.'

It was their little daily argument.

'Go and sit down at table. I'll bring it in to you.'

From his place, he could see a part of the garden, in particular the old lime tree, for which he had a particular affection. The house had been called Two Limes from time immemorial. There was only one now, full of light and shade and birdsong. Only a few leaves had begun to yellow.

The other lime tree, probably planted by his great-grandfather, had died long ago and had been replaced by birches.

No one would have thought they were in the middle of Lausanne, in a steep street too narrow for two cars to pass. A low wall surrounded the property and the wrought-iron gate was never closed.

'What is there for lunch, Mathilde?'

'Veal casserole with noodles.'

He ate quickly, looking now at the lime tree on his right, now at the wall half-panelled in dark wood. Then, bare-headed, pulling on only a shiny suede jacket, he went to the garage at the end of the garden and took out his scooter.

He had a social psychology lecture at eight o'clock and, at ten o'clock, a lecture on statistics in human sciences.

He had decided to take his degree in sociology and he was in his third and last year. He hoped to go on to his doctorate after that.

At eleven o'clock he left the Rue Charles-Vuillermet, behind the cathedral, where lectures in social sciences and psychology were held in the buildings of the law faculty.

In the dining-room nothing had changed, except that his father's cup and his had disappeared. His sister's place was still set.

He opened the kitchen door.

'Hasn't Odile come down?'

'I haven't seen or heard her.'

His sister was like her mother. In the evenings she could not make up her mind to go to bed. Even when she did not go out, she hung around as late as possible, watching television in the drawing-room, reading whatever came to hand, sometimes even comic strips, although she was over eighteen, only going to bed when she was so tired she could scarcely stand.

Their mother read too, and both of them slept late in the morning. One had to wait until lunchtime to see them. Their father went to bed early, and now he was upstairs, in his study, working quietly. They hardly saw him, except at mealtimes. He had knocked down a dividing wall on the second floor, transforming the attics into a vast library where he took his siesta after lunch, on an old red sofa.

'There is a letter for you. I put it in your room.'

Intrigued, he went upstairs and pushed open his door. The sun had moved round and was not shining on the same walls. He found the letter on his desk and was astonished to recognize his sister's handwriting. He opened it, vaguely worried. Odile had always been unpredictable, and one could expect anything from her.

According to the postmark, the letter had been posted the evening before. Now, Odile had not had dinner at home that evening. It was a common occurrence. She came and went without giving any account of herself to anyone and often came home at three in the morning.

He crossed the hall and opened his sister's bedroom door. The bed had not been slept in. There was none of the usual disorder.

He returned to his own room, sat down in his armchair, and read:

My dear Bob,

You will be surprised to see this letter. You will no doubt find it when you come home for lunch, and I can imagine you examining the postmark with your eagle eye. Then you will go to my room with your long strides and you will find it empty. At that moment I will be far away.

It was one of his sister's habits to try to guess what people, particularly those in her own family, were going to do, and one had to admit that she was rarely wrong.

The handwriting was small and regular, but the number of downstrokes varied – there could be two or four for an m, and some letters were practically indecipherable. A t, for example, could be taken for an i.

When exactly had she written these pages? The letter had been posted at six o'clock the previous evening. At the station? That was probable, since she said that when her brother read it she would already be far away. Now, leaving, for Odile, meant going to Paris, where she had only been four or five times, but which she considered the only place she could possibly live.

Lausanne and other towns were for her kinds of prisons which she put up with because she could do nothing else.

I am very fond of you, Bob. You are the only person in the world I am sorry to be leaving. I wanted to kiss you goodbye, but I was afraid I would get too emotional and burst into tears. Because, you know, it's a long, long journey I'm making, the longest that one can make.

As for Mummy and Daddy, I must confess that I don't particularly mind one way or the other, although perhaps Daddy doesn't deserve that.

He's a nice old man who has organized things so that he can live in peace. I don't know if he has found any happiness that way, but he has achieved a kind of serenity.

What I find touching in him is that we have never seen him drunk. He takes his glasses of wine in such a way that he keeps more or less sober, and in the evening only a member of the family could tell that he had drunk his two bottles of Dole.

He must wait impatiently for the time for his next glass, constantly looking at the clock.

Poor Daddy! And poor all of us! You're the only one who doesn't feel the weight of the house which is suffocating us, and I don't know how you do it. You must be a strong man. In your place, if I'd been a boy, I would have left home long ago.

You know by now that I have left for good, don't you? It isn't just an escapade and I haven't succumbed to a brainstorm. I have been thinking of this departure for a long time. A final departure. I am not only saying goodbye to the house but to life, which has become more and more unbearable for me.

I am useless. No one will be hurt by my disappearance. They will hardly notice it, except for you, and you have your work which takes up all your attention. You're very lucky in that. Nothing interests me. Life is like slightly muddy water, neither cold nor hot, tepid water, like dishwater.

There will be no scandal, for there will be no funeral either. I'll fix things so that my body is not found, or if it is, so that no one will be able to identify me.

134

It will be enough to tell people that I have gone away without leaving my address.

For some weeks, if not months, I have thought of many solutions and there are several which seem to me to be acceptable. I have not yet chosen. I am going to give myself two or three days to decide.

Daddy will be sad for a little while, but he is so accustomed to his selfish little life that he will soon take up his habits again.

As for Mummy, she's not concerned with appearances but with the family and she will only sigh:

'And to think what we've done for that child! I always said she wasn't normal.'

I have often been tempted to talk to you as I am doing in this letter, but at the last moment I would keep quiet because I was afraid that you would think me ridiculous.

All this has been going on for a long time, Bobby. When I was a little girl I always felt ill at ease in the house and my reading showed me families which were real families.

I was left to myself. I would hide myself in the garden or in the huge, dark drawing-room where nobody goes except to watch television. Once, at the end of one of my moods, Mummy asked me:

'Shall we go in to town, Odile?'

I hated those trips, held by the hand as if I were on the end of a leash. She would meet women she knew and they would chat in the middle of the pavement while the passers-by bumped into me.

She refused to buy me an ice-cream cone, because one doesn't eat those things in the street.

I had to be very tidy, very clean, very well-behaved.

I don't know how you managed to get them to leave you alone. Perhaps it has something to do with your being a boy.

And the silent meals with from time to time a sentence which found no reply!

You're a nice boy, Bob. I am sure that you will understand me, that you will forgive me. I seem to be only accusing others and to be putting all the weight of my decision on their shoulders. However, that isn't true. I realize that my real enemy is myself. You see, I don't feel at ease with life.

As long as I can remember, I have considered myself different from my friends. That is perhaps pride. I don't know. I should have had some other kind of life, but I am the first to admit I don't know what kind.

That is why I have tried a little of everything and why in the end, at over eighteen, I know nothing. I haven't even the most elementary diploma which would allow me to take up a career if I should find one I wanted to do.

If I hang about in the evenings, as late as possible, watching television or reading, it is because I am afraid to be alone with myself.

I think too much about myself, but I can't do anything else.

I had girlfriends at school. Quite frankly, I didn't like them and after quite a short time they would exasperate me.

'You must invite So-and-so or So-and-so,' Mummy would say.

Invite them to do what? They didn't have the same interests as I did. Their chatter, their senseless bursts of laughter seemed childish to me.

I am tired of writing and yet I want so much to explain everything to you. There would be at least one person who would think of me otherwise than as a weathercock, shifting constantly, or as if I were ill.

Mathilde has told me that I was never a real child, that when I was very small I behaved like a grown-up, and that my one desire was to be alone. They would find me sitting on the branch of a tree, at the bottom of the garden, or even in the cellar.

'What are you doing there?' they would ask.

I would look at them without answering. What could I have answered?

I would become very keen on a friend at school. I would invite her to the house, and after a few weeks I wouldn't be able to stand her any more.

When I went to a friend's, for a birthday tea for example, I would feel ill at ease in a flat so different from our house, where the mother would try to amuse us.

"What are you thinking about, Odile?"

"Nothing, Madame."

I was polite. I had been taught to be polite. Good morning, Monsieur. Good morning, Madame. Thank you, Monsieur.

Heaven only knows how many times I have said thank you in my life!

I really must decide to finish this letter. You have guessed that I have gone to Paris, haven't you? It is the best place to disappear.

I don't want you to feel sorry for me. Since I have made my mind up, I don't feel unhappy any more. It will be a bad moment to go through, but very short, shorter than going to the dentist.

And afterwards I shall be free. Free of myself, the person who has tortured me, perhaps without reason.

Aren't you tired of reading my letter yet? I have the feeling that I am writing to you as if I were the centre of the world. Do you understand me, or do you think me conceited? I am stupid to ask you that question, since I shall never know the answer.

Well, my dear Bob, don't think about that any more, now my

decision is taken. And don't mourn for me. It would be more painful for me to go on living than to go away.

When you see Uncle Arthur, tell him I don't blame him. It isn't his fault. I have thought about it and I have finally understood that it was I who provoked him. It's true I was only fifteen. It's true that he didn't go all the way. I didn't know that. It was only later that I understood.

I haven't been lucky with men. I say men because I have never been interested in boys of my own age. Was I wrong about that? They didn't interest me.

It doesn't matter.

You see, my great discovery is that I have never done anything for anyone. I blamed everything on other people. Then, little by little, I asked myself questions.

Even when I happened to do something generous, it was as if I was looking at myself in the mirror to watch myself making a handsome gesture.

Why then can I not finish this letter? I think it is because it lacks the most important part, that all I have been saying to you isn't what really matters.

When I began I thought that it would be easy, that I only had to let my pen run over the paper without taking time to think.

Will you understand? I hope so, even though I shan't know. Destroy this letter. Don't show it to Daddy, or to Mummy. After all, they've only done what they could, both of them.

I shall think about you a lot, Bob, in the hours following this, about your kindness, your nice, frank smile. You are a well-balanced boy who knows what he wants and who will get it. You will get married. You will have children. I only hope that you don't stay at Two Limes. I think that the lives which have been lived there, one after another, have left an oppressive atmosphere.

Well, that's that! So once more I am going off in another direction. It is time I finished. I'll give you a big kiss on your always stubbly cheeks, dear Bob. Soon you will be smiling again, or, better, you will laugh your usual loud laugh.

Bye bye!

Your idiot sister,

Odile

He stayed there for a long time, motionless, the sheets of paper in his hand. When he heard steps on the stairs, he shoved them into his pocket.

'Lunch is served, Bob.'

She did not say 'monsieur', any more than she said 'mademoiselle' to his sister. She was the one who had in fact brought them up, and they had always called her 'tu' since they were children.

'Is my father down?'

'It's half-past twelve.'

'And my mother?'

'She's at table.'

He kissed them both on the forehead, bending his long, lean figure over them. He had one of those loosely-knit bodies which made him look as if he had the suppleness of an acrobat.

'Isn't your sister coming down?'

'She isn't in her room.'

'Did she say where she was going?'

His mother, a very dark woman, wore a blue silk dressing-gown. Before she started her hors-d'oeuvre, she finished her cigarette. She smoked from the moment she got up until the time she went to bed, and at the end of the day her fingers trembled because of it.

His father had grey hair, almost white, which made his face appear youthful again.

'She didn't say anything to me, but she left me a letter.'

Marthe Pointet's eyes were almost black, and her look was penetrating.

'Aren't you going to show it to us?'

'I think I must have torn it up. She just says that she is going to Paris and that she prefers not to leave any address.'

'Did you hear that, Albert?'

'When did she go?'

'As far as I can tell, yesterday evening, on the T.E.E. at six-thirteen.'

'Do you think she was alone?'

'I imagine so.'

'There isn't a man behind all this?'

'I don't have that impression.'

The father looked at his plate without saying a word.

'All the same, it's quite unthinkable!' cried Marthe Pointet, her voice sharp. 'Imagine a girl of only just eighteen going off without saying a thing to her family. Has she any money?'

'I think she had been saving what she got for Christmas and her birthdays.'

'She doesn't say when she is coming back?'

'No.'

'I can hardly believe it. If I were to tell my friends that, they would wonder what kind of family I have brought up.'

She turned to her husband.

'And you, you're not saying anything. You're eating!'

'What could I say?'

'Anything, but don't be so indifferent. It's our daughter, after all.'

'I know.'

'I wonder if we ought to inform the police?'

'That wouldn't do any good. If she wants to disappear ...'

'What do you mean, disappear?'

'Make her life apart from us ...'

'And why should she, can you tell me that?'

'Probably because she had had enough.'

'Enough of what?'

'I don't know ... She's young. She's going ahead with her life.'

The meal had dragged on to its end in silence around the oval table where, opposite Bob, his sister's place-setting had not been removed. Hardly had she swallowed her last mouthful than Marthe Pointet lit a cigarette, while her husband got up, sighing, as if to do so were a painful exercise.

In fact, apart from his morning walk in Mon Repos Park, he took no physical exercise, and the Dole wine did nothing to make him thinner. He was going to go up to his room. In that household they were only together at mealtimes, then each person went about his own business.

'Are you going out?' Bob asked his mother.

'No. I have a bridge party here at four o'clock.'

That was what she devoted the greatest part of her days to. She had friends who came to Two Limes, or to whose houses she went in her turn. They started with tea and cakes, then, towards half-past five, these good ladies turned to whisky.

'Do you know if she has taken anything with her?' Albert Pointet asked, his hand on the doorknob.

'I didn't see the blue suitcase she was given last Christmas. Her toilet case isn't there either.'

'Any clothes?'

'I don't think there's anything missing, except her camel-hair coat. She never wanted to wear that. She found it too formal.'

'I shan't say anything to my friends about her departure,' said Marthe. 'There's no point in having everyone gossiping about it just now. Since she's certainly going to come back some day or other . . .'

'I don't think so,' answered Bob.

'What makes you say that?'

'It's just the impression I have.'

His sister's letter was certainly in her usual style, and Odile was not averse to dramatising herself. It was not the first time she had spoken of suicide, but this time the tone was different.

Albert Pointet started up the stairs. His wife followed him directly and Bob, standing in front of the window, looked at the old lime tree which he had called 'his' tree when he was a boy because he used to climb up and sit in the highest branches.

He heard Mathilde, who had begun to clear the table.

'Why didn't you tell them the truth?'

'The truth?'

'That she left yesterday evening and that she sent you a letter through the post. I know her well, and she didn't just send you a note. You had a long letter, didn't you?'

'Yes.'

'Aren't you going to show it to them?'

'No.'

'Why not?'

'Because she talks about them and what she says wouldn't make them very happy.'

'Do you really think she has gone to Paris?'

'I think so. I could be wrong.'

'What is she going to do there?'

'I don't know. What comes out in the letter is that she wants to disappear completely. That may mean that she is thinking of committing suicide. That reminds me, I want to check something.'

He took the stairs four by four and went into his parents'

bathroom, where the medicine cabinet was. Everyone in the house, now that the children were grown up, came and took what they wanted from it as they wished. He looked carefully at the bottles of tablets and what he had suspected a moment ago was shown to be so: the bottle of sleeping pills had disappeared.

He went back into his sister's room, where her guitar was in its place in a corner and several stuffed animals dating from her childhood sat on some shelves. In the wardrobe there were very few skirts, but half a dozen pairs of trousers. The jacket, exactly the same as his, had disappeared.

It was Wednesday. The school and the *gymnase* were closed in the afternoon. He went down to the drawing-room where the telephone was and rang the Dupré's house.

'Hello, madame. Bob Pointet here. May I speak to Jeanne, please?'

At school, the Collège de Béthusy, she had been in the same class as Odile for five years and they saw a lot of each other, going to each other's house. It wasn't a regular thing. It depended on Odile's mood. For weeks, or months, she would consider Jeanne her best friend, and then, suddenly, wouldn't want to speak to her any more. Now Jeanne Dupré was nineteen and in her last year at the *gymnase*. She was an open, gay girl, her eyes an almost transparent blue.

'Hello. Is that you, Bob?'

'Yes.'

'What are you doing these days?'

'Working, as usual. I wanted to ask you if you had seen my sister in the last few days?'

'Well, you know, since she left school ...'

'Yes, I know.'

She did not see her old friends, girls or boys, willingly. As far as she was concerned, they had remained children. She had joined new groups, who frequented the less desirable bars in the town.

'Wait ... About a week ago I met her in the Rue du Bourg, and she insisted on buying me an ice-cream.'

'How was she?'

'You want me to tell you the truth, don't you? I thought she was nervous and a bit odd. She asked me what I was going to do after the *gymnase*. I said wanted to study pharmacy.

' "Do you really think you'll enjoy that?" she asked me ironically.

' "Why not? It's a good career for a woman, and I hope I may have my own business some day."

' "Well, I wish you the best of luck. And for you to meet a handsome pharmacist! You could have little pharmacists then ... " ' '

'I know that mood.'

'So do I. Anyway, I asked her why she seemed so bitter. She seized me by the arm:

' "Don't pay any attention to me. I'm in the middle of making a big decision. You'll hear about it soon."

' "You're not happy."

' "I never have been happy."

' "I can remember the day when you were the life and soul of the party."

' "Because I was playing a part."

' "You're playing a part now too, aren't you?"

' "No. This time it's serious. But I don't want to say any more about it. I'm glad I ran into you. I used to be horrible to you although I am really very fond of you. You'll have a nice life, well organized, with your work, your husband, your children. You won't ask yourself any questions ... "

'Well, Bob, that's more or less what she said to me. Her features were drawn. She told me it was because she could never get to sleep before the early hours of the morning.'

'I suppose she was wearing trousers and her jacket?'

'Yes.'

'Do you remember what colour her trousers were?'

'Yes. Rust coloured.'

Now his sister had the habit of wearing the same outer clothes for two or three weeks, and the rust-coloured trousers, which Bob hadn't thought of, were not in her wardrobe.

'Be a good girl and don't mention this telephone call to anyone. She wouldn't be pleased if she learned I'd been asking you questions.'

'What are you afraid of, Bob?'

'What about you?'

142

'I'm wondering if we're thinking of the same thing.'

'She has some idea of suicide . . .'

'You're not telling me anything new. She thought about that at school, but I thought it was part of the role she was playing. Because she was playing a part . . . It wasn't always the same one. She needed people to pay attention to her. She needed them to admire her, too. And, in fact, she was more intelligent than we were.'

'Can your mother hear you?'

'No. She went out to do her shopping when you rang. I'm alone in the house. My two brothers are with neighbours.'

'What are you going to do?'

'I'm going to Paris. Do you know if any of the people she's been going around with recently live in Paris?'

'I know almost none of her new friends. My father and mother let me go to parties on condition that they are at the homes of people they know.'

She had been in love with him at one time and they had exchanged a few kisses and superficial caresses. Jeanne Dupré's voice was nostalgic, as if she hadn't yet forgotten.

'Good luck, Bob.'

'Thank you, Jeanne. All the best . . .'

He hung up and wondered whom he could ring next. All his sister's old friends would have less to tell him than Jeanne, for Odile had deliberately lost sight of them.

There was one boy she had been keen on for a while, Alex Carus, the son of Doctor Carus in the Avenue de Rumine. Bob had only been to his house once, and he had been impressed by the former artist's studio which his friend had made into his bedroom.

He rang him and was lucky enough to find him at home. It was mostly in the evenings and late at night that Alex went into town.

'Bob here . . .'

'Bob Pointet?'

'Yes.'

'What has become of you and to what do I owe this telephone call? We haven't seen each other for more than three years.'

He was nineteen, like most of Odile's friends. For a while, at the Collège de Béthusy, they talked of 'Odile's crowd'. He too had abandoned his studies. He played several musical instruments and he had formed a small group with other young people.

'What about my sister? Have you seen a lot of her?'

'I saw her one evening in the Brasserie de l'Ours, where some friends of mine and I were having something to eat. She was eating, too, at another table. I invited her to join us, but she didn't want to.'

'How was she?'

'Rather bad-tempered. I asked her if she still played the guitar, because she could have joined our group . . . I'm not saying we're a great group, but we have played several public engagements and a reputable company in Geneva has promised to cut a disc for us. She told me she hadn't touched her guitar for over a year.'

'Is that all?'

'My friends were waiting for me. I didn't have anything to say to her.'

'"Ciao!"'

'"Ciao!"'

'She went away a little later, alone, and there was something weary in her walk.'

'Thanks, pal.'

'Why are you asking me these questions?'

'Because she has gone to Paris without warning anybody.'

'She's had that idea in her head for long enough. Whenever anyone talked about the future, it was always Paris for her. She couldn't understand how anyone could live in Lausanne and she regarded those who meant to stay here somewhat scornfully.'

'Thank you. I'm sorry to have bothered you.'

'I'm expecting my friends in a quarter of an hour for a rehearsal.'

'Doesn't your father mind the noise you make?'

'I'm at the other end of the flat.'

Bob hung up and looked around him. It was the darkest room in the house and Odile was quite right in saying that it wasn't cheerful.

Their grandfather, Urbain Pointet, had been Professor of Law for thirty-five years. The house where the family lived now had been his. Bob's father and mother had come to live there at the professor's request, when his wife had died.

He had a handsome head of hair, a well-trimmed beard, at first a pale grey and then brilliant white. What was now the big drawing-room had then been his study and library. Here too panelling covered part of the walls and the rest was covered in an embossed paper imitating Cordova leather.

The bookshelves which ran from floor to ceiling contained thousands of books and bound journals and no one had ever dared to touch them.

Urbain Pointet, who had been a respected figure in the country, had died ten years previously, and, instead of taking over his study, Bob's father had continued to work in his attic, which he found more suited to him.

The door opened. Mathilde came in and unfolded the bridge table, then went to one of the cupboards to get out the cards and score-pads.

'What are you doing in here, Bob?'

'I was telephoning.'

'Did you find out anything?'

'Nothing interesting. Only that she has been planning this departure for a long time.'

'Are you going to Paris?'

'I am going up to talk to Father about it.'

'Where do you think you'll find her among millions of people?'

'She has at least one friend there, or at least it's a friend of mine whom she was very keen on. She has a girlfriend there too, Emilienne. I know her address. As a final resort, there is the police.'

'Wouldn't you hesitate before going to the police?'

'No. I can at least tell you – I am afraid for her.'

'So am I. Poor little thing! It's not her fault, you know . . .'

'I know that very well and I would be happier if I could find her . . .'

Some moments later he knocked at the attic door. A voice grumbled: 'Come in!'

His father must have recognized his footsteps on the stairs. He too had a beard, but it was red and badly-trimmed. He had bushy eyebrows, and tufts of hair stuck out from his ears.

He was seated in front of the huge table which he used as a desk. It was always covered with books, journals and notebooks.

Could one say that his professional life had been a failure? When he had taken his doctorate in history, he had probably thought of teaching on one hand, of research on the other.

Had he been disillusioned, or had he decided to choose the easier way?

He wrote fat books which were clamoured for by Parisian publishers, for they all sold in impressive numbers. He wrote one book a year on average, choosing his subject carefully to appeal to a wide public.

They were not really historical novels, but more what one might call intimate history. For example, he would bring to life a little-known conspiracy, or he would exhaust the list of mistresses of a king or a well-known personage.

He wrote in a big, clear, firm hand, with no trace of nervousness or fatigue. He knew the number of pages he must cover each day, and he did it conscientiously, rewarding himself with a glass of red wine every hour on the hour.

'Do you want to talk to me about your sister?'

'Not especially.'

'Are there things you preferred not to say in front of your mother?'

'Yes. It is quite serious. She threatens to commit suicide, and this time I think she is capable of it.'

His father held out his hand.

'May I read her letter?'

'I have destroyed it.'

'Why?'

'Because it said things which were too personal.'

'I imagine she was speaking of your mother and me.'

Bob was very fond of his father, and could have been his friend if there had been any place for such a thing in Albert Pointet's too well-regulated life. Behind his uncouth appearance he hid a sharp intelligence, but he rarely showed it.

He sighed.

'I was wrong to accept my father's invitation to come and live here with my family when he became a widower. It is an old people's house, and I can understand that young people might rebel against it.'

'I don't think that is the real reason . . . '

146

'I spend all day in this untidy attic, taking a glass of wine every hour. At half-past nine I am in bed, but I am up again at half-past five, all alone in the house.

'The only time I go out is to go to the university library or to go to Paris to see one of my publishers.

'Your mother spends a good half of her time in bed, and her principal occupation is paying bridge. By the way, have her friends arrived?'

'They hadn't a few minutes ago.'

'Sometimes I wonder if she's quite normal, or whatever it is that people say. You heard her at lunchtime – no emotion, her only reaction was that the news would get around, that her friends would find out. Sit down, my boy.'

He lit a cigar and asked Bob:

'Do you want one?'

'No, thank you.'

'What did you come to ask?'

Usually he came up to the attic because he needed money. Indirectly, that was the reason again.

'I am going to Paris.'

'Do you think you will find her?'

'I won't lose anything by trying. I know two or three people with whom she might have made, or might yet make, contact.'

'It's probably not a bad idea. You are afraid, aren't you?'

'Yes.'

'Did she say anything about it to you?'

'About dying? Yes.'

'Don't say anything about that to your mother. I have the same fear . . .'

He took a fat wallet out of his trouser pocket and counted out hundred-franc notes.

'Here's five hundred. If you need more you only have to send me a telegram. When are you leaving?'

'On the T.E.E. at six-thirteen.'

His father leaned his head forward as usual, and Bob kissed him on the forehead.

'Will you be staying in the Rue Gay-Lussac?'

It was there, to the Hôtel Mercator, that Bob, like his father, usually went. It was in the middle of the Latin Quarter, close to the Sorbonne and the Luxembourg Gardens. The proprietor was no longer Mercator, and had probably not been so for several generations, but a man whose name went well with his plump face and round body: Monsieur Bedon.

'If you don't hear from me it's because I haven't any news for you.'

His father watched him as far as the door, looked at his watch and reached out for the bottle. It was three minutes past the hour.

Chapter Two

Bob had only taken a small suitcase which held, apart from a change of underwear, a pair of flannel trousers and a pair of shoes for changing into should he be caught in a heavy shower.

When he left the house he avoided the drawing-room where his mother's friends could be heard chattering, so that he did not say goodbye to her. Instead, he went into the kitchen.

'I knew you would go,' Mathilde said. 'Move heaven and earth to find her, Bob. I don't know why, but I have the feeling that she is in real danger. I have felt for a long time that there was something unhealthy about her state of mind.'

He went out of the garden and appeared to say goodbye to his tree, into which the setting sun was sending reddish reflections. The same reddish light could be seen on the surface of the lake beyond the town.

He strode down the steep street, crossed Mon Repos Park and found a taxi.

'Take me to the station.'

He drowsed through most of the journey. In the restaurant-car, he asked the head waiter:

'Were you on this run yesterday?'

'Yes, monsieur.'

'Did you notice a very young girl who seemed upset or nervous?'

'We see so many people, you know . . .'

He showed him the photograph of his sister.

'I think she sat in that corner. A table for two. She came in alone, but the man opposite wasn't long in speaking to her, and they left the restaurant-car together.'

'What kind of man?'

'A gentleman. Still quite young. In his forties . . .'

In Paris he took a taxi to the Rue Gay-Lussac. The building

was the smallest in the street, only three floors, squeezed in between houses of five and six floors. On the other side of the desk a door was open, and he could see the proprietor, Monsieur Bedon, leaning over a pile of papers.

'Goodness, Monsieur Bob! What good wind blows you in here?'

'More of an ill wind. Before anything else, tell me if my sister is here by any chance.'

'No. It's almost six months now since she has been here.'

'Did you notice anything odd on her last visit?'

'She stayed for three days ...'

'I know that.'

'She went out the first evening, immediately after taking her case upstairs, and she told me she was going to take the air for a bit. In fact, I can tell this to you, she didn't come back until about four in the morning.'

'How did she seem?'

'Very well, it seems. It was old Victor who gave her her key. They chatted for quite a while. Is she in Paris?'

'Probably.'

'I am surprised that she hasn't come to stay here as usual.'

Monsieur Bedon frowned.

'Are you here to look for her?'

'More or less. She left home without any warning.'

'She is definitely a very independent young lady.'

'Did she come back just as late on the two other nights she spent in Paris?'

'I must confess that she did.'

'Did that happen the other times she came?'

'Never three nights in a row. She practically never went out in the daytime. She had sandwiches taken up at two in the afternoon, then she must have gone back to sleep. She didn't put her nose out of doors until dinner-time.'

'Thank you, Monsieur Bedon.'

The proprietor took down a key from the rack and handed it to him.

'It's number 12, the room you had last time.'

He recognized the room, with its flowered wallpaper, its brass bedstead and its big mirrored wardrobe.

As his sister had done six months previously, he went down-stairs again straight away, gave the proprietor a wave, and went towards the Boulevard Saint-Germain. What Monsieur Bedon had just told him about Odile's last day in Paris had reminded him of something she had said:

'I've found a fabulous *boîte* in Saint-Germain-des-Prés. There are only five musicians, but they manage to create a marvellous atmosphere. It's very small. It's called Le Cannibale.'

That was where he was heading, on the off-chance. He had some difficulty in finding the sign and the stair which led down into the basement where one could hear pop music.

It was not big, in fact. The room must have been able to hold about thirty people, but for the moment it was only half full. On a narrow stage were five musicians with very long hair, and the guitarist had the longest hair of all.

'Are you alone?' asked the proprietor in a strong Swedish accent.

'Yes.'

'That doesn't matter. Sit down at this table. What will you have to drink?'

'A scotch.'

He was served by a pretty girl wearing the shortest skirt he had ever seen.

Most of the people were couples, lovers, some of whom were dancing on a tiny dance-floor.

'Tell me, is this the same band which was here six months ago?'

'Yes, monsieur. They've been here for almost a year now. They are good, aren't they?'

'Yes, they are.'

He waited for half an hour until the music stopped. Three of the musicians stayed where they were and had a cigarette. One of them went to the bar and one went outside. It was the guitarist. Bob followed him out on to the pavement where the man was getting a breath of air.

He had wisps of a blond beard, not many, and he seemed very young, still a boy.

'Cigarette?'

The guitarist took one.

'Thank you.'

'Do you often have unaccompanied women in the *boîte*?'

'Not very often. And never professionals. The proprietor won't allow that. It's funny, but he's a real prude in his way.'

'I'd like to know if you recognize this face.'

He showed him Odile's photograph, while his companion took it over to a gas lamp to study.

When he handed back the photograph he seemed hesitant.

'What's she to you?' he asked.

'She's my sister. But don't worry. She has complete freedom and I know about most of her affairs.'

'Are you sure?'

'Yes.'

'Has she spoken to you about me?'

'Not about you, but about Le Cannibale. You have slept with her, haven't you?'

'Yes.'

'It was she who spoke to you first, wasn't it?'

'Yes.'

'I know my sister.'

'She wanted to talk about the guitar. She plays too.'

'Yes, she used to play.'

'What else did she tell you?'

'That she lived in Lausanne, in an old house dating back to her great-grandfather, and that she was bored to death there. I asked her why she didn't come to Paris to live, and she said that she didn't have any money or any profession.

'"All I could do," she sighed, "would be to stand behind a counter in one of the department stores."'

'Did she stay here until you closed?'

'Yes.'

'And she went home with you?'

Odile would not have dared to take anyone to the Hôtel Mercator.

'If one can call it a home. I have a room, badly furnished and not very nice, in a lodging-house in the Rue Mouffetard.'

'She went there with you.'

'Yes. We didn't only make love. She talked a lot. I must admit she had had two or three drinks.'

'What did she talk about?'

'About herself. She envied me having a profession, even if I earned very little. She was sorry she had given up the guitar.

' "It's like that with everything," she sighed. "I begin something with enthusiasm and I think that I am saved at last, that I have found the right thing for me. Then, one month or six months later, I feel as if I were struggling in a vacuum. Nothing exists any more. I am sick of myself . . . " '

'I know her well and she has often said the same things to me.'

'You know, she's not really interested in sex.'

'I've always imagined that.'

'She wants her partner to have pleasure through her, but she herself doesn't have any . . . I must go down now. There's another break in half an hour.'

Bob sat down again at the table and ordered another drink.

'You've never been here before?' asked the proprietor.

'No. My sister has been here several times, some time ago.'

He showed him the photograph and the man with the Scandinavian accent recognized her.

'A pretty girl. She stayed in her corner, the left-hand corner, near the band, for hours. She only left at closing time . . . How old was she, in fact?'

'When you knew her, she wasn't yet eighteen. She is now.'

'Didn't she come to Paris with you?'

'No. She came alone and I am looking for her.'

The proprietor looked automatically at the guitarist, and Bob hastened to say:

'I know. I've just been talking to him, outside.'

'Doesn't he know anything?'

'He hasn't seen her this trip. She must have got here last night.'

'I haven't seen her either. You seem worried.'

'I am. When she left home she was very depressed. In a letter she left me, she talked about putting an end to it all.'

'In that case, there isn't much chance she'll come here.'

'That's true. Did she tell you anything about herself?'

'No. I just asked her to dance, twice, and she accepted both times.'

Half an hour later, the guitarist came to sit down at his table.

'A scotch?'

153

'No. A beer. I'm hot . . . A beer, Lucienne.'

'And another whisky.'

'Was the boss able to tell you anything interesting?'

'No. He danced with her, but she hardly spoke to him. Do you think he has slept with her?'

'No, he doesn't do that sort of thing . . . And besides, Lucienne wouldn't let him. That's been going on for more than a year, the two of them.'

'Can you think of anything, even something she said by chance, which could put me on my sister's tracks?'

'Do you want to take her back to Lausanne?'

'Not necessarily. If I found her, I am not even sure I would tell my parents. I'm looking for her to stop her making an irreparable mistake.'

'She is a very intelligent girl, and she has real insight into herself.'

'I know.'

'She makes herself very unhappy. She came three evenings in a row.'

'Did you go to the Rue Mouffetard all three evenings?'

'I couldn't go to her hotel, that hotel with the funny name . . .'

'Mercator.'

'Yes. It seems all the family goes there. She even went there when she was a little girl.'

'That's true.'

'She's both a very complicated and a very simple person. Very candid. She didn't know me, yet right from the first evening she told me things that one would only tell an old friend. The second night, she asked me to bring the guitar home. She stretched out on the bed, quite naked, and she wanted me to play for her alone. That shows a romantic character, doesn't it?'

Bob did not answer. He was thinking, trying to put in order the information he had gathered.

'Here's to you.'

'And you.'

'She didn't say anything to you about any friend, boy or girl, she might have in Paris?'

'She mentioned a boy, but he was more your friend than hers.'

'Lucien Denge?'

'I don't know his name. I only know he does something in films.'

'That's him. Has she slept with him too?'

'She didn't say. She also mentioned a girl who was studying History of Art.'

'Emilienne?'

'That could well be the name she said.'

And the musician added, a little embarrassed:

'I'm sorry about what happened . . . I swear I didn't have that in mind . . . I'm not putting the blame on her, but I was quite surprised . . . I must get back to work. Thanks for the beer.'

He held out his hand.

'My name is Christian Vermeulen. I'm from Roubaix. I threw up everything, too, to come to Paris.'

His smile was open, a little shy.

'I hope we'll meet again. And I hope you find her. If she comes in here or to my place, I'll give you a ring. The Hôtel Mercator, you said?'

'Yes, in the Rue Gay-Lussac.'

Bob called Lucienne so that he could pay the bill. The proprietor shook hands with him.

'Good luck.'

No one thought he was a fool, and the people here, at least, thought well of Odile.

He walked back to the hotel. Most certainly the picture he was building up of his sister was becoming more and more clear. He was beginning to realize that he had not really known her. And yet the two of them got on very well. Was it impossible to know a member of one's family really well?

He imagined her naked on the bed in the Rue Mouffetard, having the guitar played to her and listening, staring at the ceiling.

He knew that she had had several lovers, and he had suspected that she was frigid.

What she wanted was to talk, to talk to someone who did not know her and who would listen to her with interest.

She had no confidence in herself. Or rather, that depended on the occasion. Sometimes she had too much and she went too far. She needed to find a way of exteriorizing herself, of affirming her personality, of showing that she was an exceptional girl.

155

After that would come the crisis of humility, as when she had written the letter she had sent to him. Back in his room, he read it again. He was more moved than he had been the first time, because of what the musician had told him.

Around him there were five million human beings and he was looking for only one, a young girl who did not want to be found, who was perhaps already dead.

Why did she not want anyone to find her body? Wasn't it a sort of challenge? And how did she think she would manage it?

He finally went to sleep. When he woke, in the middle of the morning, a thin, yellowish fog lay over the city. He was shaving when the phone rang.

He rushed to it, hoping God knows what, but it was his father who was at the other end.

'I don't suppose you have any news?'

'No. But I know where she spent the three evenings on her last trip to Paris.'

'Where?'

'In a *boîte* in the Boulevard Saint-Germain.'

'Alone?'

'She went there alone and she met one of the musicians.'

'I can guess what happened.'

'Yes.'

'Does he not know anything?'

'No. He talked to me a lot about her. The proprietor of the *boîte* did too.'

'What are you going to do?'

'Go on questioning people. There are two or three people in Paris whom she used to know. She may have made contact with one of them.'

'I hope so. Keep me in the picture. I haven't been able to work this morning. I am alone in my attic, kicking my heels.'

'I'll ring you soon.'

'Yes, soon. Preferably with good news.'

Bob was surprised. He was suddenly discovering a father who was different from the image he had always had of him. He remembered what his sister had said to him several times.

'Daddy is an old egoist who only thinks about his work and

156

his wine. As for Mummy, she's completely turned in on herself.'

But now, his father had just telephoned him, an act which had made him go downstairs to the drawing-room, since that was where the only telephone in the house was. He had spoken many times of having an extension put in his study, but he had never had it done.

One could tell that the man was very worried, very down-hearted.

It was only Odile who treated him as an old man, because of her own youth. In fact, he had only just turned fifty, and was in the prime of life.

Bob did not have Emilienne's address. She was more his sister's friend than his. He went to the Sorbonne, to the office. It was not an easy task. The first people he dealt with knew nothing about it.

'What course is she taking?'

'History of Art.'

'Go to Room 21.'

In Room 21, they looked at him suspiciously.

'Is she a relative of yours?'

'No. She's a friend of my sister's.'

'And why do you want her address?'

'To help me find my sister.'

'Has she disappeared?'

'Yes.'

'Of her own accord?'

'Yes.'

'How old is she?'

'Eighteen.'

'Where are you from?'

'From Lausanne.'

'And your sister has run away to come to Paris. Has she been here before?'

'Several times, but that was with my parents' knowledge.'

'I'll see what I can do.'

He went into another room. The door was open, but he spoke in a low voice and Bob did not hear what he said. When he came back after a long time, he said:

'Just a moment.'

157

Opening a metal filing cabinet full of pink cards, he eventually picked one out.

'Emilienne Lhote, Avenue de la Sallaz?'

'That's right.'

'Her address in Paris is Hôtel de la Neva, Rue des Ecoles.'

'Thank you.'

'Do you know what time she finishes her classes?'

'I'm not worried about that.'

The hotel was in fact a family *pension* in the grounds of what must have been a vast mansion. The walls were painted white, and there were green shutters, as if it had been in the country. A bench on each side of the door completed the illusion.

At the moment when Bob arrived the sun was shining full on the front of the building and the door was open. A broad, big-breasted girl was on her knees in the corridor, washing the floor.

'Would you happen to know if Mademoiselle Lhote is in her room?'

'What did you say?'

'Mademoiselle Lhote . . . Emilienne Lhote.'

'I know Mademoiselle Emilienne, but I don't know if she is upstairs. She doesn't keep the same hours every day. I'll call the landlady.'

She came from the end of the corridor, wiping her hands on her gingham apron.

'Do you want to see Mademoiselle Emilienne?'

'Yes.'

'She isn't in just now. I give my lodgers breakfast, and then dinner at eight o'clock. As for lunch, they fix it up themselves near where their work is. Are you a member of her family?'

'No. My sister and I went to the same school as she did, in Lausanne, and we were friends.'

Short and fat, the landlady made him think of Mathilde as she had been ten years before.

'You wouldn't know at about what time I would have the best chance of finding her in?'

'She usually comes in quite early, about half-past six or seven.'

'I'll come back then. Would you know if she had a visit from a girl yesterday?'

'I didn't see anybody, but I might well have been in the kitchen.'

'Thank you.'

He walked carefully through the soapy water which had covered the whole corridor and soon found himself outside again. He would come back, anyway. He knew that his sister had quarrelled at one time with Emilienne, but they had made it up again later. Odile had quarrelled with everyone in her class and with all the girls she used to go around with.

Bob had never had passionate friendships. He had never fallen madly for anyone. At school, and then at the *gymnase*, he had had several friends, but he never saw them out of class. He knew his sister's friends better, because they came to the house and they played various instruments together. He had gone out with some of them, although they were much younger than he was. He didn't remember having gone out with Emilienne, a tall, thin, bony girl whose nose was too long.

He walked towards the Rue de la Seine and found the tatty hotel where Lucien Denge lived. At the left of the door was the usual marbled sign saying:

Residential Hotel
Rooms let by the day,
by the week and by the month.

There was a window in the hall, giving on to a small room where one could see a roll-top desk, a board with keys hanging on it, and a shapeless armchair. An enormous woman, her bare legs swollen, her feet in red slippers, was reading the paper.

'Excuse me, madame. I would like to see Monsieur Denge, please.'

'He isn't in.'

'But he does live here?'

'Of course. He wouldn't find as cheap a room with running hot and cold anywhere else.'

'You don't know when he'll be in?'

'At the moment he is making a film somewhere around Paris, possibly in the suburbs. They're doing what they call exterior shots, so they work irregular hours.'

'Does he have dinner here?'

'No. He usually eats in a little place in the Rue de Buci. But when he's filming, he most often eats with the others.'

'When do you think I'd be likely to find him?'

'I don't know ... If all goes well, about ten o'clock ... If he has a drink he'll have several and he won't likely be back before midnight.'

'Thank you.'

'You're not here on behalf of his parents, are you?'

'Why? Is he afraid they'll visit him?'

'He's always afraid they'll come and look for him. You'd hardly know he was of age, he's so terrified of his mother. It seems she's a dreadful woman.'

The Denges lived in the Tunnel district of Lausanne. He had four sisters a lot younger than he was, all of them at school. Their father was a cashier in the Swiss Société de Banque. Bob had seen him. He looked pleasant, if a little starchy. As for the mother, he had never laid eyes on her.

He gave himself until the next day before telling the police. He knew there was a department devoted to searching for people on behalf of their families. As he was passing a police station, he went in, and waited his turn, leaning on a sort of counter. He was astonished to find the rooms bright and clean, the walls freshly painted.

'Have you an appointment?'

'No. I wanted some information. When a person has disappeared, what department does one consult?'

'Is it a member of your family?'

'My sister.'

'She isn't of age?'

'No. She is eighteen.'

'How long ago did she disappear?'

'Two days ago.'

'She's maybe just gone off for a few days.'

'She has never done that before.'

'Listen. In any case, it is nothing to do with me. You will find the Bureau of Missing Persons at 11 Rue des Ursins, in the IVth *arrondissement*. It's in the same building as the Department of Health and Public Safety. Ask for Room 4.'

He only had to cross the Seine. It was near the Quai aux

160

Fleurs, but he didn't dare set the police in action yet. He preferred to try all he could do himself first, and then to telephone his father.

He spent an hour reading the paper at an outdoor café on the Boulevard Saint-Germain, since it was still warm. Then he walked for a while and finally went into a cinema, for want of anything better to do.

When he went back to the *pension*, a little before seven o'clock, the woman asked him:

'What is your name?'

'Bob. Bob Pointet.'

'Just a moment.'

And, gathering her skirts about her, she started up the stairs. When she returned, she announced:

'She's coming down right away. Come this way.'

They went through a dining-room where six or seven places were set around a round table, and went into a drawing-room which smelled almost of the country, at any rate a spicy smell.

He was not welcomed with open arms. When Emilienne came in, she looked at him curiously, coldly.

'I understand you want to see me.'

'Yes. You were one of Odile's friends.'

'You know very well that Odile didn't have any friends.'

'You haven't seen her recently?'

'The last time we met was over a year ago, in the Rue de Bourg.'

'She hasn't tried to see you here, in Paris?'

'If she had asked for me, someone would have told me. Am I to understand she has disappeared?'

'Yes.'

'You wouldn't have a cigarette, would you?'

He lit it for her, then lit one himself and sat down in one of the green repp armchairs.

She sat down opposite him.

'When did this happen?'

'Two days ago.'

'Are you sure she is in Paris?'

'Where else?'

'She'll come back one of these days. She will have wanted to

161

make herself interesting once more. She has never accepted the fact that she is a girl like other girls.'

'I know. But I am still worried. She is desperate. She just wants to disappear completely.'

'Listen, Bob. Try to look at things a bit coolly. If she is desperate enough to commit suicide, there is no reason for her to come to Paris. She had as many opportunities to do it in Lausanne as here.'

'She doesn't want anyone to find her, to find her body.'

'And how is she going to do that? Bury herself? If she jumps in the Seine, her body will come to the surface some day or other.'

'She might be unrecognizable.'

'Besides, why would she come to see me? To tell me what she was going to do and make her identification more easy? There's another thing. You understand, I'm speaking frankly to you. This tale of not being found again, that's real Odile. She knows she will be recognized and that everyone who knows her will go to her funeral.'

He sighed.

'Perhaps you're right.'

'You know, she has always enjoyed complicating her life. Not long after she was fifteen, she started to whisper, to one girl and another, that she wasn't a virgin any more.

' "Are *you* still?" she would ask.

'And if we answered yes, she would look at us with both surprise and pity, as if we were ill.

' "It wasn't one of the boys at school, but a man. I wouldn't want to go to bed with a friend."

'For more than a month she battered our ears with her lost virginity. Everyone knew about it, even the boys in the class, and they looked at her curiously.

'It was round about that time that she began to get very friendly with two of the young teachers. I don't know if there was anything between them. I don't think so.

'She would go and have a fruit juice and a sandwich in the little restaurant near Bethusy where they used to have lunch and eventually they all sat at the same table and she didn't mind smoking in front of them, in spite of the rule . . . '

'I know all about that, Emilienne.'

162

'Then why are you asking me questions?'

'Because I am trying to find her. She had her faults, of course. That is no reason to let her make an irreparable mistake.'

'That is exactly what I'm trying to make you understand. She is playing a part. She has always played one part or another. When she learned that I was going to take lessons in Decorative Art at Vevey, she wanted to do the same thing, although she had never touched a paintbrush in her life. Two months later she threw it all up. She had to catch an early train and work hard, with no smoking.'

Everything Emilienne was saying was true. It really was his sister she was talking about, but she did it coldly and the picture which emerged was basically unlike her. The two girls had nothing in common.

'Oh well! Thank you for seeing me.'

'What are you going to do?'

'Go on looking.'

'She doesn't know as many people as all that in Paris. How many times has she been here?'

'Alone, four or five times. Each time for several days. When we were children our parents brought us twice and showed us the sights.'

'You're a nice boy, Bob. Best of luck.'

When he left her he was overcome by a certain uneasiness. He had no illusions about his sister's character, but it had just been dirtied for her in a few minutes. The picture which had been painted for him was true in its main outlines, but at the same time it was false, because it lacked a spark which one always felt Odile had, a certain thirst for life, for the ultimate.

He found it difficult to explain to himself what his own opinion of her was. Wasn't she worth much more than a girl like Emilienne? And than most of her friends, whom her parents held up to her as examples?

Something, some force within her, pushed her to the limits, without worrying about what anyone thought of her. It was still the guitarist who had understood her best.

He walked slowly in the direction of the Rue de Seine, and went into the Hôtel des Rapins on the off chance. The fat proprietress was busy in the kitchen.

'Has my friend come in?'

'Ten minutes ago. You're lucky. They were filming on a quay-side, near Corbeil, and he fell into the Seine. He's changing, if he has anything to change into.'

'What floor?'

'Room 31, on the third floor.'

They must have been the cheapest rooms, up there, for the stair carpet stopped on the second floor. He knocked at the door.

'Who is it?'

'Bob.'

'Bob Pointet?'

'Yes.'

'Just a minute. I'm putting my pants on.'

He opened the door a moment later. His clothes were rolled in a ball on the floor and a pool of water had formed around them.

Standing in the middle of the room, which was not very big, Lucien Denge was pulling on jeans and a yellow polo-necked sweater.

'It was that idiot of a sound enginer who knocked me into the water by moving backwards without any warning. I couldn't stay there, soaked to the skin. I had to take a taxi, as we didn't have a car available. It's a low-budget film, almost all exterior shots.'

'Are you happy?'

'Apart from my forced bath, yes. I'm second assistant director now. That's a step up. Up until last month I was only a stage manager.'

'Do you hope to become a director?'

'You bet I do!'

He was a small man, oddly built, whose feet turned out as he walked. He had an india-rubber face and a perpetual grin.

'Will you eat with me?'

'As long as we each pay our own.'

'Right.'

'To what do I owe the pleasure of your visit?'

'I'll tell you in a minute.'

Lucien pulled on his socks and put on black canvas beach-shoes.

'Come on. There's a nice *bistrot* just round the corner.'

164

It was a real *bistrot* which could only have been patronized by regulars, because there was nothing to attract the eye. There was no Formica, the tables were still of wood, the counter steel, and the proprietor in shirtsleeves and a blue apron.

'Good evening, Monsieur Lucien. What are you having?'

'A Picon grenadine.'

'And you, monsieur?'

'A glass of wine.'

'Beaujolais? I can recommend it. My brother-in-law sends it to me from down there.'

Bob drew over the slate on which the menu was written. *Moules marinières, blanquette de veau,* cheese, apple tart.

They took their glasses and sat down at one of the tables, and a tall girl in black with a white apron came out of the kitchen and went over to them.

'You're dining here with your friend, Monsieur Lucien?'

'Yes.'

'Will you have the set menu, then?'

'Do you eat mussels?' he asked Bob.

'Yes, indeed.'

'Yes, we'll have the menu, Léontine.'

'You know my name isn't Léontine.'

'I think it suits you. Your parents should have called you Léontine.'

He winked at Bob and gave the waitress a slap on the buttocks.

'Aren't you ashamed of yourself?'

'Not at all.'

'What will your friend think?'

'That we are very good friends and that you see the joke.'

As she moved off he murmured in a lower voice:

'Well, what is it?'

'I don't suppose you have seen my sister?'

'When?'

'Yesterday, for example, or the day before yesterday, in the evening.'

'It's at least three years since I saw her last. Say, she must be a very pretty girl now. She was a bit thin then, and she didn't have any breasts.'

'She does now.'

'A funny girl. She should have gone into films.'

'Why do you say that?'

'You know her better than I do, since you're her brother. But I have watched her for a long time. Suddenly she will decide to be a particular character and one would swear that she is not acting, that she becomes that character automatically. Besides, I believe she does. When she grows tired of the role, or people aren't pleased with it any more, she chooses another skin.'

'That's just about true, what you're saying.'

'That's why I'm talking about films. She would have the chance, at each shooting, to be a different person.'

He interrupted himself to speak to the waitress, who was bringing the mussels.

'A bottle of Beaujolais, Léontine. My friend says it is very good.'

Then, to Bob:

'Is she in Paris?'

'She must be. That's what she said in her letter.'

'She went off without any warning?'

'Yes. And she's threatening to disappear for ever. I'm questioning the few people she knows in Paris, in the hope that she may have gone to see one of them.'

'No good?'

'Not so far. Tomorrow I shall go to the Bureau of Missing Persons.'

'It's as serious as that?'

'You've just said so yourself. That she chooses a part and that she really becomes that person . . .'

'Poor Odile. Basically, she's a great girl. I would even say she's worth a good deal more than most of her friends.'

Chapter Three

Even if Odile had not yet put her plan into operation, she would none-the-less not have stayed all day and all night within the four walls of a hotel room.

She must have gone out, more probably in the evening – and as late as possible! – than in the morning or the afternoon.

She had no liking for the *boîtes* in the Champs-Elysées. She found them pretentious. And Montmartre, for her, was only an enormous tourist trap.

In her eyes there was only the Left Bank, and Saint-Germain-des-Prés in particular.

For want of even the slightest clue, Bob undertook to go around the more or less well-known places. Thus he went into places full of smoke and thundering music where, in the half-dark, couples had hardly room to move their feet.

'A table, monsieur?'

'No, thank you. I'm leaving again in a moment.'

He would stand at the bar and order anything that came into his mind. He would begin by looking at the clientèle, always in the hope of seeing his sister. Then, once more, he would take the photograph out of his pocket.

'Would she have been here last night or the night before?'

The bartender, who was often the proprietor, would look at the picture, frowning, and shake his head.

'It doesn't ring a bell with me. But, you know, with so many people . . .'

'If she came, she certainly stayed until you closed, and I suppose that at that time you have fewer customers.'

'Yes. They thin out as the night goes on. No! I am almost certain I have never seen her.'

He had begun in the Rue Saint-André-des-Arts. Then it was the

167

Rue Sainte-Geneviève, the Rue Saint-Jacques, the Rue de la Bûcherie. He had once, during one of his stays in Paris, made the tour of all the *boîtes* in the quarter.

Some had disappeared, while others had sprung up.

He would order a gin and tonic, take a sip, take the photograph out of his pocket and ask the inevitable question. As it grew later and later he found his idea less and less good, and he wanted to go to bed.

'Just one more!' he would promise himself. That would be the last.

Saying each time that this would be the last, he went to more than twenty *boîtes,* each one narrower and more smoke-filled than the last.

On the way, he remembered what the guitarist had told him: it was to his hotel room in the Rue Mouffetard that he had taken her, and where she had stretched out, naked, on the bed, listening to him play the guitar.

It had been on an earlier trip, but it must have remained a bright spot in his sister's memory. That was why Bob went to that area. The *boîte* he went into, still promising himself it would be the last, looked more like an ordinary *bistrot*, its walls none too clean, with a hippy clientèle for the most part. A dark, greasy-haired woman sang among the tables, accompanied by a guitarist whose hair was as long as hers.

There was no trace of Odile. He almost left. Nevertheless, he went over to the bar, where the enormous thickly-moustached proprietor stood. His chest seemed to have been poured into the vest, over which he wore no shirt.

'A rum, please.'

He suddenly wanted to change his drink, and he had just caught sight of a bottle of rum straight in front of him.

'The singer isn't part of the set entertainment here, you know. Here the customers do their own entertaining. There are some who only come for that. If they're not too bad, I give them a drink on the house.'

He looked at Bob and asked:

'Are you a student?'

'Yes.'

'I thought so. Few students come here. Lots of young English kids. Scandinavians too. All more or less hippies, but very pleasant.'

'Have you see this girl before?'

He held out the photograph without the slightest hope. The proprietor scarcely glanced at it.

'If you had been here last night, you would have seen her at the third table, where those two blacks are sitting now.'

'Are you sure?'

'As sure as I see you.'

'What was she drinking?'

'Gin and tonic.'

It was Odile's favourite drink. She only drank whisky when there was no gin.

'What was she wearing?'

'Is this a test?'

'I'm trying to make sure it was really her. Was she alone?'

'She was alone when she came in, yes.'

'What time was that?'

'About a quarter past midnight. A South American who must have had some Indian blood in him was playing a strange flute. You get all kinds here, and the evenings are never the same. When the musician had finished playing, I saw she had changed places and had sat down at his table.'

'What was she wearing?'

'Dark brown trousers and a yellow pullover, with a suede jacket.'

It was the outfit Odile wore most often.

'Did she drink a lot?'

'Three or four glasses. The Indian didn't drink spirits.'

'Did they leave together?'

'I don't think so. I didn't have any reason to watch them any more than anyone else. In any case, I saw him alone at the table later. Is she your girlfriend?'

'No. She's my sister.'

'Is she a student too?'

'No.'

'Have you both been in Paris long?'

'Three days. But we've been here before.'

'Together?'

'No. At what time do you close?'

'When the place begins to empty. Usually between two and three in the morning.'

'I'll stay, just in case.'

He sat down in a corner. His head was spinning a little because, going from bar to bar, he had drunk more than he had thought.

'Could I have a very strong coffee?' he asked the waitress.

'I'll go to the kitchen to see if the percolator is on yet.'

She soon brought him a cup of coffee as thick as soup. The woman who had been singing had left. A group of five tourists came in, looked at the customers around the tables, and beat a quick retreat. It was not picturesque enough for them.

So, he had not been mistaken. Odile had gone out the evening before, but she had not gone to see her guitarist. She had wanted to see something new. Had she gone the rounds of a few *boîtes*, as he had?

Bob's eyes were growing bleary. Why did Odile not want anyone to find her body or, at least, to be able to identify it? It was an absurd idea, and he could not guess how she expected to carry it out.

If she were to throw herself into the Seine . . . But she knew how to swim and it would be difficult for her to drown herself. Or else she would be caught up in the propeller of a motorboat, or else, after some days, her body would come to the surface.

She didn't have a gun. Or did she? He nearly rang his father straight away, but he, in his bedroom, would not hear the telephone ringing in the drawing-room. There was a revolver in the house. It must have been there for years, and Albert Pointet kept it in a drawer in his study where, however, there was no risk of his being attacked in broad daylight.

Bob wanted to know as soon as possible if the gun had disappeared. He would ring at about six in the morning, when his father would be alone, drinking his big cup of coffee before taking his walk.

Each time the door opened he had a surge of hope. The guitarist was playing again, on his own, as if for himself, his head a little on one side. Some people were listening to him. He played not badly.

He paid his bill, sighing, for the customers were thinning out.

He was on the point of going back to his hotel in the Rue Gay-Lussac but, on reflection, he went in the direction of the *boîte* where he had gone the previous evening.

Odile was not there. There were only five or six people there and the little band was playing softly. The proprietor came over to shake his hand.

'You haven't found anything?'

'I know where she was last night.'

The guitarist was not long in joining them.

'She hasn't been here?'

'No. Have you any news?'

'She is alive. At any rate, she was alive last night and she was in a *boîte* in the Rue Mouffetard. It's called the Ace of Hearts.'

'I know it. They're only amateur musicians, but it's quite a nice place. Did she leave alone?'

'The proprietor says she did.'

'I've remembered something she said to me when she came to Paris the last time . . .

' "There are some people who are satisfied with themselves. I envy them. I hate myself. As long as I can remember I have hated myself." '

'Do you remember what she was drinking then?'

'Gin and tonic.'

Bob was beginning to feel the effects of tiredness and of his drinks. He went straight to bed after setting his alarm for six in the morning. He would telephone his father, who would be downstairs at that time, and then he would be free to go back to sleep.

Suddenly it was morning and the sun was rising in a slightly misty sky. There were lorries going by in the street. He had a terrible taste in his mouth and was not very pleased with himself.

He rang Lausanne. The phone rang for a long time at the other end before anyone picked up the receiver. It was his father.

'Who is that? Is that you, Bob? Have you found her?'

'No, but she was still alive and kicking the night before last. It appears that she goes to little *boîtes* in Saint-Germain-des-Prés.'

'Alone?'

'Apparently. But that's not why I'm ringing you. Can you tell me if you still have your revolver?'

'What revolver? Oh, yes? That old thing a friend gave me when I was about twenty. It must be in a drawer in my attic.'

'Would you go and look?'

He had to wait for a long time. At last his father's voice, out of breath, said:

'I can't find it. And yet I am sure I didn't put it anywhere else. I have just asked Mathilde if she hasn't seen it while she was cleaning. She doesn't know what has happened to it either. Do you think Odile has taken it?'

'I don't know. The bottle of sleeping pills has disappeared from the bathroom ... The revolver has disappeared from your study ...'

In fact, his sister wanted to die, but didn't know how she would set about it. And that did not keep her from spending a part of the night in the district around the Place Maubert.

'Have you gone around the hotels?'

'No. There are too many. And I think she won't have picked one in the Latin Quarter, where she knows we go ...'

'What are you going to do?'

'First of all, I'm going to the Bureau of Missing Persons.'

'Don't forget that we are Swiss citizens.'

'But she has disappeared in Paris.'

'Can you prove that?'

'I shall try to, anyway. Have a good walk. I'll do all I can.'

He went back to sleep until ten o'clock. He felt no better. He drank his coffee and ate his breakfast without taking any pleasure in it. A little after eleven o'clock, he was in the Rue des Ursins. He followed the arrows painted on the walls of the corridor. In that way he reached Room 4 and entered the room before reading 'Enter without knocking'. There was a uniformed policeman behind a light-coloured, almost new desk.

'Can I help you?'

'I should like to see the director.'

'There is no director. There is a chief superintendent. Do you want to inform us of a disappearance?'

'The case is quite complicated. I should like to see the chief superintendent in person.'

The policeman pushed a pad towards him. The sheets were

printed with several questions. He filled in the spaces in pencil, and the policeman disappeared down a corridor.

'The superintendent is engaged. He will see you when he is free.'

'Do you think that will be long?'

'Your guess is as good as mine.'

'Have I got five minutes, at least?'

'Certainly.'

'I'll be right back.'

He went down the stairs four by four and went into the first bar he saw.

'A glass of white wine.'

'Vouvray?'

'That'll do.'

He needed to clean his mouth out. His coffee and his breakfast were sitting heavily on his stomach.

It was a small glass, and he drank it at a swallow.

'Another one.'

He almost ordered a third, but prudence stopped him. He already felt a little better. He paid, rushed out, and in a minute had taken his place again in the room where the uniformed policeman was.

'The superintendent hasn't called for me?'

'No . . . Wait a moment . . . That is his visitor leaving now.'

He could hear voices in the distance, then steps in the long corridor.

'Will you come this way?'

The superintendent was a broad-shouldered man smoking a very black cigar.

'Take a seat.'

He himself sat down at his desk.

'Who has disappeared?'

'My sister.'

'Is she a minor?'

'She has just had her eighteenth birthday.'

'Has she ever run away before?'

'No.'

'Why is it you who has come? Are your parents no longer alive?'

'Yes, they are. But my father does not leave home any more if he can help it.'

'You have put down the address of an hotel on this slip of paper. I suppose that is not your home address. Where is your home?'

'In Lausanne.'

'You are Swiss? Are you studying in Paris?'

'No. I am a student in Switzerland.'

'And your sister?'

'She has been here for four days . . . no, three. I don't know any more. I am so confused.'

'In fact, the case which is worrying you is no concern of ours. Even if you lived in the provinces, in France, you would have to go to the Prefecture, which would in turn consult us. Besides, your sister has only just disappeared. Have you any proof that she is in Paris?'

'Yes. I picked up the scent last night in a *boîte* in the Rue Mouffetard. The proprietor recognized her photograph. He also gave me an exact description of her clothing.'

'Give me that description.'

'Dark brown trousers, a yellow pullover and a suede jacket like mine.'

'What was the name of the *boîte*?'

'The Ace of Hearts.'

'I know it. Could she not be staying with relatives or friends?'

'I have seen the few friends we have in Paris.'

'There might be some you don't know about.'

'I've met one already, a guitarist in Saint-Germain-des-Prés, with whom she went out on her last trip.'

'So she has been here before?'

'Yes, with my parents' permission.'

He took the photograph out of his pocket and held it out to the superintendent, who looked at it carefully.

'What kind of girl is she?'

'Rather odd. She left school before the last year . . . Then she tried various things . . .'

'And men?'

'Yes. She had her first experience shortly after she was fifteen.'

'Still with your parents' permission?'

174

'No. I was the only one she confided in. Right from the start she was disappointed with sex, but she went on anyway.'

'Did she have any girlfriends in Lausanne?'

'When she was at school I knew them. Afterwards she became more independent. She would often go out in the evenings and come in at one or two in the morning.'

'Did your parents accept this situation?'

'It wouldn't have done them any good to argue with her. She would still only have done what she wanted to.'

The superintendent chewed on his cigar without hiding his surprise.

'What does your father do?'

'He writes history books. You must have seen some in book-shop windows, for his publishers are in Paris and his books are very popular. He writes under his own name: Albert Pointet. He could have taught at the University of Lausanne, because he has his *agrégation*.'

'If I understand you rightly, he is not very interested in you or in your sister.'

'I think he has lost heart.'

'And your mother?'

'My mother sleeps and plays bridge.'

'Does she drink?'

Why did he ask that question?

'Two or three whiskies towards the end of the afternoon.'

'So in fact your sister enjoys perfect liberty . . . Why did she come to Paris?'

'Because for her Paris is the only place in the world. Not just Paris. It was Saint-Germain-des-Prés which fascinated her.'

He was annoyed with himself, in a superstitious way, for having used the past tense, and he corrected himself:

'. . . which fascinates her . . .'

'I don't see, given these conditions, what my men can do. Even if we find her we can't take her back by force to Lausanne, where your parents are not going to chain her up.'

'Read this letter. She posted it, probably at the station, just before she caught the train, and I received it the next morning.'

The superintendent read the letter very carefully.

'I understand your concern now,' he said at last, pushing it

175

back to Bob. 'Leave me the photograph anyway. I'll have a number of copies made and pass them round to our men.'

'You don't think it will be too late?'

'We shall do all we can, Monsieur Pointet. But you must admit your sister is not a very calm person.'

'That is true. May I have the photograph back this evening? I need it to show to people.'

'Come back about five o'clock. The man on duty will give it back to you and he will be able to give you two or three copies too.'

He stood up, drew on his cigar and shook Bob vigorously by the hand.

He had stayed in the district and he had lunch in a little local restaurant which he found without any difficulty, since they can be found almost anywhere in Paris.

Seated alone at a table, he watched the people passing by, but it was of Odile that he was thinking. Would she be eating too, in a *bistrot* of the kind she liked?

Was it not more likely that, especially if she had gone to bed late, she would content herself with nibbling a sandwich in bed as she so often did at home?

Not without an uneasy feeling, he wondered if she had already put her plan into effect or if she had given herself a few days more respite.

Was she still in the same state of mind as when she had written him the letter posted at the station? If not, if that had only been a transitory depression, would she not be regretting now having sent it to him?

So many thoughts came into his mind that he had the impression that he had done nothing since his arrival in Paris. And yet he had almost found her, at the Ace of Hearts. If he had gone there one evening earlier, he would have found himself face to face with his sister.

He had not tried all the restaurants. It was an almost impossible task for one man alone. In the Latin Quarter alone there were hundreds. There were at least as many hotels to which she might have gone.

He toyed with the idea of asking the newspapers to publish her photograph. He could easily write a short paragraph which would move her. He had almost mentioned it to the superintendent in the morning, but at the last moment he had kept silent, believing that he might precipitate matters by doing that.

She was sensitive to the opinion of others. It was difficult to explain. She did all she could to shock those with whom she lived, but she remained attentive to the opinion they had of her.

She despised them, found them idiots and old-hat. At the same time she wanted to be loved, and that was why she was so generous.

When he left the restaurant he took a taxi and asked to be taken to the Forensic Institute where an official in a waiting room asked him:

'Have you come to identify a body?'

'I don't know. My sister has disappeared, and I have exhausted most possible places of finding her.'

'Did she have any reason to commit suicide?'

'She said she would, in a letter.'

'What name?'

'Odile Pointet. She wouldn't necessarily have her bag and her papers on her.'

'That is what happens most often, in fact. How old is she?'

'Eighteen. She is blonde, quite tall, and thin. She was probably wearing brown trousers . . .'

'When did she disappear?'

'She was last seen the night before last in the Rue Mouffetard area.'

'In that case, she is not here. We have had three bodies in the last twenty-four hours, but none of them was a girl or a young woman. Leave me your address, just in case.'

He had already begun to feel more cheerful when that sentence, spoken quite naturally, indifferently, chilled him.

He wrote his name and the address of the hotel in the Rue Gay-Lussac on a sheet of paper.

'Did you say that she told you she was going to commit suicide?'

'Yes. That was about four or five days ago.'

'In that case there is little chance that she will. When one really wants to die one doesn't worry about other people and one does it straight away. The moment one takes time to think . . .'

A little later he stopped at a kiosk and bought a map of Paris. The list of hospitals was on a blue page. There were fifty, some of them near the Latin Quarter, others more or less farther away.

He went to the first one which was on his route. A middle-aged woman in a white overall and cap sat in a glass cage in which there was a small opening.

'If you wish to visit someone . . .'

She pointed with the end of her pencil to the notice giving the days and hours when visiting was permitted.

'No. I am looking for someone.'

'Someone you think may be here?'

'I don't know. It's a girl of eighteen.'

'Has she had an accident?'

'Not as far as I know. She's my sister.'

He was upset, and the severe expression of the woman did nothing to reassure him. He became muddled in his explanations.

'What I am afraid of is that she has tried to do away with herself.'

'What makes you think that?'

'A letter which she sent to me, in which she spoke of committing suicide.'

'What is her name?'

'Odile Pointet.'

'What district does she live in?'

'She lives in Lausanne, but I know that she was in Paris the night before last.'

She consulted a list.

'There's no girl of that name here and there has not been a suicide for a week.'

'A week ago she was in Lausanne.'

That was true. He could hardly believe it. Four days ago, Odile was still sharing family life at home. A life which suddenly in the bustle of Paris, seemed so strange to him that it became unbelievable.

He had always taken for granted that things in the Avenue de

Jaman were as they should be. His father had a rather idiosyncratic way of arranging his days, but was that not through lack of contact with his wife?

He never saw them together in the drawing-room, not even in front of the television, which did not interest his mother.

She came to life particularly in the afternoon, to play bridge, and in the evenings she would go to the Nouveau Club, in the Avenue de Rumine, to play bridge again.

He himself paid little attention to Odile. It was true that his course of study was very difficult and that he had very little free time.

He went into another hospital where his welcome was a little more friendly.

'A young girl, did you say? And recently? Just a moment, while I ask Matron if there have been any admissions in the last few hours.'

She disappeared at the end of the corridor where a patient was waiting on a trolley.

'No, young man. Nothing like that . . . I hope you get the same reply everywhere.'

He finally found himself at the bottom of the Rue Saint-Jacques again, in the district where most of the hospitals are. He went round them all, patiently. He repeated the same things. They received him well in some cases, badly in others. It did not matter to him.

'No, monsieur.'

He waited in vain for one of them to add:

'I'm sorry.'

He went by the Rue Gay-Lussac to check that there had been no letter or message for him. For his sister would know that after receiving her letter he had taken the first train for Paris. And the family always stayed at the Hôtel Mercator.

'Nothing for me? No letters, no messages? No telephone call either?'

'Nothing at all. Listen, you look exhausted. You would be better off going to bed early this evening.'

He smiled with some bitterness. It was precisely in the evenings that he had a slight chance of running into Odile.

'I'll do my best,' he promised.

At five o'clock he went to the Rue des Ursins, where he was given half a dozen photographs.

He couldn't take any more and he went back to the hotel, where he stretched out on his bed. He fell asleep immediately and when he woke night had fallen and his room was only lit by reflections from a street-lamp.

He showered and dressed. He thought he could hear thunder in the distance, but he was not sure. It was ten o'clock in the evening. He went into the first bar he came to and had three sandwiches and a glass of beer because he did not feel up to sitting in a restaurant.

Did the rolling thunder sound like the noise of a train? In any case, he thought of a train, of his sister, her blue suitcase in hand, getting out on the platform.

If she had taken her suitcase, that meant she did not intend to commit suicide straight away. She knew she would not stay in the Rue Gay-Lussac where the family would easily find her. She had never stayed at any other hotel in Paris.

Why not stay near the station? There were many hotels of all kinds. In the continual coming and going, she would be less noticed than she would anywhere else.

He took a taxi to the Gare de Lyon. Here he only had to say her name, as travellers were obliged to show some form of identification.

'Mademoiselle Pointet, please.'

'Is she supposed to be staying here?'

'I don't know.'

'We have no one of that name.'

He went from one hotel to another. Each time they shook their heads.

Until one of the night porters said in the most casual way:

'You have just missed her.'

'She was here?'

'Yes.'

'When did she leave?'

'Yesterday, at the beginning of the afternoon. She took a taxi.'

'You didn't hear what address she gave?'

'I'm not here in the daytime.'

He wanted to be sure that it was really Odile.

'Did you see her?'

'Certainly. When she came in at night it was always me who was on duty. A very nice girl, but not very happy.'

'Was she wearing trousers?'

'Yes. She didn't change her clothes. She always wore the same brown trousers.'

She had not gone to the station to catch a train, for she would not have taken a taxi. Why had she changed hotels?

'May I use the telephone?'

'A local call, in Paris?'

'Yes.'

'You will find the phone box on the left, in the hall. Wait, I'll give you a token.'

He rang the Bureau of Missing Persons and asked to speak to the chief superintendent, whose name he did not know.

'You really want to speak to Monsieur Lebon? I'll see if he is free.'

The slightly rough voice of the superintendent said:

'Who is that speaking?'

'I came to see you this morning.'

'Are you the Swiss who was looking for your sister? Have you found her?'

'No, but I have found the hotel where she spent her first three days. She checked out yesterday afternoon and went off in a taxi. I'm sorry to disturb you at this hour. I am leading such a life that I don't realize what time it is any more.'

'In the police force we don't keep set hours. You are lucky that I had a report to finish and I came back to the office after dinner. What you have just told me is very interesting. That could actually serve as a starting point. What is the name of the hotel?'

'Just a minute. I didn't note it, but I can read it from here. It's an odd name: the Hôtel Héliard.'

'Opposite the Gare de Lyon?'

'Yes.'

'I know it. My men will see to that tomorrow.'

'Thank you.'

He was quite pleased with himself because he had had the idea of looking near the station. But why had Odile suddenly left a hotel where she had every reason to believe that no one would come to look for her? Was it too far away at night, when she left the Latin Quarter? Had she gone some place near Saint-Germain-des-Prés?

He began with the basement bar with the big Scandinavian proprietor. He found the same musicians there, including the guitarist. He went to the bar and ordered a scotch. When the music stopped, the guitarist came over and sat on the next stool.

'Have you seen her?'

He shook his head.

'But I heard a friend of mine, who eats in the same *bistrot* I do, speak of her. He's a guitarist too. He doesn't belong to a group and he gets what work he can. He is often at the Ace of Hearts, a *boîte* in the Rue . . .'

'I know. I went there the night before last. My sister was there the night before. They noticed her because she isn't the usual type of person there. They were able to describe her to me exactly. What astonishes me is that, knowing you, she didn't come here again. Unless she is avoiding this place precisely because she is afraid to see you again.

'She is fairly sure that I am in Paris. She is running away from me. Perhaps she imagines that my father is here with me. I'll wait here a little, anyway.'

When the music started again, he went over and sat down in a corner where a beautiful girl who could not have been wearing anything under her black silk dress came over to him and said:

'Are you dancing, lover?'

'No, thanks.'

'Will you buy me a drink?'

'Get one at the bar and put it on my bill.'

'Don't you like my company?'

'It's not that, but . . .'

He stammered, taken by surprise, and she sat down calmly opposite him.

'Whisky?' the waitress asked her as if she had known her tastes for a long time.

'A double.'

She seemed overcome by scruples.

'I hope you're not one of those?'

He shook his head.

'You're not from Paris?'

'I'm from Lausanne.'

'That's in Switzerland, isn't it? I heard someone talking about Switzerland not very long ago . . . Yesterday or today, but I can't remember where it was.'

'Was it a girl?'

'I don't know. I have the feeling it was a woman's voice.'

'In a restaurant?'

'That's possible. I always eat at the Bilboquet, in the Place Maubert. But I don't think it was there.'

'Do you live in a hotel?'

'No. I have a room of my own, where I can cook if I want to. I'm thinking . . . Switzerland twice in two days, you must admit that's a strange coincidence . . .'

She was watching him as she talked and seemed to find him agreeable.

'Are you in Paris for long?'

'I don't think so.'

'Are you a student?'

'Yes.'

'Here's to you.'

On any other occasion he would certainly have gone to bed with her, because she seemed like a nice girl and her body was very attractive.

He signalled to the waitress.

'Are you going already?'

'Yes. I have to catch up on my sleep.'

He paid. The girl sighed:

'Just my luck!'

He waved to the guitarist and went out. It was raining, a fine drizzle which the Parisians had been waiting for for a long time, since here as in Switzerland September had been completely without rain.

On the off chance he went to the Ace of Hearts, where the proprietor gave him a glass of rum on the house. He did not want it, but he did not dare say so.

'She hasn't been in?'

'No.'

There were three this evening, all with long hair, playing music as they moved about the room.

The glass of rum made him have trouble moving his legs, and he had some difficulty getting back to the Rue Gay-Lussac.

He slept until ten in the morning and woke once more with a foul taste in his mouth.

Chapter Four

'Bob leaves the house before the post comes. If the postman gives the letter to Mathilde, she will take it up to my brother's room.

'If by chance she leaves it downstairs and if by an even greater chance my mother gets up early, she will recognize my handwriting and won't be able to resist her curiosity.'

That was her state of mind in the train. Her thoughts were not dramatic, and she avoided thinking of the action she was going to take and of the manner in which she would disappear.

What would her brother think when he read the letter? Would he discuss it with his father? It was possible. The pair of them got on quite well and Bob often went up to the attic to talk.

Would he tell him about the suicide? Or only about the disappearance, a kind of running away, in fact?

There was every chance that Bob would come to Paris to look for her, but among five million inhabitants there was little chance that he would find her.

Night fell and she left the dining-car to go back to her seat. A middle-aged man, holding a morocco leather briefcase on his knees as if it were something precious, stared at her and when she happened to turn her face towards him, would smile at her in what he thought was an attractive way.

It was on the station platform that her mind suddenly seemed to go blank. People were rushing about and many of them bumped into her as they went by. She stood there without moving, in the grey light of the dirty lamps, and everything, even her journey, seemed unreal to her.

At a loss, she wondered what she had come for. She nearly got into a taxi and went to the Hôtel Mercator in the Rue Gay-Lussac, where she would find herself in a familiar atmosphere. She could not go there. It was there that all the family had stayed for years and there where Bob would undoubtedly go in the first place.

Opposite the station there was a row of hotels where only a few of the lights were kept on in the hall at night.

She went into the first one she came to, without looking at the name. The night porter, a sad-looking man, asked for some identification. She had not thought of that. It would be the same everywhere, and she took her passport out of her bag.

Her room was quite big, but ugly, a dull ugliness, old, and of doubtful cleanliness. In the bathroom the water dripping from the taps had left a long brown stain on the enamel.

Then, sitting on the bed, she began to cry. She felt alone, without anything to hang on to. No one had ever paid any attention to her and held out a hand to help her. Had anyone ever helped her to live?

It was stupid. Everything was stupid. Existence had no meaning, no purpose. She had been battering herself against the walls like a large fly on a hot summer's day.

She almost went out, went anywhere, just to see the people walking, the cars, the lights. To escape from this emptiness which surrounded her.

Outside it would be the same. She would still be alone, and the passers-by could do nothing for her.

She took the bottle of sleeping tablets from her toilet case and was tempted to swallow the entire contents.

Not yet. She wanted to give herself the time to live her death. She was still lucid. She took only one tablet and swallowed it with a little water from the tooth glass. Then, lying on the bed, she cried a little more.

She did not dare to undress, as if she did not feel safe in that hostile room, and she eventually went to sleep fully clothed.

In the morning she found the same décor, which was no more attractive in daylight. It was almost midday. She did not feel up to taking a bath or a shower and going out. There was a telephone on the bedside table and she asked if she could have sandwiches brought up.

'What kind, mademoiselle?'

'Two ham and two cheese.'

She ate them in front of the window, watching the taxis coming and going, taking passengers to the station or bearing them away.

She slept again and did not wake until four o'clock. She washed and dressed then, in a hurry to be out of doors, to escape from those four walls.

She walked along the Seine thinking automatically of drowning. She could not drown herself. She was too good a swimmer and would instinctively save herself.

She had dinner in a little restaurant on the Quai de la Tournelle. She did not yet feel a sense of reality. She had real dizzy spells. Her head was spinning. She wondered if she were ill. It was a thought she had often had, for several years.

'I shan't live to make old bones ... '

She had said that to Bob two years before, and Bob had laughed at her.

'Ah, that's just your nonsense, my dear.'

'Then why do I always have these sicknesses?'

'Everyone has, but they don't pay any attention to them.'

She ended up in a little *boîte* in Saint-André-des-Arts, watching the couples dancing.

They were happy. There were such things as happy people. She drank gin and tonic which made her even more sad.

She would have liked to talk to someone. To her brother, for example. No. Rather to a doctor, a specialist who would perhaps find the root of her illness.

But what illness was it? What had she done with her life until now? And it was no one's fault, not even the lugubrious atmosphere of the town.

She alone was responsible. She was unable to think of anything but herself, her illnesses, the future which she was incapable of imagining.

She was useless. She gave nothing. On the contrary, she was a burden on others.

And now there was nothing beyond the present.

She had taken a decision. She had written to Bob and tried to tell him everything. Bob was her opposite, a serious boy, stable, sure of himself. What had he thought when he understood her message?

At that very moment he was probably in the train, the same T.E.E. in which she had come to Paris.

187

She was tempted to allow him enough time to arrive, to go and see him in the Rue Gay-Lussac, to tell him that she would give up her plan if he would promise not to tell their parents or anyone else where she was.

She would not go back to Lausanne. What would she do? She had left school too early to have a diploma which would be any use for anything. It was the same with her guitar lessons, her English lessons, her dancing lessons.

She would suddenly take off in a new direction and for a couple of weeks she would feel a sort of euphoria. She would want to go more quickly than her teachers, who tried to calm her fever.

Then, from one day to the next, nothing mattered any more. She would leave a note for Mathilde before going to bed.

'Don't wake me tomorrow morning. Ring the English class and say I am ill.'

Then she would isolate herself in her room and would only come down for dinner. She would sleep, play records, read whatever came to hand.

A middle-aged man sat down beside her.

'This is the first time you've come here, isn't it?' he eventually asked, leaning over her.

She looked at him as if she didn't see him, and he appeared embarrassed. She paid for her drinks and took a taxi back to the hotel. She had not much money, hardly more than five hundred francs. What would she do when that was finished?

She was stupid. Had she not found the solution before she left Lausanne? She would disappear. She did not wonder any more what to do so that her body should not be found or identified. She had had the idea in Switzerland. It was too romantic. Besides, it was proving to be impracticable.

She would suffer the fate of all suicides. The police would be called in. Her body would be taken to the Forensic Institute for the autopsy.

Her parents would rush to the scene, would stay in the Rue Gay-Lussac, and would have the body taken back to Lausanne.

That was the part which upset her most. And yet, when it was all over, she would not feel anything any more. And would there be a short church service? There would, unfortunately, be articles in the papers, and her former friends, girls and boys, would be at the funeral, as well as the tradesmen and her mother's bridge partners.

She would be in a long varnished box where she would suffocate. It was stupid to think like that. She would not suffocate, of course. But was it certain that one did not feel anything any more?

She took another sleeping tablet, as she had done the previous evening. She got up shortly after ten o'clock and, after eating breakfast, she washed and dressed.

She put on the same clothes as she had the day before. She usually wore trousers and clinging blouses, to show off her body.

She was not pleased with her body. She had almost no breasts or hips. At home, she weighed herself two or three times a week, disappointed when she had not put on a few grammes.

She lunched in a restaurant, in a street whose name she did not notice, behind the church of Saint-Germain-des-Prés. Things were not going as she had imagined. She had not thought that she would be alone, that she would have no one with whom to talk. She could not walk the streets indefinitely.

She went back to lie down and stayed in bed all afternoon.

She kept putting off the moment of doing the final act. Not from fear, but because she felt a need for this slow goodbye to life.

It was a sort of preparation. No one among those she passed in the street or who spoke to her in the hotel would guess the thoughts which were running through her head.

She went out in the evening, of course. She just had sandwiches in a bar, for she was not hungry. Bob must have arrived. How would he set about it? Where would he start to look? He would certainly go to Le Cannibale, because she had once told him that she had gone there and that she had had a good time.

She had been in a state of euphoria then, and she remembered with nostalgia the guitarist who had taken her home with him. She would have liked to see him again, to talk to him, perhaps to tell him of her decision.

It was too dangerous. Bob would almost certainly go to Le Cannibale. Would he speak to the musician? Would he tell Bob what had passed between them?

What did it matter, in fact? She was not ashamed of the life she had been living for several years now. The worst memory was that of Uncle Arthur, who did not seem to be embarrassed himself since he still came to the house from time to time. He remained the same, pleased with himself, a joke always on his lips.

'Well, my beauty, how many victims have you had now?'

He was her mother's brother. He made quite a lot of money. He was constantly on the move, at the wheel of a flashy car, going from farm to farm selling agricultural machines. Almost everywhere they would give him a drink, which he never refused.

Odile had another relative in Paris, an aunt of her mother's, who had never married.

She must have been over eighty and she lived alone in a flat in the Rue Caulaincourt. She had worked for more than forty years in the same office in the Rue du Sentier and she must have had some savings in the bank, as well as a small pension.

Odile had only seen her once, when her mother had taken her to Montmartre to see her. The flat was sparkling clean and they had to wear felt pattens so as not to mark the waxed floors.

What could she have told her aunt? And would she not have informed her parents straight away?

It was funny to think of her, a stranger in fact, at this moment. If she gave up her resolve, would she not become like her aunt?

She looked for a *boîte* where she could spend part of the night. It must not be too well known, for she was afraid of meeting Bob, who would be looking for her.

She ended up at the Ace of Hearts. A woman was singing. A guitarist accompanied her. When a girl with nails which were varnished but dirty asked her what she wanted to drink, she ordered a gin and tonic.

It was one of the two young teachers whom she used sometimes to meet in the *bistrot* who had given her the taste for gin.

She had imitated. She had always imitated someone. She had no thoughts of her own. She realized that. What was disturbing with her was that she understood herself very well but was incapable of changing herself.

She looked at the lovers who were holding each other round the waist and kissing. The man had his hand on one of his companion's breasts and it embarrassed neither of them that there were twenty or so people looking at them. Were they really looking at them? Wasn't everything permitted here?

At the table next to her were two men, quite young, with long hair and jeans.

'Are you waiting for someone, mademoiselle?'

'No.'

'In that case would you like to join us?'

They were drinking beer. She went over to their table.

'What are you drinking?'

'Gin.'

'Drink up so we can buy you another.'

She did so, docilely.

'Are you French?'

'No.'

She was already beginning to have a faint smile on her lips.

'Belgian?'

'Not that either.'

'You speak French without any accent.'

'I'm Swiss.'

'From Geneva? I've been to Geneva twice, and once to Villars for the winter sports.'

'My parents have a chalet at Villars, and when I was a child I went there every year.'

'We might have met. Don't you go there any more?'

'My parents still do. I prefer the sun and I take my holidays on the Mediterranean.'

'Are you a student?'

'Yes.'

'In Paris?'

She had to be careful, for they might be students and they would recognize a lie straight away.

'No. In Lausanne. I have come here for a few days.'

She had often lied in such a way. It was not to make herself seem more than she was, but because the truth was too complicated. One could not talk about holidays as far as she was concerned since she did nothing all year except take one class or another, for a short time.

'Have you been here before? Do you know Old Moustaches?'

That was the proprietor, because he had enormous black moustaches.

'This is the first time I have been in this *boîte*.'

'It's a bit of a lottery. Some evenings it's fantastic, and others it's nothing. It depends on who comes. The guitarist isn't a professional. He comes here to play for his own pleasure. The singer too.

'Some evenings there are six or seven musicians. The proprietor knows what's what. He doesn't interfere. Even when half a dozen drunken Americans come in and threaten to break the place up.

'Do you know Paris well?'

'I've been here quite often.'

'With your parents?'

'Only when I was small. I've been coming alone for quite a while.'

'Always to the Left Bank?'

'Yes. This is where I feel at home. I have never visited the Louvre or any museum. I can hardly have been on the Champs-Elysées more than once or twice.

'Are you both students too?'

'My friend Martin is at Nanterre . . .'

She looked at him with some admiration.

'I'm taking my degree in English and then I'll try to do a doctorate.'

She had not expected to meet such serious boys in this *boîte*.

'Haven't you any girlfriends?'

'We do sometimes, but nothing permanent. We prefer change. We seize whatever opportunity comes.'

'And when you invited me to your table you thought I was one of those opportunities . . .'

They both laughed. The student from Nanterre was not particularly attractive, but the other had a frank, infectious laugh.

'Do you speak English?'

'No. I studied it for six months and the results were disastrous. Like everything I do.'

'What do you mean?'

'That everything I try fails lamentably.'

She was surprised to find herself smiling too.

'What faculty are you in?'

'Arts.'

'Do you want to be a teacher?'

'No.'

'A literary critic? A novelist?'

She was quite surprised to hear herself laughing. But was she not the centre of attention of the two young men? They were paying attention to her. They thought she was interesting. She was acting, and she hardly noticed that she was lying.

'Have you any brothers or sisters?'

'Only one brother.'

'Older than you?'

'He's four years older.'

'Is he at the university too?'

'Yes. He works hard.'

'What faculty is he in?'

'Sociology.'

'Like me,' said the student from Nanterre. 'What year is he in?'

'Third year. Then he goes on for his doctorate.'

'I'm doing mine now.'

It was a banal conversation, and it was comforting. She was not thinking of herself any more, or of her plans. They chatted lazily, with a reassuring casualness.

'Would you like to dance?' the boy sitting next to her asked.

'Yes.'

There was very little room between the tables and it only took three couples to fill the available space.

'Are you in any hurry to get home?' asked the student in a low voice.

'No. There's no one waiting for me.'

'When I get rid of my friend we could go for a walk together, through the night. Do you like walking?'

'Yes.'

It was not true. She only walked when she could not do anything else. In Lausanne she would take her scooter just to go down to the Rue de Bourg, five hundred metres from home.

He pressed her fingers as if they were already two conspirators.

'Then we could go and have a last drink at my place.'

She said nothing. Neither yes nor no.

'I'll tell you in a little while.'

She had not envisaged this when she left the Hôtel Héliard. They sat down again and ordered more drinks.

There was a silence. The student was now a little embarrassed about the proposition he had just made. But it was two in the morning, and wasn't she alone in a *boîte* of doubtful reputation? What did she want, if not an affair?

He pressed his knee lightly against hers and she did not draw away.

'Do you see those two hippies opposite us? They are smoking marijuana.'

'What if the police come in?'

'The police know about it. As long as there's no trouble and there's no LSD, they prefer to keep their eyes shut. Except for pushers, of course.'

'Have you tried it?'

'Yes. Twice.'

'Did you like it?'

'No. It made me sleepy instead of exciting me.'

'What about LSD?'

'I was as sick as a dog. You see, there are still some very ordinary young people around the Place Maubert. Your health ... My name is Martin. My friend's name is Louis, but we usually call him the Terror because of his fierce expression.'

He gave her a questioning wink and looked at his watch. She blinked her eyes as a sign of agreement.

'Well, Louis, shall we go?'

'Right. It's your turn to pay.'

Louis left them on his own initiative because he had a scooter at the door. Odile remained alone, in the long, badly-lit street, with the one called Martin.

They walked for a long time in silence and they could hear the noise of their footsteps. Then something happened which made Odile tremble, something which she had not been expecting. Gently, hesitatingly, her companion had slipped his hand under her arm, so that they were now walking along like lovers.

It was hardly anything, but she was moved by it. It gave a

different colour to their meeting. She did not remember a man ever having walked arm in arm with her.

'Do you live around here?' she asked, just to say something.

'Nor far from here. In the Rue de Bac. We mustn't make any noise on the stairs or going through the drawing-room.'

He laughed, and his laugh was very youthful.

'The house is an old mansion divided up into flats. My land-lady has rented a wing on the third floor for a very long time and, since it's too big for her alone, she sublets two furnished rooms.

'She insists that her tenants obey two conditions. The first is not to cook in the rooms nor, in principle, to eat there. The second is not to bring in women.'

'A condition which you don't fulfil very often, I should think.'

'On the contrary. It's very rare that I take anyone home, and old Madame Boildieu has never caught me out. She must have been very rich, because the furniture is wonderful. The carpets too . . .'

There was a door in the hallway and he had the key. They went up to the third floor silently, switching the light on again at the second.

He put his finger on his lips and took another key out of his pocket. All was darkness and silence. Only in the big drawing-room was there a little light coming through the shutters.

He took her by the hand to guide her and they reached a cor-ridor, where he stopped in front of a door. He only had to turn the handle to open it, then he closed it again. The key was on the inside.

'Here we are!'

He put the light on and kissed her. It was all happening as if in a dream. The room was very big, high-ceilinged, and crimson silk curtains covered the windows.

The bed was turned down for the night.

'Don't be afraid,' he whispered. 'We can do anything we like from now on, except talk out loud.'

'I'm not afraid.'

If she had met a boy like Martin before, she would perhaps have fallen in love and things would have been different.

He kissed her tenderly and she felt that he really did feel tender-

195

ness towards her. It was a little as if he realized that in spite of her self-assurance she was only a child.

'What would you like to drink? Cognac or wine? It's all I have here, and the wine isn't very good.'

'Cognac, then.'

While he went to get the bottle and the glasses from an old cabinet, she took her jacket off with a natural movement. The furniture was Louis XV and the wood was beautifully polished.

'Your health . . .'

'To both of us,' he corrected. 'I would like you to have a happy memory of this evening. I don't know if I'll see you again, because you will undoubtedly be going back to Lausanne.'

'I am going away, yes.'

Speaking like that in hushed voices and having to strain their ears gave their meeting a mysterious, romantic character.

'It's a pity,' he said, 'that I didn't meet you sooner.'

'I think I'm sorry about that too.'

With gentle, easy movements he unbuttoned her blouse and took it off, then took off her bra and laid them both on the chair.

'My hands aren't too cold?'

'No.'

Of the affairs she had had, none had been like this. He tried to take her trousers off, but that was more difficult.

'Leave it. I'll do it.'

And she sat on the edge of the bed to free her legs. She felt no embarrassment, no shame. All she had on was a tiny pair of pants, and she took those off too.

'Aren't you going to undress?'

'There's too much light, isn't there?'

'The bedside lamp would be enough, wouldn't it?'

The lampshade was red and bathed the room in a rosy light.

He was the less at ease of the two. Odile was thinking:

'This is the last time, my girl.'

He slid down beside her and caressed her.

'I'm too thin, don't you think?'

'You're slim and tall, but not thin.'

'I should weigh five kilos more.'

'And where would you put them? You want to get fatter, while most women are torturing themselves to lose weight.'

When he caressed her more intimately, she closed her eyes, and soon he was on top of her, entering her slowly. For a moment she thought that for the first time she was really going to feel pleasure. There was a beginning, and she stayed as if suspended there, holding her breath, but the sensation disappeared.

She did not let him notice anything. She had opened her eyes and was looking at him. He looked so happy! Rarely had she seen such happiness on the face of a man.

'You don't need to take any precautions.'

That had no more importance now. She would not have time to be pregnant.

She had been wrong to think of that. When she felt him come in her tears rolled down her cheeks. Not violently. She was not sobbing. She just moaned a few times.

'Did I hurt you?'

'No. Don't pay any attention.'

'It isn't the first time, is it?'

'No. I'm not reproaching you for anything. It's a personal matter. I'm a fool . . .'

The tears were still running down, very warm, and they had the same taste as the tears at Ouchy.

She had been eight years old at the time. One day her mother had scolded her severely because she had hidden in the drawing-room while her mother and her friends were playing cards.

On being discovered, she had been shaken very hard.

'Go to your room and don't let me catch you hiding any more.'

What she felt most was the sense of injustice. She had not thought of listening to what the grown-ups were saying. Or had that really been a little bit of her intention?

'She hates me and I hate her too.'

She spoke to herself.

'I'm going to rid them of my company and then I shall be rid of theirs.'

She tiptoed downstairs. She crossed the garden and went through the gate. She went down the street straight in front of her and shortly afterwards crossed Mon Repos Park, which she knew very well. She had been there countless times to play, but she did not look around.

She continued the conversation with herself.

'How can grown-ups spend all their afternoons playing cards? She does nothing else. It would never enter her head to help Mathilde, who is old and has to do everything. Of course there is Olga, the cleaning woman, but she only comes four times a week, just for the morning . . . It seems she's very ill and doesn't know it.'

She went on walking. She wanted to go very far from the house. She did not ask herself what would happen after that.

Was it a way of punishing her mother? Now she was walking through streets she did not know and she was quite surprised to find that she was beside the lake and had arrived at Ouchy.

She sat down on a bench where she could be alone. And it was then that tears sprang from her eyes, hot, salty tears, accompanied by just a few sobs. She had no handkerchief to wipe them away. She was wearing the smock she wore at home.

'What's wrong, little girl?'

The lady must have been old. Almost all people were old to her, even her mother and father.

'Nothing, madame.'

'Is anyone with you?'

'No.'

'Do you live near here?'

'No.'

'Do you know where you live?'

'In the Avenue de Jaman.'

'And you walked here?'

'Yes.'

'Do your parents know you are here?'

'I didn't tell them I was going.'

'Where do you want to go?'

'I don't know. Anywhere. My mother scolded me and shook me. I wanted to punish her.'

'Come with me. I'll take you home.'

She took her hand and led her to a taxi rank.

'What number in the Avenue de Jaman?'

'The house is called Two Limes, but there's only one.'

It was her father who opened the door, because his wife had

told him what had happened. She was searching all the streets in the district, and Mathilde was doing the same.

'Thank you, madame. I must admit I was very worried.

'Your daughter is a very intelligent, very nice girl.'

She did not only remember the tears, but the words which had been spoken. Her father had taken her in his arms, which he almost never did, and had kissed her. Her mother had been the first to come back.

'Is Odile back?'

'She's playing in her room. A charming old lady brought her home. You'd better not go up now, and don't say any more about it.'

After all that time she still remembered her tears, and she cried as she had then, naked in the arms of a naked man whom she had only known for a few hours.

'Don't pay any attention to me.'

And she said to herself again:

'It's the last time.'

He went to the dressing-table drawer to look for a handkerchief to dry her tears and threw it to her, joking:

'Here, blow your nose.'

He began again a little later, and she did not cry any more. She felt well. Her body was relaxed. She did not think of anything. She would have liked to stay in that bed until morning, with this big, kind boy.

He filled the glasses again with cognac.

'To our loves.'

She sighed, knowing what those words meant for her.

'To our loves.'

She had never loved. She would never love. She had only just found, and then only by a fluke, arms in which she felt at ease. Wasn't it time for her to go now?

She went into the bathroom for a minute, then came back and dressed. Martin was almost ready.

'You don't have to take me back,' she said.

'You're not going back alone. Where are you staying?'

'Not far from here. Just let me out of the flat.'

This time he took a little electric torch. Taking her hand to guide her he crossed the drawing-room, and when they reached the hall they saw a sort of ghost, a very thin woman in a night-gown who was watching them, her arms crossed over her chest.

Martin hastened to shine the torch on the front door and the figure disappeared.

They hurried down the stairs. On the pavement, Martin pretended to laugh.

'I'm sorry. You're going to be chucked out because of me.'

'Don't be sorry. I was beginning to get tired of that atmosphere. It's too well-upholstered for my taste. Where shall I take you?'

'I've already told you: nowhere. I have to go back alone. It will let me think.'

'Do you have a lot to think about?'

'Yes.'

'Serious things?'

'Some of them.'

'I suppose I'm not part of your worries?'

'I've just spent one of the happiest hours of my life.'

'And yet you cried.'

'Exactly.'

He put his arms around her shoulders and kissed her for a long time, more gently than before.

'Shall I see you again?'

'I don't think so. It's time for me to go back to Lausanne. If I should stay any longer I shall go to the Ace of Hearts from time to time and then we shall meet again.'

'I'll drop by every evening.'

He watched her go off and turn the corner of the Boulevard Raspail. She walked with long strides, breathing deeply. It was her night. She did not know why she thought that, but it was like a signature tune.

If she were to marry a man like Martin . . .

It was too late, much too late. And if she told him about all the affairs she had had, he would be disheartened. Perhaps at first he would gloss over her affairs. But later? Would reproaches not come then?

She suddenly wondered how she had begun. Most of her friends at school swore they had never had relationships with men, apart from a few kisses and sometimes a furtive touch. She knew that two of them were lying, but they were the two girls in the class who mocked at everything.

One of them, Emilienne, must have been living round about where she was at this minute. It was she who had studied Decorative Arts at Vevey.

And because she was at Vevey, where she went by train every morning, Odile had gone there too. For several months they had been very close friends. Emilienne had told her about her affairs. She found it natural to have sexual relations with men.

Other people must have known about it. But no one accused her. She stayed on good terms with her girlfriends, except for Odile, whom she reproached for being uppish and disagreeable.

She was now in Paris, where she was taking a course in History of Art. She would get married. She would have children. And all her affairs would be forgotten for ever.

And then there was the case of Elisabeth Ajoupa. She was dark, with large dark eyes and a lazy walk. She was well-formed, a woman already, at sixteen.

Odile envied her because of her breasts. They had become friends, and one Saturday afternoon they had gone to the pictures together.

'Have you ever made love yet?' Elizabeth had asked her when a rather daring scene had just been shown on the screen.

'No. Have you?'

'Yes, I have. But don't tell anybody. I think my father would kill me if he found out. The first was a friend of the family, a married man with a very beautiful wife, much more beautiful than me. He rented a studio in Pully where we used to meet.

'After that I had others. Three of them.'

She held up three fingers, as if that was important.

They had lost touch with each other. A year later Odile had received a wedding announcement from Beirut. Elisabeth Ajoupa was marrying a doctor with an almost unpronounceable name.

She had not noticed how far she had been walking. Now she was walking beside the Seine and the moon was reflected in it. She was not afraid. She did not think that anyone could want her handbag. Two policemen on bicycles turned round to look at her in astonishment, and one of them almost went back to warn her.

It had not occurred to her to take a taxi. She wanted to think, to think until it hurt. She smoked cigarette after cigarette. The two cognacs, after the gins, had made her walk a little unsteady, and perhaps her mind too.

'I must, mustn't I?'

She was not fighting against it. She had taken her decision. She had informed Bob about it. Perhaps he would have told their father.

Oddly enough, at this distance her father was becoming a more sympathetic character. He made her think of a big dog whose size is frightening but who is really gentle.

There had been one when she was a little girl, a Saint Bernard who belonged to the people next door. He used to come into their garden, particularly when she was playing there.

He must have realized that he looked fierce, because when he wanted to get close to her he would get down on his chest and crawl towards her. He had become her great friend and she would run to the kitchen to get pieces of sugar or sweets for him.

It was Mathilde who would scold her, for she had an almost pathological fear of dogs.

'How can you play with that huge beast?'

'He isn't a beast. He's a dog.'

'A dog who would eat you up in one mouthful.'

'When I give him something to eat he takes it so delicately that I can't even feel his rough tongue.'

Why did that memory come back to her? Oh, yes, because she had been thinking of her father. When had he hidden himself in his attic, and why? She would never know. He was already installed there when she was born. Their grandfather lived in the house and what was now the drawing-room was his study.

No one had the right to go in there without being invited. She particularly remembered his white, well-trimmed beard through which he ran his fingers mechanically.

For a long time she and her brother had had their meals in the kitchen. Then, when she was about six, she had been given the right, along with Bob, to eat in the dining-room, on condition they did not speak.

Now the grown-ups did not speak either, so that meals passed in silence. Her grandfather paid no attention to them. She still did not know that he had never recovered from the death of his wife and that he had spent the last ten years of his life longing for death.

One evening, there had been comings and goings on the staircase, and voices in the old man's room.

A car had stopped at the gate. Odile had not dared to open the door, and Bob was asleep. For at that time they slept in the same room.

The next morning she learned that her grandfather was dead. He had called for his son, had spoken to him for a long time in a low voice, and then it had ended before the doctor arrived.

Chapter Five

She nearly telephoned her father, without thinking that it was four in the morning and that she would be making him come down to the drawing-room in his pyjamas.

She did not even know what she would say to him. A week before, she had hated him, considering him horribly selfish. Suddenly she saw him in another light, a man who was resigned to life, who had made himself a little world to suit his circumstances.

She wanted to hear his voice. What would she have talked to him about? Two Limes seemed less gloomy to her from this distance, as did the life she had led there.

She had always thought of herself. She never thought that she might be disturbing other people, finding it natural that they should put themselves at her disposal, even for a passing fancy.

Was that not the reason why she had lost her friends? Afterwards she would hate herself for it, would beg forgiveness. She was sincere. She would see herself with a cruel objectivity, but a week later she would begin again.

If she did not ring her father after all, it was not from respect for his sleep, nor to avoid upsetting him, but because at the last moment she found nothing to say.

A moment ago, while she was walking by the Seine, she had been full of ideas which seemed good to her. At that moment she needed to exteriorize herself, and she would have confided in the first person who came along. She needed a contact.

She wanted to be listened to, understood, encouraged.

Now, in her ugly, badly-lit room, she was empty. She had never felt so alone. Stretched out on her bed, fully dressed, she stared at the ceiling.

Why should she not telephone Bob, who was almost certainly in the Rue Gay-Lussac? He knew what was going on. He would be relieved to have news of her. She would hear his voice. She felt she needed to hear a familiar voice.

Then she pushed that idea away as quickly as it had come.

What would have fixed everything up would have been for her to have fallen ill, not here in her hotel room, from where she would obviously be taken to hospital, but in Lausanne. They would call Doctor Vinet. He knew her well. It was in his office that she would unburden herself when she didn't feel all right within herself.

She did not know what illness she would have liked to have. Something which would scare everyone else but which was not likely to be fatal. Something also which would not make her ugly or leave her crippled.

That was an idea which came from way back. She couldn't have been more than ten years old when she had thought from time to time of what she called 'a good illness'.

She had had one, when she was five. Her parents, Mathilde and Bob took it in turns to be at her bedside. She had a fever, which distorted her vision and thoughts. The room around her seemed misty and people's faces were blurred.

Doctor Vinet came to see her twice a day.

'It is too late to isolate her. You have all been in contact with her.'

The doctor was very fond of her. Even now, he was the only one to look at her indulgently, and even with a sort of complicity. When she needed someone to pay attention to her she would telephone him.

'This is Odile.'

'How are you?'

He had known her since she was a baby and he still called her 'tu'.

'Not very well. I would like to see you.'

He was very busy. He hardly ever managed to have a full night's sleep. And yet he always managed to give her an appointment.

As soon as she was in his surgery she felt better.

'I don't feel well, doctor. I'm sure there's something very wrong.'

Didn't she end up by believing it?

205

'What are your symptoms?'

'You don't believe me, do you?'

For the doctor's eyes were sparkling with malice, but an affectionate malice.

'I'll tell you that when I've examined you. What's wrong with you?'

'First of all, I feel so tired I can hardly climb the stairs. I tremble all over. Look at my hands. And finally, I have a perpetual headache. It couldn't be a tumour?'

'No.'

He examined her carefully.

'Well, my girl, I may perhaps be disappointing you, but there's nothing at all wrong with you. You think too much about yourself. You spend your time wondering what could be wrong.

'Do you know what's wrong with you? You're using illness to try to escape from reality.'

She knew that he was right, but she did not like him to say so.

'You sound like Bob.'

'How many cigarettes a day do you smoke?'

'Two packets.'

'You realize that that's enough to make you tremble?'

'I can't do without them. Nor can you, anyway. I've often heard you tell my father you wouldn't smoke any more, and several days later I would see you with a cigarette in your mouth.'

'I'm not eighteen any more, my child.'

To be ill for ever. To have everyone standing anxiously around her, just as when she had had scarlet fever.

She stretched out her arm to the bedside table and took a sleeping tablet. Out of habit, for she would have slept without that. She had taken the whole bottle from her parents' medicine cabinet, for she had thought at the time that she might kill herself that way.

She wasn't so sure of that now. She had read an article on suicide in a paper or a magazine. It talked of barbiturates and other medicines. Apparentiy too strong a dose, contrary to popular opinion, rarely produced death because it brought on vomiting.

She did not know the dose. She did not want to be found in a bed full of vomit.

It was for a similar reason that she did not like the idea of using her father's revolver. To make sure of success, she would have to shoot herself in the head, at the risk of taking away half her face.

She did not want to die here, in this room which she detested. Why did she not go on thinking about the delightful evening she had had? For once luck had been with her.

The young man whom she had not known a little while earlier had been very attentive and very tender. She remembered the moment when he had put his arm under hers quite naturally.

And that climb in silence up the darkened staircase. And the ghostly figure of the old woman who appeared before them as she was leaving.

It was all good. It was life. Unhappily, that didn't happen even once a year, and there were all the other days, all the other nights to spend.

She slept at last. She did not get up to undress herself. She jumped when someone knocked at the door. She looked at her watch and saw that it was past noon.

She was just going to open the door when the chambermaid slipped a pass-key in the lock.

'Ah! I see you're up. I'm sorry I knocked, but I thought you had gone out.'

It was not true. It disturbed her work if a guest stayed in bed until the middle of the afternoon.

'I'll be out in half an hour.'

She wanted to leave immediately. She was suffocating in that room. She took a shower, flung her things any old how into the blue suitcase and into the toilet case.

'Are you leaving?'

'Yes.'

And she carefully did not leave a tip. On the ground floor, she went to the desk.

'May I have my bill, please?'

'Are you leaving?'

'Yes.'

'Are you going back to Lausanne already?'

'Yes.'

She paid. If she were to take a taxi in front of the hotel, they would know she was not going by train. That was why she walked across the road, went into the station and came out again by another door.

The taxi-driver turned questioningly towards her.

'Where shall I put you down?'

She did not know. It was important, because it would be the place where she would spend the last hours of her life.

'Put me down in the Place Saint-Michel.'

She felt a little lost there, carrying her suitcase and her toilet case. But she was on the Left Bank, where she felt more or less at home.

She went down a street on the left, a street she did not know, the Rue de la Harpe, and she walked along the pavement for some time, looking at the signs.

Finally she found herself in front of a hotel which had just been repainted. There was a big green plant on either side of the door.

The interior, in a light-coloured wood, smelled strongly of polish. The woman behind the desk was young and pretty, and there was a baby crawling about on the linoleum floor.

'Have you a room free?'

'For how long?'

'I don't know.'

'We don't usually like to rent a room for one night alone. Almost all our people are weekly or monthly. There are some who have lived here for several years.'

'I shall certainly stay for several days.'

'Can you show me some identification?'

She liked the place.

The woman took a key from the board and picked up the child and put it under her arm.

'Excuse me, but at this time of day I haven't any one to look after him.'

They stopped on the second floor. There was no lift. The carpet was new. The room too, which was very bright, had been repainted.

'We don't do main meals, but we serve breakfast.'

'Thank you. That will do very well.'

She opened her case and unpacked the contents into the cupboard and drawers. She put the bottles from her toilet case on the shelf in the bathroom.

She looked around her, discomfited. She very nearly asked herself what she was doing there.

It was a nice place. It was clean. It was sparkling.

She was hungry and she went downstairs and found a little restaurant with gingham tablecloths a little farther down the street.

Her last meal? Probably. And yet she was not moved. It was in the arms of the young student that she had cried. Now her eyes were dry. She watched the bustle in the street through the window. It would be the same the next day and all the other days. The life of Paris would go on in the same rhythm. And so would that of Lausanne. And her father would take his constitutional every morning in Mon Repos Park and then go up to work in his attic. Her mother would play bridge with her friends. They would mourn her at first. Then they would not think any more.

She was no use to anybody. And nobody was really concerned with her.

'Yes, the calf's head, please. And then the lamb chops.'

Here too the décor was pleasant. A little artificial, an imitation of an old inn, but still very pleasant. Why shouldn't she have a gin?

That had no more importance. She could do anything she wanted. In an hour or two, in any case before nightfall, it would all be over.

'Waiter! A gin and tonic, please.'

She drank two. She was no longer afraid. She felt calmer and more lucid than usual.

What she had always lacked, and what she still lacked, was someone to pay attention to her. Someone who knew all her faults, who would protect her from herself, who would tell her what to do or what not to do.

Someone like a Doctor Vinet for her own personal use exclusively.

No such person existed, obviously.

Her mother had played this rôle until she was about three. Then it was Mathilde who had taken care of her.

Bob was very fond of her. She was fond of him too, but he had his own life and they saw each other relatively little apart from at mealtimes.

Would Martin, her young man of the previous evening . . . ? In his arms she had felt at ease. Contact had been established. But would it be like that if it happened every day?

In fact she was looking for something which did not exist, someone rather, who would sacrifice his personality and his private life for her. It would need to be someone very sweet, very reassuring, someone too with whom she would not get bored.

She smiled ironically. Without moving her lips, she was carrying on an interior conversation with herself:

'That's you all over again, my girl! Just when you are going to give up life, you start dreaming of what has never existed.'

It was a sunny day. There were two tables out on the terrace, but no one was sitting at them.

'Like this? A little more?'

The waiter who served her had an Italian accent, and he was quite handsome.

'Just a little more, thank you.'

She ate heartily, while at home they accused her of merely picking at her food.

Where would Bob be just then? Probably having lunch, too, in a little restaurant. He was a well-balanced person. He would be a good husband, capable of understanding his wife and children.

What did he think of her? He had always had, in spite of himself, a slightly protective manner, a little as if he considered her to be an invalid.

Was she mentally ill? She had often thought about that. It was one of the reasons why she asked to see Doctor Vinet so often.

And Vinet too had astonishing patience with her. Was it because he knew that it was not her fault that she was as she was?

The lunch was good. She had ordered red wine. She looked vaguely at two men opposite her who were discussing real estate. Wasn't it odd that so many people worried about so many things which had no importance at all?

'For dessert, mademoiselle?'

'What do you have?'

'Plum tart. I can recommend it.'

210

She ate the tart, then lit a cigarette, refusing the coffee, which would increase her tremblings.

And that was that. She was in the street. She had nothing more to do. People were coming and going, taxis, lorries. Everyone was rushing to a destination they considered important. What importance had she not given in the past to her weekly marks? She did not even know any more what had become of her old exercise books.

It was after two o'clock and the shops were open again. She went into a chemists'.

'A packet of razor blades, please.'

'Any particular brand?'

'No.'

She wanted to laugh. Did the chemist imagine that she was going to shave the hair under her arms, and perhaps her pubic hair?

She must not go too far in the direction she was going, or she would come to the Rue Gay-Lussac.

She walked slowly. She was annoyed with herself for not showing more determination. It was not because she was afraid. She was not hanging on to life.

On the contrary, the idea of leaving it soon gave her a sort of lightness of spirit which she had never known. She had no more need to carry the burden of her small body around with her, or to worry about her future. One could do nothing more for her or against her.

She looked in the shop windows, surprised at what was displayed there, as if she had never looked in shop windows before. A chemist in a long grey smock was piling plastic buckets on the pavement near the open door. Two women were waiting, motionless and silent, in a hairdresser's shop.

It was a long time since she had had her hair set, or even washed. She was almost tempted. She would have liked at least once in her life to be beautiful.

She went in and spoke to the girl at the counter.

'How soon will the hairdresser be free?'

She could hear him working on the other side of the flowered curtain.

'I'm afraid he isn't free today. These ladies are waiting and

211

at four o'clock he has an appointment and another at five.'

'Thank you.'

Too bad! She wasn't going to go all round the district to find a hairdresser who was free.

Her legs were tired. She had walked a lot the previous evening.

She turned round and went back to her hotel, which was called prosaically Hôtel Moderne. She smiled at the young woman at the desk. The baby was no longer there. He would probably be sleeping in another room.

'Would you like your key?'

'Yes, please.'

'Have you had a good lunch?'

'Very good.'

'At Mario's, I suppose.'

'I didn't see the sign. It's about a hundred metres from here.'

'That's Mario's. It's very clean and the cooking is very good.'

People spoke just for the sake of speaking. When you got down to it, they were perhaps afraid of silence. Was it not that which made her so ill at ease in the house in the Avenue de Jaman?

Her father was hardly ever heard. Even when one knew he was upstairs one did not notice his presence. Her mother spent part of the day in her room and the rest with her friends, either in the drawing-room or at the house of one of them, or at the Nouveau Club.

There was only Bob, who could be heard coming up the stairs four by four when he came back from his classes.

She went upstairs slowly, stopping on the first landing to look around.

It was the end. She could not go back. One could see a certain melancholy on her face.

If only she had been stronger . . . ? Strong enough to try once more? But she had tried so many times.

She turned the key in the lock. A ray of sunlight shone across the room.

Would it not be easier if she waited until night? She was thinking too much for that. She did not want to think any more. She was tired of it.

She shut the window which the cleaning woman had left open and the breeze from outside stopped puffing out the curtains.

She brushed her teeth automatically. Then, slowly, she undressed and ran the water in the bath.

As she looked at herself in the mirror, she suddenly felt again the need to talk to someone for the last time.

She only knew the first name, Martin, of the young man of the previous evening, and he had not thought to give her his telephone number.

When the bath was full and the taps turned off, she went into the bedroom, where there was a writing pad on the table. There were three sheets of paper in it and three envelopes with the name of the hotel. She had to hunt around in her bag for quite a time to find a ballpoint pen with a chewed end.

She was sitting naked on her chair. At home, in her own room, she often sat like that.

She nibbled the end of the pen for a minute before writing:

Dear Bob,
This time it's final. When you get this letter I shall be dead. I hope someone in the hotel will be good enough to stick a stamp on it and post it. I have taken my clothes off and I haven't the strength of mind to get dressed again and go down.

I can't remember any more what I told you in my last letter, which was written in the emotion of my departure. Now I am not nervous, and I find that it is easy to die. If I have allowed myself four days – I haven't counted them because the time has gone by so quickly – it is because I wanted to give myself a sort of respite. I don't regret it.

I have been thinking a lot in these last few days and I'm not angry with anyone any more. I think I have learned a lot. I don't see people and things in the same way any more.

I had a tendency to blame my perpetual depression on the atmosphere pervading the house. I still think it's not very cheerful, but Daddy and Mummy can't help that. I am sure other houses are much gloomier and the children are happy.

Besides, the proof is that you've become the strong man you are.

Do you know, I've often envied you? And even hated you for your strength of character! Your look always made me a little afraid, because I expected to read irony or pity in it.

I know now that was wrong. It's like my attitude towards Daddy, whom I no longer find ridiculous. He does lead a monotonous life, but no more so than men who go to the office and return at fixed times.

Even Mummy, who has found an inoffensive passion in life . . .

In all this rather sordid story there's only one person to blame. Me. I've sometimes thought that before, but straight away I would see myself in a favourable light.

By the way, while I remember, give my guitar, since you don't play, to someone who can't afford one. Give away my skis and skates too. I'll count on you to do that.

I don't want anyone to keep anything in the house which belongs to me. I don't like souvenirs. It's a good thing I haven't had too many photographs taken. Goodness! There's another case of my misinterpreting things. At Emilienne's house there were lots of photographs of her, in every conceivable pose. Her father took them.

I told myself that Emilienne was beautiful and that was why they took so many pictures of her. I know I'm not beautiful, and there was no one, not even you, to take my photograph.

I have spent four days reflecting on myself, to the point where my head started to spin. I'm not a dreamer, you know. I'm not a romantic either. I have rather a tendency to look at things and people coldly.

I think I've discovered the chink in my armour. It's my difficulty in establishing contact with people. Did I tell you that in my letter from Lausanne? Perhaps I did. In that case, I'm sorry.

At school there were groups of people, as there were in your time. I would be asked to join one of them. I was always made very welcome. For two or three weeks, perhaps longer, everything would be fine. They liked me and found me full of good ideas.

Then, for no apparent reason, I felt myself different from my friends. Then they would look at me curiously. There was always at least one who would say:

'Have we done something to annoy you?'

'No, why?'

'Because you're not the same any more. You hardly look at us. You go home straight after school and you always find an excuse not to go to anyone's house.'

It is true. It is even true for the places where I find myself. I'll stop on the edge of the pavement and ask myself:

'What am I doing here?'

It is at those moments that I feel dizzy. I have the feeling that I'm whirling, on the point of falling. I very nearly stop a passer-by:

'Monsieur, could you take me back to my house? I don't feel well.'

You know all that, and you have often said I was imagining things. Doctor Vinet did too, though he prescribed sedatives.

If I am suffering from some illness, why does no one tell me? Perhaps that would take away the agony with which I live.

Guess what! Here in Paris I have walked ten times more than I do in Lausanne and I haven't felt tired. At this moment I don't have a headache. I have no aches anywhere, and I could go on writing to you for hours.

It seems I've still so many things to say. Soon I shall not be speaking any longer. Communication with people like myself will be cut for ever. People like me? I hope for their sake that they are not like me. I am obviously not the only one of my kind, but we haven't met each other.

Well, I must make up my mind to leave you. I believe it's of you I shall be thinking at the last minute. Think of me too from time to time, will you?

I would like to be near you and have you hug me close to your chest, stroking my head absentmindedly as you sometimes do.

You can see I have good memories of you.

I'm not going to read this over. Excuse the repetitions and the mistakes, if there are any. Excuse the cigarette burn too.

If he mentions me, tell Doctor Vinet that I got up to three packets a day and that little by little I got a taste for gin.

Ciao! A big hug. Goodbye, Bob, dear brother.

Your Odile.

She stopped for a moment and gazed into space, then she added, below her signature:

P.S. As with my first letter, I must ask you not to show this to Daddy or Mummy. I would like this to remain between us two and no one else to know anything about it. Thank you.

She wrote her brother's name on an envelope, with Hôtel Mercator, Rue Gay-Lussac as the address. Then she added 'Express'.

She searched in her bag and brought out some change which she laid on top of the letter to pay for the postage. Then she thought about the rent.

Dear Madame,

Forgive me for the disturbance I have caused you. The two hundred francs should serve to pay my rent and for the unpleasantness caused you.

You have been very kind and I am grateful to you.

She placed this note under the two banknotes and got up. She had finished. She walked over to the window through which she saw the street a little mistily because of the net curtains.

The street would be the same, with the same sounds, the same ordinary people on the pavement, tomorrow, the day after and for years and years to come.

She lit a cigarette and with a firm step went into the bathroom and put her leg over the edge of the bath.

She had to get out again because she had left the razor blades on the shelf. She took one and sat in the water with her legs stretched out.

The cigarette smoke made her blink. She was not afraid. She was calm. She had promised herself she would take two or three sleeping tablets just in case, but she had no need of them.

She looked for the vein in her wrist and made a long cut with the blade.

There was someone in the room, someone who was doing something to her arm and who smelled strongly of tobacco. She was surprised to be still alive and at last she opened her eyes.

A tall, red-haired young man, his face and arms covered in freckles, was putting a tourniquet on her arm. The bath-water, in which she was still sitting, was slightly pink, and that made her heart miss a beat.

'What are you doing here?'

'You can see. A tourniquet. Don't be afraid. It's a clean handkerchief which I got from my room. Yours were too small.'

His skin had the same texture as an orange, and his eyes were a very pale blue.

'Why are you here?'

'Because you called out.'

'I did?'

He had finished and he had also applied a temporary dressing.

'If you'd like to get out of the water . . . Have you a dressing-gown?'

'There's one in my suitcase.'

He saw a bathrobe which was hanging behind the door and held it out to her.

'Here! Put this on.'

She could not read any thought from his expression.

216

'What do you mean, I called out?'

'You gave a sharp cry, and because there is just a partition between your room and mine, I realized it was a cry of anguish. I was afraid I would find the door locked but it wasn't.

'You had fainted. I ran into my room to get a clean handkerchief and a toothbrush which would do instead of a stick for the tourniquet.'

'I wanted to die.'

'I had in fact realized that you didn't slash yourself like that for fun.'

'Is it deep?'

'Not very. When you saw the blood, your instinct was to stop and you cried out. Just once. A very loud cry.'

'I don't remember a thing about it.'

He helped her out of the bath and handed her the white bathrobe.

'I'm not quite a doctor, but I'm in the fourth year of my medical studies and an assistant at the Cochin Hospital. It's lucky that this afternoon I had some theoretical work to finish . . . How do you feel?'

'I'm flabbergasted.'

'I'll go and get a glass of spirits to set you up again.'

He came back with a bottle of cognac and rinsed out the toothglass.

'What about you?' she objected.

'I haven't cut my wrist.'

'Are you going to make me another dressing?'

'I'm going to take you to the hospital where they'll take care of you much better than I could do here.'

'Don't take me to the hospital, please. They'll realize it's an attempted suicide and they'll tell the police.'

'Are you afraid of the police?'

'They'll tell my parents. And I don't want to go home at any price.'

'Sit down. You can't be too steady on your feet.'

'It's funny. I don't remember feeling any pain.'

'You didn't feel any pain. It was anguish which made you cry out at the same time as you let go of the blade.'

He seemed to hesitate.

'Do you live in Paris?'

'No. I'm from Lausanne.'

'Do you have any relatives here?'

'Only an aunt of my mother's, whom I haven't seen for at least ten years. I don't want to go home. If you want to speak to someone who knows me, I can ring my brother, who is almost certainly staying in a hotel in the Rue Gay-Lussac.'

'Is that letter addressed to him?'

'Yes.'

'Did he come to Paris to look for you?'

'Yes. I had written to him and told him that I was leaving home for ever and that no one would hear of me any more.'

She had a slightly bitter smile.

'It's funny!'

She looked at the place where she had sat down to write her letter, then she looked at the time. Less than twenty minutes had passed since she had sealed the envelope.

'When can I see your brother?'

'As soon as he gets back to the hotel. You can call now. You'll see if he is staying there.'

'I have more urgent things to do. You must promise to stay here like a good girl and wait for me. I'm going to the chemist's to get what I need.'

'You're not going to take me to the hospital?'

He looked embarrassed.

'You're lucky that I'm not a doctor yet, because if I was, I'd have to inform the police about you. It's splitting hairs a bit. I hope you can keep your mouth shut.'

'I promise you that.'

She lit a cigarette with one hand, while he went downstairs without putting his jacket on. He was tall, broad, and had rather thick features.

She did not remember crying out, but it came back to her now that she had had a sensation of falling and that she had tried to hang on to something, probably the edge of the bath.

Did the red-haired student believe her? Wouldn't he suspect her of having pretended to commit suicide knowing that she would call out at the last moment?

She hadn't known that he was there and that he was an assistant in a hospital. He had never seen her in the hotel, where she had only arrived that morning.

He came in, his arms full of little packets. Then he went into his room to get a spirit lamp.

'Does that hurt?'

'A little. Hardly at all.'

'I'm going to be the one who has to hurt you.'

He disinfected his instruments by putting them in the flame of the lamp and he made five stitches.

Each time, she gave a start, clenching her teeth because she did not want to cry in front of him.

'Now I want to take the tourniquet off.'

'Is that all?'

'For the moment, yes. Tomorrow I'll have to take the dressing off to see how the wound is.'

His glance fell on the bottle of cognac.

'How would you like another?'

'I think it's doing me good.'

He gave her some and sat on a chair turned backwards, one leg on each side and his arms leaning on the chairback.

'Are you pregnant?'

She started, more surprised than annoyed.

'Why do you ask that?'

'Because it's often because they're pregnant by a man they can't marry that girls try to commit suicide.'

'That's not my problem. You said try. Are there many who come back?'

'A good half.'

'If you hadn't been in ...'

'I know. Ring your brother now.'

She asked for the Hôtel Mercator and recognized Monsieur Bedon's voice.

'Hôtel Mercator here.'

'Is Bob Pointet staying with you?'

'He's staying here, but he went out about an hour ago.'

'You don't know at what time I'd be likely to find him in?'

'A little before dinner, because he likes to take a shower at the end of the day.'

'Thank you.'

'Can I give him a message?'

'Tell him that someone rang and will call back. He'll understand.'

She put down the receiver.

'It's just as I thought. He'll only come back just before dinner to take a shower.'

She took another cigarette and he held out a match for her.

'May I?' he asked, taking a pipe from his pocket.

'Please do.'

'How do you feel, being alive?'

'I'm more tempted to wonder how I would have felt being dead.'

'A love affair gone wrong?'

'No. I'm not in love.'

He looked as if he was thinking, then sighed.

'Have you ever done that before?'

'No.'

'You've never been tempted to?'

'Often. Every time I have a period of depression, and I often have . . . '

'Who's your doctor?'

'The family doctor, Doctor Vinet.'

'Have you talked to him about this desire to commit suicide?'

'I tell him everything.'

'What treatment has he given you?'

'He tells me to give up smoking, to take a tranquillizer three times a day, and two sleeping pills in the evening, because I can't sleep otherwise. It was the same when I was a child.'

She felt at ease with this big, pleasant man in shirt-sleeves on which there were a few little drops of blood.

He did not smile. He was not trying to appear amiable or the reverse. He was looking at her carefully, as if he was looking for an answer to a question he was asking himself.

'Have you had a blood test recently?'

'Less than two months ago. We usually go, in our family, for a complete check-up and laboratory analysis every year.'

'Are you still at school?'

'I should be at the *gymnase*. We don't have quite the same school system as in France.'

'I know. Why did you say "I should be"?'

'Because I'm not. I left school without finishing. I have no diploma or certificate.'

Someone was taking an interest in her, and it was a young man who seemed to understand the human heart. She had only just escaped death and she found herself quite whole again. She hoped he would ask her a lot of questions.

'Weren't you working just now?'

'Yes, I was working, but that can wait. May I ask your father's profession?'

'He's a writer. A historian, rather. He usually writes historical biographies.'

'Albert Pointet?'

'You know him?'

'I've read three or four of his books. According to the papers he writes one regularly every year.'

'That's true.'

The telephone rang. Odile hurried over to it, then she panicked, then caught hold of herself and had to make an effort to pick up the receiver.

'Hello,' she said.

'So it's you!'

Bob was on the end of the line.

Chapter Six

'Where are you?'

'Not far from the Hôtel Mercator.'

'Are you all right?'

'Quite all right. I mucked it up, of course. Being me, I couldn't have done anything else.'

She smiled at the student, who looked embarrassed.

'Can I come to see you, or are you going to come and stay here?'

'I'd rather stay here, for the moment at any rate.'

'Then I'll come. Where is it?'

'The Hôtel Moderne, in the Rue de la Harpe.'

'I'll be there in ten minutes.'

The red-haired young man was still examining her with a curiosity which he did not try to hide. He was surprised by her, that was certain. He was trying to understand her. He could feel that there were undercurrents which were escaping him.

'I intrigue you, don't I?'

He didn't say yes or no. He watched her steadily, his face expressionless.

'I shouldn't think,' he said, as if to himself, 'that, knowing what I know about your father, you had an unhappy childhood, did you?'

'No. But I don't have any happy memories either. They often used to find me, silent and motionless, huddled in a corner of a corridor or in the garage at the end of the garden.'

'Why?'

'I don't know. Perhaps because I felt ill at ease with my mother, for example, or with anybody ... I realized later that it was a little as if I didn't feel I belonged to the same race as the others.'

'Didn't you ever play?'

'Very rarely. And when I did it was without much conviction.'

'Can you remember now what you used to think about?'

'No. I don't think I thought at all. I would stare straight in front of me. I must have stayed for hours staring at a spot on the wallpaper.'

'Didn't your parents get worried?'

'They thought it would pass. I would often hide myself in the house until I was found.'

'Was it a way of getting them to pay attention to you?'

'It might have been.'

'Didn't you have any childhood illnesses?'

'Scarlet fever. It's my happiest memory. I was in bed, with magazines. The maid would come up twenty times a day to make sure I didn't need anything. My mother's friends had stopped coming to play bridge because they were afraid they would catch it. My room had become the centre of the household. My mother came to see me, too. My father would come down and sit by my bed.'

'Did you lack affection in the normal run of things?'

'I can only say yes. It was I who didn't understand. I had the impression that each person was only interested in his own private life and that I was more of a burden than anything else. May I get up? I want to go into the bathroom to dress.'

The bathtub was full of pinkish water, and she pulled the plug. In her suitcase she found a pair of grey trousers and a paler grey sweater. Then she ran a comb through her hair. She heard voices in the next room and rushed through, knowing it was her brother.

'Oh, Bob!' she cried, burying her head against his chest, just as she had dreamed of doing.

'Dear little pussy.'

He sometimes used to call her that, when he was being sentimental.

'Let me look at you. No, you don't look ill.'

She felt happy, detached. She had two men in her room, when the odds were that she would have remained alone in the bath until the next morning.

'Let me introduce you.'

She turned towards the student.

'I'm sorry, but I didn't even think to ask your name.'

'Albert Galabar.'

'My brother Bob.'

'Pleased to meet you.'

'And to meet you.'

Their manner was awkward. They seemed to be measuring each other up.

'If I've got it right, you came to Paris to look for your sister?'

'And I only just missed her. First of all, in a *boîte*, they told me they'd seen her the evening before. Then this very afternoon, in an hotel she had just left, opposite the Gare de Lyon.'

'You found the Hôtel Héliard?'

'I couldn't visit all the hotels on the Left Bank. I guessed you would be scared you might run into me. When you got to the station you rushed into the first hotel you came to, thinking no one would look for you there.'

She shivered as she thought of her room.

'It was such a miserable place.'

'Weren't you afraid to stay so close to the Rue Gay-Lussac?'

'I wasn't running any risk, because I'd decided to end it all today.'

'What happened?'

He was holding her by the shoulders and he was so relieved to have found her that he looked more like a lover than a brother.

'I cut my wrist and apparently I gave a loud cry. Albert Galabar has the room next door. I didn't know that. I'd never seen him. When I opened my eyes I was still in the bath and he was putting on a tourniquet. He's a medical student, an assistant in a hospital.'

The two men looked at each other again.

'It was by chance that I was in my room.'

'Would the wound have been fatal?'

'Very probably.'

'Is this letter for me?' asked Bob, pointing at the envelope on the table. 'Why is there some change on top of it?'

'To pay for the stamp.'

'And that money?'

'It's for the room.'

They both looked at her in surprise.

'You thought of all that before cutting your wrist?'

'I was calm, not at all nervous. Before that I had gone to a restaurant a little way down the road, where I had a good lunch. After that I almost went and had my hair washed and set, but I would have had to wait too long.'

'May I take the letter?'

'It's yours. Don't show it to anyone, particularly not the family.'

'Shouldn't you ring Father?'

'I think I must.'

She frowned. It was already a contact with the Avenue de Jaman, and it seemed to her she was going to be caught up in its meshes again.

'I shan't tell him I'm going to come back. I'll just speak to him.'

He asked for the number. It was Mathilde who answered.

'It's Bob here, Mathilde. I want to speak to my father. Mother isn't in the drawing-room with her friends, is she?'

'No, she has gone out shopping.'

'So much the better. Father will give her the news.'

'You have good news, haven't you? I can tell that from your voice.'

Some moments later his father was at the other end of the line.

'Is there any news, Bob?'

'Very good news. I've found Odile. Or rather she found me.'

'How is she?'

'Very well, apart from a cut on her wrist. It's not serious and she has been cared for very well.'

'When are you both coming home?'

'I'll probably come back tomorrow, because I've already missed several important classes. I don't know about her . . .'

He signalled to his sister to come and take the telephone.

'I'll put her on.'

'Hello, Daddy.'

'What a way to scare us! When did it happen?'

'This afternoon.'

'And you're up already?'

'Of course. I've never felt so well.'

As she said that she threw a quick, conspiratorial glance at the student.

'Aren't you coming back at the same time as your brother?'

'I'm going to wait until I'm rested and my wound has begun to heal properly.'

She could hear sadness, or at least a resigned melancholy, in her father's voice.

'I understand,' he said. 'Are you staying in the Rue Gay-Lussac?'

'No. If you need to get in touch with me, I'm at the Hôtel Moderne, in the Rue de la Harpe.'

'I hope you'll be home soon. You can't imagine how empty it feels.'

'If I were to get married, it would be the same, wouldn't it?'

'You don't intend to come back for good?'

'No.'

'Do you think you'll stay in Paris?'

'Yes. You know that's always been my dream.'

There was silence. Someone on the line asked:

'Have you finished?'

'No, mademoiselle. Don't cut us off, please.'

'I'll come home next week to see you, then I'll come back to Paris to look for work. I haven't much to offer, I know. I don't have any diploma, but I hope I'll still find something to do. Have you seen Doctor Vinet?'

'I asked him to come round and see me. Why do you ask?'

'Because I was sure you would consult him. Not about you, but about me. You asked him what he thought about my running away, and if I would really commit suicide.'

'That's right, I did.'

'What did he say?'

'He wasn't very optimistic. I'll phone him right away and tell him the good news.'

'Do that. Tell him I send him a kiss. A big kiss for you too, Daddy. I've been thinking about you a lot and I love you more than ever.'

'Thank you, my dear. Don't hang up. I can hear someone coming in. It must be your mother.'

She heard voices away from the telephone and then her mother's voice, saying:

'So, you're alive! Thank God! Tell me what's happened.'

'Daddy will tell you, because I'm a bit tired now.'

Besides which, she didn't know what to say to her mother.

'Are you coming home tomorrow?'

'No. I'll come and see you in a few days. Daddy will explain. And Bob, who is leaving tomorrow, will tell you both all the details.'

The face of the doctor-to-be showed astonishment. She had just escaped from a voluntary death and she was already occupied in organizing the future.

She put down the receiver.

'Whew,' she sighed, dropping into the only armchair in the room. 'That's one thing done.'

She appeared to have shed a load and to be finding her feet again. She lit a cigarette.

'What did you say your name was?'

'Albert Galabar. My family comes from Toulouse.'

'What I can't understand,' murmured Bob, with a shiver as he thought of it, 'is that you waited four days, almost five . . .'

'It was my holiday.'

'What did you do?'

'Don't you know me well enough to guess? I went to *boîtes* every night.'

'All alone?'

'I did that in Lausanne too.'

'Did you drink a lot?'

'Not much. A few glasses of gin. That makes me thirsty for another drop of cognac. May I, Monsieur Galabar?'

'Of course, but call me Albert.'

'Albert then. I have a reputation for being too familiar rather than too formal.'

She was not drunk, but she was getting light-headed. Wasn't an event like that worth celebrating? It seemed to her that she was definitely saved, that she had lost the worst part of herself.

'By the way, ask Daddy to send me some money, will you? I left home with about six hundred francs in my pocket. I changed them in the first hotel I stayed at, but I have almost nothing left.'

'I'll give you a little now.'

He took his wallet out of his pocket, counted the notes and took out three.

'Will that be enough until you come home?'

227

'I think so. Since I'm going to keep the room, I won't have to pay for it straight away.'

'I'll leave you,' said Galabar, getting up from his chair.

And, to Odile:

'I'll come and see you tomorrow. At what time will I disturb you least?'

'Well, you know, I'm a night bird.'

'You'd be better not to tire yourself out too much today. Buy a thermometer at the chemist's just down the street. Take your temperature when you come in, and if you have one don't hesitate to knock on my door.'

'Thank you. And thank you for everything you have done.'

'Better thank Providence which kept me in my room this afternoon.'

He shook her good hand.

'Don't drink too much either.'

The two men shook hands.

'I may not have the chance to see you again before you leave. I'm very glad to have met you.'

'And I to have met you.'

When they were alone she threw her arms round his neck.

'It's so good, Bob.'

'You can't know how afraid I was.'

'Did you think I'd do it?'

'I know you, don't I?'

'I think you're the person who knows me best.'

'Let me look at you again. You have stayed quite the same, except now there's a little light in your eyes.'

'Don't tell anyone, but this time I think I've fallen in love.'

'May I be allowed to ask you with whom?'

'You've guessed already, haven't you?'

'Things move quickly with you. Is he the reason why you're going to stay in Paris?'

'No. But I couldn't stand the atmosphere of the house any more. Here! While I fix my face and hair, you read this letter. That'll save me having to tell you everything again. Although I can't remember any more what I wrote. I went out to buy razor blades. Oh! You can have the ones that are left. I had run the bath and I was already undressed and I started to write. I put down on paper everything that went through my head. I suppose it's stupid . . .'

It was such a short time ago that she had been sitting, quite naked, on that chair, writing with a ballpoint pen with a chewed end.

'You can't know how good it is . . .'

'I have a phone call to make.'

'To whom?'

'You'll see.'

He asked to be put through to the chief superintendent at the Bureau of Missing Persons.

'Do you wish to speak to Chief Superintendent Lobeau?'

'Yes.'

'I'll see if he is free.'

A few minutes later a deep voice asked:

'Who is speaking, please?'

'I don't know if you remember me. I'm Bob Pointet and I came to see you to inform you of my sister's disappearance. I have found her.'

'Is she all right?'

'Yes.'

'Where was she today?'

'In the Latin Quarter.'

'What put you on her track?'

'She telephoned me.'

'I'm happy for your sake, and for hers. I'll close the file, then. Goodbye, Monsieur Pointet.'

'Did you understand that?'

'I got the idea.'

'There are thousands of hotels in Paris, hundreds on the Left Bank alone, where I thought at first you would come. As I couldn't visit them all, I went to the Bureau of Missing Persons.'

'Shall we go out? I think the fresh air will do us good. Then we can both have dinner in the little restaurant where I had lunch. I was sure it was my last meal, and yet that didn't lessen my appetite. On the contrary! Read the letter quickly. I'll be right back.'

She made herself up more carefully than usual, and brushed her hair, looking at herself in the mirror with satisfaction.

Why had she always thought she was ugly? She thought she was pretty today, and she noted her good points with pleasure.

When she went back into the bedroom, her brother was slipping the letter into his pocket. He seemed moved.

'There. You've read it. You have understood. Now we won't talk about it any more.'

'All right, Odile.'

His voice was a little hoarse.

'You're a funny girl, you know. I hope you meet someone who will understand you. It isn't easy.'

'Come on.'

She took her handbag and picked up the money on the table.

The baby was in his place on the floor again, in the office, and he was playing with bricks.

'Good evening, madame. This is my brother Bob.'

'I'm sorry I don't have any more rooms.'

'Oh, he's been staying in the Rue Gay-Lussac for several days. I hope I won't be back too late.'

'Well, you know, I'm used to it. Besides, my husband takes my place in the evenings.'

Out on the sunny pavement, she took her brother's arm.

'It's wonderful, Bob.'

Everything was wonderful. The breeze in the air, the shop windows, the passers-by.

'I'm going to show you my little restaurant. And I'm going to have a gin straight away. I don't really like cognac, but Albert didn't have anything else in his room.'

She had ordered a gin and tonic and her brother a whisky.

'Did you know this place?'

'No. It seems nice.'

'And the food's good, you'll see. It seems funny to me to be talking about food on a day like this, doesn't it?'

'Perhaps it does a little.'

'At lunch I ate twice what I usually eat at home.'

They both smiled and gave each other conspiratorial looks.

'It's good to see you, Bob. Do you know what I like about Albert? It's because he's like you in some ways.'

'Shall we have dinner? I'm the one who's hungry now.'

She saw a word she didn't know on a menu.

'Waiter! "Porchetta." What's that?'

'Sucking pig, stuffed and roasted.'

'Would you like that, Bob?'

'Yes.'

'Two porchettas. Will you have a light chianti with that?'

They were both in a gay mood.

'What time is your train tomorrow?'

'One-fifteen.'

'I'll go with you to the train.'

'I hate saying goodbye on station platforms. I'll come by your hotel to say goodbye to you.'

They stayed for a long time at the table, while at home one only sat down for the precise length of time it took to eat. Once the meal was over there was a kind of stampede to get away.

'Shall we have a coffee with brandy?'

'We'll have something to drink later.'

They went along the Boulevard Saint-Michel where the crowded terraces were brightly lit. Odile stared at the spectacle hungrily, as if she had never seen it before. From time to time, when she made a sudden movement, she felt a stab of pain in her wrist, but it did not really hurt.

They did not have a continuous conversation. It was not really a conversation at all. One of them would say something and the other would echo it. After that they walked in silence for most of the time.

'I've always known you wouldn't stay at home.'

'Even when I was a child?'

'From the time you were ten or twelve. You were very precocious.'

'Is that bad?'

'No. Don't you think it's a little late for you?'

'You are forgetting what a terrible girl I am.'

When they got to the corner of the Rue Gay-Lussac they turned around. They were holding hands and Bob was humming.

'You like me, don't you, Bob?'

'Yes.'

'Why?'

'I'd find it difficult to say.'

'I'm unbearable, aren't I?'

'Not if one knows you.'

He thought of the medical student. He did not want to hurt his sister, or to discourage her. That was why he added:

'Not even if one doesn't know you at all.'

'If I understand you properly, it's the bit in between that's dangerous.'

'You're a sweet girl, Odile. You only have one enemy.'

'Who?'

'Yourself.'

He led her to a terrace where there was a free table.

'We'll have a last drink and then we'll go quietly off to bed.'

'Already?'

'What did your student tell you?'

'Yes . . . I'd be better to rest.'

'Well, between ourselves, when do you expect to come to Lausanne?'

'In about a week, if my wrist gets on all right.'

'Are you going to spend some time with us?'

'I don't think so. Two days, maybe? Just enough time to pack up my things.'

'Shall I still give the guitar away?'

The question embarrassed her a little.

'No. I think I'll take it with me. It's still what I do least badly. And since I only play for myself . . .'

'Mother will be furious.'

'I know. But Daddy will understand. He must have known too, a long time ago, that I would go away one day. Did you know Albert has read several of his books?'

'That doesn't surprise me.'

They stayed there for a quarter of an hour, relaxed, with no need to talk for the sake of talking.

'What surprises me is the number of people sitting alone . . .'

He did not point out to her that that would be her lot too, in a week or two.

'Let's go now.'

He took her back to her hotel.

'Good night, Bob.'

'Good night, Odile.'

She watched him striding away. It made her sad to lose him. It was true that in Lausanne she hardly saw him except at mealtimes.

There was no light showing under the door next to hers. She stopped anyway and listened for a minute, but heard nothing.

She put on her pyjamas, then took her make-up off carefully, and gently rubbed in a little face-cream for the night. Then she took two sleeping tablets. After a moment's thought, she took a third.

She fell asleep almost at once and if she dreamed she did not remember her dreams in the morning.

It was a knocking at the door which woke her up.

'Come in!' she said, thinking it was Bob.

She had not looked at her watch.

'The door is locked.'

It was Albert Galabar's voice.

'Have I disturbed you?'

'Just a minute. I'm putting my dressing-gown on.'

She also ran a comb through her hair.

When she opened the door she saw that he was rather embarrassed.

'I woke you up, didn't I? I forgot to tell you yesterday. It's one of the days when I go on duty at the hospital at eleven o'clock. I don't finish until six. I'd prefer to do your dressing before I go.'

His shyness contrasted with his height and his broad shoulders.

'You haven't been in too much pain? Could you sleep?'

'I fell asleep straight away.'

'At what time?'

'Eleven o'clock. And I've only just woken up.'

She lit a cigarette.

'Sit down. Let's see how that wound is getting on.'

He removed the dressing of the day before very carefully. The flesh on either side of the cut had not swollen, and it was hardly red at all.

'It's coming on very well, isn't it?'

'As far as I'm concerned, I can hardly feel it.'

'I'm going to put on a new dressing and you'll be all right for twenty-four hours.'

'How many stitches did you put in?'

'Five. I thought I'd better play for safety. Your skin is very fine, very delicate.'

She took that as a compliment and she was pleased.

'Are you going to have a busy day?'

'At the moment I'm on casualty, and one hardly has time to breathe.'

'Accidents?'

'Everything.'

They were speaking with their lips and the words were only there to hide their thoughts.

She liked him at least as much as she liked Bob, but in a different way.

'Do you go home often?'

'My two sisters are married. They both live in Toulouse. My father and mother are alone at home. I usually try to spend half of each vacation with them in Royan. We rent a big house and my sisters come with their husbands and children.'

She was staggered. It was a kind of life which was totally alien to her. She could not see herself at the seaside with parents, married sisters and their husbands and children.

'Do you expect to settle in Paris?'

'If I can. I'll see you tomorrow, Odile. It'll be Saturday, won't it? In that case, I can come an hour later.'

She took her bath as well as she could, trying not to wet the dressing. It was a sort of acrobatics. Then she put on the trousers she had worn the night before.

She opened the window wide. What direction were her thoughts taking? The idea of death had left her. And yet she came back to it indirectly. She was waiting for Bob, and he was going to take the train. She imagined the long platforms and suddenly she found a solution to her problem which had escaped her.

God knows why, a few days before, she had wanted her body not to be identifiable. She believed she had thought of everything and each time she found an objection which had made the solution impossible.

The train! She had not thought of the train. If she had bought underwear and a dress in a cheap chain store . . . If she had gone to one of the stations in Paris just when an express was arriving

234

. . . She could even have jumped off a railway bridge just before one went by . . .

She felt dizzy thinking of it. Just to think that she escaped that made her feel sick and dizzy. For if that idea had occurred to her she would probably have done it.

What had been wrong with her? She did not understand the decision she had made any more. She tried in vain to discover how she had arrived at it.

She rang for the boy to bring up her breakfast.

'May I have two fried eggs?'

She was hungry. Usually she just had toast and marmalade.

'And a big glass of orange juice, please.'

She did not know what to do or where to go. Normally she was still asleep at that time and there she was, all ready.

But ready for what? She had nothing to do.

Bob arrived while she was eating by the window.

'I see you're not lacking in appetite.'

'No. Do you know, Albert has been in already to put a new dressing on. He's on duty at eleven o'clock.'

'Did you sleep well? You didn't feel any pain?'

'I slept as I have rarely done and when I woke up I had forgotten I had a cut on my wrist. Would you like something to eat? Aren't you going to have any lunch?'

'I'll have lunch in the train.'

She lit a cigarette and he took one too.

'I want to ask you to do something. It's not to wait a week before you come home. Our parents are going to be very upset, particularly when they know your decision. They mustn't think that you're leaving home because of them.'

'I'll promise you that, Bob.'

'When they see you looking so well, they'll think that for one reason or another you pretended to commit suicide.'

'Did you ever think that?'

'No. But I haven't got a suspicious character. Mother is naturally suspicious.'

'I know. Do you like this room?'

'It's more cheerful than the one I had at Monsieur Bedon's. It must be more expensive, too.'

'I haven't asked the price.'

'That's just like you.'

'I'll try to stay here.'

'Have you any plans?'

'Not real plans. I must take my ignorance into account. I must find a job that's easy and at the same time not too unpleasant. I wouldn't be able, for example, to work in a factory. I couldn't be a shampooist in a hairdresser's, either.

'If I could choose anything I wanted, I'd be a nurse. In Lausanne, I found out about the courses. I don't have enough basic education to be good at it.'

'Poor Odile! Here am I asking you such a question today and not letting you draw breath!'

'You were right to. Don't think I'm not thinking about it, even when I don't talk about it. There are two things I could do. I could be a receptionist in an office – that doesn't need special skills – or a telephonist. But telephonists are almost always shut up all day in a little room, and the time must drag for them.'

'Do you know, you've had a good idea.'

She shrugged her shoulders.

'I've always had plenty of ideas, dear Bob, but at the last moment they would fade into nothing. I can see myself very well in a doctor's outer office, or a dentist's, or a lawyer's. I'd prefer a doctor's, or a dentist's.'

'I hope that's what you'll tell us when you get back home.'

'I'm going to start going through the advertisements in the papers. If there's nothing there, I'll put one in.'

'It's time for me to go now.'

'Haven't you any luggage?'

'I have a suitcase I left downstairs.'

'I suppose you'll get a taxi in the Boulevard Saint-Michel.'

'Yes.'

'I'll go with you. Don't worry, I won't go any farther.'

She put her jacket on and picked up her handbag.

She remembered to lock the door as she went out, and gave the key to the proprietress. The baby was not on the floor.

'Is he having a nap already?' she asked.

'He has his bottle at noon and goes to sleep straight after.'

Bob almost forgot his suitcase.

'Hah! And I'm the one who has accused you hundreds of times of being scatterbrained!'

They only had two hundred metres to walk. There was a whole row of taxis. Most people were having lunch. One could see some of them, too, in the bars, having a drink just before lunch.

'Good-bye, Bob. And thank you again. You don't know how happy you've made me by coming . . .'

'Ssh, little sister. Be good. Get your emotions in order again and come and see us in good form.'

He gave her a kiss, put his hand on her shoulders and looked her straight in the eyes.

'Don't be afraid: you'll never be all alone.'

He got into the taxi and she could not ask him what he meant. Was he talking about himself? It was unlikely and out of character. Did he mean the medical student? Was he trying to make her understand that there would always be a man in her life?

She walked as far as the Boulevard Saint-Germain and turned to the right. There were a lot of free tables on the terrace at Deux Magots and she sat down and ordered a gin and tonic.

She must get out of the habit of drinking. Before, she only drank fruit juice. It was in the *boîtes* in Lausanne that she had taken up the habit of drinking spirits.

She had chosen the one she found had least taste: gin.

But it was the same with drinking as with smoking. It became a habit. She used to have a bottle in her room, she who had been annoyed with her mother for drinking two or three whiskies while playing bridge.

Now she was on vacation, between two periods of her life. She had to keep her mind free and let herself live. She would need no effort for that. The late autumn was magnificent and the sun was dancing about in the leaves of the trees. Most women were still wearing their summer clothes.

She half shut her eyes. Blurred figures passed by in front of the terrace and she told herself it was good to be alive.

Chapter Seven

Albert came to see her every day, to take off the old dressing and put on a new one. The wound remained clean, without the slightest inflammation.

Contrary to Odile's expectations, he became more distant as time went on. Preoccupied, he hardly spoke to her, or if he did, it was to ask banal questions.

'If I understand you rightly, you've always lived in the same house. Is that so?'

'So has my father. And my grandfather, who had a beautiful white beard and who died when I was nine.'

She bought several newspapers and read the advertisements carefully. They asked for typists, shorthand-typists with a perfect knowledge of English, specialists of all kinds.

Once someone wanted a telephonist, but she had to speak German as well as English and French.

She did not grow discouraged.

'Do you still take the tranquillisers your doctor in Lausanne prescribed?'

'Yes.'

'You don't need them any more. You could do without them very well. The best thing would be to talk to him about it when you go home.'

Once he asked her a more personal question.

'Why did you leave school?'

'Because I was bored. It seemed to me that what they were teaching me was useless. I had begun to go out in the evenings. In the mornings I felt sleepy. All the girls were against me . . .'

Seen in perspective, all that had lost its importance, and she laughed at herself for having made a song and dance about it.

She went to the cinema almost every day, and tried out new restaurants.

'Arriving Saturday's T.E.E.'

She had sent that telegram to Bob and she was surprised to see her father on the station platform. As she moved along with the queue of travellers, she looked at him and found that he was different. It was impossible that he had changed in two weeks. It was she who was seeing him differently.

He had always been plump; now she saw him as fat and flabby. Even the station seemed less big, something of a backwater.

'Have you any bags, Mademoiselle Pointet?'

'I only have this little case.'

Her father watched her approaching and seemed moved. He kissed her on both cheeks, awkwardly, because at home they kissed each other very little.

'Your brother has been very kind. He let me take his place.'

He was pretending to take his meeting very lightly.

'Give me something to carry.'

To make him happy she gave him her toilet case.

'Have you had a good trip?'

'It's so short, you know . . . '

'You haven't got any thinner.'

'No. I'm eating very well.'

'Your mother has been very worried.'

They walked through the underpass, coming up not far from the taxi rank.

'Avenue de Jaman. The first house on the right.'

'I know where it is, Monsieur Pointet.'

Everything had changed, the place and the people. She did not feel at home any more. She felt like a traveller in a strange city.

She had lived here for more than eighteen years. Her father and mother had spent all their lives there.

Her mother ran out as soon as they opened the garden gate.

'My poor little girl,' she said, kissing her.

She was sniffing. She was crying. She was looking at her as though at a ghost.

'Have you been in a lot of pain?'

'I haven't had any pain at all.'

'Come inside quickly. It's colder here than it is in Paris. You're thinner, aren't you?'

'No. I think I have even put on some weight.'

The three of them went into the house.

'Your brother has a class. He'll be back soon.'

She did not know what to say to them. She felt with them the way she did with strangers. The drawing-room seemed more dismal than her room in the Hôtel Héliard, opposite the Gare de Lyon. And yet her grandfather had worked in there for more than forty years and it was there that her mother played bridge with her friends!

She had promised herself she would stay for two days. Now she was wondering how she could manage to cut her stay short.

'Have you any gin?' she asked her father.

He was surprised and nodded.

'Could I have one? The train has upset me a little.'

It was not true, but she needed something before she faced the house.

Mathilde came in her turn to give her a kiss.

'But you look very well!'

She was sniffing too, and wiping her eyes with a corner of her apron.

'I hope you won't be going away again this time. There's no-where better than home.'

They were all three looking at her, and she decided to get to the point straightaway.

'I'm going away again in two days' time.'

'Going where?' her mother asked suspiciously.

'To Paris, of course.'

'And you've made this decision alone, without discussing it with us?'

'I have the right to make a decision on which my whole future depends.'

'And what are you going to do there?'

Her voice was getting aggressive.

'I shall work.'

'What at? You haven't any training.'

'I'm going to be a doctor's receptionist.'

'Have you found a job already?'

She lied:

'Yes. And I've taken a little room at the hotel.'

Her father gave her a drink and had one himself at the same time.

'Your health.'

She knew he would back her up.

'So, you're going to leave us and live alone in Paris.'

'I couldn't live here any more. I've tried. You know what happened.'

'Don't you think that after a few weeks you'll have had enough?'

'If I've had enough I'll come home.'

'Well! If I only believed that! How's your arm?'

'My arm is getting on very well. The wound will soon have closed over and I won't even need a dressing.'

'Aren't you hungry?'

'No. I ate on the train.'

It was almost seven o'clock. The lights were lit. They had to be lit early as the house was dark.

'Won't you eat with us anyway?'

'If you want me to.'

They could hear Bob's scooter. He put it in the garage and came in to the house.

He hugged his sister, crying:

'Not too upset to be back in our old house?'

He winked at her.

'No, not too upset.'

He looked at his parents and, seeing his mother's pinched face, understood what had happened.

'When are you going back?'

'In two days' time.'

'How did you know she wasn't going to stay here?' his mother asked.

'Because I know Odile and I saw her in Paris.'

'Do you know what she wants to do?'

'No.'

'She wants to be a doctor's receptionist.'

'That's not a bad idea.'

'Do you think she's right?'

'She's old enough to decide. After all, it's her life.'

Mathilde came in to tell them that dinner was served. Before leaving the drawing-room, Odile drank a glass of gin at one swallow.

'Did you start to drink in Paris?'

'No. It was here. Everyone in the house drinks except Bob, who rarely does.'

'Everyone isn't eighteen.'

Dinner was torture for her. She had a sensation of stifling. Except for her brother, they looked at her one by one as if she had suddenly become a freak.

Her mother was the most bitter and the most incredulous.

'Who are you going out with in Paris?'

'With no one.'

'Isn't there someone you're going back to be with?'

She almost blushed, thinking of Albert. Bob gave her a stealthy glance.

'I'm not going back to be with anybody.'

'Do you think it will be fun living on your own every day?'

'I've just had some experience of that and I haven't been bored for a minute.'

'While you do get bored here?'

'I didn't say that.'

'But you were thinking it.'

'I like to live on my own.'

She hardly knew what she was eating, and she thought of her good appetite in Paris.

When the meal was over she said goodnight.

'I'm going up to my room. I need to organize my things.'

Bob carried her case up for her, went into her room and sat down on the edge of her bed.

'You really take the bull by the horns, don't you?'

'I had to. Tomorrow it would have been worse.'

'Maybe you're right.'

'I'm sorry for Daddy – I've hurt him. He seemed older to me, less sure of himself.'

'You're forgetting he's already had his two bottles.'

'I know, but I didn't see him like that. It's not the first time I've been away for a few days. This time I feel everything has changed.'

'Even me?'

'Stupid!'

'You know, I'm very likely to lead a life like theirs one day. Not in this house, which has had its day. But a well-regulated life, centred about my work.'

'And about your wife.'

'If I get married. At the moment I don't have any desire to. How's your young doctor?'

'He isn't a doctor yet.'

'All right. Your young student.'

'He's been in every day to put a new dressing on.'

'Are you in love with him?'

'I don't know.'

'What about him?'

'He gets shyer and shyer.'

'Because he's scared to say anything.'

'I thought that for a moment, but I'm not so sure any more.'

'Have you kept your room?'

'Yes.'

'Is it true, this story of you being a receptionist?'

'No. But I hope it will be. I'll put an advertisement in the papers when I get back.'

She opened her wardrobe and threw down in a pile on the floor all the clothes she had not thought she would wear any more.

'When I think I was keeping all these old things!'

'You can't wear jeans when you're a receptionist.'

'I'll wear a dress.'

He watched her in amazement as she moved around. The house had not changed. Nor had their parents. It was she who had changed.

'Are you going to see Doctor Vinet?'

'Why should I? I'm not ill.'

It was the first time she had ever said that. Before, she had always been worried about her health and complained about the most unlikely illnesses.

'He'll be sad if he learns you've been here without seeing him.'

'I'll see tomorrow. I might ring him.'

'It's Sunday.'

'He has been to see me on a Sunday before, or else I've been to his surgery.'

He looked at the pile of clothes and underwear which she was getting rid of.

'You won't have anything left to wear, will you?'

'If it had been possible, I would have thrown out everything, everything which reminds me of the past, and I would only wear new things.'

She laughed.

'You see, I'm still extravagant.'

'I'm going to miss you.'

'I'll miss you too. You're my only friend. I hope you'll come to see me from time to time.'

Albert Pointet kept the same timetable on Sundays as on other days. After his walk he would go up to his attic, carrying his two bottles, and he would sit down at the table he used for a desk.

He heard light footsteps on the stairs at about nine o'clock. He did not think it could be his daughter at that hour and yet it was.

'Am I disturbing you?'

'No. Sit down. Have you had your breakfast?'

'I've just had it.'

'Is your mother up?'

'If she is, she hasn't come down yet.'

'Don't be angry with her. It has given me a shock, too. We're used to there being four of us here, to seeing each other twice a day at table.'

'Where nobody says anything.'

'Because everyone has different interests. Have you ever thought that for parents of children who have grown up, it's possibly out of a sense of modesty. We don't want to bore you with tales of what we are doing, and we don't dare to ask you what you do.'

He looked at her with a melancholy expression.

'How are you going to do for money?'

'I shall be working.'

'I know, but you won't be earning enough to live in the way you are used to. I thought about it in bed last night. We provide for Bob until he finishes his studies, and I give him pocket money as well.'

'That's natural, isn't it? If one didn't do that there wouldn't be any students.'

'Let's suppose that you were in the same state, that you had been continuing your studies, here or in Paris. I would underwrite your needs until you earned enough to live on.'

'I hadn't thought about that.'

'What you're going to do is a sort of training. So I'll do as if you were a student, and I'll give you an allowance until you're twenty-five.'

She stayed still for a moment, staring incredulously at her father.

'Will you really do that?'

'Yes.'

Then she rushed to him and kissed him very hard on his bearded cheeks.

'You're lovely, Daddy.'

'You don't need to tell your mother about it. Not yet. I'll know when it's the right moment to tell her the truth.'

'You do understand, don't you, that I'm not running away from you?'

'I understand. When you were a little girl you often used to come up to see me. You would sit in a corner and watch me writing. Is it tomorrow you're going away?'

'Tomorrow evening, on the T.E.E. again.'

'This time I won't be at the station. I don't want to show everyone my feelings.'

Chapter Eight

She had gone back to her room in the Rue de la Harpe. She had had dinner in the train. It was after eleven in the evening, but she needed to go out and feel herself rubbing shoulders with the crowd. There had been no light under Albert Galabar's door, and she had been disappointed at that. Was she jealous already? Perhaps.

Wasn't it normal that at his age he should have one woman or more in his life?

She found a bar with high stools near Saint-Germain-des-Prés. She asked for a gin.

She looked around her greedily and she wanted to listen to music. There was some not far from there. She felt a little ill at ease on finding a very chic, very dressy clientèle.

Her father had been marvellous. A little before she left, he had come up to her room to give her a banknote for a thousand Swiss francs.

'I'll send you the same amount every month, by banker's order. You'll need extra money at first.'

'I asked Bob to send my scooter. Is that all right?'

'Of course. It's yours.'

'I'm taking my guitar too. It's the only thing I do reasonably well.'

She liked to sit on the edge of her bed and run her fingers over the strings.

'I've taken my record-player too . . . I hope you're not angry with me.'

'No. I understand.'

He had not wept. He had taken her as far as the taxi, with Bob. Her mother had stayed in the drawing-room, where she had pulled aside the curtain.

'I only ask you to be careful.'

'I promise you that. I'd rather no one came to the station.'

Her luggage was bulky, and she had to get a porter.

'Are you going to live in Paris?' the man asked, surprised.

He knew her well. He had often carried her bags.

'Well, I've grown up now, haven't I?'

She went back to the hotel and decided to unpack her bags. She put the guitar in a corner of the room, the record-player on one of the two bedside tables. She put a record on while she hung her clothes in the wardrobe and in the cupboard. There was just enough room. It was the same with the drawers, which would not have held more than the underwear she had with her.

She took her sleeping tablets. She had not seen Doctor Vinet. She had tried to ring him on Sunday morning, but he must have been away for the weekend with his wife.

She could not reach him the next morning either, for he was on duty at the Nestlé Hospital.

She put her empty cases in the corridor. She felt she was at home at last, and it didn't take her long to go to sleep.

She got up a little before nine o'clock and had her breakfast sent up. Then she took a bath and dressed. Her movements were a bit slow and she felt a little like a convalescent. She must work herself slowly into her new life.

The student must have heard her moving around, for he knocked on her door at ten o'clock.

He looked at her with some curiosity.

'I didn't know you were coming back so soon.'

'I couldn't have stayed any longer. I felt a stranger there, and I hated myself for it.'

'Did you see your doctor?'

'No. He wasn't at home on Sunday and he's on duty at the hospital on Monday mornings.'

'You haven't had any pain?'

'None at all.'

They each sat down in their usual place and the young man took the dressing off.

'That's marvellous. It has already begun to heal over. I think I'll just put on a piece of gauze held on with adhesive tape.'

'I have some good news for you.'

'What?'

'I have a job starting next month.'

'You've found a job? In Paris?'

'And with a doctor. Thanks to my dressing, in fact. I went to have dinner in the restaurant-car. I was put at a table for two. Opposite me there was a middle-aged man. He seemed quite pleasant.

'Towards the middle of the meal he asked me if I had been severely hurt.

' "Do forgive me for speaking to you when we haven't been introduced. I am Doctor Le Flem." '

'The cardiologist?'

'I don't know. He didn't tell me what he was a specialist in. He lives in the Place Denfert-Rochereau. I felt at ease with him. I was sure that he wouldn't try anything on with me. I told him I only had a cut on my wrist and it was almost healed.

'He didn't ask me how I had hurt myself, but only if I lived in Paris and I told him I was in the process of moving there.

' "Are you a student?"

' "No. I've never passed my *baccalauréat*."

' "What are you going to do?"

' "I'd like to find a job as a receptionist, preferably with a doctor or a dentist."

'He began to think, then he took a visiting card out of his wallet.

' "Listen. Here is my address. I'm always in my office in the afternoon. Come and see me. I may be able to give you a job. My receptionist, who got married last year, is expecting a baby round about Christmas. I must have a word with her and ask her what she is going to do. Where do you live?"

' "Until now I have lived in Lausanne with my parents. I've just told them that I'm going to live in Paris. Here I'm in a hotel in the Rue de la Harpe."

' "It's not far away."

' "I have a scooter." '

Albert was looking at her closely.

'Will you stay in this hotel rather than take a room nearer to your work?'

'I'm staying here.'

He did not ask why.

'Would you feel better with a lighter bandage?'

'Yes. Thank you, doctor.'

'May I shake your hand to congratulate you?'

He seemed strangely moved.

'I'll leave you now. You must have to sort out your things.'

'I did almost all of that last night.'

'You're going to be working during the day.'

'I'll get used to it. You can see I'm already dressed and have had breakfast.'

She took her guitar from the corner and, alone in her room, began to play some chords. She was suddenly a little afraid. Things were going too well. She knew her own character and since her trip to Lausanne she knew she would never go back to her former life.

She had not heard her neighbour go out. She took something out of her briefcase, her father's revolver, which she had forgotten to mention to him.

The next moment, she was knocking on the door next to hers. He was sitting at his table, which had notebooks spread all over it.

He watched her come towards him, the gun in her hand. There was a moment of surprise in his look.

'Would you look after this for me?'

'Of course. Are you still afraid you might?'

'I don't think so. It's more a symbol, you know.'

He began a sentence which he did not finish.

'Why . . .'

He was going to say:

'Why me?'

Then he looked at her, his arms dangling.

She said, quickly:

'I'll let you get back to work.'

'Yes.'

Later, perhaps.

He watched her as she went towards the door.

Epalinges, 4 October 1970

The Cat

Translated by Bernard Frechtman

Chapter One

He had let go of the newspaper, which first unfolded on his lap and then slid slowly over his knees before dropping to the polished floor. One would have thought he had just fallen asleep, were it not that a narrow slit could be seen between his eyelids from time to time.

Was his wife taken in by this? She was knitting in her low armchair on the other side of the fireplace. She never seemed to be observing him, but he had known for a long time that nothing escaped her, not even the barely perceptible quivering of one of his muscles.

The steel jaws of the crane opposite crashed heavily against the ground near the concrete mixer with a clanking din. The shock shook the house each time, and each time the woman started and put her hand to her chest as though the noise, to which by now she must have been used, reached to her very vitals.

They were observing each other. They had no need to look at each other. They had been observing each other that way for years, slyly, constantly refining their game with new subtleties.

He was smiling. It was five minutes to five according to the black marble clock with bronze ornaments, and one might have thought he was counting the minutes, the seconds. Actually, he was counting them mechanically, he too waiting for the big hand to be vertical. The noises of the mixer and the crane would then suddenly stop. The men in raincoats whose faces and hands were dripping with rain would be motionless for a moment before heading for the wooden shed that had been put up in a corner of the building site.

It was November. Since four in the afternoon they had been working by the illumination of floodlights that would be turned off in a moment, and then, without transition, there would be darkness and silence. The alley would be lit up only by a single gas light.

Emile Bouin's legs were numbed by the heat. When he opened his eyes, he saw the flames, some of them yellow and the others bluish at the bottom, spurting from the logs on the hearth. The fireplace was made of black marble, like the clock and the four-branched candlesticks on either side of it.

Except for Marguerite's hands and the faint clicking of the knitting needles, everything in the house was silent and motionless, as in a photograph or a painting.

Three minutes to five. Two minutes. Workmen were beginning to trudge to the shed to change their clothes, but the crane was still functioning and a last jawful of cement rose up to the framing that marked the first storey of the structure.

One minute to. Five o'clock. The hand quivered hesitantly over the pale face of the clock, and then five spaced gongs rang out as if everything in the house had to be slow.

Marguerite sighed. Her ear was alert to the sudden silence outside that would last until the following morning.

Emile Bouin was thinking. Smiling vaguely, he watched the flames through the slit of his eyelids.

One of the logs, the one on top, was now only a blackened skeleton from which streaks of smoke rose up. The other two were still glowing, but the crackling announced that they were going to collapse before long.

Marguerite wondered whether he would be getting up, to take a couple of fresh logs from the basket to put in their place. Both of them were accustomed to the heat from the hearth and did not move their chairs back until the skin of their faces actually stung.

His smile broadened. He wasn't smiling at her. Nor at the fire. He was smiling at a thought that flashed through his mind.

He was in no hurry to translate it into action. They had time, both of them, all the time that separated them from the moment when one of them would die. How could one tell who would go first? Marguerite surely thought of it too. They had been thinking of it for many years, several times a day. It had become their main problem.

Finally he sighed too, and his right hand left the arm of the leather chair and felt for the pocket of his cardigan. He drew from it a little notebook that played an important role in their domestic life. The narrow pages had dotted lines that made it possible to detach neatly strips of paper an inch and a quarter wide.

The cover of the notebook was red. A thin pencil fitted into a leather loop.

Had Marguerite given a start? Was she wondering what the message would be this time?

She was certainly used to it, but she could never know what words he was actually going to write, and he purposely remained motionless for a long time, with his pencil in his hand, as if he were thinking.

He had nothing in particular to communicate to her. He merely wanted to upset her, to keep her on tenterhooks, at the very moment when she felt relieved by the end of the din in the building site.

Several thoughts occurred to him, and he rejected them one after the other. The rhythm of the knitting needles was no longer quite the same. He had succeeded in disturbing her, at any rate in arousing her curiosity.

He made the pleasure last another five seconds, during which time they could hear the footsteps of one of the workmen moving towards the end of the alley.

He finally wrote, in block letters:

THE CAT.

Then he remained motionless again for a while before putting the notebook back into his pocket after tearing out a strip of paper.

Finally, he folded the strip up very small, the way children do with a piece of paper that they shoot with a rubber band. He did not need a rubber band. He had become amazingly clever at the game, almost Machiavellian.

He placed the paper between his thumb and middle finger. He cocked his thumb and suddenly shot the message into Marguerite's lap.

He almost never missed. He rejoiced inwardly each time.

He knew that Marguerite would not bat an eyelid, that she would pretend to have seen nothing, would continue to knit, moving her lips as if in prayer while she silently counted the stitches.

She sometimes waited for him to leave the room or turn his back in order to put fresh logs on the fire.

At other times, after a few minutes of apparent indifference, she would let her right hand slide over her apron and pick up the message.

Although their acts were always more or less the same, they did occasionally introduce variants. Today, for example, she waited until all the noises from the site had stopped, until silence invaded the alley at the end of which they lived.

She put her knitting down on a stool as if she had finished her work, and, with her eyes half closed, she too seemed about to doze off, lulled by the warmth of the logs.

She then pretended, much later, to notice the folded paper on her apron and picked it up with her delicately wrinkled fingers.

It looked as though she were going to throw it into the fire, as though she were hesitating, but he knew that that was part of the daily play-acting. He was no longer taken in.

Children play the same game every day at the same hour over a more or less long period of time, and they do so without losing their apparent belief in what they are doing. They act 'as if'.

The difference here was that Emile Bouin was seventy-three years old and Marguerite seventy-one. Another difference was the fact that their game had been going on for four years and that they did not seem to tire of it.

In the warmth and silence of the living room, the woman finally unfolded the paper and, without putting on her glasses, read the two words that her husband had written:

THE CAT.

She did not turn a hair. There had been longer, more unexpected, more dramatic notes, some of which were veritable riddles.

This note was the most trivial, the one that recurred most often, while Emile Bouin could think of nothing more clever.

She threw the paper into the fireplace where a thin flame shot up and died immediately. With both hands on her stomach, she sat there motionless; the only life in the living room was that of the hearth.

The clock quivered and struck once. Marguerite stood up as if at a signal. She was small and slender.

Her woollen dress was pale pink, the pink of her cheeks, and the checked apron was light blue. There were still blonde glints in her white head of hair.

Her features had sharpened with the years. For others, for those who did not know her, they expressed gentleness, melancholy, resignation.

'Such a long-suffering woman! . . . '

Emile Bouin did not snigger. Both of them were beyond such obvious manifestations of their states of mind. A shudder, a curl of the lip, a fleeting gleam in the eyes – these were sufficient.

She would look around, as if hesitating about what to do next. He would sense her move, as one foresees one's opponent's move when playing draughts.

He had not been wrong. She was walking over to the cage, a big white and blue standing cage with gold bars.

A multi-coloured parrot was standing motionless on a perch and staring fixedly, and it took a good moment or two to realize that the eyes were made of glass and that the parrot was stuffed.

She nevertheless looked at it tenderly as if it were still alive, and, moving her hand forward, she slid a finger between the bars.

Her lips were moving, as they had been a while before when she was counting her stitches. She was speaking to the bird. One almost expected her to feed it.

He had written:

THE CAT.

She was replying silently:

THE PARROT.

The classic answer. He was accusing his wife of having poisoned the cat, his own cat, which he had loved long before he knew her.

Every time he was seated by the fire, dulled by the waves of heat from the logs, he was tempted to reach out and stroke the furry, black-streaked animal that used to curl up in his lap as soon as he sat down.

'A common alley cat,' she would maintain, in the days when they still spoke to each other, almost always in order to start an argument.

Though the cat was not pure-bred, it was not an alley cat either. Its long, supple body glided along the walls and furniture like the body of a tiger.

Its head was smaller and more triangular than that of the domestic cat and its gaze was intense and mysterious.

Emile Bouin claimed that it was a wild cat that had ventured into Paris. He had found it as a kitten on a building site at the time he was still working for the Paris highways department.

He was a widower and lived alone, and the cat had become his companion. At the time there were still private houses on the other side of the alley where a big block of flats was now going up.

When he had crossed the street to marry Marguerite, the cat had followed him.

THE CAT.

The cat that he had found one morning in the darkest corner of the cellar.

The cat had been poisoned by eating the food that Marguerite had prepared for it.

The animal had never got used to Marguerite. During the four years he had lived in the house opposite, it had never accepted food from anyone but Bouin. Two or three times a day, its master would signal to it by simply clucking his tongue, and it would follow him on the pavement of the alley as if it were a trained dog.

He was the only one who had ever stroked that cat until the day they entered a new house in which there were unfamiliar smells.

'He's a bit shy, but he'll get used to you.'

It had not got used to her. It was mistrustful and never approached either Marguerite or the cage of the parrot, a big brightly coloured macaw that did not speak but which uttered horrible cries when it was angry.

Your cat . . .

Your parrot . . .

Marguerite was gentle, almost bland. One imagined her young and slender, already dressed in pastel tones and strolling poetically on the bank of a river with a parasol in her hand and a big straw hat on her head.

Besides, there was a photograph in the dining room that showed her like that.

She was as thin as ever, except that her legs had swollen a little. She faced life with the same too-sweet smile that she had formerly put on for the photographer.

The cat and the parrot, which were equally mistrustful, observed each other from a distance, and with a certain respect. When the cat began purring on its master's knees, the parrot would stop moving and observe it with its big round eyes as if it were perplexed by that regular and monotonous sound.

Had the cat discovered the power it had over the macaw? Did it watch the bird with quiet satisfaction through its half-closed eyes?

It was not in a cage. It shared the pleasant warmth with its master, who protected it.

A moment would come when the parrot, tired of studying a problem to which there was no solution, would become irritated and angry. Its feathers would quiver, its neck would grow tense, as if there were no bars around it, as if it were going to swoop down on its enemy, and the house would respond with its piercing cries.

Marguerite would then say, 'You'd better leave us for a moment . . .'

'Us' meant herself and her bird. The cat would quiver too, knowing that it was going to be picked up and carried into the cold dining room, where Bouin would sit down in another armchair.

Marguerite would open the cage and speak in tender tones, as if to a lover or a son. There was no need for her to extend her hand. She would go and sit down again in her chair. The macaw would look at the closed door of the living room and listen to assure itself that there was no danger, that the two strangers, the man and his animal, were no longer there to threaten it or to make fun of it.

Then, with a great leap, it would fling itself on to the back of his chair, for it did not fly. In two or three hops, it would reach its mistress and alight on her shoulder.

She would go on with her knitting. The play of the gleaming needles fascinated the bird. When it had enough, it would rub its huge beak against the woman's cheek and then on the softer skin behind the ear.

YOUR CAT.
YOUR PARROT.

The minutes would flow by, with Emile in the dining room and Marguerite in the living room, until it was time to prepare dinner.

In those days, it was still she who did the cooking for both of them.

At the beginning, Emile had continued to prepare the food for his cat. One week when he had flu and had stayed in bed for three days, she availed herself of the opportunity to buy lung at the butcher's, cut it up into small pieces, cook it, and mix it with rice and vegetables.

'Did he eat it?'

She had hesitated.

'Not immediately.'

'Did he finally eat?'

'Yes.'

He was almost sure that she was lying. The following day he had a high temperature, and she said the same thing to him. The next day, while she was out shopping on the Rue Saint-Jacques, he went downstairs in his dressing-gown and found the food of the previous night under the sink. It was untouched.

The cat, which had followed him, had looked at him reproachfully. Emile had mixed the food again and offered the plate to the animal, which did not make up its mind at once.

When Marguerite got back, she found the plate empty. The cat was not on the ground floor, but in the bedroom upstairs, lying against its master's legs.

That was where it slept every night.

'It's not hygienic,' she had protested the first new nights.

'It slept with me for years, and it didn't make me ill.'

'Its snoring keeps me from sleeping.'

'It doesn't snore. It purrs. One gets used to it. After all, I got used to it.'

She was partly right. The cat did not quite purr like other cats. Rather, it made a snoring sound, which was as sonorous as that of a man who has drunk too much.

Now, standing near the cage, she would stare at the stuffed parrot and move her lips as if she were talking to it tenderly.

Emile, whose back was half turned to her, had no need to see her.

He knew that game just as he knew Marguerite's other games. He smiled vaguely, still gazing at the charred logs. Finally, he got up, took two new logs, and put them into the fireplace, arranging them with the help of the tongs.

Outside it was now quiet except for the pattering of the rain and the thin jet of the fountain in the marble basin. The alley contained seven houses, side by side, all exactly alike, with a door in the middle, two windows at the left, those of the living room, and at the right the window of the dining room, behind which was the kitchen. The bedrooms were on the floor above.

Two years earlier, replicas of these houses, the even-numbered ones, stood on the other side of the street. The enormous iron ball of the demolishers had knocked them down as if they were cardboard toys, and the entire view now consisted of a building site cluttered with cranes, girders, steamrollers, planks and wheelbarrows.

Three residents of the street had a car. Even with the blinds closed, one could hear if someone went out in the evening. And from outside one could tell in which room the people were sitting.

Few tenants drew their curtains, and one could see families at table, a man with thinning hair reading in his armchair under a tarnished picture frame, a child bent over a notebook and sucking its pencil, a woman peeling vegetables for the next day.

Everything was mild, soft, muted. Actually, one really heard the fountain only once one was in bed and had put out the light.

The Bouins' house, which was still called the Doises' house, was the last in the row, against the high wall that closed the alley. At the foot of the wall was a statue, a bronze Eros holding a fish.

A thin jet of water that spurted from the fish's mouth fell into a marble shell.

Marguerite had gone back to her chair in front of the fire. She had stopped knitting. Wearing her silver-rimmed glasses, she was turning the pages of the newspaper which she had picked up from the floor near her husband's armchair.

The black hands of the clock advanced slowly, trembling hesitantly on the hour and half hour.

Emile was not reading or looking at anything. He sat there with his eyes closed, perhaps thinking, perhaps dozing, and occasionally shifted the position of his legs because of the heat.

When the clock struck seven, he stood up slowly and, without looking at his wife or at the cage of the stuffed parrot, walked to the door.

The hall was not lit. The front door, in the middle of which was an empty letterbox, was at the left, and the staircase leading to the first floor, was at the right. He switched on the light, shut the door behind him, and opened the door to the dining room, with its cold stagnant air.

The house had central heating, but it was turned on only on very cold days. Besides, they no longer used the dining room. They ate in the kitchen, where the gas stove gave a feeling of warmth.

Bouin, who was careful and methodical, put out the light in the hall, closed the door behind him, walked to the kitchen, and, when the light was on there, turned off the light in the dining room.

He had adopted his wife's economical habits, and he had an additional reason for doing what he did.

He knew that Marguerite had started squirming in her chair as soon as he had stood up. She did not want to follow him too closely. She was waiting a little. When she got up with a sigh, she would have to extinguish the lamps in the living room, put on the light in the hall, then extinguish it, and also shut each door behind her.

These movements of each of them had become ritual gestures and had a more or less mysterious meaning.

In the kitchen, Emile Bouin took a key from his pocket before opening the cupboard on the right, for there were two cupboards. The one on the left, which was older, had already been there in the time of Marguerite's father.

The one on the right, which was painted white, had been bought by Bouin on the Boulevard Barbès.

He took from it a cutlet, an onion, and three cooked endives, which were left over from lunch and which he had put into a bowl. He also took a half-empty bottle of red wine and poured himself a glass before attending to his butter, oil, and vinegar.

After lighting the gas, he melted a knob of butter, sliced the onion, and, when it began to brown, put the cutlet in the frying pan.

Marguerite had appeared in the doorway, pretending not to see him and to ignore the fact that he was there, to ignore even the smell of the onion.

Taking a key from her belt, she opened *her* cupboard.

The room was not large, and the table occupied a good part of it. They had to move carefully to keep out of each other's way. They were so used to it that they hardly ever grazed each other.

They no longer used a tablecloth but made do with the checked oilcloth.

Marguerite also had her bottle. It did not contain wine, but a cordial that had been popular at the beginning of the century and that her father had given her at lunch and dinner when she was still an anaemic girl.

On the label, which was old-fashioned, were unidentifiable leaves and ornate lettering: Cordial of the Alps.

She poured herself a tiny cordial glass and wet her lips with relish.

When the cutlet was cooked and the endives were reheated, he put the food on a plate and sat down at one end of the table in front of his bottle, his bread, his salad, his cheese and his butter.

Apparently indifferent to what he was eating, she spread her supper at the other end of the table: a slice of ham, two cold potatoes which she had wrapped in foil before putting them into the refrigerator, and two thin slices of bread.

Her husband was ahead of her. One of them would sometimes sit down to eat when the other had already finished. It did not matter, since they ignored one another.

They ate in silence, just as they did everything else. Bouin was sure that his wife was thinking: 'There he goes eating meat twice a day again! And he fries onions on purpose.'

It was partly true. He liked onions, but he did not necessarily want them every day.

At times, in order to make her angry, he would prepare complicated dishes for himself, dishes that would take an hour or two to cook. This had meaning for him. It proved that he had not lost his appetite, that he still was a gourmet, that he didn't mind attending to his food himself.

Some mornings he would bring back tripe, the mere sight of which disgusted his wife.

In the evening, as if to emphasize her frugality, she would make do with a slice of ham or cold veal, a bit of cheese, and at times a potato or two left over from lunch.

That had a meaning too. Several meanings. In the first place, it established the fact that he spent more money on food than she did. Secondly, that she refused to use the frying pan after him. When it was necessary, she would wait for him to clean it, even if it meant eating much later.

They chewed slowly, she with barely perceptible movements of the jaws, like a mouse, and he, on the contrary, noisily manifesting his appetite and pleasure.

'You see! Your presence doesn't disturb me in the least . . . You thought you were punishing me, that you were getting the better of me . . . Well, I'm very happy, and I haven't lost my appetite.'

Of course, their dialogues were silent, but they knew each other too well not to divine every word and every intention.

'You're a vulgar man . . . You eat sloppily and you stuff yourself with onions like a common person . . . As for me, I have always had a bird's appetite . . . That's what my father called me . . . His little bird . . . And my first husband, who was a poet as well as a musician, called me his fragile dove.'

She would laugh, not outwardly. Inwardly. Her laughter was no less apparent.

'It's he, poor thing, who died . . . He was the fragile one . . . '

Her gaze would glide over her second husband and would harden.

'And you who think you're so strong, you'll go before I do too.'

'I'd have gone long since if I hadn't been careful . . . Remember the bottle in the cellar?'

Now it was his turn to laugh, inwardly. Despite the fact that they were alone in the silent house and condemned themselves to muteness, they nevertheless indulged in fierce repartee.

'Just wait . . . I'm going to spoil your dinner for you.'

He took the notebook from his pocket, wrote four words, detached the strip of paper, and skilfully tossed it on to his wife's plate.

She unfolded the note without surprise.

CAREFUL ABOUT THE BUTTER.

It was more than she could take. She stiffened. She had never been able to quite get used to that particular joke. She knew that the butter was not poisoned, since she kept it under lock and key in her cupboard, even though it got soft and sometimes runny.

She nevertheless hesitated to eat any more of it and managed to do so only at the cost of an effort.

She would take revenge later. She did not yet know how. She had time to think about it. Neither of them had anything to do.

'You're forgetting that I'm a woman and that a woman always has the last word, just as a woman lives three to five years longer than a man. All you need do is count the widows . . . They're far more numerous than widowers.'

He had been a widower, but it was by accident, it didn't count. His wife had been run over by a bus on the Boulevard Saint-Michel. She had not died at once but had dragged on helplessly for two years. He was still working. He had not yet retired. When he returned in the evening, it was to take care of her and look after the house.

'She took her revenge, didn't she?'

An emptiness. Silence. The rain in the yard.

'I sometimes wonder whether you finally didn't get tired of it and end by getting rid of her . . . With all the medicines she took, it was easy . . . She wasn't as careful, as shrewd as I am . . . She was a nobody, with big red hands, who had milked cows in her youth . . .'

265

Marguerite had not known her. The couple had lived in Charenton. It was Emile who had spoken to her about the red hands, had spoken tenderly about them, at a time when they were still on speaking terms.

'It seems odd to me to see you with such white hands, such delicate joints, with almost transparent skin . . . My first wife was a country girl, well built, with sturdy red hands.'

He would take from his pocket a packet of Italian cigars, the black, twisted, very strong kind known as coffin nails.

He would light one, puff a blast of pungent smoke into the air, and use the match to pick his teeth.

'A lesson for you, old girl . . . That'll teach you to be so delicate.'

'Wait . . . You'll get all that's coming to you.'

He would empty his wine glass, finish the bottle, then, after a moment of immobility, lumber to his feet and go to the sink, where he would turn on the hot water.

While she finished her meal in dainty mouthfuls, he would wash his dishes, clean the frying pan, first with a piece of paper and then with a cloth, and carefully wrap the bone and fat of the cutlet in an old newspaper which he then threw into the dustbin under the staircase. Not forgetting, of course, to lock his cupboard.

A slice of the day had thus been nibbled away, and he tackled the last slice by going back to the living room and turning the knob of the television set. It was time for the news. He would change the position of his chair. The logs on the hearth were almost burned out, but it was no longer necessary to look after the fire, for the room was now filled with a pleasant warmth.

Then she would wash her dishes. He would hear her moving about. She would join him, but she would not turn her chair towards the television set immediately. The news did not interest her.

'It's all dirty politics, accidents, and brutalities,' she used to say.

She would pick up her eternal knitting. Then, when a programme of songs was announced, she would shift her chair, first slightly, then a little more, and then completely. She did not want to seem too greatly interested in such nonsense. Nevertheless, she sometimes wiped her eyes during a sentimental, sad ballad.

Bouin got up to take the dustbin and put it at the edge of the pavement. The rain was icy. The alley was lonely with its seven houses in a row, its few lighted windows, the three cars that were waiting for the following morning, and that awful building site where walls were beginning to look up beside gaping holes.

The fish in the fountain kept spitting its jet of water into the shell, and the bronze Eros dripped with rain.

He locked the door behind him and shot the bolt. Then, as he did every evening, he lowered the blind in the dining room and then the one in the living room where the television was on.

It was only a silvery gleam, but that gleam enabled him to see in a flash that his wife had a thermometer in her mouth.

She had managed! It was her little revenge, her riposte to the matter of the butter. She imagined that she was going to worry him by making him think that she was sick.

In the past, she had spoken about her chest, her bronchitis, and at the slightest drop of temperature she had wrapped herself up in shawls.

'You can drop dead, old girl.'

He did not just think that. He wrote it on a slip of paper which she received in her lap when she wasn't expecting it. She read it, removed the thermometer from her mouth, looked at her husband pityingly, and then, taking a piece of paper from her pocket, she wrote:

YOU'RE GREENISH ALREADY.

She did not throw it, but laid it on the table. Let him be inconvenienced. She did not fortify herself with a notebook of detachable slips. Any old bit of paper would do, even a piece of newspaper.

He would not dare to get up immediately. Despite his curiosity, he would wait as long as possible.

She found the way to make him move. All she had to do was get up and turn to another channel. He could not stand having to watch a programme other than the one he had chosen.

So, as soon as she got back to her chair, he stood up, changed the channel, and, in passing, picked up the note as if accidentally.

Greenish! he laughed. He laughed on purpose. He laughed

badly, not quite heartily, for it was true that he did not have a good complexion. He noticed it every morning when he shaved.

At first he blamed it on the light in the bathroom with its frosted glass. He had looked at himself elsewhere. He had, of course, lost weight. When one gets older, it's better to get thin than fat. He had read in the paper that insurance companies make fat men pay a heavier premium than thin ones.

All the same, he had difficulty getting used to the man he had become. He was tall. In the past, he had been broad, heavy, husky.

On the job, he had worn huge boots and, in summer as well as winter, a black leather jacket. He ate and drank whatever he pleased, without bothering about his digestion. For more than fifty years, it had never occurred to him to weigh himself.

He now felt skinny in his loose clothes, and occasionally he felt a pain, sometimes in a foot or a knee, sometimes in his chest or at the back of his neck.

He was seventy-three years old, but, apart from growing thin, he refused to consider himself an old man.

And she – did she consider herself an old woman? When he got undressed, she would look at him mockingly, without realizing that she was in much worse shape than he.

Another of their games! They would play it later, around ten o'clock, when they would go upstairs to bed. There were three bedrooms on the upper floor. The night of their marriage, they had quite naturally slept in the same one, which had been the bedroom of Marguerite's parents and the one she had shared with her first husband.

She had kept the old oak bed, the feather mattress, and the enormous quilt. Bouin had tried to get used to them. After a few days, he had given up, especially since his wife refused to sleep with the window open.

He had not gone so far as to change bedrooms. He had brought his own bed and set it up next to his wife's.

The wall was covered with flowered paper. At first, there were only two enlarged photographs in oval frames on it, one of Marguerite's father, Sebastian Doise, and one of her mother, who had died of tuberculosis when Marguerite was still a small child.

Later, when they had stopped speaking to one another, Marguerite had put up, next to her father, a photograph of her first husband, Frédéric Charmois. According to the photo, he was a slim, distinguished-looking man, with a poetic air about him. He had a thin moustache and a pointed beard. He was first violinist at the Opéra and gave lessons to a few pupils during the day.

Less than a week later, Bouin responded to the provocation by hanging up a picture of his first wife at the head of his bed.

Thus, each flouted the other, as they seemed to flout each other when they undressed. They could have gone to another room, but they did not want to change in any way the habits of the early years.

Bouin almost always undressed first, as discreetly as possible. Nevertheless, there was a moment when he showed his naked chest, his ribs, which stood out more and more, and his hairy legs and thighs, from which the muscles had melted away.

He knew that she was watching him, delighted to see him withering away, but a little later it was his turn to glance furtively at his wife's flat, skinny chest, her drooping buttocks and swollen ankles.

'You're a sight, my dear girl!'

'And you, you think you're handsome?'

They still did not speak to each other. They measured each other in silence. Each went to brush their teeth in turn, for the bathroom was the only room in the house where they were never together.

Bouin would get into bed heavily and put out his bedside light. His wife would slip between the sheets more delicately. And he knew that she kept her eyes open for a long time waiting for sleep to come.

He fell asleep almost immediately. Another slice of the day, the last one, was consumed. Tomorrow would be another day, pretty much the same.

It was good to sleep. It was particularly good to have dreams in which he was ageless, in which he was not old. He would sometimes see landscapes as he had seen them in the past, landscapes that were alive, with vibrant colours, landscapes that smelled good. At times he would even run until he lost his breath in search of a spring whose murmur he could hear.

He never dreamed of Marguerite, and rarely of his first wife, and when he did it was always of her as she had been shortly before their marriage.

Did Marguerite dream too? About her first husband? About her father? About the time when she wore broad-brimmed straw hats and strolled along the Marne under a parasol?

What did it matter to him? Let her dream about her first husband the musician and about her childhood if she felt like it.

He didn't care, did he?

Chapter Two

He woke up at six o'clock, as he did on other days, as he had done all his life without ever using an alarm clock. His father, too, always got up early. He was a bricklayer, at a time when cranes were not yet used in building and when walls went up brick by brick.

They lived in a small house in Charenton just behind the lock that linked the Marne canal to the Seine. People in the neighbourhood thought that his father had grey hair because it was sprinkled with plaster and mortar.

There was no bathroom in the house. They washed in the yard, near the pump, bare-chested in winter and summer alike, and once a week, on Saturday, they went to the public baths.

Bouin had been a bricklayer too. He had started as an apprentice at the age of fourteen, and his work had consisted chiefly in buying bottles of red wine for the entire gang.

He went to night school. He didn't get much sleep. He was already married when he took his foreman's examination and then, much later, his examination as building inspector.

The name of his first wife was Angèle, Angèle Delige. She came from a village near Le Havre; when she was sixteen her parents sent her to Paris, as they had done with her four sisters. She had been a nursemaid, and then a salesgirl in a delicatessen.

It was true that she had milked cows and that she had big red hands.

They had rented a flat not far from the lock, on the Quai de Charenton, and in those days Bouin still went to hug his father and mother every morning before going to work.

There was no bathroom on the Quai de Charenton either. He continued going to the public baths, the corridors of which were invaded with steam that had a human smell.

'Why don't you use the bath?'

He was sixty-five when he remarried, and she sixty-three. They were very awkward with each other, more intimidated than very young lovers.

Were they really in love?

'I prefer showers . . . '

To be stretched out in warm water filled him with anguish. He felt seized with a numbness that did not seem natural. He preferred to soap himself under the shower and then to run cold water over his naked body for a long time.

'Are you going to go on getting up so early when you have nothing to do all day long?'

To him, the bed was somewhat like the bath. He felt comfortable in it at night and sank quickly into sleep. But at six o'clock, and often earlier in the summer, he felt the need to return to life. In order to please her, he had tried to linger between the sheets, but it gave him an uneasy feeling in the chest.

He would get up noiselessly and make his way to the bathroom, where he would shut the door and bolt it. After showering and shaving, he would slip on a pair of old corduroy trousers that were too big for him, a flannel shirt, and go downstairs in his slippers so as not to make any noise.

He was convinced that she was awake, that she pretended to be sleeping, that she was listening attentively to every sound.

In the kitchen, he prepared a big bowl of coffee for himself. After making sure that he had his key in his pocket, he went to the front door and out into the alley.

At that time of year, it was still dark, and the street lamp was the only source of light.

For years his cat had followed him with an almost solemn pace, as if that stroll in the empty streets was an important act to him, a kind of mass which they both celebrated in silence.

Bouin did not have a cat on the Quai de Charenton. During the last two years of his wife's life, when the accident had crippled her, he had had no time to go walking. He looked after the house, put things away, washed, scrubbed, prepared Angèle's breakfast.

Before the accident, he spent at least a half hour strolling along the quays, observing the canal boats, the barrels that were to be delivered to a big wine-merchant, the tugs coming from above Corbeil which drew four or five barges of sand.

He now invariably made the same tour. The alley branched out from the Rue de la Santé, halfway between the prison and Cochin Hospital. Lower down was the lunatic asylum, which he passed before going up the Rue du Faubourg Saint-Jacques.

At the corner of the Rue de la Tombe-Issoire and Place Saint-Jacques, he would see St Dominique's church, where Marguerite went to mass on Sundays. In the summer, she sometimes went on weekdays too.

There was a time when she received Holy Communion every morning. In those days she was very friendly with the priest, whom she helped decorate the altars and to arrange the flowers in front of that of the Virgin.

What had come between them? What had been the cause of their quarrel? The fact remained that she had stopped seeing him and taking part in parish affairs. Instead of occupying a personal pew, she contented herself with a rush-bottomed chair at the back of the church.

Except for the day of his marriage, Bouin had entered the church only once, out of curiosity. He had been baptized. He had received his first communion. But nobody in his family went to mass, which had not prevented his father and mother from having religious funerals.

He had only one sister, who had got off to a bad start in life. For years the family had been without news of her. They did not know whether she was living or not. Then one day, a letter that had been forwarded to various addresses, with an envelope containing comments by various postmen, had finally reached Emile. His sister informed him that she was married to a miller from the neighbourhood of Tours, that she had two children, a big house on the banks of the Loire, and an American car.

He had not seen her again. He had merely written, saying that he was a widower and that he was nearing retirement age.

He would turn to the right on the Avenue du Port-Royal, then right again on the Rue de la Santé, which was always as empty as when he had left.

In the course of a fifteen-minute stroll, he passed a hospital, a prison, an asylum, a school for nurses, a church, and a fire station. Wasn't this a kind of summing up of life? The only thing lacking was the cemetery, which was not so very far away.

When he returned, one of the neighbours, Victor Macri, who had a solemn gait, would be emerging from number 3 and starting his car. They would exchange greetings. First the car would let off smoke before the engine gradually got into its stride, and Macri would head for the big hotel on the right bank where he was a porter.

Marguerite and he knew all the residents of the alley. Marguerite was the owner of the row of houses that remained. A few years before his death, her father had sold the opposite row where a big block of flats was now rising.

Emile Bouin took the key from his pocket. After three years, he still missed his cat, and almost every morning he hesitated slightly as if to let the cat in first as he used to do.

He would hear footsteps on the upper floor, the water flowing into the bathrub. He would raise the blinds. Before long, the darkness outside would be less dense, the light from the street lamp would grow pale, and he would hear a slamming of doors and footsteps moving towards the Rue de la Santé.

Neither the loneliness of the hour nor the emptiness around him weighed upon him. All his life, he had been in the habit of going through the same routine at given times.

Certain gestures, certain schedules, had changed. He had known different periods, but each had been marked by a definite rhythm, which he avoided breaking.

It was now the time, as it had been when he got ready to go out on a job, for red wine, bread and salami.

His father, before leaving for work, used to eat a big bowl of soup, a steak or a stew, which did not keep him from taking food along for a mid-morning snack.

His mother was small and rather stout. He mainly remembered her doing the washing, which she then hung up in the yard. There were no washing machines. Even if they had existed, they would have been too expensive. And probably his mother would have been scared by them as she was scared by everything that was electrical.

She would put the clothes to boil in a huge galvanized kettle, and she had to start her washing early, because she needed her husband or son to help her remove it from the stove before leaving.

There were the ironing days, the evenings devoted to mending socks, the afternoon for the copper pots, with the result that the week was a succession of different images and smells.

Curiously, as he grew older he became almost insensitive to smells. Nor did he see the streets as he had seen them in the past, when they offered a constantly changing spectacle of which he never wearied.

He had then had the impression, when he plunged into the crowd, of being part of a whole, of participating in a kind of symphony, each note of which, each spot of colour, each gust of heat or coldness, enchanted him.

He could not have told when the change had taken place. No doubt gradually, as he aged, without his being aware of it. For he had never realized that he was getting older. He did not feel old. He was really amazed when he thought of his age.

He had not become wiser, nor more indifferent. He still had the thoughts and odd ways and made the gestures of the youngster he had been.

On Place Saint-Jacques, he had bought the morning paper, which he glanced at while eating. Marguerite spent a long time upstairs washing and dressing. Three years earlier, when they spoke to each other, he had pointed out to her that it was dangerous to bath in a locked room, for she might have a fainting spell and nobody would realize it.

It had become a habit of his, even though they were at war, to cock his ear while she was in the water. This was easy because the bathroom was directly above the kitchen. The drainpipe went through the kitchen, to the right of one of the cupboards, and made a racket every time the bath emptied.

He would drink two glasses of wine, from a thick glass, as in the country. He would drink a third glass later, around the middle of the morning, when he got back from his shopping.

It was seven-fifteen by the alarm clock. He had the impression that its ticking was louder in the morning than during the rest of the day. He had also noticed that it was quicker than that of the clock in the living room. He wondered why, since they kept the same time.

He would light his first Italian cigar and go down to the cellar, which was lit by a very weak bulb that hung from the ceiling.

For about a quarter of an hour he would cut wood, for it was more economical to buy it in big pieces than already cut to the dimensions of the fireplace.

He would fill the basket and take it up to the living room. Then there was the delicate job of lighting the fire while listening to the news on a portable radio.

Actually, the news did not interest him. It was a habit, a pebble to mark one step in the unfolding of the day. He would hear Marguerite enter the dining room and then the kitchen. Outside, the rain fell in a whitish fog.

He did not have to keep an eye on her, since his food was under lock and key in his cupboard. She would then prepare her coffee, caffeine-free coffee, for she was convinced that she had a heart ailment.

Or was it only an alibi, a reason for complaining or for assuming sickly expressions?

She would have her coffee with three or four buttered rusks, and therefore she had hardly anything to wash up afterward.

The fire would begin to take the chill off the living room. Although the daylight was still dismal and indecisive, he put out the lights and went upstairs, where he had to make his bed. He made the bed carefully, without leaving a crease in the sheets, blankets, or counterpane.

Marguerite would then go up. They did not greet each other, did not exchange a look. Each went about his business, glancing furtively at the other only when they believed themselves unobserved.

She was ageing. To be sure, she was no longer a young woman when he met her but middle-aged, and somewhat delicate, which perhaps added to her distinction.

She had a clear, pink complexion beneath her silky white hair, and her face had a gentle, kindly expression.

The shopkeepers on the Rue Saint-Jacques adored and respected her. She did not belong to their world, but to a world apart. She was a kind of aristocrat in the neighbourhood where her father had built the houses in the alley that was named after him.

For more than thirty years, she had lived with a man as distinguished as herself, a musician, an artist, the first violinist at the opera, who could be seen at night in a black cape and evening clothes and who for a long time had continued to wear a top hat.

He too had that vague, gentle smile, that politeness which was both shy and a shade condescending.

'He's such a good teacher . . . This year again, one of his pupils got first prize at the Conservatory.'

At that time, in the alley one could hear for hours on end the same musical phrases being repeated by a violin which the professor accompanied on the piano.

The piano was still in a corner of the living room, encumbered with photographs and fragile curios. Marguerite had played it until the death of her first husband, and when she returned from the funeral she had decided that she would never touch the instrument again.

Bouin had insisted at first. She would answer with gentle obstinacy:

'No, Emile. It was his piano . . . It's still a little of his life . . . '

He had once lifted the lid and run a finger over the ivory keys. She had come rushing down, indignant and unable to understand how he could have been so bold.

In her eyes, the piano was part of her husband. It was a holy relic, as was the violin which was locked in a cupboard. Of course, another man now shared the bedroom that Frédéric Charmois had occupied with her for more than thirty years. He washed in the same bathroom. In the beginning, they had tried to have the same intimate relations.

Things had not worked out. They were both intimidated and had the impression that at their age the gestures which they made so awkwardly were ridiculous, that they were a kind of parody.

Who knows? Perhaps Marguerite regarded it as a sacrilege. She would lie there with her eyes closed and her lips tightly pursed. She was resigned. Since they were married, her new husband had the right to her body.

But that body remained stiff, on the defensive.

'Why don't you go on, since you want to?'

'How about you?'

'I don't know.'

Perhaps she had felt like it, before. Perhaps on falling asleep at night she sometimes dreamed of pleasures which she had known in the past. At the moment of resuming them, her feelings rebelled.

'We'll get used to it ... '

They had tried several times.

'I thought you loved me.'

'I do love you. Forgive me ... '

'What's holding you back?'

'Forgive me,' she would repeat. 'It's not my fault.'

And tears would tremble at the edge of her eyelashes.

Instead of working out, things had become very bad. As soon as he approached the oak bed, he would see Marguerite's body shrink away, her eyes become harder, almost hostile.

He was the male, the brute who thinks only of his personal satisfaction. She had already suffered from his heavy step, the way he moved about the house where formerly everything had been discretion and delicacy. She had never quite got used to his cigars, which, in the beginning, he had smoked in the doorway.

As for the cat, it inspired her with an almost superstitious terror.

On the very first day, the animal had stared at her as if it were trying to understand why she was butting into their shared existence.

It would sometimes follow her through the house and up the stairs as if to assure itself that she was not a threat, and its golden eyes, which were full of mystery, seemed always to be asking questions.

It slept on Bouin's bed, against his legs, where, before letting itself fall asleep, it waited for that strange creature who slept in a neighbouring bed to be completely motionless.

At that period, Marguerite alone looked after the house.

'Aren't you going to take your walk?'

She did not like to see him wandering about the house while she was cleaning. He would take his coat and go walking in the streets, sometimes far away, for example, along the quays, which he sometimes followed with his even gait as far as his former neighbourhood.

He was neither happy nor unhappy. He would stop to have a glass of wine in a small café, as in the past, when he would go off for a drink during the morning break.

278

The difference was that formerly he was surrounded by people like himself, who were covered with dust or mud. They would speak loudly, they would laugh, the glasses would clink.

'This round's on me, Alice!'

He had worked for a long time in the very centre of town when the Boulevard Haussmann was joined to the Grands Boulevards. He had also taken part in the transformation of the outer boulevards when the old ramparts were demolished.

Wherever they were, the workers would discover a cosy little bar where they met several times a day. Often they ate there, taking their food from their knapsacks. His first wife, Angèle, found that life quite natural. They had no children and did not try to find out whether it was his fault or hers.

Angèle was not distinguished. She was gay, noisily so. She loved the cinema. She sometimes went alone in the afternoon, and often, in the evening, she asked him to go with her to see another film. On Saturday nights they went dancing.

In the summer, on Sundays, they took a train to the nearby countryside. They met friendly couples and drank with them.

They were warm, they sweated, they bathed in the river. Angèle did not know how to swim and splashed about near the shore.

On the way home, they would have a funny taste in their mouths, the taste of the fried food which they had just eaten, of the mud of the river. Their heads would spin a little, for they had drunk rather heavily. His wife's hand on his arm felt heavier as they approached the house.

'I'm dizzy.'

It amused her to feel drunk.

'Aren't your legs wobbly?'

'No.'

'I bet you'll want to make love.'

'And why not?'

'I'd like it too, but I don't think I'm up to it. Your hard luck if I fall asleep . . .'

Nothing was important. Nothing was serious, nothing was dramatic. Sometimes the meal wasn't ready or the bed was unmade.

'Just imagine, I slept almost all day. It's your fault too. If you hadn't been at me until two in the morning . . . '

Marguerite would have found her vulgar. She was, but it was a good and healthy vulgarity and resembled her husband's.

'Tell me, have you ever slept with other women?'

'Occasionally.'

'You still do it?'

'From time to time, when there's a chance. There are almost always young women prowling around the site.'

'Aren't you ashamed to take advantage of them?'

'No.'

'Is it the same with them as with me?'

'Not quite.'

'Why?'

'Because I love you. With the others it's like having a drink.'

'If they knew what you think of them . . . '

'They don't worry. Sometimes we pass them on to one another . . . '

Who knows, perhaps Angèle deceived him too. He preferred not to think about it, but he did not reject the possibility. She was free in the afternoons. She would go into town and visit the shops, not to buy, because she could not afford it, but for the fun of it. Every cinema poster tempted her, and she would go off to sit in the darkness.

Didn't any man try his luck then? Not only old ones, for whom it's a kind of disease, but young ones who had the day off?

'Have you ever deceived me?'

'Why do you ask that?'

'Because you've just asked me the same question.'

'Do you think I'm going to give the same answer? Are you jealous?'

'Perhaps I am. Perhaps not . . . '

'What would be the point? You're enough for me, aren't you?'

It was not an answer. He would sometimes think about the matter and scowl, but he could not be said to be anxious.

Perhaps yes, perhaps no. Anyway, she was a fine girl who did her best to make him happy.

He was happy. He had no desire for change. He was satisfied with his life. Later perhaps he would buy a car and go driving with Angèle on Sunday instead of taking the train or bus.

He did not foresee that his wife would be run over one autumn afternoon on Boulevard Saint-Michel or that, when the time came to retire, at the age of sixty-five he would marry a woman almost as old as he.

By ten o'clock he would finish his share of the household work. She had not asked him to help. It was he who had decided, the day after they had stopped speaking to one another, that he would not be indebted to her. At that time, their anger was still hot. They would sometimes mutter in a low voice. Each felt himself a victim and regarded the other as a monster.

Almost in a fury, he had begun to clean the living room, dining room, and even the kitchen, where he got on his knees and washed the floor with soapy water, as he had seen his mother do in the past.

Because there was only one vacuum cleaner, he had to wait until he no longer heard the noise of it in the bedroom, which was Marguerite's domain, to go and get it. Strict justice would have required that she give it to him halfway down the stairs.

Once a week he waxed the living-room floor, not in order to give pleasure to the old woman but because he liked the smell of the polish.

It was after that that the little game began. It had just begun. He did not like the word 'game'. Marguerite probably did not like it either. But how did she refer, in her own mind, to what took place every morning?

The word 'game' implies a certain gaiety which neither of them felt, except from time to time, and which they were very careful to hide.

Seen from another point of view, their actions and gestures were tragic or grotesque rather than comical.

This morning, Marguerite had not forgotten the comedy which she had begun the night before with the thermometer. She had it in her mouth again when he went up to get the vacuum cleaner. Her hair was covered with a pale blue kerchief as it was every morning. Was her colour really bad? Was it the light of this rainy, foggy day? The air outside was slightly yellow.

And what if she really fell ill ? She had never been ill, in spite of her complaints. He had never been really ill either, and they both seemed destined to live to a ripe old age.

Marguerite on the upper floor and he on the ground floor were now waiting to see who would leave the house first. He had already put on his mud-coloured raincoat and his galoshes. His cap was within arm's reach.

She must have been ready too. The day before, he had lost patience and had gone out with a shrug of his shoulders.

Today, after a ten-minute wait, which she had no doubt spent, ready to leave, with her umbrella in her hand, standing in the bedroom, she decided to go down and get her shopping bag in the kitchen.

He had one too, almost the same as hers. The street door shut behind his wife, and then he too left the house.

He saw her on the pavement, small and slender, clumsy on her swollen legs when she tried to avoid puddles of water, with the purple umbrella swaying above her head.

She knew that he was following her. On other days, it was she who trailed him, never at a great distance, for he was careful not to walk too fast.

She turned to the right towards Boulevard de Port-Royal and crossed the street opposite Cochin Hospital, where there were ambulances in the yard in which housemen in white coats moved about rapidly.

A little later they would enter, separated by a distance of a hundred feet, the busy Rue Saint-Jacques, where the shops were full of housewives.

He was asking himself, 'Is she going into the grocer's ?'

Rossi's grocery was an Italian shop. The store was dark and deep and overflowing with food. It specialized in prepared hors d'œuvres, small artichokes in oil, fried fish in a spicy sauce, and marinated octopus about an inch long of which Emile was very fond.

He needed sugar and coffee. When he entered, Marguerite was looking at the shelves and ordered spaghetti and three tins of sardines.

She did not look as if she knew he was there. They ignored each other in public as well as at home, and the local shopkeepers had got used to seeing them enter one behind the other without so much as looking at each other.

Every man for himself. Nevertheless, they spied on each other, and if one of them ordered something expensive or original, the other tried to outdo him.

'Have you got any cannelloni?'

'Freshly made this morning.'

'Give me four.'

They were long and generously stuffed. She must have started.

'Let me have three slices of Parma ham,' she said. 'Not too thick. I have such a small appetite!'

She wore a shawl under her coat, like someone who does not feel well and is afraid of catching cold. It also made her look older, more broken-down with age.

'Aren't you well, Madame Bouin?'

People always hesitated to call her by that name. The old-timers had known her first as Mademoiselle Doise. That name had great glamour for them, for they sold Doise Biscuits and Doise Cookies.

It was Marguerite's grandfather who had created the biscuit factory whose tall chimney with a capital D painted in white halfway up still stood on the Rue de la Glacière.

Here, among the metal boxes with glass covers that contained biscuits, were several boxes with the name 'Doise', followed, it is true, by the mention: 'V. Sallenave, Successor.'

For more than thirty years, too, they had called her Madame Charmois, and they had never quite got used to her present name of Bouin.

Madame Rossi was waiting on her.

'Anything else, Madame?'

'Let me look at my list. Do you still have the same chocolates you had last time?'

'Those with hazelnut filling?'

'That's right. I'll have half a pound. I only take one occasionally . . . So they last a long time.'

As for him, he did not forget the sugar and coffee. He added a quarter of a pound of salami and of mortadella. Unlike his wife, he felt no need to furnish explanations.

Marguerite was taking coins from her purse.

'How much do I owe you?'

He lingered in front of the shelves so as not to approach the cash desk until the moment she was leaving.

A few steps farther was the butcher's shop. The clients lined up. Raoul Prou joked with the housewives as he cut up his meat.

Emile waited until two customers had lined up behind Marguerite before he entered the shop.

What was said about them when they left? It was unthinkable that Prou, in any case, did not make any comments.

'See those two cranks? They're husband and wife, and every morning they arrive one behind the other looking as if they didn't know each other. Each buys for himself . . . I wonder what they do all day long in their house . . . But she was a fine woman. Her first husband played the violin at the opera and gave lessons . . .'

'It's your turn, Madame Bouin . . . Have you got a cold?'

'I think I'm beginning to come down with bronchitis.'

'Be careful . . . Mustn't play around with that kind of thing at your age . . . What will you have today?'

'Let me have a little veal cutlet, very thin . . . You know . . .'

He knew. She spoke to them all about her birdlike appetite, as if to avoid the accusation of avarice.

'Please trim the fat.'

'There won't be much left.'

'It'll be quite enough for me.'

They must have pitied her, must have blamed him for the situation. When he married her, he still looked like a husky brute, for it was only recently that he had begun to shrivel. He smoked his strong little Italian cigars. He would spit a yellowish jet of saliva on the ground, and he could be seen going into the cafés for a drink. Marguerite's first husband would never have behaved in that way!

And didn't some people maintain that he had managed to put one over on her, and that he had married her just for her money?

That was false. He was about as rich as she was. There was no telling exactly, for she was discreet about such matters. When they had married, she had retained legal control of her own estate, but she did not seem to have any direct or indirect heirs.

As for him, in addition to his savings he had his pension, and if he died before her she would receive three quarters of it for the rest of her life.

Which of the two, therefore, was self-seeking?

Both of them? Either?

'Have you got a nice veal kidney?'

She had opened her purple umbrella as she left the butcher's shop and headed for the dairy.

He joined her there while she was paying. He had not seen what she had bought. He knew only that it had cost her two francs forty-five centimes.

'A quarter of a pound of Münster cheese.'

A cheese that had a strong smell and that she loathed.

'A dozen eggs.'

He would buy a quarter of a pound of mushrooms and that evening, before the cheese, he would prepare a creamy, lavish omelette, the kind he liked. She would look disgusted. Perhaps she would leave the table, as she sometimes did, especially when she saw him unwrap the Münster.

She was standing in front of the stall of the vegetable seller, from whom she was buying potatoes. She loved potatoes, whether hot or cold, and ate them at almost every meal.

'Let me have a quarter of a pound of mushrooms.'

He did not add, as she would have done: 'It's for an omelette.'

'Anything else, Monsieur Bouin?'

He needed potatoes too, and he had the stallholder put them at the bottom of the bag so that they would not crush the other things.

'Some onions ... Preferably red ones ... '

'Shall I give you half a pound? They keep very well.'

'I know ... Some parsley ... Two pounds of potatoes ... Not those ... I prefer these, a little shrivelled ... '

The shopkeepers must have thought that he remained a gourmet and continued to indulge himself while his poor wife merely nibbled a few crumbs.

He did not need anything else. He watched his wife enter the chemist's with the green front, and he saw the pharmacist showing her several boxes and tubes of pills, no doubt medicines for a cold. She was asking questions, hesitated, and finally chose lozenges. That was not all. She also bought something which he recognized from afar. Mustard plasters.

That evening, before going to bed, she was going to apply one to her chest, after moistening it. Then she would twist and squirm in order to place a second one on her back. It was difficult. He pitied her each time, and he was tempted to put out his hand to help her, but he knew that she would have regarded such a gesture as an insult.

Then, while the two plasters were producing their effect, she would nervously walk back and forth between the bedroom and the bathroom until the pain became unbearable.

She was capable of keeping them on for a long time. One would have thought that it was a self-imposed punishment, and when she removed the mustard plasters her skin was as red as a fresh wound.

Was that all, this time? No, she also wanted to exchange a book at the secondhand bookshop which exchanged volumes for fifty centimes. She invariably chose novels of the beginning of the century, sad stories that contributed to her melancholy.

He would glance at a few paragraphs when she was not in the living room. There was always a proud, courageous victim who suffered every possible misfortune but who nevertheless kept her head high.

'Poor woman ...'

He often thought that. He, too, sometimes regarded himself as a brute. Then he would start brooding over the memories of the last three years and would end by writing a little note:

THE CAT.

It was doubtless she who had put rat poison into the animal's food. She had taken advantage of his being in bed with flu.

In the evening, he had been surprised that the animal had not jumped on his bed.

'Have you seen him?'

'Not since this afternoon.'

'Did you put him out?'

'I opened the door for him at about five o'clock, when he wanted to go out.'

'Did you stay outside with him?'

It was midwinter. A crust of snow covered the pavement of the alley. The demolition work across the way had not begun, and the two rows of houses faced each other as in the time when Sebastian Doise had constructed them.

'Hasn't he scratched at the door since?'

'I haven't heard anything.'

He was already beginning to get out of bed.

'Don't you want me to go and see?'

'I'm going myself.'

'Are you going outside in spite of your fever?'

It seemed to him that there was something false in his wife's voice. Until then, he had found her uncomplicated, often tormented by fixed ideas, some of which were a bit silly, but it had never occurred to him that she might be vicious.

It was the cat, and the cat alone, that had become the object of her bitterness. Every time it touched her, she would jump aside and let out a scream. She overdid it. He was convinced that she was putting on an act. During the very first week of their marriage she had insinuated that he might get rid of the animal by giving it to friends, for example.

'I've been afraid of cats all my life. I might perhaps get used to a dog. We had one, when my father was alive, and it used to follow me around when I was little and seemed to protect me. Cats are treacherous. You never know what they're thinking . . . '

'Joseph's not like that.'

For Joseph was the name he had given the animal that he had found one evening on his way home.

That shocked Marguerite.

'I don't think it's right to give an animal the name of a saint.'

'It's too late to debaptize it.'

'How can you utter that word? As if one baptized animals!'

'Why not?'

That had been their first quarrel. There had been others, all of them about Joseph, who listened to them as if he knew what they were discussing.

'He's not even pure-bred.'

'Neither am I.'

That was to tease her. It was part of his character, one of his habits. On the job, the men were pretty rough with each other,

287

which did not prevent them from going off and drinking together when the whistle blew.

With Angèle, too, he spoke quite freely, and sometimes went rather far.

'Come here, mulehead.'

'Why do you call me mulehead?'

'Because you're like all women. To look at you, one would swear that you work yourself to shreds to satisfy me, that nothing counts but me. In reality, you're like a mule, you do exactly what you feel like doing.'

'It's not true. I always obey you.'

'In a sense, that's true. When you feel like doing something, you convince me that I'm the one who wants it. Don't deny it, old girl . . . Go on, I know you! You're as big a slut as the others.'

'Aren't you ashamed?'

'No.'

They would end by bursting out laughing and, most often, by rolling on the bed.

With Marguerite, it was different. There was no question of rolling on the bed or of using coarse language. Crude words made her shudder, and she would immediately withdraw into silent disapproval.

She still went to communion every morning, and late in the afternoon she would sometimes kneel in the dark church, near a confessional.

'Well, did you go off to pray?'

'I prayed for you, Emile.'

He did not hold it against her. Rather, he was annoyed with himself for having married her, for he was not the man to make her happy.

How did the idea ever occur to him? He had often thought about it. Which of the two had made the first advances?

He lived opposite her, on the spot where the crane was now set up. He had taken a room on the upper floor of the home of a young couple for whom the house was too large and the rent too high.

That was why he had left the Quai de Charenton. He felt lost in the flat which he had shared with his wife. Usually he ate in a restaurant. A big room and a bathroom were enough for him.

His armchair was near the window, from which he could hear the water in the fountain. In the evening, when he did not go out, he watched television.

He had made some friends at the café on Place Denfert-Rochereau where he went to play cards. As for women, there was always Nelly, even though it wasn't very comfortable. He attached little importance to the matter.

In the morning, he would see the little lady from the house opposite go shopping, and he found her distinguished. She resembled the women on old-fashioned calendars with their gentle smile of resignation.

He knew that she was the owner of the opposite houses, that was all. Although he knew her name, he did not associate it with the biscuits that he had eaten when he was a child.

They would return home, she with her umbrella and shopping bag which would sometimes knock against passers-by, and he with his small cigar and his face wet with raindrops.

They would find themselves in the same quarters, each with his thoughts, each with his little packages, waiting for the time to prepare lunch.

On Place Saint-Jacques he would stop and, letting her go on ahead, would go into a bar for a glass of red wine.

The boss's wife served at the counter. She was as old as Marguerite and had a hard bun on top of her head and big flabby breasts that hung down above a big stomach.

'It looks as if it's going to snow,' she said, looking at the colour of the fog.

Chapter Three

He had gone downstairs, with his woollen dressing gown over his pyjamas and his bare feet in his slippers. He had looked everywhere, in the living room, in the dining room, in the kitchen, and, what with his fever, he finally got a headache as a result of bending down to look under the furniture.

From time to time he would emit the faint whistle to which the cat was accustomed, and he would sometimes call out, in a gentle voice in which anguish was apparent:

'Joseph . . . Joseph . . .'

Then he had put on his galoshes and slipped on over his dressing gown the first thing he found on the coat hanger, the old black leather jerkin. He didn't give a damn about looking ridiculous.

'Emile!' called his wife from the top of the staircase. 'Don't go out. It's bad for you.'

Nevertheless, he went through the alley, in the darkness, over the crackling snow, and he almost slipped and fell on the pavement two or three times. At the lighted window of one of the houses, the second one, a child watched him with its face glued to the pane and then turned around to call its mother, who could be seen through the open door of the kitchen.

His outfit frightened children. He walked to the Rue de la Santé. When the cat was let out to attend to its needs, it never went beyond the invisible line that separated the street from the alley.

'Joseph!'

He felt like crying. He would never have thought that the absence of the cat could move and distress him to such a point.

Two dogs lived on the street, a brown dachshund that belonged to a spinster and a Pomeranian that a twelve- or thirteen-year-old girl took out on a lead. There had never been any trouble between them and Joseph. When the latter met them, he disdainfully looked elsewhere and, if necessary, stepped off the pavement to let them go by.

He had left the door ajar. He pushed it open, took off his leather jacket and galoshes, and went up to the bedroom. His gaze was hard and his features were drawn. As he was about to get into bed, he thought of the cellar and went downstairs. Marguerite, visibly nervous, followed him to the ground floor.

'Did you get wood?' he asked her.

'I had to warm the house, after all . . . '

He did not yet accuse her, but he was beginning to suspect her. In the cellar, he lit the feeble bulb and began to search among old boxes, bottles and logs.

'Joseph!'

He found him, at the very back, against the damp wall, behind a pile of firewood. The animal was stiff, its eyes open and motionless, its body twisted. It seemed much thinner than when it was alive. Slobber had stuck under its mouth, and there was greenish vomit on the ground.

Emile took it in his hands and vainly tried to close its eyes. The contact with the almost icy body had given him a curious sensation in his spinal column.

He was not a quick-tempered man. He had, on rare occasions, got into fights, especially in cafés, only once at work, and each time he had kept his self-control.

But now his face had an evil look. Holding the animal in his hands, he looked around as if searching for something. And he found it.

There were many rats in the alley. At times they could be seen prowling at night around the dustbins, and Marguerite was very afraid of them.

'Do you think we have any in the cellar?'

'It's possible.'

'If I were sure, I'd never dare go down again.'

He had bought a product with an arsenic base that was sold everywhere. From time to time, in the evening, he would spread it on slices of bread and leave them in a corner of the cellar.

All he had ever found was the corpse of a single rat, an enormous one, to be sure, almost as big as Joseph. Perhaps others had gone to die elsewhere.

The metal container of the rat poison was kept on a crude shelf where they put various objects that had no place elsewhere.

He put the cat down for a moment, struck a match, and saw the former circle that the container had left on the dusty wood. There was another circle.

Picking up his dead cat, he had gone upstairs, slowly, so slowly, so heavily, that Marguerite on the ground floor must have felt the menace.

She wanted first to take refuge on the upper floor, but as he barred the way she rushed into the living room. When she tried to lock the door, he moved his foot forward, forced his way in, went up to her with the same slow gait, and, with his left hand, grabbed her hair.

At the same time, with his right hand he raised Joseph's corpse in front of the frightened face.

'Look, you bitch! Take a good look!'

With her whole body trembling and her eyes bulging from her head, she had cried for help in a shrill voice. She had lost all self-control and looked as if she were insane.

'Emile! Emile! Please, pull yourself together ... You're frightening me ... '

He continued rubbing the cat's fur over her face until she fell to her knees, then dropped forward, as if she had fainted.

'I know very well that it's an act. Everything you do is an act, you slut! I wonder what keeps me from going and getting the poison and forcing it down your throat.'

He was breathing hard, his head was spinning. He must have been crimson, frightening.

She did not move. And he, in order to release his fury, put out his arm and swept away all the knicknacks and photographs lined up on the piano.

After that, without looking at his wife, he went upstairs, still holding the cat, which he placed delicately on the chest.

His temperature must have gone up. He felt a spell of dizziness. He lay down, put out the light, and remained motionless, with his eyes open.

At first, nothing moved in the house. For more than a quarter of an hour, there was silence. Then there were indistinct noises, scratchings. A door was opened cautiously, then another.

Marguerite had crossed the dining room to go to the kitchen, probably because she felt the need of a dose of her famous cordial. He later found the glass beside the sink.

It was almost an hour before she dared go upstairs, and she waited a while longer listening, with her ear against the door. Finally she entered the bedroom, hesitated, and lay down on her bed without undressing.

Neither of them had slept much. Emile had difficulty breathing. He dozed off several times, and each time he was awakened by nightmares which he vainly tried to remember later.

At six o'clock he opened his eyes for good. His head ached. He almost remained in bed. He had perspired a good deal, and his pyjamas and pillow were damp.

His wife was sleeping. She had been incapable of remaining on guard to the very end, and her pose was almost as tormented as that of the cat in the cellar.

He felt drained, unable to think. He slipped on his dressing gown mechanically, took the cat by two paws, as if it were a rabbit, and went down the stairs.

Joseph was no longer a companion, a living thing that had shared part of his life and exchanged so many looks with him. The animal was now only a corpse, an inert thing, which was beginning to smell.

He remained standing in the hall, finally opened the door, and took three steps to the dustbin. The dustmen had not yet called. Raising the lid, he placed the now limp body in the bin.

After that, he washed his hands in the kitchen and prepared his coffee.

He had no doubt about Marguerite's guilt. Wasn't it established by the fear she had displayed when he had gone down to the cellar?

He drank only a few mouthfuls. The coffee sickened him. He stood up, opened his cupboard, and took the bottle of wine that was already started. It was, as usual, red table wine. He drank two glasses one after the other, with his elbows on the oilcloth of the table. It was still a long time before daybreak. It was December, and the night before the sky had seemed heavy with snow.

He first thought of going away. But where? Should he take a furnished room in a small hotel while waiting to find another flat? In that case, he had to remove his furniture, put it in storage somewhere.

From his first marriage, he had kept the bed, his armchair in the living room, the television set, and, upstairs, a desk that Angèle had given him. It was a Christmas present. Christmas was approaching again.

He would not accept a gift from Marguerite, who usually gave him slippers or shirts or socks. He would not give her anything either.

It was over between them. She had just revealed herself as she was, as he had often suspected her of really being beneath her saccharine manners.

He poured himself a third glass. He had no desire to be upstairs again with her. Let her sleep. Let her sweat it out. He would never again speak to her.

They were both old, even if they did not realize it in the usual course of events. In a few years they would be dead. Was he, because of a cat that had been picked up in the street one evening . . .

He mustn't weaken. It was not only Joseph who was involved. It was he himself that she had been aiming at through the animal.

As soon as he had entered that house, in fact as soon as they were married, he realized that Marguerite was bent on changing nothing.

A grandfather Doise named Arthur who wore side-whiskers, a frock coat, and a very high collar had founded the biscuit firm on the Rue de la Glacière. Little by little he made a prosperous business of it.

He had only one son, Sebastian, and a daughter, Eleonore, a yellowed photograph of whom was in the blue leather family album.

Eleonore had died at the age of thirteen, of tuberculosis, as did Marguerite's mother later.

When Sebastian married, he was already a corpulent man close to forty who also wore a frock coat with a double watch chain on which charms were suspended.

Little by little, a Doise state of mind had been created, a Doise atmosphere, a Doise ritual. The alley had been constructed at a time when buildings were regarded as the safest investment and when whole streets emerged from the ground here and there in Paris and on the outskirts of the city.

Later, Sebastian had ordered the fountain, and the word 'alley' had been changed. On the blue and white street plaque, as well as on notepaper and visiting cards, appeared the name Square Sebastian-Doise.

Old Arthur had died. Sebastian's wife had died. All that remained was a daughter, Marguerite, and her father took her walking in her laces and embroidered dresses on the Champs-Elysées and in the Bois de Boulogne.

There existed a photograph of them in a hired carriage. Sebastian did not devote all his time to the biscuit business, as old Arthur had done. He frequented clubs and spent afternoons at the races, wearing a grey bowler and with field glasses slung over his shoulder.

Marguerite had a governess, Mademoiselle Piquet. There was a cook in the house and a cleaning woman several days a week.

A young man came to give piano lessons to the young girl, Frédéric Charmois, whom she finally married.

The house seemed safe against any attack from without.

However, a certain Victor Sallenave worked on the Rue de la Glacière. He had begun as a book-keeper for old Arthur. When the latter died, he became increasingly important in the firm and before long brought his son Raoul into it.

Exactly what had happened? Marguerite remained vague and contented herself with allusions to these events. Emile had had difficulty in getting her to admit that two women in the family had died of tuberculosis. When he had asked her whether her father had been a gambler, she had replied with an innocent air:

'Why should he have been a gambler?'

The Doises must remain spotless even once they were dead. All the family stories gradually took on pastel tones. Everything was pure and delicate, like the poetic profile of the violin player.

And yet Sebastian Doise had found himself one day facing bankruptcy, a word even more unmentionable than the word 'tuberculosis'.

In order to avoid scandal and the inevitable smirch, he had preferred to turn the business over to the Sallenaves, father and son,
with the result that Raoul Sallenave, whose father was now dead,
was the master on the Rue de la Glacière and on the Quais d'Ivry
where he had constructed new buildings.

What was the son of a Charenton bricklayer, what was this
brute of a foreman, doing in the house?

Had she not often made him feel the abyss that separated them
and that nothing could fill?

She had married him out of the fear of remaining alone, of
having no one to look after her in an emergency, because a man
was needed in the house, if only to cut and bring up wood and to
take out the dustbin.

Perhaps too the ageing widow had been stirred by the contact
with the male who came for a cup of tea almost every day.

It had been a failure. She had stiffened at their first physical
contact, and the two beds were a symbol of their botched union.

In short, he was only an intruder and, in her heart of hearts, she
must have accused him of having wormed his way into her life by
trickery.

As if it hadn't been she who had called out to him!

He was at his window one hot August morning. When he was
with Angèle, he would sometimes take a holiday, go to the sea-
shore or to the country. But since he was a widower, he seldom
left Paris. What would he have done all alone, away from home?

Marguerite, across the way, had suddenly opened her door with
a dramatic gesture. It was ten o'clock. All through the alley,
blankets, sheets, and mattresses were being aired at the windows.

Looking anxiously about, she sought someone whom she could
call upon, and she was obviously in a panic.

'Monsieur!' she had cried out to him from the pavement.

He had stood up.

'Won't you come down? Please come quickly, because the
whole house will be flooded . . . '

He had come down as he was, without his jacket, and had
crossed the street.

'What's happening?'

'A leak in the bathroom . . . I don't know what to do about
it . . . '

He went up the stairs in that house which he did not know but which resembled the one he had just left. A pipe had burst in the bathroom, and a veritable geyser was spurting in an almost boiling stream.

'Do you have tools, a big monkey wrench?'

'I don't think so . . . No . . . I've never bothered about those things . . . There were tools in the cellar, but they were rusty, and I got rid of them . . .'

'I'll be back in a moment . . .'

He returned with tools from his own flat.

'Where's the meter?'

'Under the stairway . . . Good God! The ceiling's going to be damaged.'

Five minutes later, the water had stopped spurting.

'Let me have a bucket and a rag.'

The water on the bathroom floor was a few inches deep, and, despite the woman's protests, he had carefully mopped it up.

'Please don't bother . . . I'm ashamed to have called you . . . Someone I don't even know!'

'Well, now you know me.'

'Let me finish the job . . . That's no work for a man . . .'

'So that you can get soaked too?'

He worked quickly, without impatience, like a man who had used both hands all his life.

'Do you have a clean towel?'

He set everything in order, and when he had finished, one would have thought that nothing had happened.

'The pipe is old, in bad condition. It probably dates from the time the house was built, and that wasn't yesterday.'

Had he irritated her?

'I didn't know. What should I do?'

'I could solder it, but it wouldn't last long . . . Better change it up to the main . . . Wait . . . Ten feet . . . Fifteen feet . . . Do you have a plumber?'

'I don't remember ever having needed one, in any case not since the death of my husband . . . Before that, I didn't bother about those things . . .'

She seemed so frail, so bewildered, alone in that house, that he had suggested:

'Would you like me to take care of it?'

'Are you a plumber?'

'Not quite . . . But I know something about such things . . . '

'Would it be expensive?'

'The cost of fifteen feet of pipe.'

They went downstairs one behind the other.

'What can I offer you? Won't you have a drink?'

That day he had made the acquaintance of the famous cordial.

'Don't you like it?'

'It's not bad . . . '

'When I was a girl, I had to take it against anaemia . . . Just a little glass before lunch . . . I've never been very strong.'

That had amused him. He had gone back to his room to change, then he went to an ironmonger's to buy the piece of pipe. When he rang at the door she had had time to put on an old pink dress and to arrange her hair.

'Back already! Are you sure that I'm not imposing on you? Don't you have other things to attend to?'

'I have nothing to do all day long.'

'It's true that I often see you sitting near your window . . . You live alone too?'

'Ever since my wife died . . . '

'Don't you work? You used to leave early in the morning and return only in the evening.'

'I retired six months ago.'

She dared not ask him what he had done before. He had brought a blowlamp and a tool kit, and he had a little more than an hour's work.

'It's so nice of you! A woman alone feels helpless and quite lost as soon as the slightest thing happens.'

'If there's another leak, or anything else, don't hesitate to call me.'

'How much do I owe you?'

He took the ironmonger's bill from his pocket. It came to fifteen francs and a few centimes.

'What about your work?'

'You're not going to pay me for that. I'm only too glad to have been able to be of use to you.'

'Will you have another drink?'

'To tell the truth, I only drink wine.'

'And I who don't have any in the house! Listen . . . Come back this afternoon and I'll have a good bottle . . . '

'Ordinary red wine will do . . . I'm not used to fancy labels.'

The sun was shining. The two of them were smiling on the threshold.

He did not care to remember it.

He stood there, miserable, in his dressing gown, barefoot in his slippers. The kitchen had not been heated. His nose was running and he constantly had to wipe it.

He had gone to get one of his Italian cigars from the living room, and the tobacco had a bad taste. He had not smoked during the three days he had spent in bed. He had hardly eaten anything.

He had drunk jugs of hot lemonade sweetened with honey that Marguerite brought him. She had prepared custard for him. She was displeased that he refused the mustard plasters which she would have liked to apply, very hot, on his chest and back.

And now? He heard the tap running above his head and deduced from it that she had just got up and was brushing her teeth. She must have been afraid. He wondered whether she would come downstairs after dressing.

How many glasses of wine had he drunk? The bottle was empty. He stood up to get another from the cupboard, for there was still only one cupboard for the two of them.

As a rule he drank moderately, and one could count on the fingers of one hand the number of times he had got drunk.

That morning, the blood had rushed to his head. He must have been flushed. It seemed to him that something crucial had happened, something whose consequences he could not yet foresee.

Since Marguerite had poisoned his cat, everything had become false. He had already suspected that things were false between them, though he had not wanted to believe it. He recalled certain images, remembered certain phrases and glances.

They had never uttered the word 'love'. They were too old for that. Had he really loved Angèle, his first wife, and, despite her smirks and smiles, had Marguerite really loved her first husband?

It was now hard to say which of the two had been the first to envisage a life in common.

They were separated only by the width of the alley. Neither she nor he had known a long solitude. They were both used to being part of a couple.

He was alone in his room, above the young couple which had just had a baby. She was no less alone in a house where she felt somewhat lost, somewhat frightened.

When he went to see her in the afternoon, she would be charming, easy to get on with. Perhaps she spoke a bit too much about the great days of her family and of her gilded childhood.

Nevertheless she looked upon humanity with an amused kindliness, except for the two creatures who assumed in her mind the quality of traitors in a melodrama, the two Sallenaves, father and son.

They had grown rich with the fortune that should have gone to her. Raoul Sallenave lived in a big apartment on the Boulevard Raspail, and he had built a luxurious villa on the Seine, near the forest of Fontainebleau.

The Doise Biscuits! The Doise money! The Doise honesty, which had forced them to sell one of the rows of houses on the square which bore their name!

There was already talk at the period of demolishing everything in order to put up blocks of flats, and Marguerite had received offers.

'Of course, I refused. I'd rather go without bread . . . '

He should have been wary. He listened with a smile. She asked him a few questions about himself, and that should have alerted him.

In short, the only living creature that interested her was herself. She was part of the procession of her dead family which continued to surround her with a kind of protecting halo.

He now understood. She did not want a servant or a cleaning woman because she would not have been able to put up with a person of her own sex in the house.

Yet she needed help. She might need it. An illness, a broken leg, would be sufficient. She did not even have a telephone to call for help, for she had had the line disconnected.

300

'No one has any reason to telephone me. I'd jump with fright every time someone got a wrong number.'

He had suspected her of avarice. And he was now sure that she was miserly and that avarice had played a role in their marriage: she would have someone at her disposal day and night without having to pay.

Bouin had a pension. He had once mentioned, casually, that in the event he remarried his widow would continue to receive two-thirds of it.

As for her, she never spoke of what she owned. One side of the alley continued to belong to her. Once every quarter the tenants came to pay their rent. Each entered the dining room in turn. Bouin did not know what they paid, just as he did not know what his wife did with the money.

Did she deposit it in a bank? Did someone take care of investing it for her?

She alluded only to expenses, to repairs that were requested of her, to the roofs that leaked, to windows and doors that needed to be fixed.

'You'd think that they damaged things out of spite. The rents aren't enough for the upkeep of the houses.'

She felt no affection for him. She had proved it when she had remained stiff and frigid in his arms. For her, he was a kind of servant.

Had he gone too far? Perhaps. He had a right to go far after what she had just done to him. He also had a right to drink. And to smoke his cigars.

What happened when he lit one in the living room after dinner, in front of the television set? She would open the window wide and cover herself with her heaviest shawl, which did not keep her from shivering so as to get across to him that she was risking pneumonia because of him.

That was just one detail. There were a hundred others. There were a thousand. For example, after they got married, he had suggested that they share household expenses. As he saw it, it was a matter of each one's paying a monthly sum to be fixed by mutual agreement.

However, after doing the shopping, she would take all the

shopkeepers' receipts and classify them in a drawer with the bills for electricity, water, sewage and refuse collection.

He had been surprised, at the end of the first month, when she had declared: 'I've done our accounts.'

With her glasses on her nose, she had demanded that he check with her the bills of the shopkeepers, the laundry, etc.

'Check the addition . . . Yes, I insist!'

She had divided the sum in half.

'We'll do the same thing every month. That'll avoid any arguments.'

He had gone to get his money in the bedroom. He kept it in a drawer of the chest. He did not have the key to it and was not concerned about it.

What was the meaning of doing things this way? Was it love, was it affection, confidence?

When they went to the cinema, each paid for his own ticket.

'It's fairer that way.'

She would observe him when he ate, assuming a look of disgust when, for example, he would use a matchstick as a toothpick. By seemingly trivial words and by meaningful looks, she would underscore each of his bad manners.

Everything about him shocked her. It was not only the cat that slept against his legs every night.

'My first husband's skin was as smooth as a woman's,' she once remarked when he was walking bare-chested in the bedroom.

That amounted to saying that the dark thick hair with which he was covered repelled her.

'She has always detested me.'

The way she detested the Sallenaves. Perhaps out of a need to detest someone. Perhaps to fill her empty days.

He felt her always watching him from behind, furtively.

'Well! You've had something besides wine to drink today . . . '

She was not mistaken. He had met an old friend and they had had two or three apéritifs.

She knew everything. She wanted to know everything. She took her time before asking seemingly innocent questions. None of them was really innocent. Some of them had to do with events that were several months in the past and about which she remembered everything.

She would compare the answers with others that he had given. 'But you told me . . . '

At times he felt as if he were at school, facing the teacher who was trying to pin a fault on him and who wasn't satisfied until he blushed before confessing.

'Is it true that your first wife wasn't jealous?'

'That's right.'

'Then she didn't love you.'

'I think she did . . . We got on very well.'

'Were you happy with her?'

'I didn't feel unhappy.'

Angèle did not ask questions. There were no rules between her and him. They did not eat at a definite hour. If dinner was not ready, they would go to a restaurant.

Their rare disputes were rather part of a game.

'Did you take advantage of it?'

'Of what?'

'Of her not being jealous.'

'Sometimes I did.'

'And now?'

'So far I haven't.'

He was lying. She could feel it. She had actual antennae.

'But you hope you will?'

'I hope nothing. I don't plan ahead.'

'Your first wife wasn't very proud.'

'Why?'

'Don't you understand?'

'No.'

'To see one's husband come home after having just dirtied himself in the belly of another woman, of a woman he hardly knows and who perhaps has given him a nasty disease. To sleep in the same room as he, to share a bathroom . . . '

He found nothing to answer and would look at her with stupefaction.

'I wouldn't stand for it . . . I'd say to him, "You'd better leave."'

As if talking to a servant!

Did Marguerite ever follow him in the street when he went out in the afternoon? He had suspected her of doing so. There were times when he turned around suddenly. He had, to be sure, seen her twice in the course of several months, the first time entering a store, the second suddenly turning about. He had not questioned her when he got home.

He preferred not to think of those more or less disagreeable things in order to retain some pleasure in life.

Too bad for her if she was going to start spoiling things between them. He managed to fill his days with little pleasures, and he always had Joseph as a faithful companion, Joseph who sometimes seemed to reproach him for having changed houses, for having imposed a foreign presence upon him, in short, for having betrayed him.

Did she dare to beat the cat in his absence? He doubted it, because she was too afraid of it.

She had done better. She had killed it. And it was not only Joseph that she had thereby attacked, it was he himself, Emile, whose presence and smells she no more liked than she did those of the animal.

She had waited for the opportunity for years. She had not had the patience to wait longer, a year, perhaps two, until the cat died a natural death.

Bouin drank, but he felt cool and collected. He was convinced that he saw things more clearly, more objectively than ever.

She was a bitch. One had only to look at the photographs and see the awkward bearing of her first husband, the famous first violinist of the opera, to know that he was a weakling who had let himself be led by the nose for more than thirty years.

As for her father, Sebastian, that bloated half-wit, decked out with a charm-studded watch chain, he was so much in need of forgiveness for his many sins that he let his daughter get away with anything whenever he was home.

A bitch already when she went driving in the Bois de Boulogne in a carriage drawn by two horses. A bitch the day she married Frédéric Charmois. For there was, naturally, a wedding photograph too. The album was overflowing with photos. The biscuit factory seen from the street. The yard of the biscuit factory with the entire staff lined up in rows around Sebastian Doise.

Old Arthur Doise, in his armchair. The same in his office. His sister, with a hair-do like that of the Empress Eugénie. Other

Doises, particularly old ones, a few babies on bear-skins, finally Marguerite, photographed by her fiancé on a riverbank, with her big hat and her parasol with the pointed tip.

The album sat in state on the piano, like a treasure.

Bouin did not have access to it. She had never asked him for a picture of himself. When they were married, she had not suggested that they be photographed.

Only one dog in the lot, a sleek, pedigree animal, as distinguished-looking as the violinist husband.

No other animals. There was no place for animals, except for the parrot that Marguerite had bought a few weeks after Charmois's death, to replace him.

A parrot that did not talk. Wasn't that better? Did Charmois talk? He gave violin lessons. In the evening, he put on his dress clothes and white tie and took the Métro at Denfert-Rochereau for the Opéra, where he proudly walked in by the stage door.

'God damn it to hell!'

He was in a fury. He felt unhappy. She had touched him in a sensitive spot, and he found no way of retaliating.

He hated her. Despised her.

'A bitch, that's what she is . . .'

He missed Angèle, he felt like weeping over Angèle, talking to her, being comforted by her.

Angèle was a woman, a real one, a female, who did not come from sickening biscuits. Even the Doise biscuits were a bad memory, especially those that were baptized French Kisses. Pretentious and saccharine drivel typical of the female's mentality.

Actually, the plant manufactured cheap stuff, the kind of sweets that one doesn't buy for oneself but that one gives to children when one goes visiting and doesn't know what else to give them.

The French Kisses were made of cheap dough. One got the impression that one was eating sand. But they were sugar-coated in various colours and decorated with floral and arabesque designs.

When he was four or five years old, an old neighbour used to call him when he was playing in the street.

'Come here, child . . . I've got something good for you.'

She would get her box of biscuits, Doise biscuits, and open it as

305

if it were a jewel case. She would say to him, expecting to delight him, 'Take one.'

She lived alone. The neighbours thought her a bit mad. They said that she had been an actress. She was the only one on the street who used make-up, and he was almost afraid of her coal-black eyes.

'The bitch . . . '

He was not drunk. She did not dare come down. From time to time he heard light footsteps above his head. Devious footsteps. Everything about her was devious.

'Do you want to go out, Emile? It's time for Coco's exercise.'

For, of course, the parrot's name was Coco. It was stupid. It was bad-tempered. Like its mistress, it did not forgive Bouin for having invaded the house, and particularly for having brought with him an odd animal.

He was brooding over his grievances. The wine helped him. As one refills a stove, he kept finding grievances to add, and suddenly he stood up, bent on showing her who he was.

Did he have a definite aim when he entered the living room hesitantly?

He began by raising the blind, which had not yet been touched that morning. The snow was beginning to melt. There were still patches of it on the pavements on both sides of the alley. A little boy tried to slide on it, and Bouin was surprised to discover that outside life continued as on other days.

A sewer man, who was standing near a manhole, was beating his arms in order to get warm. He caught sight of Bouin behind the curtain and must have envied him, as though he himself would not reach the age of sixty-five, and be able to retire. And what of it? What would he do with himself?

Was Marguerite finally going to come downstairs? She had heard the sound of the blind. He imagined her with her ear glued to the door of the bedroom. She was wary of everything, particularly of him.

The parrot, in its cage, let out one of its piercing screams, and Bouin turned around with a hard and evil look on his face.

Now it was his turn to be vicious. She who always spoke about justice must have been expecting it.

Staring at the bird, which stared back at him, he strode over to the cage. He opened it and extended one arm cautiously. The wings unfolded. He managed to grab one of them, while the bird sharply pecked at one of his fingers, drawing blood.

It was impossible to remove the bird by force through the narrow opening. He might have strangled it. He had just grabbed it by the neck, but that was not what he wanted. Putting his other hand into the cage, he pulled out a feather from the tail, the longest feather, a bright red one. He had to pull hard. He hadn't thought that the feathers were so firmly planted in the flesh. He pulled out two, three, four ...

'You'll see a thing or two, old girl.'

Five ...

It was as if he were pulling out the feathers of the Doises.

Six ...

Smaller and lighter feathers were coming out by the handful. Blood was flowing, from his hand and from the bird's behind.

He finally stopped, exhausted, slammed shut the cage, and, bending over, picked up the feathers from the floor.

He was nauseated and exhausted. He had no other desire than to go back to bed and sleep.

He looked at the multicoloured feathers in his hands. They formed a kind of bouquet. In a vase, on the piano, there had always been a bouquet of immortelles.

He removed the flowers and replaced them by the feathers, and he could not refrain from smiling slyly.

When he got to the entrance door, he opened it and threw the immortelles on the powdery snow, where they scattered.

He and she met on the stairs. She must have seen the blood flowing from his hand, and she rushed to the living room. She uttered only one cry. He had reached the top of the stairs. He turned around, but even though there was a soft thud, it did not occur to him to go down again.

Chapter Four

It was not his fault. Marguerite was so aware of it that when he tossed a note into her lap reminding her of the cat's death, she dared not reply:

THE PARROT.

He felt sick, feverish. Because of the blow she had just dealt him, he had drunk more than usual, and he lived the last half hour in a nightmarish fog.

He remained standing a moment longer, tottering in front of the open door of the bedroom. His wife's bed was made. The room was tidy. His own bed was ready to receive him with fresh sheets and a clean pillowcase.

Wasn't that still another way of showing him that she was a perfect wife, that she knew her duties, that all the wrongs were on his side, and that she was the victim?

The proof was that she was taking care of him despite his cruelty, that the evening before she had suggested that she apply mustard plasters, that she was worried about his comfort, that she changed the sheets of his bed even though it wasn't the day for it.

Was she still on the floor of the living room, in a faint, or pretending to be? She was hoping that he would get worried, that he would come downstairs, would get panicky, beg her pardon, perhaps send for a doctor.

He hesitated and finally, with a stony face, went to his bed, though he left the door open.

He kept listening. The fever took him back a long way in time, to the days when he was a child and had a sore throat or a bad cold. His sensations, his thoughts, which were sometimes vague and sometimes very precise, and the images that resembled dream images, had a somewhat childlike quality, and hadn't he just behaved like a furious child downstairs?

It had relieved him for a moment. Had he really been relieved? Had he not forced himself to go to the very limit of his impulse, of the diabolical idea that had suddenly occurred to him?

He felt ashamed. He did not admit it to himself. Above all, he did not want to feel guilty towards her. What he would have liked, as when he was little, was a good sickness, a real one, that would endanger his life and oblige the doctor to come to see him two or three times a day.

Marguerite would be frightened, in spite of everything. She would be torn by conflicting feelings, and she would finally recognize that she was wrong and would be ashamed, instead of him.

He would not be sick. He would have to make do with a hang-over. Coughing, wiping his nose, sweating in bed without anyone's pitying him.

Nobody had the right to claim that he was asking for pity. He didn't like to be pitied. He was a man and had always been self-sufficient.

Was it absolutely true?

He was faking, was rejecting thoughts that were not yet formed and that by taking shape might become unpleasant. He kept listening. He still hesitated about getting up and going downstairs.

'You're beginning to realize that this time it doesn't work, old girl.'

It was funny. At times, he confused Marguerite with his mother.

She was moving about below. He caught the slightest noise, the slightest rustle of cloth. She was probably getting up slowly, she too listening intently. Then she stood up, and she probably looked at the cage and the plucked bird, for he could hear her sobbing. Between her sobs she stammered words that he could not make out, and then she walked to the hallway.

At the right was a bamboo coat hanger that must have been there in the time of Sebastian Doise. The leather jerkin was hung on it, and on the other side an old grey coat of Marguerite's.

She must have slipped it on and put her galoshes on over her shoes. The front door opened and shut, and he could hear footsteps on the pavement.

He ran to the window and saw her walking hurriedly towards the Rue de la Santé. Her hands were empty. He could sense that she was agitated, and, though she was not gesticulating, she was probably still mouthing her dramatic monologue.

Where was she going? He wondered for a moment whether she was not on her way to the police station to complain about what he had done, but as soon as he got back to bed he fell asleep.

He continued to be conscious of the situation. Something very serious had happened. The rest of his life might very well be changed as a result. Nothing enabled him to foresee exactly what would happen.

So what! Much better that way! It was bound to happen one day or other, something was bound to explode. He had put up with the old woman's sneaky attacks long enough.

For, though he did not feel old, he saw her as old. Older than his mother, since the latter had died at fifty-eight.

She would find a way of having the last word. Who knows if she had not got it into her head to go and see a lawyer?

A half-hour went by, and he started every time he heard a sound in the alley.

All her life, Marguerite had foreseen misfortunes from which she suffered in advance, even though they never took place. Her avarice, for example. She had a sickly fear of the future, and she remembered her father's ruin, the business falling into the hands of strangers.

She might fall sick, find herself suddenly immobilized for ever. If she had counted on him to look after her, she no longer did. She would need a nurse. Would she be able to pay for one for years?

The word 'hospital' haunted her. She was seized with panic at the thought of finding herself at the mercy of everyone, in an unknown bed and surrounded by the curious eyes of eight or ten sick persons.

She needed money, if only to pay for a stay in a private clinic.

She had already thought of the matter when Frédéric Charmois was still alive, perhaps during her father's lifetime too.

She was afraid of everything, of the wind and the thunder, and above all of poverty.

'She'll bury me . . .'

He had often thought that. He had said it to her. She had once murmured:

'I hope so.'

She had added:

'It's less painful for a woman to remain alone than for a man ... Men are unable to look after themselves ... They're softer than we are.'

She always finished by being right. The proof was that whereas she was bravely walking in the cold and snow to go God knows where, he remained wallowing in his bed, groaning and disgusted with himself.

Footsteps ... Footsteps of two persons ... One of them was a man ... The key entered the lock ...

'Come in, Doctor.'

He did not understand why she had brought back a doctor, unless it was not for herself but for him. And what if she had gone for a psychiatrist with the thought of having him committed?

They entered the living room, the door of which then shut, and Bouin could hear only a hushed murmur. It went on a long time. He tried in vain to understand. After all, the man she had called doctor must have been a vet.

That was it. She had gone for a vet to treat the parrot. He was not mistaken. The living-room door finally opened and then the front door, and when he rushed to the window, he saw a man, from the back, carrying off the cage, which was covered with the flannel cloth that was used at night.

He got into bed again, waited a while, and finally fell asleep.

Later, he heard familiar sounds, very far off, in another world. He recognized the old woman's step on the floor of the bedroom, and there was the noise of a plate or a cup against the marble of the bedside table.

He did not open his eyes. The footsteps moved off. She went down the stairs. He did not move, and he felt beads of sweat forming slowly on his forehead. It became a game. He tried to guess where the next drop was going to emerge. Sometimes it was near one of the temples, and sometimes in the middle of the forehead, and from time to time there was also one near the nostrils.

Opening his eyes, he saw the bowl, which was still steaming

slightly. He was not hungry. He refused to touch the food that she had brought for him out of duty or pity.

Who knows whether she did not intend to get rid of him as she had got rid of the cat?

It was the first time that the idea occurred to him. The thought was still vague, and he did not really believe it. It was part of the fever, and the wine he had drunk had something to do with it.

'That would suit her. She would inherit the pension without having to put up with me any longer.'

There was a contradiction in this which he preferred not to see. If she had married so as not to be alone and to be assured of free help in case of need, his disappearing would be of no advantage to her.

But was she thinking about what she was doing? Wasn't she steeped in hatred? A hatred that did not date from that morning, that had nothing to do with the parrot, but that went very far back. It was idiotic to say so, but perhaps it dated from before she knew him.

He remembered her cold, hard look when, after having hesitated for a long time, he had stretched out over her with the intention of making love. When, not without difficulty, he had entered her, her whole body had suddenly stiffened as if it were instinctively repelling the male.

For perhaps a moment, he had hoped that she was going to relax, but she did not. He had withdrawn shamefully, muttering excuses.

'Why?' she asked in a toneless voice.

'Why am I apologizing?'

'Why don't you go on and why don't you have your fun? I married you. It's my duty to submit to that too.'

The 'too' had recurred to him many times. What exactly did it mean? What else was she submitting to out of a Christian sense of duty? His cigars? His uncouthness? The fact of sharing the same bedroom?

There were two empty bedrooms on the second floor. One served as a storage room and the other had been her room when she was a girl; she had kept it intact, with all the objects in place, and probably considered it as a kind of sanctuary.

She had shown it to him only once, from the threshold; he had

312

not been asked to step in, and the door was always locked. She opened it only when he was not there, at least that's what he supposed.

She was in the kitchen. She was eating, in spite of her grief. He made an effort to overcome his dizziness and, resting on one elbow, he took the bowl that contained the now tepid vegetable soup.

He sniffed at it mistrustfully, put his lips to it, and found that the liquid had an odd taste.

Could it be that it was now he who was putting on an act? If she meant to poison him, she would not do it so soon after the death of the cat or after the incident of the parrot.

Nevertheless he got up and went, in his bare feet, to pour the contents of the bowl into the lavatory, eating only the biscuit that was on the plate.

He was not hungry. He had not shaved, nor had he taken a shower, and he felt dirty.

It was a painful afternoon, the kind that one later tries to forget about. He slept, woke up several times, once when it was dark and the street lamp was lit in the alley.

He listened but heard nothing. For more than a quarter of an hour, he lay there on watch, and he became aware of his loneliness. He felt that Marguerite was not in the house. He was left to himself, and he was filled with anxiety.

Finally he made up his mind to go downstairs, which he did on tiptoe. There was no light in the living room, no fire on the hearth. It was very cold. The absence of the cage left a void, and the room seemed larger, the piano enormous.

The dining room was not lit either, nor was the kitchen, but everything was tidy.

He drank another glass of wine, defiantly. He had no desire to drink. The wine seemed bitter to him. Then he went upstairs very quickly, afraid that his wife might find him on the ground floor.

He had never been so concerned with Marguerite's doings, which now assumed enormous importance.

He dozed off once again, but nevertheless heard her come in. They were both used to the noises of the house, of the slightest displacement of air.

She did not light a fire in the living room. Perhaps there were

313

no split logs in the cellar; the supply upstairs had been exhausted for three days.

She stayed in the kitchen. Later, she went upstairs and remained standing in front of him, watching him by the light of the hall lamp.

He pretended to be sleeping. She took away the cup and plate. He then had to go to the lavatory, and he almost did not flush the bowl so as not to betray his presence there.

He slept again. She must have lain down, since, when he awoke in the middle of the night, he heard her regular breathing.

The next day was much the same. She went out twice, the first time to do the shopping and the second probably to go to the vet's, the way one goes to see a sick person in a hospital.

Was Coco going to die? He hoped not, although he was frightened of the thought of their future encounters in the living room in the presence of the tailless bird.

He took advantage of his wife's being out to go downstairs and eat some bread. He felt worse that afternoon, and he vaguely saw her in front of him, with a blank look on her face and her eyes cold as when he had naïvely lain upon her.

'Do you want me to call the doctor?'

He shook his head.

'Do you need anything?'

He made the same movement. He was not putting on an act. He was very far away from her, in an incoherent world.

She went out again at about five o'clock, and he again went downstairs to eat something. His legs were weak. His head was spinning. He clung to the banister as if he were afraid of toppling forward.

He found a slice of ham in the refrigerator and ate it, holding it with his fingers. Then he ate a piece of cheese. It was Marguerite's dinner, but she could go and buy something else.

The following day, he knew it was Sunday because of the silence. The universe was motionless. There was only the sound of church bells in the distance.

She had gone to mass. He no longer felt sick. He was very hungry. He felt a particular need to get rid of the smell of sweat and to shave.

He was weaker than he had expected, but all the same he took a

314

shower. His hands trembled as he ran the razor over his cheeks. He sucked two eggs. In order to cook them, he would have had to use the frying pan or a pot, and he did not have the heart to wash them afterward.

What was it going to be like between Marguerite and him now that he no longer had any reason for staying in bed?

Wearing a pair of clean pyjamas and his dressing gown, he went down to the cellar, split some logs, and carried them to the living room, where he lit a fire. As if to inform his wife that he was up and about, he opened the blinds. She would thus be warned before entering the house, which would give her time to compose herself.

It was for her to choose, not him. The house belonged to her. Most of the furniture was hers. Many of the objects were in the same place where they had been when she was born. Frédéric Charmois, even though he had lived there more than thirty years, had merely passed through and had left few traces, only some photographs and a violin in a locked closet.

Bouin could have gone off while Marguerite was away. A wheelbarrow would have been enough for him to remove his things. He had thought of doing so. He would think of it again when he was steadier on his feet.

He was anxious. The minutes and seconds were slow. The key fumbled before entering the lock and making the familiar click. If, in a period of a few years, he had so accustomed himself to the sounds and smells of the house, to the very quivering of the air, what effect would the slightest change have on Marguerite, who had lived there the seventy-one years of her existence?

She entered the dining room where they had never had a meal but where a family had formerly gathered around the oval table beneath the kerosene chandelier, which had been successively transformed for lighting by gas and then electricity.

She was in the kitchen. She did not stay there long, but she had opened the refrigerator and therefore knew that he had eaten two eggs.

She went upstairs and entered the bedroom which had been hers when she was a girl. He was impatient, resented her keeping him on tenterhooks. Wasn't she doing it on purpose, in order to punish him?

The bedroom was decorated with flowered cretonne. In a corner was a little writing desk on which, fifty-five years before, she had perhaps confided her girlish thoughts and feelings to a diary.

If he had known her at that time . . . But he was then only a rough-mannered bricklayer's apprentice at whom she would not have deigned to look.

The door of a car slammed. It was the engineer, who had started his engine and then had gone to get his family. At that time of year they did not go to the country. Probably they would be spending the Sunday at the home of the parents of one or the other or of a sister or brother in the suburbs or elsewhere.

Everyone lived in a more or less limited circle. His and Marguerite's circle was limited to the walls of the house.

He had never had that impression with Angèle, perhaps because they almost never stayed at home, except for occasional meals, for making love, and for sleeping.

Yet they had few friends. They went anywhere and drifted with the crowd, where they did not feel lonely.

Had Bouin felt alone when he lived opposite, and had only a room and a bathroom? He never thought about it. He was neither sad nor melancholy, and he never had the agonizing impression of moving about in the void.

Here he sometimes wondered whether the objects, the furniture and knicknacks, were real. Everything was in its place, immutably, for eternity.

When Marguerite watched television, he would sometimes notice her profile, and she too was so frozen that he was surprised to hear her breathe.

It was she who had wanted him, out of fear of that immobility, of that silence. When they had both sat down in the kitchen to drink a glass of her sickening liqueur, she had suddenly realized that something was changed, that a quiver of life had entered the house.

In order to make the man stay, to be able to live as a couple without sin, she had had to marry him.

An old faded couple. Did the people who saw them, the neighbours and shopkeepers, find them pitiful or grotesque?

What would they have thought if they had observed them both in the house?

A door shut. Footsteps. Another door. He waited for her to come downstairs. She reached the hall and hesitated.

Finally, stiff and expressionless, she came into the living room. She faced him. Their gazes met, without warmth, without possible contact. With thin, trembling fingers, she handed him a piece of paper.

He stood there for a moment without reading what was written on it and finally glanced at it while she moved towards her armchair. Before sitting down, she picked up the knitting that was on the seat. He read:

I HAVE THOUGHT IT OVER. AS A CATHOLIC, I AM NOT ALLOWED TO DIVORCE. GOD HAS MADE US HUSBAND AND WIFE AND WE MUST LIVE UNDER THE SAME ROOF. HOWEVER, I AM NOT OBLIGED TO SPEAK TO YOU AND I REQUEST THAT YOU NOT SPEAK TO ME.

She had signed the note, with the angular, regular penmanship that she had learned from the nuns: 'Marguerite Bouin'.

The game had just begun.

The next day, for the first time since he had lived in the house, he made his bed, while she was making hers.

He was not trying to provoke her. He was no longer sick. His mind was clear. Since they no longer spoke to each other, since there were no further bonds between them, except for their signature on a register, it was natural to accept nothing from her.

It was perhaps childish, but he was determined about it, and when he saw her getting ready to go out to do the shopping he wrote on a slip of paper:

I'LL EAT OUT.

He was being strictly honourable in not having her cook for two, for he had decided not to eat anything that she prepared.

He took his meal at a small restaurant in the neighbourhood and did not speak to anyone, and he avoided going to the café where he would have met people whom he knew.

Without admitting it to himself, he was in a hurry to get home, to know what she was doing. When he got to the house there was no one there, and he did not know what to do. It was confusing. On other days, he never wondered how to occupy himself.

It was three in the afternoon. He opened the refrigerator to try to see what she had eaten. He found a bit of paté, two potatoes separately wrapped, and some string beans in a bowl.

The two preceding days, she had left later. Did that mean that today she was going somewhere else?

He was worrying for no reason. He went up to the bedroom floor, opened the wardrobe, and saw that she had not taken her woollen coat but the fur coat that as a rule she wore only on Sunday.

He would not be able to question her when she got back and would have to be satisfied with observing and trying to guess.

Was the parrot dead?

He was annoyed with himself, though he was never going to admit it. Did she regret having poisoned the cat?

He lit the fire and was reading his paper when she returned. She went to the upper floor and then down to the kitchen. She made only a brief appearance in the living room to get her knitting.

Was she going to install herself in the dining room or the kitchen, where it wasn't warm enough?

Empty hours, without colour, without light or shade, with only the kind of thoughts that one isn't proud of, futile, if not ridiculous, questionings.

'Who knows if she's not going to try to poison me?'

And he suddenly wondered:

'Would I be sad if she died?'

No! Not sad. Not unhappy. Perhaps he would miss her. He did not like people to die. It was not because he liked them, but rather because he dreaded death.

At their age, what chance did either of them have of living much longer?

Sometimes, when he lay in bed, he crossed his hands on his stomach, and if he noticed it before falling asleep he hastily changed his position, for the other was too reminiscent of a corpse in a funeral chapel.

Where would the mortuary chapel be set up? In the bedroom? In the living room? He imagined it in detail, the arrival of the coffin that smelled of freshly sawn wood.

He did not want to die first. Nor did he want her to die. He had to think of something else. He preferred to go off, to walk in the streets, despite the cold and the wind. For the wind had succeeded the snow and was driving the clouds across the sky.

He had not dared drink his glass of wine in the kitchen, where Marguerite was. He was not far from Nelly's place. He decided to go over, without any definite intention. It was not like the other times.

He had know Nelly a long time, more than ten years, almost fifteen. He already frequented her little café on the Rue des Feuillantines during the lifetime of her husband, Théo, as everyone called him.

You went down a blue stone step. The floor was paved with red tiles on which sawdust was sprinkled.

The bar was at the back, near the glass door of the kitchen that was covered with a thin curtain.

When Théo was still alive, there were first and foremost the regulars, at all hours of the day. In the morning it was mainly workmen, who drank coffee or white wine before going back on the job. Later came the shopkeepers and artisans of the neighbourhood, who appreciated the Loire wines and Théo's good humour.

The colour of his face was almost as glowing as that of the tiles. His main activity was to disappear by the trap door behind the counter at about ten o'clock and bottle the wine in the cellar.

His wife took his place and stood right above the trap door.

'That way, you're sure he won't escape,' the customers would say jokingly.

Nelly was a juicy girl, twenty years younger than Théo. Bouin was not the only one to take advantage of her temperament.

She was always ready to make love, which she did as naturally as the clients drank their glass of wine. Once when Emile asked her whether she never wore panties, she replied, banteringly but sincerely:

'And run the risk of missing an opportunity?'

It is true that Théo's almost continuous presence, the fact that the café was open to everyone, and the topography of the place made amorous exercises rather difficult and brief.

Early in the morning, at about eight o'clock, it was still easy, because then Théo was doing his shopping in the neighbourhood. A look at Nelly as she leaned idly on the bar was sufficient for her to understand. She would answer likewise with a look. It was either yes or no. Almost always yes.

After a brief moment, she would head for the kitchen, where Bouin would follow her. With the door closed, she could see through the curtain whether anyone entered the café, while she herself remained invisible.

It had to be done standing up, always in the same place. She would lift up her skirt with a gesture that was so natural that it was not indecent, and she would offer a white, fleshy rump.

Did she really get to enjoy herself too, or did she only pretend? He had asked himself the question without being able to answer it. It was possible that if she was always ready it was because she never quite made it.

If a customer or even Théo arrived, the manoeuvre was easy. One simply left by the second door, which led to the hallway of the building, and went directly to the street.

She must have aged since the first time he had ventured to court her, but, as he had aged along with her, he hardly noticed it.

'A glass of Sancerre.'

'A big one?'

She had emerged in blue slippers from the depths of the kitchen where she had put a pot on the fire. She ran a hand through her hair, which fell over her cheeks as always.

'I thought you were dead.'

It was hardly the moment to utter that word, when he was living with the thought of death, that of Joseph, perhaps the parrot's, who knows, his own one day or other.

'Is it true that you've remarried?'

Her lips parted over her fine teeth, and her eyes were moist. Leaning on the bar, with her chin on her hands, she offered Bouin a view of her white breasts.

He had always known her dressed in black. One might have thought that she wore the same dress over the years.

'It's true.'

'It seems you've made a fine marriage, a rich wife, who has a street of her own.'

He did not like that subject of conversation and emptied his glass.

'Let me have another . . . Will you have something?'

'A small cassis.'

They did not quite know what to say to each other. He wondered whether he was going to give the usual signal.

'It's not the small old lady dressed in magenta I saw you with last autumn on the Rue Saint-Jacques?'

It must have been a fine sunny day, for Marguerite's magenta suit was rather light, and she usually wore it with a white hat.

'Life moves on. Too bad we don't see you more often . . . Have you retired?'

'I retired some time ago . . . '

'Things are quiet here . . . The old-timers are disappearing one after the other . . . The young ones don't appreciate places like this . . . They think they're old-fashioned, and they're not far wrong . . . There are days when I wonder whether I'm not going to put the key under the door and end my days in the country.'

How old could she be? As far as he could tell, she had been about thirty when he had followed her into the kitchen for the first time. Théo had died of a stroke seven years ago. She must be around forty-five, and her face was still smooth.

When she became a widow, her behaviour in no way changed.

She was free. She no longer had to account for herself to anyone. Yet she had never invited him to go up to her bedroom. He had never seen her entirely naked, and their relationship had remained rather furtive.

She belonged to everyone, almost like a woman of the streets. Nevertheless, she felt the need to have a personal domain, a place to which nobody was admitted.

'You've become thin.'

'A little, yes.'

'Aren't you well?'

'I've just had the flu.'

'Troubles? Things not going well with your wife?'

'Oh, it's all right.'

She looked at him as if she were reading his mind. Her cat looked at him in exactly the same way.

'Oh, forget it!' she exclaimed, as if in conclusion to confidences which he had not made.

And, straightening up, she gave him the signal, a wink, a barely perceptible movement of the head.

He dared not say no. On entering the café, he must have expected that that would happen. Wasn't that why he had come? Wasn't it a kind of test?

He followed her. She looked at him laughingly.

'Admit that you hesitated ... For a moment I thought you were going to refuse ... You didn't look very gay ... Let's see if you're still the same ... '

It amused her. Perhaps that was her entire secret. If she accepted men's caresses so easily, if she provoked them with calm immodesty, it was probably less out of sexual need than because they amused her.

'Fine! ... That's better.'

He had feared that he would not make it, and now he found himself in a familiar belly, as when he was fifteen years younger, as in the time of Angèle, before he married Marguerite.

A childish thought occurred to him. He would have liked his wife to loom up, to see him as he was at that moment. It was of her that he was thinking, of the magenta suit that had just been mentioned, of her expressionless face of the day before and of that morning.

From here, the house in the alley became unreal. Marguerite too, and her ancestors the Doises, the man with the watch chain and the founder of the biscuits, the husband with the violin who left in evening dress for the opera, the semi-darkness in the rooms, the cheerless fire and the evenings passed in silence, in the darkness, in front of the television set.

He would have liked it to last a long time, so that he could remain in that state of mind.

'Are you keeping an eye on the door?' she asked, out of breath.

For it was up to him to be sure that nobody came in.

'I am ... '

He stood motionless for a moment, catching his breath, while Nelly let her skirt down.

It was over. All that remained was a kitchen that was not much lighter than their house, a smell of leeks mixed with that of armpits and the whiffs of wine that impregnated the whole building.

'Satisfied?'

'Thanks.'

He said it sincerely. He would have liked to express his gratitude to her. She had given him pleasure so often, without asking for anything, without expecting anything in return.

Others who had taken advantage of her as he did must have spoken of her as a whore once they were with their friends.

Emile had a feeling of gratitude and warmth towards her. He would have liked to talk with her, to have gone up to her bedroom, to have shared a real intimacy with her.

When he became a widower, he thought seriously about her several times, for Théo was already dead.

It annoyed him, of course, that so many men had been in the kitchen, like himself. He suspected that she would never become a faithful wife. But had Angèle been faithful to him? He did not know and preferred not to raise the question.

What he liked about Nelly was that she was real. He was fond of her. He now was sorry that he had waited so long before going to see her.

If he had come more regularly to the café perhaps he would not have let himself be taken in.

For he had let himself be taken in and had lost touch with the rest of the world. He rubbed shoulders with people in the street, but did not really see them. He no longer knew what a woman was, or a child, laughter or tears.

He lived in a ghostly world that was both precise and inconsistent. He knew every flower on the wallpaper in the living room, the spots that had been made in Charmois's time, the photographs, the steps of the stairway that creaked, and the crack in the banister.

He knew the light at every hour of the day, in every season of the year, and Marguerite's face, her thin figure, her even thinner lips, the too white and too delicate skin of her chest when she undressed for the night.

It was an obsession. He had let himself be locked in and now he was a prisoner for life. He ought not to have burned the note. The text of it was eloquent. She regarded him as her property and, in the name of religion, did not allow him to regain his freedom.

'What are you thinking about?'

He tried to smile.

'Nothing definite.'

'All the same, you're not the kind who's sad after making love.'

It was nice of her to say that.

'Lots of men are ashamed and don't dare to look at you. Are there women like that too?'

He almost replied that he knew at least one who was ashamed even before beginning.

In general, Nelly was right. He searched among his memories.

'Maybe we're more realistic,' she said.

Two customers came in, metalworkers or typographers, judging from their grey smocks.

'Two small white wines.'

They waved a greeting, glanced at Emile, then continued with their conversation.

' . . . So I said to him, straight to his face: If that's the kind of customer you are, you can repair it yourself. Can you beat it? Twenty francs for a job that would have taken me more than three hours!'

Nelly winked at him, and, since the café was dim, stretched out her arm to turn on the light.

'Your health, Justin.'

'Yours.'

They must have been around sixty. They did not yet realize the speed at which they were going to age.

'How much do I owe you?'

'Three Sancerres and one glass of white wine . . . For you, it comes to two francs and eighty centimes . . . Actually, it would be the same price for anyone else.'

He was in the street again. There was the wind, the lights, the displays, the smells of the shops. There were also men, women, children being dragged by the hand, infants pushed in prams. They had always been there. They would always be there. Life flowed around him, but he did not have the sensation of flowing with it.

He had become a stranger. Marguerite had become one before

him, and who knows, perhaps she had always been a stranger.

That little girl who looked as if she had stepped out of a bandbox, whose photograph he had gazed at, wasn't she already outside the world?

As one looked at the photograph, one felt like shaking her, waking her up, saying to her:

'Look!'

Look and feel! Touch! The trees, the animals, the men ... There's the sun ... A fine, useful rain is falling ... It's going to snow, it's snowing ... And now the wind is starting up ...

You're cold ... You're warm ... You're alive ... You're vibrating ...

He was walking mechanically, with his head down, without having to watch his way, like an old horse returning to the stable.

He turned the corner of the alley. Silence reigned. A few windows were lit, with a dismal yellow light. A house, then another one, all of them alike. The last one. The fountain in front of the end wall, and the naked little figure that held the spitting fish.

He took the key from his pocket, sniffled before opening, wiped his nose, and, while he was at it, wiped the wetness on his cheek.

Chapter Five

For five days, he had eaten out, without pleasure. He would get up at six o'clock, lock himself up in the bathroom, go downstairs, and prepare a cup of coffee or even drink his glass of red wine immediately.

In the silence and emptiness of the ground floor, he would then do his part of the household chores. He did his job very carefully, as if he feared a comment or reproach. It was becoming a kind of mania, and the piano had never shone so brightly.

His last job was to go down to the cellar, split wood, bring up a basketful, and light the fire in the living room.

Marguerite would come down at about half past eight, already fully dressed. Without seeming aware of the presence of a man around her, she would prepare her breakfast, then, putting on her everyday green coat, she would head for the Rue Saint-Jacques.

He would sometimes follow her even if he did not need anything, simply for want of anything else to do. When she returned she would put her purchases into the refrigerator and the cupboard, and she would go upstairs to tidy herself up and take her fur coat with her.

Twice a day, in the morning and afternoon, she would go off to a mysterious appointment, probably with the vet who was looking after the parrot.

Bouin did not know either his name or his address. He knew only, because he had seen him through the window when he was carrying off the cage, that the vet was a short man with a limp and that he wore a tight overcoat.

He dared not go back to the café, perhaps because the pull was too strong. He was suspicious of the way he thought about Nelly and he realized the danger.

With her, he had no need to watch himself. He relaxed. The complications of the alley disappeared, lost their importance, or seemed absurd. If he let himself go, he would end by getting used to remaining there. It would become a weakness. He would drink his small glasses of wine and make use of Nelly when he felt like it.

He had no projects. Nothing was yet standard in the house. Each of them came and went, seeking his place, his rhythm, his schedule, somewhat in the way the members of an orchestra tune up their instruments in the pit.

On the fourth or fifth day – he had stopped counting – he followed his wife from a distance when she went to her afternoon appointment. It was already dark.

She went down the almost deserted Rue de la Santé, passed the prison and then the asylum. There were few people in the street, and one could hear their footsteps from a distance.

She then took the Rue Dareau, which was hardly livelier, and finally arrived at the Rue du Saint-Gothard, near the railway.

She did not try to see whether she was being followed. She walked rather fast for a person of her age. She stopped in front of a curious building, which seemed to be an ancient farmhouse, with an inner yard beyond the gate. It was a rustic house, and there were other buildings that were as low as stables.

When she crossed the paved yard, dogs barked in these buildings. Then she went up a short flight of steps, rang a bell, and waited for the door to open.

After she had disappeared inside, he went up to the gate and read on an enamel plaque:

DR PERRIN
VETERINARY CLINIC

She went there as one goes to see a patient in a hospital, and her visits indicated that the parrot was not dead.

He regretted what he had done, even after the poisoning of his cat. He would have liked to tell her so, but it was too late. Besides, he did not wish to give her the satisfaction of seeing him humiliating himself.

Did she too regret what she had done? No. She was not the kind of woman to have regrets. She was always right. She was sure of herself. She took the right course. It was enough to see her look of assurance when, particularly on Sunday, she returned from church. Her clothes then smelled of incense. One would have thought that her eyes were clearer and purer, as if she had just caught a glimpse of the beatitudes of heaven and of eternal life.

He hated Sunday, the quietness of it, the lowered blinds of the shops, the people one met in the streets where they had nothing to do. They did not walk the way they did on weekdays. They were not going anywhere, or, if they did have a goal, they were not in a hurry.

They were bored too in their Sunday clothes and were afraid that their children would get themselves dirty. When he was young, quarrels broke out almost every Sunday between his father and mother, who were decent people all the same, used to knuckling under and to taking life as it came.

'Go for a walk.'

He would go along the canal or along the Seine. They would give him a coin to buy ice cream in summer or sweets in winter, and he always chose hard sweets that lasted as long as possible.

Even on the barges, the families seemed frozen, and, towards the end of the afternoon, one was sure of meeting men who were drunk.

That Sunday he found his usual restaurant closed and had to go as far as the Avenue du Général Leclerc for lunch. Later, he went by Nelly's café, the blinds of which were lowered too.

What did Nelly do on Sunday? She certainly didn't attend mass. She probably stayed in bed late, loitered about her bedroom, in the kitchen, in the dark little café where nobody came to bother her.

In the afternoon, perhaps she went to a film. He had never seen her in the street. He knew her only in her black dress and her slippers.

Marguerite had not gone to the clinic, which was also closed on Sunday. She did not go out in the afternoon, and they remained sitting in the living room in front of the television set watching a soccer game, a few songs, a cartoon film. Finally a Western.

They were making time pass. She was knitting. Two or three times it seemed to him that her face was softening, that as she raised her head she was about to speak to him.

He pitied her a little. Since she was unable to make the first gesture, he was tempted to make it himself. He too opened his mouth, to say, for example:

'We're acting like children . . . '

No. She would not accept that definition of their attitude.

'Listen, Marguerite, let's try to forget.'

Nor that either. She was forgetting nothing. She remembered, with supporting dates, each disappointment, each offence since her childhood, each of her sorrows.

She needed to be unhappy, a victim of men's wickedness, and to forgive them with her lips.

'Poor woman . . . '

It was he who had been wrong. He ought not to have married her. What was it that had made him come back so many afternoons to the little house where she offered him a cup of coffee and, later, a glass of wine?

Was he not impressed by the fact that she was the owner of half of the street, the daughter of Sebastian Doise, a delicate creature, with a slightly faded elegance in her pastel-coloured clothes?

He had not thought of money. Not crudely. Money nevertheless did appear as a kind of background of that row of houses that belonged to Marguerite, and the little figure with the fish took on a symbolic quality.

Bouin had just entered, almost by accident, a world which he had glimpsed only from a distance and to which it had not occurred to him that he would ever be admitted.

Was he really admitted? He had stopped a simple leak. The woman had offered him a glass of cordial, as to a workman who has finished a job in the house.

'Why not come back tomorrow for a cup of coffee?'

In the kitchen. It was only after two weeks that she had taken him into the living room.

The photos had impressed him, particularly that of the carriage drawn by two horses, and also the one which showed her walking by the water in her big straw hat.

He remembered his childhood when he had seen an elegant woman lift her skirt to enter a carriage or when, in the Bois de Boulogne – he had been there only two or three times, for it was far from home – he admired the women on horseback.

'Did your father have horses?'

'He could have had them. He preferred to hire a carriage by the day. I took riding lessons in an academy.'

The horses in particular set him dreaming.

'Only in the academy?'

'We used to go riding in the Bois de Boulogne with the teacher.'

In the beginning, she liked to talk about her life, jumping from one period to another.

'Twice a week my husband took me to the opera in the evening. I had a reserved seat.'

She had kept the Liberty silk evening gown, embroidered with pearls, which she wore on those occasions and the white, elbow-length kid gloves.

'Don't come tomorrow. My tenants will be queuing up to pay the rent.'

What could the seven houses that she still owned bring in? He had no idea, but the thought of her receiving people who came to pay tribute to her in the overheated living room was glamorous to him.

She had no need to do housework. She had told him so.

'I'd be bored if I did nothing, and if I got bored I'd fall ill. I'd become like so many women of my age who think only of their little ailments.'

He protested with a gesture.

'Tut, tut! I know what I'm saying. I'm not forgetting my birth date. But I swore to myself never to complain. It's when one starts coddling oneself that one gets old.'

He and Angèle had also gone strolling on Sunday along the Marne, near Lagny. They would push each other for the fun of it and, when no one was around, they would take a roll in the tall grass. He remembered Angèle's smell, her laugh, for she often laughed when making love.

'Don't you think it's funny? I don't know who invented this business, but he deserves a statue.'

When they kissed on Sundays, their saliva had a taste of the countryside.

Marguerite was dreamy and distant in the photograph. She looked so vulnerable that he would have liked to protect her.

At bottom, it was to some extent the photographs that he had married, the baby grand piano that gleamed in the semi-darkness, the Louis Philippe and Second Empire furniture, the fountain in the alley, and the high chimney on the Rue de la Glacière.

He should have said no. He had been naïve and foolish enough not to understand, and he had made her unhappy.

'How about a film?'

For he had tried to take her out.

'What's on?'

'A Western.'

'I hate fighting and shooting.'

He would sometimes take her to a restaurant. She would look around suspiciously, would wipe the knife and fork, would sniff at the dishes before eating.

'It's cooked in margarine.'

Or: 'The waiter ought to wash his hands before serving.'

She lived in a world of her own, an invisible world that she coloured to suit her taste. And now she had to put up with a real man, a noisy man, with a heavy gait, who smoked foul cigars and emitted an animal smell.

To top it all, he had introduced into her carefully protected domain an animal that crept along the furniture the way a wild beast rubs itself against the bars of its cage and that stared at her but accepted familiarities only from its master, its god.

For Emile Bouin was a god to Joseph, and that annoyed her.

Bouin had sacrificed nothing for her, had not tried to integrate himself into her universe.

They had thus lived in their corner, each growing irritated with the other's gestures and intonations.

Had they not ended by taking a secret pleasure in their relationship? Children play at war. They were doing the same thing. But more passionately.

Each thought of the death of the other, each, in a more or less avowed way, wished for it, wished to be the survivor.

Marguerite had already got rid of her obvious enemy, of the cat whose mere presence was a defiance of the Doises and their sensitivity.

Why would she not get rid of her husband some day in the same way?

He had read in a paper that most acts of poisoning were committed by women. The article added that there were probably ten times as many cases as were discovered, for the family doctors, in the case of a sick or elderly person, signed the burial permits without investigating closely.

It was not yet fear, but he was beginning to be wary. He had another reason for not eating his wife's cooking. His decision to owe her nothing, to share in the household chores.

Since he had made his bed, split the wood, lit the fire, polished the floor, and took out the rubbish, why should he not also prepare his food, thus avoiding the necessity of going to the restaurant twice a day?

Just as he did not share Marguerite's bed, so he did not want to mix up his food with hers, and it did not displease him to surprise her and even enrage her.

On Monday afternoon, he went to a furniture store on the Boulevard Barbès.

'Don't you have one that locks?'

A cheap white lacquered pinewood kitchen cupboard with two doors.

'Locks can be put on for a slight additional cost.'

'Good locks,' he insisted. 'Not the kind that can be opened with a hairpin.'

The cupboard had been delivered on Thursday morning. That day, Marguerite had not gone out to visit the parrot, and she had cried part of the day. She was on edge, her eyes were red and her cheeks swollen.

She had watched with amazement as the huge yellow delivery lorry with its large black lettering manoeuvred before it was able to enter the alley.

She watched the delivery men who brought the cupboard into the kitchen and who asked:

'Where'll we put it?'

It was to her that they had put the question, and, without deigning to reply, she left the room.

'Here . . . To the right of the sink.'

'Don't you think it's too big?'

It just about fitted into the space that Emile had intended for it.

That day he went on a spending spree, came back with tinned goods, bottles of oil and vinegar, and all kinds of packages.

At noon, while his wife was upstairs, he had prepared his lunch, a huge steak, browned potatoes, peas.

When she came down, she found him at the table, and she in turn prepared her snack.

The kitchen looked out on a yard six feet wide, on a blank grey wall. As they avoided looking at each other while eating, that was the only view they had. The sounds of the alley, of the city, did not reach them, except occasionally the distant zooming of a plane high in the sky.

The construction work on the other side of the street had not begun. All they knew, from hearsay, was that certain tenants had been asked to leave. There was talk of building a school for nurses, others spoke of an office building, a modern garage, deluxe flats.

It was all the doing of the accursed Sallenaves, who had extorted half of the alley from a too-credulous Sebastian Doise. With the money from the land, they were going to enlarge the new biscuit factory in Ivry.

A month went by. Marguerite received a letter that upset her. She dressed hastily and left the house rapidly. As he was not yet dressed to go out, he could not follow her.

He waited. They spent as much time waiting for each other as spying on each other, for they felt ill at ease when they were alone in the house. The absences of one partner or the other were like a kind of menace, especially if they occurred at unusual hours.

Where had Marguerite gone?

Where did Bouin go more and more often at about four in the afternoon?

They sometimes followed each other without concealing themselves, looking innocent, as it were.

Marguerite's return that day was as unexpected an event as the intrusion of the furniture lorry in the alley. For the first time since he had known her, she came back in a taxi. The driver left his seat to help her remove the cage which they must have had difficulty getting into the car. Coco's cage, obviously.

He watched them from the living-room window. She insisted on carrying the cage herself, and she put it down carefully on the pavement, long enough to take out her key and open the door.

When she paid the fare, she uttered some words that Bouin

333

could not hear, picked up the cage, which was covered with its flannel cloth, and a few moments later, without looking at her husband, set up the object in its usual place.

He remained near the window without moving, surprised and uneasy. He saw her remove the flannel and look tenderly at the parrot, which was standing on its perch.

It had all its feathers, and the tail was more brilliant than ever. Its protuberant eyes were staring straight ahead, and Bouin felt uncomfortable as in the presence of an incongruous spectacle. He suspected something unnatural. The bird did not move. Neither did Marguerite. She was communing inwardly, as if in the presence of the corpse of a beloved person.

He finally discovered the truth. The animal was dead. It had been stuffed, its feathers had been replaced, and its eyes were made of glass.

After a while, Marguerite turned to him and looked at him sternly and defiantly.

Then she went to a small table on which were paper and a pencil. She wrote a few words, placed the sheet on the piano, and went to the hall to remove her hat and coat.

Emile read:

IF YOU TOUCH IT, I'LL NOTIFY THE POLICE.

She did not return to the living room immediately, leaving him time to digest the warning. When she went back and sat down in her chair, not far from the parrot, he was sitting too, on the other side of the fireplace.

He wrote something on the page of a notebook, folded the paper very small, put it between his thumb and middle finger, and shot it into his wife's lap.

This time he missed.

He was to become more skilful later. The message struck Marguerite's knee and fell on the floor. She pretended to have seen and felt nothing. They remained motionless for a long time, as if in a state of suspended animation. Several times she looked at the parrot.

Finally, she let fall her ball of wool and, in picking it up, took the piece of paper, which bore a message for the first time:

THE CAT.

They were even.

His memory was not so good as in the past. He remembered events very well, remembered having been in such a place when it was raining or sunny, comments exchanged with the local shop-keepers, the huge lobster he had bought to astound Marguerite, the first removal van in the alley two houses below.

He remembered the text of his notes, of those that his wife, pursing her lips contemptuously, had left for him on the piano or bedside table.

But his memory was not reliable in the case of dates, in the sequence of facts. He had a tendency to telescope happenings, whereas they might have taken place over a period of two years. In order to establish the time, he was obliged to refer to the seasons, to the clothes that he and Marguerite wore.

The first removal, for example, had taken place during the first half of March, a month of March that was particularly radiant, for the newspapers quoted statistics and published photographs of the chestnut trees in bloom.

When all the windows were open in the alley, the latter was less dismal, less silent. A quiver of life ran through it, voices could be heard from one house to the next, or a child playing in the streets and called by its mother, a gramophone record, a radio, and the background noises of cars on the Rue de la Santé and distant echoes from Carrefour Saint-Jacques.

Leaning at the window, he contemplated the furniture piled up in the removal van, thus discovering the tastes and a bit of the private life of people whom he had encountered only in the alley. He was surprised at the typewriter of a former officer, at a huge painting in a gilded frame representing a naval battle in the time of the buccaneers.

Marguerite also looked out from the second floor, but her window was closed, and she stood behind the curtain, without showing herself. She seemed to be suffering, she ate less than ever, and she began to show her age.

There were times when she did not put on make-up, whereas a discreet make-up had always given a certain freshness to her complexion. She seemed to have faded, grown grey, almost overnight.

335

She never entered the living room without first pausing for a moment in front of the parrot's cage, moving her lips as if in church.

Bouin could not get used to that silent presence. The dead parrot was more encumbering than the live one had been. In ceasing to move, it had taken on a mysterious and threatening expression, like that of certain African sculptures which he had seen in the window of a picture dealer.

There was no longer any need to cover the cage with the flannel cloth in the evening.

He hesitated to place the exact time of Madame Martin. Was it during the removals that had followed each other in the houses opposite? At that time, there were unusual comings and goings in the alley.

Men would arrive in cars, would move about with briefcases under their arms, would consult plans, would stop, gesticulate, and then leave.

They were the architects and contractors and their technicians. After a moment, Marguerite would shut the windows so as not to see them.

He hoped at times that she would give in, would change her attitude, would turn towards him with a human look, with gentler eyes, and speak to him.

To say anything. For example, simply:

'It's time for lunch.'

As elsewhere, in all houses, wherever human beings lived together.

He would have forgotten about the cat. Perhaps. Perhaps not for long. Especially as he had discovered other grievances.

At bottom, what he did not admit to himself was that he was afraid of her. She had more persistence than he, more energy, more self-mastery.

He would have been willing to go back to their old life, even if it meant quarrelling after three days and returning to communication by notes.

But not she. Her face and gaze were as rigid as the parrot's body.

He pitied her. That tension was bound to become painful, and he was afraid that she might crack up.

He would immediately reply to himself. 'Don't worry! A woman like that will never crack up. Not while you're alive. She wants your hide, and she knows that she'll finally get it. Until then, she'll hold out against everything.'

It was in the summer. About the month of August, for the butcher and the Italian grocer were on holiday, and they had to go some distance to find shops open. There were signs everywhere on the closed blinds of the shops, and they had to change laundries three times.

Bouin had got into the habit of following his wife when she did her shopping, although it was not yet a daily routine. On certain days he left the house first. On others, he went out later, at around eleven o'clock, in order to have an apéritif on the way back.

He drank more than before, always red wine. It made him sleepy after meals, and he did not mind that drowsiness which gave him dreams that were closer to reality than his dreams at night. A foggy reality, voices, and postures that were slightly distorted.

He would remain seated in his armchair, with his head a bit heavy and his eyes half closed. For a while he would continue to see the shiny feet of the piano, the lions' paws in their glass supports. The image would gradually become cloudy and would be replaced by a tree in the forest of Fontainebleau, and he would imagine that he was hearing the coarse, vulgar, but vivid voice of Angèle.

When they had brought her back from the hospital, after her accident, and he had bought her a chaise longue, for she could only take a few steps with crutches, he knew, as the doctor had told him, that she would remain crippled, but he was certain that she would live.

A year later, an ambulance took her to the hospital again, and for months he went to see her three times a week in a ward where other husbands sat like him and whispered at a bedside.

'Are you managing? It's not too bad?'

She acted gay.

'I have a good friend, the little redhead two beds away. Her name is Lili. She was a salesgirl . . .'

They gave her back to him six months later, without concealing the fact that her state was worse but that there was nothing more they could do for her. A local doctor looked after her. An old cleaning-woman, Madame Blanquet, spent most of the day with her and prepared her meals.

Her legs swelled up. Then her stomach became enormous. The kidneys were affected. She had uremia. She did not know it, and she would call out to him while he was washing her:

'Goodness me! You'd think I was pregnant.'

One evening, a Friday, May the seventeenth, he was in charge of a job near Porte de la Chapelle. Leo, the foreman, was an old friend.

'How about a drink?'

'My wife's waiting for me. You know she's laid up.'

'A quick one!'

He had not lingered more than five minutes. When he got home, Madame Blanquet got up precipitately from her chair. Her eyes were red, and she watched him closely, as if she were afraid of a violent reaction on his part.

'I didn't leave her for a moment, I swear to you.'

Angèle was dead. The old woman had closed her eyes. She seemed as enigmatic as Marguerite's parrot now did.

'When did it happen?'

'Half an hour ago.'

He had taken her hand, which was still soft, but had not been able to kiss her.

His mother had not even had a Madame Blanquet at her side when her time came. She was alone. He was already married. She had not been feeling well for some weeks, but continued to get up to look after the house.

He went to see her every evening, took her delicacies or fruits. He had found her on the kitchen floor, with her eyes open.

He would sometimes be afraid of coming home and finding Marguerite dead in one of the rooms.

There was no resemblance among the three women, between his mother and Angèle, between the two of them and Marguerite, and yet, in his somnolence, they had a tendency to merge. Especially their voices, the words, the phrases they uttered. Perhaps a certain questioning in their looks.

Who knows whether the common element was in him rather

than in them, a feeling of fear, as when he was a child and there was always something with which to reproach himself, an uneasiness, the sensation of being behind-hand, of not doing all that he should, of deserving to be scolded?

It didn't matter whether it was in June, July, or August. The period, in any case, when Marguerite was most edgy and could not sit still.

Two or three days went by without his following her when she went shopping. He felt a need for Nelly, He finally went to see her, and, as usual, he asked the silent question, received the signal, and followed her into the kitchen.

'You seem to have gone back to your old habits. Isn't your wife jealous?'

'We don't talk to each other.'

'You're not joking?'

'It's true.'

'Wait ... You're hurting me.'

A long silence. He was out of breath. Then she continued, letting down her dress without losing the thread of the conversation:

'You mean to say that you both live in the same house without talking to each other?'

'I swear.'

'And when you have something to say to each other?'

'We write notes.'

'For example: I feel like making love.'

'We've never made love.'

'Doesn't she appeal to you? Or doesn't she want to?'

'Both ... I don't know ...'

He had felt a need to talk, and he was already annoyed with himself, as if the fact of mentioning Marguerite to Nelly were a fault, a lack of delicacy.

He stood at the bar, with a glass of Sancerre in his hand when, as he turned to the sunny street, he saw his wife on the pavement in the company of a woman about ten years younger than she, whom he had already noticed with Marguerite. They were both walking slowly, as if to make the conversation last.

Was Marguerite likewise talking about him?

She was about to pass the café when she turned her head. She must have seen him, despite the semi-darkness inside. She saw everything, sensed everything, especially when it had to do with him, particularly when it had to do with something he wanted to hide from her.

'Is that her?'

'Yes.'

'Which of the two?'

'The older. The one in a pink dress.'

'Does she always dress like that?'

'She wears only light colours, a little faded.'

'She saw you.'

'I think so too.'

'Do you mind?'

'No.'

'I'm not so sure. You're not going to be afraid to go back?'

'Afraid of what?'

'Tomorrow?'

'Probably.'

'Here's to you.'

But the next day he did not go to see Nelly. Something had happened in the house at the end of the alley. At about four o'clock, someone had rung at the door, which was rare. Without hurrying, Marguerite, who seemed to be expecting someone, had gone to open the door.

'How are you, Madame Martin?'

She was very dark, vigorous, with a man's shoulders and the shadow of a moustache.

'Am I disturbing you?'

Marguerite knew that Emile was in the living room, in his shirt sleeves, reading a magazine. In spite of it she brought in the visitor. He made as if to get up and greet her. Madame Martin hesitated and almost put out her hand, but she was already interfered with.

'Sit down here, please. It's the most comfortable chair, the one my mother seemed to prefer. I hardly knew her! Will you have a cup of tea?... Not now?...'

Madame Martin looked at him curiously, and he was embarrassed. Nevertheless, to leave the room would be to lose ground, and he remained where he was, pretending to read.

'I have very few visitors, you know. I'm almost always alone. You're one of the rare people who visit me.'

She added, following Madame Martin's gaze, 'Don't pay any attention to him. I married him because I was sorry for him, I suppose. He was a widower. He seemed unhappy. He lived right across the street in one of the houses they're going to tear down. I used to see him spend his days at his window.

'One day I invited him over for a cup of coffee, and he made a rather good impression. I realize now that he was intimidated. Intimidated and a hypocrite. For I've never known anyone as hypocritical as that man. Maybe it's not his fault. I discovered, too late, that he's not quite like other men. When he spoke to me, he was rude, so I asked him to be silent.'

'Doesn't he speak to you any more?'

Just like Nelly a day earlier! Only Marguerite was being more cruel, more vicious than he had been on the Rue des Feuillantines.

'For several months . . .'

'Not a word?'

'Not a word . . . Sometimes he rolls up a note and tosses it to me, and I don't even read it.'

'Why?'

'Because I know in advance that it contains insults. The proof that he's not all there is that when his cat died, an old alley cat that he picked up somewhere or other, he accused me of having poisoned it. Me who had put up with its presence in the house and at night in our bedroom without saying a word . . . It slept on its master's bed and kept me from sleeping with its snoring.'

She looked at her husband severely, with a spark of triumph in her eyes. She had discovered a new way of taking revenge. The next day and the day after, Madame Martin would repeat the story in all the shops on the Rue Saint-Jacques, and the shopkeepers would look at him with mingled pity and disapproval.

'Do you know what he did the day after?'

'The day after what?'

'The death of the cat . . . You see my parrot . . .'

'Yes, it's a beautiful bird . . . Does it talk?'

'It's dead.'

'I was surprised that it didn't move for such a long time.'

'It was the most intelligent, most affectionate bird in the world.

That man was jealous of it. The parrot didn't like him. So, during a fit, I can't call it anything else, a real fit of blind rage, he tore the feathers out of its tail and to mock me put them into a vase.'

Madame Martin expressed her disapproval by shaking her head, and at the same time she observed Bouin out of the corner of her eye.

'He looks calm,' she muttered, as if to soothe him.

'He appears to be. I'd rather you didn't see him when he is angry. If he hadn't vented his rage on Coco, I'd probably have been his victim.'

'Aren't you afraid?'

'You know, at my age . . . '

She must have been rejoicing inwardly, and he suspected her of having rehearsed the scene for a long time. He did not want to leave. It would be like running away.

'Will you come to the kitchen with me? We'll go on chatting while I prepare the tea.'

Madame Martin had no desire to remain alone with the man who had just been described to her, and she hastened to follow Marguerite. He could hear the two women talking in low voices, and he wondered what else the old girl would be inventing.

If anything happened to his wife thereafter, the whole neighbourhood would consider him guilty. So fine, so gentle, so distinguished a person! A woman who had lived in the same house ever since she was born and whose first husband had been respected by everybody?

Where had she picked up that brute? It's true, isn't it, that one should stick to one's own class?

Actually, where did he come from? Did anyone know? Did anyone know his past?

The women returned. Marguerite was carrying the silver tray that was never used.

'Two lumps of sugar?'

'Please.'

'A small cake? These almond cakes . . . They're excellent.'

'Your father was a biscuit manufacturer, wasn't he? It seems to me . . . '

'You're right, Doise Biscuits. That's a whole story in itself. Another story that turned out badly. Almost for the same

342

reasons. He took on, because he was sorry for him, a man who didn't amount to much, someone named Sallenave . . . His wife was sick, his son refused to study, he himself was in poor health, in short, the old story. He gave him an important job. Then, when the son was old enough, he took him on too. You may not believe it, but fifteen years later it was my father who found himself at the door of his own business. And half of the alley that they're going to demolish passed into the hands of the Sallenaves. They sold the land. The houses are going to be torn down. A block of flats of I don't know how many storeys is going to be put up, and we'll never again see the sun. I'll be lucky if they don't set up a garage and a service station right in front of my windows. As for me, I've refused offers. If I had given in, the alley that bears my father's name would disappear. Have another cake.'

While Marguerite went on in this feverish vein, Madame Martin kept glancing now at Emile and now at the parrot.

She sensed that there was something abnormal in the atmosphere of the house.

From time to time, she also looked at Marguerite, the way women sometimes look at each other.

Did she perhaps wonder which of the two was not quite right in the head? Perhaps both of them?

Chapter Six

He held out for four days, four chaotic days, with the feeling that they were going to win out. It was a conspiracy against his nerves.

Never, in all the years that he had lived in the house, had Marguerite brought in so vulgar a woman as Madame Martin. He now saw her as a veritable local witch. She had dark eyes, and her lips and cheekbones were reddened by excessive make-up. She wore a dark dress beneath which the structure of a corset could be discerned.

She would arrive at the stroke of four, as she did the first day. He would first hear her steps in the alley. Then she would pass in front of the first window, disappear for a moment and loom up behind the second.

The next moment, the doorbell would ring. He did not move. He refused to give up any territory to them. He realized that if he yielded an inch, he would gradually lose all his living space.

The invention was diabolical, and he had only to look at Marguerite to be sure that she was pleased with it.

She would go to open the door.

'How nice of you to have come.'

'I'm so delighted to chat with you! It's not every day that one meets a woman of your quality. It's so warm today! It's cool in your house. In my flat, it's stifling, and I have to put up with the neighbours' radio all day long. If only they had taste. But no! All they listen to is silly songs.'

'Come in, my dear. Tea's ready.'

A glance at Bouin, who was always in his chair in shirt-sleeves. He stayed there. He had the right to be there, just as he pleased. It wasn't he who was being visited. They ignored him. Or rather they treated him neither more nor less than like a household animal, like the stuffed parrot in its cage.

'I hope you had a good night?'

'You know, at my age one doesn't need sleep. No sooner do you get into bed than all your troubles rise up.'

The witch looked at Emile.

'Have you had any new difficulties?'

'It's always the same thing. I've got used to it. If my nerves weren't solid, I'd have been dead or in an asylum long ago.'

He hated both of them. For he finally dared to admit to himself that he hated his wife. She had brought in outside help. The fight was no longer equal. Who knows if she would not pick up other Madame Martins in the streets and surround herself with a herd of shrews?

He was drinking too much. It was no longer to obtain a moment of pleasant somnolence. He needed a glass or two of wine every hour to give himself courage.

His wife was on the watch. Although he kept the bottles under lock and key in the cupboard, she saw how many he brought back in the morning and she was aware of the reason for his increasingly frequent visits to the kitchen.

Who knows if she did not speak of his drunkenness to anyone who was willing to listen? Madame Martin would serve as a witness. Not having been able to obtain his death and not daring to cause it more directly, perhaps Marguerite was having his funeral in mind?

He was scared. Even when they did not talk about him, he remained in the background of their conversations, which were punctuated with eloquent sighs and looks.

'One can't say, my dear lady, that you've been spoiled by life, and God knows you'd have merited a better one.'

'I've never complained. If that's God's will . . . '

'Luckily you have your religion. I always say that when one has religion . . . '

'I pity the people who don't believe in anything.'

Her eyes would fix Emile Bouin.

'Don't they lower themselves to the level of animals?'

'That's not quite the same. Animals have no choice.'

The tea. The silver tray. The little cakes. Once he went to the kitchen to get a bottle of red wine and a glass and began to drink in front of them.

That was a mistake. He mustn't do it again. His instinct warned him that no good would come of it.

He had got into the habit of going for a drink several times a day at a little bar and grill opposite the prison. The restaurant served meals to well-to-do inmates.

The boss would give such orders as:

'Two pork chops for the Jerk ... With a lot of potatoes and salad.'

'Chicken in wine sauce for the Notary.'

Almost all the prisoners had a nickname. Nobody was surprised that they lived behind bars, between four walls.

'Did they keep My Eye in the infirmary?'

'He got out yesterday. The doctor discovered that he's no more ill than I am.'

He would drink his glass of wine at the bar. They did not yet know him, and they were observing him.

'You're not from the neighbourhood, are you?'

'I am.'

'Your face looks familiar to me.'

'I live on Square Sebastian-Doise.'

He felt the need to justify his presence, as if he were taking an entrance examination. Unlike at Nelly's place, here there was a continual flow of customers, with some rather strange people among them, who spoke in low voices in the corners, called the proprietor, whispered in his ear.

'You're not the husband of the old crackpot?'

He nodded, as if the allusion could not be to anyone but Marguerite.

'Why didn't she sell?'

'Sell what?'

'Her house, of course. There was talk of demolishing the alley to put up a new building. They offered her a fortune, and they had to change all their plans because of her stubbornness.'

He returned to Nelly's place too but did not suggest that they go to the kitchen. She realized at once that he was depressed.

'Something wrong?'

'They're doing all they can to get me down ... That Madame Martin is a ... a ...'

'A rather dark, husky woman with heavy make-up?'

346

'Yes ....'

'The one who was with your wife the other day? Two years ago, she was still telling fortunes. I don't know what happened, but the police went after her. She no longer does anything. It seems that she has money put aside.'

'I can't stand them any more.'

'Why do you stay with them?'

'Because if I left the room, they'd consider it a victory.'

'You're a funny fellow. There are times when I'd swear it amuses you ... Are you sure you wouldn't miss your wife?'

'I hate her.'

'All right, drink your wine, and try to think about something else, trees, the little birdies.'

'I'm serious.'

'So am I.'

There was even the smell. Madame Martin drenched herself with cheap scent that permeated the living room. Marguerite, who could not bear perfumes, said nothing, which revealed a kind of connivance between them.

He sometimes still followed his wife when she went shopping. She was no longer content with seeing Madame Martin in the afternoon but met her, as if by accident, at the Italian grocery or at the butcher's shop, where they queued together.

On the morning of the fifth day, he had had enough, and when he entered Nelly's café she realized that he had not come only to drink a glass or two or to spend a moment in the kitchen.

'You look really done in ... What have they been up to now?'

'I've got to talk to you.'

He was embarrassed and dared not go into detail.

'After all, a man does have his dignity, you realize ....'

She laughed to herself. She knew men better than he and knew from experience that when they talk about their dignity it means that things are bad.

'Let me have a drink.'

'Is that your fourth glass?'

'You too?'

'Why do you say that?'

'Because my wife keeps account of what I drink. She watches my every movement. It's worse than if I were still a child crawling on all fours. When I come home, she manages to pass near me so that she can smell my breath. The bathroom is the only place where I can lock myself in.'

'Poor Emile!'

She took nothing tragically. For her, marital troubles were all alike.

'Well . . . You were talking about your dignity.'

'How many rooms do you have upstairs?'

She frowned, for she was not expecting that.

'Two. Why?'

He felt ashamed and continued in a low voice:

'I'm an old fellow, I know. I'm not suggesting that I live with you as . . . '

'As two lovers, I know! In the first place, my boy, I've never been able to sleep with a man. It's a matter of contact, of smell. Making love on the sly, that's all right. But to sweat side by side, to bang against an arm or a leg when I'm not expecting it, no! I tried, in the beginning, with Théo. He was my husband. Because of the business, we got married. Well, after a few days, I asked him to go buy a bed. He slept in the back room. Yet we were fond of each other.'

'Did he know you deceived him?'

'What do you mean?'

'Nothing, I beg your pardon. What I'd like is to become a kind of boarder. I'd pay. Name the figure. I wouldn't bother you. I'm not troublesome.'

'Would I have to prepare your meals?'

'Perhaps . . . I'd prefer that. But I'd eat out if I had to.'

'For how long?'

'I don't know. Perhaps always.'

'Does your old lady bother you as much as that?'

She was thinking.

'How much would you be willing to pay?'

'I don't care. I receive a good pension from the city. I have savings . . . '

'You won't be hanging around the café all day? The customers don't like that, you realize.'

'I know. I'll do whatever you like.'

'And what if friends come?'

He looked at the door of the kitchen.

'That's your business.'

'You won't get jealous?'

'Why should I get jealous?'

'What you've just said isn't very nice.

'That's true.'

'Give me time to think it over.'

'How much time?'

'Let's say until you come in tomorrow morning.'

'Couldn't it be today?'

'Is it as bad as that?'

He did not answer, but he seemed exhausted, and he looked at her entreatingly.

'All right! Come back in half an hour.'

'How much do I owe you?'

'Might as well start an account right away.'

The same as for the regulars, whose drinks she recorded in a notebook.

'When do you get up?'

'At six o'clock. I can get up at any time. I can take in the dustbins, open the blinds, sweep the café. I'm used to that.'

'Go for a little walk.'

He obeyed. He did not remember ever having been so anxious. In his eyes, it was the only possible salvation. At Nelly's place, he would stop thinking about Marguerite and Madame Martin and the threats that hung over him in the house in the alley.

Nelly understood him. She understood everyone. She had no prejudices and saw only the good side of people and events.

The rooms were on the mezzanine and the curved windows could be seen from the pavement opposite. The ceiling must be low and probably one could hear all the sounds in the café and the kitchen.

Wasn't it an ideal refuge? He might almost think that he was with Angèle. Nobody would spy on him. He would go out whenever he felt like it without looking back to see whether he was being followed.

The two harpies would no longer be able to run him down in his presence or watch his reactions so as to be able to use them against him.

He walked around the block, first in one direction, then in the other, frequently consulting his watch, and finally he entered the dark, cool café.

There was a customer at the bar, a workman whose smock was spattered with plaster. His face was covered with plaster too, especially eyebrows and lashes, which made him look like a pierrot.

He was afraid to disturb them. It was not the moment to irritate Nelly. He paused and was about to leave again, but she indicated to him that it was not a customer for the kitchen.

'What'll you have?'

'A small white wine, as usual.'

'A small one or a big one?'

'A big one.'

A trick, in short. He was seventy-one years old and did not have to account to anyone. Why had he said a small one when he knew that she would serve him a big one?

'We still have a week's work in the neighbourhood,' continued the man. 'It's not unpleasant. There are three of us, and we get on well. Can I have a bottle to take to the others?'

'The same?'

She went to draw the wine in the cellar, opened the trap door, and gradually disappeared.

Théo had had a fine life, even if it had ended badly, for he had died young, at the age of sixty-two or three.

'Thanks.'

The plasterer could not help letting his eyes rest on the rounded bosom. If he worked another week in the area, he would probably take advantage of her like the others. He was fair-haired, not more than thirty, and had laughing eyes.

'Well?'

'Let's give it a try.'

'When can I come?'

'Whenever you like. I just have to remake the bed. No one has slept in it since Théo died.'

He did not ask about the price.

'I'll bring my suitcase right away, after lunch.'

'You're not going to move all your things, I hope.'

He was so relieved that he felt like whistling in the street. It was a deliverance, and he wondered how he had not thought of Nelly earlier.

When he entered the house, his eyes were sparkling with mischief. Marguerite was going to have the surprise of her life. Her victim was escaping her. She would find herself alone, without anyone to spy on, and he tried to imagine the conversation that the two women would have that afternoon when they drank their tea.

'Did he take everything?' that snake of a Madame Martin would ask.

'No. Only a big suitcase.'

'Perhaps he went on a journey? Someone ill or dead out of town? . . .'

'He has no family left. He never gets letters, only circulars.'

'How did he look?'

'As if he were mocking me.'

'I'm sure he'll be back.'

'Do you think so?'

'Didn't you follow him?'

She must have blushed, for she had actually followed him. But he had played a good trick on her, thus proving that he had regained his equilibrium.

The suitcase was heavy. He had lugged it to Place Saint-Jacques, where there were always two or three taxis.

Marguerite did not hide herself. She walked about ten yards behind him; when he turned around, he could see the distraught look on her face.

'You'll see, old girl.'

In her haste, she had neglected to take her handbag. She was therefore without money. He had stepped into the first taxi, and had called out to the driver:

'Gare de l'Est.'

The station from which he had left for the front in 1914.

She stood there at the edge of the pavement not trusting her eyes. After a few minutes, he leaned forward and said. 'Drive around for a little while, anywhere. Then I'll tell you where to go.'

'What about the Gare de l'Est.'

'I've changed my mind.'

'You're the one who's paying.'

Finally he murmured, calculating that Marguerite had had time to return home:

'At the corner of Rue des Feuillantines.'

'What corner?'

'Whichever you please.'

A hot sun was shining. Paris smelled good. It was years since he had smelled the odours of the city as he was smelling them now.

He had played a good practical joke. She would at last realize that he was not a household pet that one buys and domesticates.

She was in the process of eating, alone at the table, alone in the kitchen, alone in the house, posing as someone who isn't hungry, who never has an appetite.

A pure spirit floating above vulgar contingencies!

'Already? You said . . .'

Nelly was eating, alone too, but with a hearty appetite.

'I'll drop off my suitcase and leave. I didn't have the patience to wait and have lunch again in her presence. I'll go to the restaurant.'

She hesitated to propose that he share her meal, which was appetizing, Toulouse sausages cooked in red cabbage. They were plump and juicy and smelled agreeably of garlic.

She preferred not to create a precedent. She was a practical woman with both feet planted firmly on the ground. She knew men. If she got along with them, it was because she did not ask them for more than they could give.

'Have a pleasant meal.'

'You too.'

He smiled at her gratefully and went off feeling rejuvenated.

Throughout his life, often without realizing it, he had made for himself a series of habits, a more or less rigorous schedule.

It would last for weeks, months, or years and would then give way, for no apparent reason, to a different rhythm, other rules, other schedules.

There had been the life in his parents' home, first as a young man, then in the early days of his marriage with Angèle. It had not always been easy, for his mother found her daughter-in-law's presence a burden. As for his father, he was prudent or resigned and avoided interfering.

His mother, in particular, was strict about mealtimes, and when she was cooking she did not want anyone under her feet.

'Go for a walk. I don't want you getting in my way.'

Consequently, they spent a great deal of time out of doors. They would walk. They knew the quays from Charenton to the Pont Neuf, and they would sometimes stroll along them late at night.

When they rented their flat, above a café, they often ate in the restaurant, either because Angèle had got up too late or because they wanted a special dish. They enjoyed discovering pleasant, inexpensive little places where the customers' napkins were kept in individual pigeonholes.

There had been a time when they frequented the Mélanie, near the Wine Market; then the Père Charles, Rue Saint-Louis-en-l'Ile, and others. Each had its very own smell and colours.

It had been the same on Sundays. One spring he bought a motorcycle on which they drove to the forest of Fontainebleau, but after barely avoiding an accident, Angèle had been frightened and he had sold the machine.

For two years they had regularly taken the train to Lagny, and they knew all the pleasant places in the area. They had danced in the country cabarets. He had taken up fishing, and his wife had tried to emulate him.

Then there had been the hospital, where he would arrive ahead of visiting hours. He would sit on the same bench and read the evening paper which he had just bought, grumbling when the bell announced the time for visits before he had read the headlines.

His solitary life in the alley as a widower, the novels he had devoured near the window, the screams of the baby downstairs, the games of cards in the afternoons at the Denfert-Rochereau café . . .

Marguerite . . .

And now he was once again in a new world into which he was trying to integrate himself.

Nelly's room looked out on the street, but his did not. From his window he could see only another window, which was so dirty that it was not possible to guess what there was behind it.

Somewhere, in an invisible workshop, a hammer kept striking metal in a slow, regular rhythm.

He did not complain. He was happy to have escaped the atmosphere of the alley.

'What do you do with your days?'

'I walk, I read . . . '

'If you can't see well enough in your room, you can sit in mine, near the window, providing you don't smoke your awful cigars.'

He did not resent her saying that, as he had resented Marguerite's attitude.

'I'd like to lend you a hand.'

'We'll see about it.'

He could guess from the look on her face that she was none too pleased about having accepted his presence.

'You're an odd fellow.'

He had bought secondhand books, five or six, quite a stock. For the first time, he had returned to the café on Place Denfert-Rochereau. The proprietor had recognized him.

'Welcome back! Have you been ill?'

He looked at him with solicitude, as if Bouin were not looking well. It was true that he had lost a great deal of weight.

It was particularly obvious at the neck. His shirt collars yawned and revealed a prominent Adam's apple with skin sagging on both sides.

He looked towards the table near the window where his friends had been in the habit of playing cards.

'Are you looking for the old-timers? Big Désiré died a year ago. The Colonel, as they called him, though he had only been a sergeant . . . '

'What was the matter with him?'

'It happened in the street . . . The stout little fellow . . . Wait. His name is on the tip of my tongue . . . Loireau? . . . Voiron? . . . . The one who had the stationery shop at Porte d'Orléans . . . It doesn't matter . . . He went back to his village in Dordogne . . . I don't know what's become of the others. They come and go . . . What'll you have?'

'A red Bordeaux.'

'Joseph! A red Bordeaux. And you? Everything all right with you?'

'I'm not complaining.'

'Your wife died, didn't she? As the result of an accident? . . . You see, I remember my customers. Sometimes the name escapes me, but I remember the faces. Do you still live in the neighbourhood?'

'Near Place Saint-Jacques.'

'It's not you who . . . I remember! . . . You married the owner of a whole alley.'

'Only a row of houses,' he corrected.

'All the same, that's quite a pile. They're building a new block of flats opposite, isn't that right?'

'Not yet. The work hasn't begun. Certain tenants aren't moving out until next month.'

'Would you like some partners for a game?'

'Not particularly.'

He did not know the players who had taken the place of those of the old days. They were younger.

'They're bridge players. They stay until eight o'clock . . . The belote players arrive about four.'

He returned to the Rue des Feuillantines by a long detour in order to go through Montsouris Park. He almost went by the Rue de la Santé to catch a glimpse of the house at the end of the alley, but it was a ridiculous idea and he gave it up.

He entered by the tenants' hallway, opened the door of the kitchen a crack, and called out, 'I'm going up.'

He was being discreet. He had hardly arrived and was afraid that Nelly might tire of his presence. It was better to live on tiptoe. He read, went out for a moment to smoke a cigar, went back, and watched people go by in the street.

He liked the smell in Nelly's room, a rather strong smell, that reminded him of the brief moments with her in the kitchen.

At about seven, he went down again to have supper. She was behind the bar, facing half a dozen customers. He read his newspaper while he was eating, imagined Marguerite all alone in her kitchen, unless she had invited Madame Martin.

It would have amused him to hide in a corner when Madame Martin arrived in the afternoon at the stroke of four.

Marguerite must have sighed: 'Good riddance!'

'It's a shame after all you've done for him. When I think that you picked him up the way one picks up a cat in the street . . . '

If Madame Martin had said that, she had made a blunder, for it was preferable not to mention cats in the house. Perhaps she had spoken of a dog.

'Aren't you a little afraid, in his state of mind . . . '

'Afraid of what?'

'I don't know . . . A man who's not all there . . . '

Had his wife heard when he had told the driver to take him to the Gare de l'Est? If so, she would wonder where he might be going. He knew nobody east of Paris, neither in the suburbs nor in the more distant towns. It was only because of the First World War that he had taken a train at that station. Later, with Angèle, he had never gone any farther than Lagny. When he got back, Nelly was eating at one end of the table.

'Did you have a good supper?'

'A steak and fried potatoes.'

'I love fried potatoes, but I never make them because they smell up the place and the customers don't like that. I sometimes go out and eat them on Sunday, when I make up my mind to leave the house.'

'What do you do the other times?'

'I sleep, I listen to the radio, I read, not much, because I don't care much for books. The stories are always the same, and there's almost nothing true about them.'

'When do you close?'

'When I feel like going to bed. Hardly anyone comes in the evening. A customer from time to time. For a quick drink.'

'I'll be going.'

'Why?'

'I'm afraid of disturbing you . . . I promised you I wouldn't.'

'Actually you're shy. I'd never have thought it. You didn't go prowling around the Rue de la Santé by any chance?'

'What on earth for?'

'I don't know. Maybe to get a glimpse of your wife, to see how she took the shock. You want me to tell you something? You both need each other as much as two newly-weds. Don't say no. You'll see. You'll be back with her in two weeks.'

'I'd rather . . . I don't know what . . . Anything . . . '

'All right, then I'm wrong. You know what? While I do my

356

dishes, you can put out the dustbins. You'll find them in the yard at the end of the hall. The ones with a red circle. Each tenant has his colour or initials, otherwise we'd get mixed up and drag around some other person's rubbish.'

She read the newspaper. She was interrupted twice by customers, and both times he left in the event that she needed the kitchen.

'Look here, stop going in and out like the weatherman in a Swiss barometer. What do you think? That I offer my arse as a tribute to all my customers? All right! You're not the only one, and there'll be others. But since I do it to please myself, I have the right to choose.'

They went upstairs at about ten o'clock. It was he who had closed the blinds.

'Do you go to bed early too?'

'Yes, unless there's an interesting programme on television.'

'I don't have television. It's expensive.'

He promised himself that he would buy her a set the next day. It would be pleasant to watch the programmes in the evening at her side.

Without realizing it, he was already building up a little world rather similar to the one which he had just fled.

'I don't have a bath, only a shower. That door over there. The water's not heated in summer. It's true that you don't need hot water . . .'

She was taking off her dress. The door between the rooms was open. He removed his jacket and took off his tie and waited hesitantly before undressing further.

'What did you do this afternoon?'

'I had a drink at Denfert-Rochereau. A café where I used to play cards almost every day. The old timers have gone . . . I don't know the newcomers.'

'And then?'

'I went to Montsouris Park and sat on a bench.'

'Watching the children play?'

She was poking fun at him.

'Or throwing crumbs to the little birds?'

'Why do you laugh at me?'

'For no reason . . . Life's funny . . . Don't you think it's funny?

357

Look, here you are, good as gold, so I don't shut the door before I'm all undressed. You know my arse, but you've never seen me naked. Confess?'

'Yes . . . I often thought about it at night.'

'While trying to fall asleep in your own wife's room! All right, if you feel like it, we'll inaugurate your stay by making love. Not on my bed or in my room . . . In yours . . . '

When she was naked, she put away her clothes, moving about without embarrassment.

'Well?'

'All right . . . ' he murmured.

'Are you staying like that?'

He was still wearing his shirt and trousers.

'I'd rather . . . '

He did not dare undress any further. His face might possibly give a different impression, but his skinny body was that of an old man, and he was afraid of a pitying or mocking look.

'Do you want me to lie down or what?'

In spite of the presence of the bed, they ended by doing just as they did behind the door.

'All right! Now I'm going to shut myself in and sleep. Good night.'

She mockingly kissed him on the forehead, and retired to her room where he heard her get into bed.

The following day was much the same, with the difference that in the evening the television set was already installed in the kitchen. When the set was delivered, Nelly's way of thanking him was to say:

'You're not so dumb.'

'Why?'

'Oh, no reason . . . That'll give us something to do in the evening. Did you and your old lady watch television?'

'Yes.'

'And with the other one?'

'We didn't have it then.'

On Sunday morning, she stayed in bed until eleven o'clock, and when she opened the door she was still half asleep.

'Haven't you gone out?'

'I was waiting for you to get up. I want to invite you to lunch in a good restaurant, wherever you like, in Paris or out in the country.'

'Are you as rich as that?'

'It would give me pleasure. You'll be able to eat fried potatoes.'

'How about Saint-Cloud? There used to be a kind of place where you could dance, with real arbours. I went there with Théo. I wonder whether it's still there.'

They took the Métro. It was the first time he had ever seen her out of doors. She was wearing a cotton dress and white shoes. They looked for the dance hall along the Seine and finally found it, and they had to wait almost an hour in order to get a table.

'Do you know how old I was the first time I came here?'

'Twenty?'

'Eighteen . . . I was still a whore on the Boulevard Sébastopol. Théo picked me up as he would have picked up any other girl. There were three of us girls at the same street corner, and in the darkness he chose at random . . . When it was over, he didn't leave right away. He started asking me questions. I didn't like that . . . There are loads of fellows who pay a girl just so she'll tell them her life story, and other who weep over their owns troubles . . . He came back, invited me to lunch, and brought me here, I'll have you know, in a taxi! . . . I had no idea that I'd be married to him three months later. Isn't that a riot? And now here I am in the same place with you, who . . . '

She did not continue. He would have liked to know what she had been about to say, but he dared not insist.

When they got back, after walking along the Seine and looking at the barges, she said, 'All right, you can eat with me here this time . . . On Sunday evening I make do with ham and cheese.'

They watched television. She did not understand the serial because she had not seen the earlier episodes, and he told her what it was about. They did not go upstairs until eleven o'clock and separated immediately.

'I'm in a hurry to get into bed. I bet I'm sunburned. I so rarely go out.'

He had surprised her on Monday morning by sweeping the tiles, tidying up the kitchen, and preparing coffee before she came down. He was behaving somewhat like a dog that has

359

found a new master and tries to please him. He, too, was afraid of being kicked out into the street, and he suspected that Nelly's infatuations did not always last long.

She put up with him, found the situation amusing. How long would it last? He made himself inconspicuous, rendered little services, and hastened to disappear when he was no longer needed.

He returned to Montsouris Park, where he did watch the children play. He had not had children himself. As for his friends, or rather his cronies, he would meet them in the café, rarely at home, or else it was in the evening and the children were in bed.

He observed them with amazement, as if he were discovering youth after the age of seventy. What surprised him most was the tough speech they used in front of their indifferent mothers.

Had it been like this when he was young? At the age of thirteen, he would not have dared tell his mother that he had learned from fellow pupils how babies were born.

'Sit up straight ... Don't put your finger into your nose ... Eat properly ... Where did you pick up all that mud? ... Wipe your feet ...

If he had had children, they would be married by now, would have children of their own.

Would Bouin be happier if he had had them? Was he unhappy? Had he ever been really unhappy in his life?

Square Sebastian-Doise? Obviously. There had been that period. He had fretted and fumed, especially since the matter of the cat. His wife hated him. He hated her too. One day when she had constantly been putting her hand to her chest as if her heart were going to stop beating, he had written a note to her:

YOU CAN DROP DEAD.

Did he really mean that? In any case, it was a reaction to her nastiness. She found subtler things to say to him and diabolically managed to put him in the wrong.

It was established once and for all that he was a monster and she an innocent victim.

What was the use of thinking about it now? He had escaped

from her. He was free. He liked the little café with the red tiles, the kitchen that smelled good, the two rooms, the place that was already his during the day, near the curved window.

It was pleasant to see Nelly open her door in the morning, heavy with sleep, in her creased nightgown and, in the evening, leave the door open while she undressed.

'Will you sell me a bottle of red Bordeaux? I sometimes feel like having a drink upstairs and I don't want to disturb you.'

'Corked wine at a franc a glass?'

'Right.'

'I'll get it from the cellar a little later.'

There! Life was getting organized. He had found a new spot for himself.

Chapter Seven

It lasted a little more than a week, exactly ten days, including two Sundays, the one when they went to Saint-Cloud and the Sunday of the storm which they had spent idling on the ground and upstairs, finally ending up, bored and sullen, in front of the television set.

Later, he probably would have had difficulty in admitting that his life with Nelly had been so short, for, in his mind, Nelly was to join the women with women he had lived for a long time, his mother, Angéle, Marguerite.

She would end up by merging with the others.

It was hard to explain. He remembered words, gestures, phrases, particularly looks, and even more his reaction to those looks, but he did not know whether it was an unconscious memory of one or the other of the lives that he had led.

One morning, at about ten o'clock, he was reading the paper near the sickle-shaped window.

He read more papers than in the past because he lacked the courage to start a long novel. One had to read a certain number of pages to familiarize oneself with the characters and their names, and he was often obliged to turn back.

There were more slack hours than in the alley, for he made a point of not disturbing Nelly when customers might drop in. He went for long walks. That was not enough to fill his days. He continued sitting on a bench in Montsouris Park, and he had lunch and dinner out except on the two occasions when he had been asked to stay.

That morning, he raised his eyes and saw her on the opposite pavement. It was Marguerite. She was standing there motionless, with her shopping bag in her hand, and looked at him with a pained expression that was new to him.

He was so struck that he almost spoke, as if there were no

distance between them. The window was open. If he had raised his voice, she would have heard him.

He had not imagined her like that. Her stiffness and assurance had disappeared. She was no longer the former Mademoiselle Doise, but a worn-out, tired, anxious, and perhaps sick woman.

She had hastily put on an old dress that did not become her. And she had aged.

Was he mistaken, or were Marguerite's lips actually moving as if in prayer?

He was disturbed and embarrassed and tried not to stand up, not to move. He tried to look away. People passed on the narrow pavement and grazed and pushed her as they went by. She watched, fascinated, and did not move.

Then, slowly and regretfully, she trudged to the corner of the Rue Saint-Antoine.

He had remained in his chair a good quarter of an hour without reading his paper. He had gone down. Nelly was at the bar serving the locksmith from the end of the street.

'A glass of white wine.'

She observed him with curiosity, served him with a mechanical gesture, and continued what she was saying:

' ... if there's been one, there'll be others ... The weather is murky, and it'll be a few days before it clears up ... '

He finally gathered that she was talking about the storms. There had been one the night before, the third in four days.

'All I want,' grumbled the locksmith, 'is nice weather on Sunday. I promised the kids I'd take them to the country, and ...'

He went off, wiping his mouth. Nelly and Bouin looked at each other.

'Well?' she asked.

'Well what?'

'Don't tell me you haven't seen her?'

'I did.'

'What did it do to you?'

'Nothing ... Why?'

She too pretended that she could read his thoughts. He resented it. It annoyed him to discover that she was like the others.

He had not come downstairs in order to confess. He did not

363

know why he had come down. Certainly not to hide behind his mother's skirts.

He almost murmured:

'She's aged a lot.'

He said nothing, for she would deduce that he felt pity. For the first time, he was not at ease in Nelly's presence, and he began to have doubts about her.

'Where are you going?'

'For a walk.'

Not to join Marguerite. He went in the opposite direction. He tried not to think about her.

It was an unpleasant day. He spent more time at the window than on the other days. All the same, he went to Montsouris Park, where he remained on his bench only a few minutes.

He was expecting it. The next day, at the same time, he saw her in the same place, in almost exactly the same pose. Her eyes were raised, and there was something pathetic about that frail little old woman who made him think of those one sees in churches addressing their prayers to the statue of the Virgin.

This time, Nelly did not refer to her, but she was not as much at ease with him as she had been. She seemed to be thinking:

'My boy, you're in a bad way.'

It was true. He was upset. He had thought that he had freed himself, and he was beginning to discover that it was only an illusion.

She returned a third time, a fourth. She looked heart-rendingly frail, as if she were about to drop on the pavement with exhaustion. One afternoon, in the street, he turned around mechanically and saw that she was following a hundred feet behind him.

It was the hour for Montsouris Park. He did not chance either his habits or his itinerary. He stepped out briskly as always. He heard hurried little footsteps behind him, and after a while he slowed down because she must have been winded.

She was visibly suffering. She missed him. She had lost her equilibrium in the empty house, and her presence behind him was an admission, a prayer.

He tried hard not to be moved. He sat down on his bench while she remained standing at the corner of a walk.

'Did you go there?'

Nelly questioned him when he got back. How could she have guessed that Marguerite had followed him, that he had been tempted to . . .

'No.'

'You know, Emile, you mustn't worry about me . . . I'll understand . . .'

He resented her saying that. He had always hated being judged, and it annoyed him even more when people foresaw what he was going to do while he himself did not know and was debating inwardly.

He did not want to return to the alley. He was happy here. He had his little ways and habits.

But he no longer had the feeling of release he had had the first few days.

He had almost succeeded in forgetting about Marguerite. And now she was imposing herself upon him, timidly, with a humility he would never have suspected of her.

Had Madame Martin advised her to act this way? Did the two women still see each other every afternoon in order to talk about him?

He asked himself questions, these and many others, to the detriment of his peace of mind.

'Are you going out?'

'I need air. It's been a stifling day.'

That evening, at nightfall, he headed almost directly, with a detour that was just sufficient to make him seem to hesitate, for the Rue de la Santé, and he passed in front of the alley, saw the lamp post, and heard the jet of water. He was unable to tell from a distance whether or not there was a light in one of the windows of the last house.

Nelly did not ask him anything. When he got back, she was in bed. He shut the door of his room, mumbling in a very low voice, in case she had fallen asleep:

'Good night.'

'Good night.'

It was a bad night. He got up at least five times, gave himself the excuse of having to urinate, and fell asleep again each time with difficulty. He got involved in labyrinthine dreams which he was unable to remember when he awoke. All he knew was that he thrashed about. He was resisting something. He was unable to tell what it was that he was resisting so fiercely, but he was overwhelmed at the fact that everyone was against him and that he stood alone.

At six o'clock he got up, worn out, swept away the sawdust, washed the kitchen floor, and took in the dustbins. He drank red wine from a bottle, and when Nelly came down in slippers and practically naked under her black dress, he found nothing to say to her.

She came, as he expected, she stood exactly in the same spot, in the same pose, and turned the same questioning look upon him, the memory of which he was unable to shake off.

Her eyes were pale blue, but when she was upset the blue turned a dirty grey, and her face lost all its luminosity and became a sickly ivory.

She looked as if she were extinguished, as if she were no longer struggling.

He refused again to let himself be influenced, but he was not quite successful. He was not hungry at lunchtime and left half of his meal on his plate, though he had chosen his favourite restaurant and ordered a veal dish of which he was particularly fond.

'Anything wrong with it?' asked the proprietor anxiously.

'No, but I'm not hungry.'

'It's the heat. You don't seem to be able to take the heat.'

He, too, scrutinized him as if to detect on his face the traces of God knows what ailment.

Couldn't they leave him alone? He did not have to justify himself to anyone, and everyone was observing and judging him.

Was he judging Nelly? Had he ever judged Angèle, his mother, Marguerite?

He finally got angry, lumped them all together, regarding them as enemies. Now, if men did the same . . .

He did not return home but jumped on a passing bus. He got off on Boulevard Saint-Michel and made for the quays. He walked for a long time, but without looking at the barges that were unloading, a thing that had always fascinated him.

He hardly looked at his former house. As for the home of his parents, of his childhood, behind the lock at Charenton, it had long since been demolished to make way for a low-cost housing project.

He was too tired to walk to the Rue des Feuillantines. He waited for a bus, feeling sullen and anxious. He had a smell of dust in his nostrils, and his shoes hurt him. He had not taken such a long walk in years.

He almost entered by the hallway, but he finally went into the café. Nelly was not behind the bar. He noticed a moving shadow behind the curtain of the kitchen door.

He felt no jealousy. She joined him, straightening out the bottom of her dress; a few minutes later, a man appeared on the pavement, his face ostensibly turned the other way.

'She came . . . '

He said nothing. He had nothing to say.

'She seemed confused . . . '

Perhaps because he had not taken his usual walk to Montsouris Park. Perhaps she thought he was ill.

'This time, she crossed the street.'

'Did she come in?'

'No . . . She almost did . . She touched the lamp post with her fingers . . . She looked at me as if she were going to photograph me, then she turned away and left.'

He did not ask:

'How did she look?'

He realized what an effort it had been for Marguerite to cross the street and approach the house. She had been on the point of entering . . . She would have been obliged to talk to Nelly. What would she have said? . . . Would she have dared ask for news about him? . . . Would she have begged Nelly to give him back to her?

'You'd better make up your mind.'

'About what?'

She shrugged, as if he were a child asking a foolish question.

'The two of you are playing cat-and-mouse.'

'I don't know what you mean.'

'You know very well, and you know how it will end.'

'How?'

She shrugged again.

'Here! Drink . . . '

They hardly said a word to each other as they watched television. It was as if each were alone in front of the screen. They went upstairs and said good night on the landing.

He slept better, though still oppressed, but he was less agitated than the night before. It was Nelly whom he now resented. He did the morning chores mechanically, and when she came down they avoided looking at each other.

Marguerite was there again at ten o'clock. He did not look her in the face either. His gaze became shifty, as if he wanted to keep a secret that the others were trying to wrest from him.

She finally left. His eyes followed her until she disappeared at the corner.

There were customers downstairs. He could hear the cheerful voices of the workmen who were treating each other to drinks during the morning break. He had done the same kind of thing when he was in charge of jobs and would accompany a foreman or contractor to a bar.

He was standing in front of Nelly's bed, a brass bed of the kind that was common when he was young. He went back to his room and opened his wardrobe, where he kept a bottle of red Bordeaux which he himself had drawn from the barrel in the cellar.

Like Théo . . . Théo who was dead . . . Death had taken him suddenly, when he was not expecting it, as it had taken his mother.

It would happen to him . . . It could happen at any moment to Marguerite, who had returned to her house and was alone in the kitchen.

Who would discover her body? And when?

He struggled and tried not to give in. Nelly was right. He really knew how it all would end. Then why not end it all now?

She was laughing downstairs at a coarse joke of one of the customers, but he was sure that she was listening to his footsteps on the floor above.

The suitcase was on top of the wardrobe. He reached up to get it, took his clothes off the hangers, and jumbled his linen with his extra pair of shoes.

He didn't care about what she would say or the way she would look at him. He was tired of being the object of other people's comments. He had the right to live as he saw fit, to follow his impulses.

He looked at himself in the mirror and thought he looked old.

What was the use of understanding? He had questioned himself during the last few days until his head ached.

He went down the stairs slowly, with his suitcase in his hand. He could have gone away without being seen, could have gone directly to the street and turned left.

He owed her money. He had not paid for his room or for the bottles he had emptied or for the glasses he had drunk at the bar.

The workmen had gone. The only one left was the plasterer with the head of a clown. He had become a regular visitor. Had he been on the other side of the door, with his eye on the kitchen curtain?

Nelly looked at him without manifesting any surprise.

'I suppose you want your bill?'

She was not angry. She spoke to him as usual. She looked for his page in the notebook.

'I'm not going to count the room.'

'I insist.'

'I don't know what it's worth nor even how many days you stayed.'

'Eleven.'

She seemed surprised that he had counted.

'Have it your own way. Let's say three francs a day.'

'That's too little. At least five.'

'Let's not argue about it. Fifty-two francs for your drinks.'

'Plus two meals.'

'Then I ought to deduct the lunch at Saint-Cloud . . . You were my guest.'

The red-headed plasterer waited without quite understanding what was going on. Bouin took a note from his wallet.

'Have you got the change?'

'Not enough.'

There was none in the till either.

'I'll go and get some.'

She left, crossed a spot of sunlight, and went to the pastry shop, the bell of which tinkled as she entered.

'Here we are! I think that does it. A Sancerre?'

He could not refuse. She poured herself a glass too.

'This one's on the house,' she said ironically.

He gulped down his drink and muttered a clumsy farewell. He left without turning around, feeling the eyes of Nelly and her companion on his back.

In a moment, they would be making love behind the door, and the thought pinched his heart.

He followed the familiar itinerary, one that he had followed for years. In the yard of the hospital, women, children, and old people were queuing in front of the door of the dispensary. Farther off, a Black Maria was waiting in front of the prison.

He turned to the left, into the alley. On one side, the houses were empty. The blinds were closed on the ground floor. The windows on the upper floor were without curtains.

The line that separated light and shadow ran right down the middle of the gutter.

He did not use the key, which he had kept without meaning to. He put down his suitcase on the pavement and rang the bell. He listened attentively and was surprised by the silence inside. He started when the door opened and when he saw half a face through a slight opening.

He had prepared a slip of paper which he did not flick with the familiar movement of the thumb and middle finger. When the door opened wide, he handed it to her without a word.

Marguerite took it. She did not say anything, but looked anxious. She took her glasses from the pocket of her apron. She read it and, leaving the door open, entered the living room.

He crossed the threshold and recognized the smell and density of the air. In the living room, he saw the cage and the rigid parrot.

Marguerite was leaning over the piano and writing. His note was a question:

MADAME MARTIN?

And also a condition for his surrender. He was not coming back with his ears stinging. He was not begging for permission to resume his place in the house.

He was tempted to go upstairs at once and empty his suitcase, but he prepared to wait. Marguerite did not hand him the message which she had just written. She placed it on the piano. Sitting in her armchair, she picked up her knitting as if to make him realize that nothing had changed.

He walked over hesitantly and put out his hand:

I KICKED THE HARPY OUT.

She waited a long moment before raising her eyes to see whether he was satisfied. Then, as if nothing had happened during the last two weeks, she began knitting again and moving her lips.

It was not until the following spring that the demolition began. To begin with, cars drew up in front of the empty houses for several days, and groups of strangers kept coming and going. At times, workmen were with them, and occasionally one was startled to see them appear on the roofs, engaged in some kind of mysterious work.

Marguerite was very nervous and kept going to the window every half-hour to watch.

One morning when they went to do their shopping, one following the other, they found a cordon of police on the Rue de la Santé. Bouin thought at first that a prisoner had escaped, but when he returned, still following his wife at a distance of ten yards, he understood.

An attempt was being made to get a huge crane into the alley, and a crowd had gathered to witness the spectacle. The tractor moved forward, stopped, backed up, and started again cautiously, while a whole crew busied itself all about.

Marguerite went by disdainfully. He found her purchases abandoned on the kitchen table. When he went upstairs, he discovered that she had locked herself in the bedroom and he heard her crying.

It took the entire day to bring the crane as far as the front of their house, and the bronze Eros was almost knocked over.

A painful period was beginning. The following day, a lorry brought a huge iron ball to the site.

For two months, it was like a circus. The first blow was given on a Monday. The preceding days, veritable acrobats had balanced themselves on the roofs and then on the beams and fragments of walls and had tossed armfuls of tiles into the alley, where they broke with a great din.

He felt like saying:

'Don't stay at the window.'

Every new noise made her start, and she put her hand to her chest twenty times a day, as if she were suffering from a heart disease.

When the ball rose into the air, they both watched, each at a bedroom window. Down below, a man in a leather jacket had a whistle in his mouth. The alley was blocked off by a red and white barrier.

The ball first swung in the void like a pendulum, describing an arc that kept getting larger. At its highest point, it almost reached the walls. The progression was slow. Finally it struck, and a crack ran down house number 8 from top to bottom.

He was almost sure that he would hear Marguerite's scream, but he could not be sure because of the din.

The ball returned, struck again, and a wall collapsed in a cloud of dust. A fireplace remained suspended in space, stuck to what was left of a room with yellow-striped wallpaper.

The rubble had to be carried off day after day. The lorries worked in relays. When Marguerite and Bouin returned from their shopping, they were obliged to say who they were, for only residents of the alley were allowed to pass.

At five o'clock, everything fortunately calmed down, but it all began again the following morning at seven o'clock. Floors hung in mid-air for two or three days. A flight of stairs led nowhere.

And men were continually doing acrobatic tricks as they stood silhouetted against the sky.

The houses were knocked down one after the other and left holes like decayed teeth. Marguerite shuddered as she looked at them.

Several times during that period, he almost spoke to her; he wanted to say something, anything, appeasing words. He realized that it was too late now and that neither of them could turn back.

She even became aggressive again after sleepless nights. One day, eager to watch the demolition, in which he had come to take a passionate interest, he did not take his shower. Later in the day, he found a note on the piano.

372

Neither of them had the right to disarm. The game had become their life. It was as natural and necessary for them to send venomous notes to each other as for others to exchange pleasant words or kisses.

He was sure that he hated her, even if he did sometimes pity her. However, he did not hold it against her that she had brought him back to the alley by trickery, by displaying false anguish beneath the window on the Rue des Feuillantines.

Several times since then, he had seen a quickly repressed smile on her lips, no doubt when she thought about her victory.

She had triumphed over a woman much younger than she, a woman with whom he certainly made love.

She, the old woman, as the two of them must have called her, had therefore lost none of her power.

The crane departed, with the same difficulties as when it had arrived. It left behind heaps of broken bricks, plaster, scrap metal, and rubbish of all kinds, and then, for a month, there was no one to be seen. There was silence, complete calm, except at night when the rats began to prowl around the dustbins.

To be sure, there was almost nobody in the row of untouched houses. Everybody was in the country or at the seaside, some in Spain or Italy.

Even for someone other than Marguerite, someone who had not been born in the alley and lived all his life there, it was a depressing sight, to say nothing of the smell, a pervasive indefinable smell that recalled that of cemeteries where new graves have just been dug.

At the beginning of September, the lorries came back and the crane started functioning again to remove the rubble. When it was over, all that remained was the spectacle of the cellars, where a few sets of shelves and a broken barrel still lingered.

The gangs changed, as did the gestures and accents of the workmen.

It was now the turn of the excavators and the power drills, and Bouin, deafened by the noise, resumed the habit of spending part of the afternoon in Montsouris Park. He would take a book and sit on a bench, his former bench in the time of Nelly.

After two days, Marguerite, who must have followed him, sat down on another bench, almost opposite him, with her eternal knitting.

Tenants rang at the door, and he could hear them complaining vehemently in the living room.

There was nothing she could do about it. She was not even able to tell them when the work would be finished, and the family from number 5 moved two weeks later. The house remained empty, despite an advertisement in the newspaper.

The contractors must have fallen behind schedule. Instead of finishing at five o'clock, the work continued until seven, and when the days grew shorter they installed electric floodlights.

Was it a matter of bad organization? Suddenly the site was a veritable anthill in upheaval and then, abruptly, there was no one on the site for weeks. In the café where Bouin went for his glass of wine, people said that the construction company had run out of funds and that the work would be taken over by another firm with the help of a big bank.

Whom was one to believe? There were all sorts of rumours. The winter went by with alternating periods of deafening noise and silence.

Marguerite dragged about like someone who has received a fatal blow. She was more and more colourless, and when she did her shopping, she sometimes stopped to put her hand on her chest and forced a smile so that the passers-by would not notice.

She did not want people to pity her or ask her questions about her health. When she stopped in the street, she pretended to be looking in a window. Then she would walk on with a less assured gait.

Perhaps she was simply putting on an act for Emile. He knew she was capable of it, and that was why he was never alarmed for very long.

When the butcher's wife asked her, 'Aren't you well, Madame Bouin? You look a bit tired,' she had replied, 'I'm fine. Let me have a very small cutlet.'

The butcher's wife was from the south, and in her language, being a bit tired meant being at death's door.

Bouin also began to feel the effects of what was going on and started walking almost as she did. He would start and sigh as soon as one of the machines began to operate.

He avoided the Rue des Feuillantines, made an effort not to think about it. What was stranger was the fact that that thin slice of life now seemed to him almost incredible.

He had difficulty convincing himself that he had really lived there, that he had been free, that he had played at being the keeper of a café, and that at night an opulent woman with firm flesh undressed in front of him without any shame.

He had only to say a word, to make a gesture . . .

They had had lunch together on Sunday at Saint-Cloud, in a dance hall, like lovers, like a young couple . . .

Then, to take revenge, he took out his notebook with the thin slips of paper and printed in block letters:

THE CAT.

Chapter Eight

How much time had gone by since the morning, when, in spite of the flu, he had gone down to the cellar and found the stiff corpse of his cat?

He did not know exactly. The dates got mixed up. Besides, it was of no importance. Three years? Two years?

There had been Madame Martin. He had seen her again only once, from a distance, several months before. But she had probably left the neighbourhood, or else she did her shopping elsewhere.

There had been Nelly . . .

There had been Marguerite on the pavement opposite . . .

There had been the ball that swung against the sky and struck the walls between which human beings had lived and which still bore their traces . . .

There had been wind, rain, hail, snow . . .

The excavator had dug deeply into the ground. It had encountered pipes and cables and had burst a sewer pipe which had made the neighbourhood stink for three days.

There had been workmen with various accents, Italians, Spaniards, and, in the end, Turks . . .

There had been fierce notes from both Marguerite and himself . . .

There had been . . .

He was alive. He would get up at six o'clock, take his shower, shave, go downstairs, bring in the dustbin, then do his part of the household chores after drinking one and more often two or three glasses of wine.

Then the wood. He mustn't forget to split the wood. He mustn't forget anything. The routine had to be followed scrupulously.

November . . . The crusts of snow . . . The walls that were

beginning to rise up across the way, the girders in which iron rods were set before the concrete was poured.

It was five in the afternoon, and he had done everything that he had to do, his shopping, his cooking, his dishes. He had dozed in the armchair in the living room until semi-darkness had set in, and he had seen Marguerite sitting in her place.

She was as motionless as the parrot . . . She did not look at him . . . They had stopped looking at each other long ago . . .

He walked . . . He felt the need for fresh air . . . He had had a drink in a café . . . He was never drunk, but he drank, he drank a lot . . . He had better control himself.

'The bitches.'

He was not thinking of anyone. It was mechanical . . . The words recurred to him from time to time, like an incantation . . .

When they had still spoken to each other, in a distant past, Marguerite would murmur when he least expected it:

'Jesus, Mary, Joseph . . . '

And as he expressed surprise, she explained to him that she thereby acquired three hundred days of indulgence, three hundred days, if he understood correctly, that she would not have to spend in Purgatory.

He could have gone to Nelly's. She would have looked at him with a compassionate smile, for he had aged even more. Would he still have had the desire, the strength, to go behind the kitchen door with her?

Two years? . . . Three years? . . .

The fact is, he no longer knew. People went God knows where. Their comings and goings had no meaning, nor did the lighted shopwindows, which were depressing, since nobody looked at them because of the wind . . .

In the cinemas, people sat motionless, in rows, looking at photographs that moved . . .

It was he who was tired. He had expected it. Women have more endurance. The statistics were right . . .

When Angèle . . .

No, it was Nelly . . . But a Nelly who had Marguerite's smile . . .

Actually, they all had the same smile, a smile that meant that they would end by winning out . . .

. . . with her big hat and princess dress, a parasol in her hand, on the riverbank . . .

It was she who had told him that the dress was called a princess dress. He had seen them in the street, a long long time ago . . .

Cochin Hospital . . . Farther off, to the right, the prison . . . Between the two, the alley, which now had only one row of houses and where one was surprised to see from a distance windows that were lighted . . .

There were no lights in his house, that is, in Marguerite's house. He took the key from his pocket. He nervously opened the door in the darkness and silence.

He switched on the light and entered the living room. Nobody. The knitting on the floor. Nobody in the dining room, or the kitchen either. He went up as fast as he could. She had probably gone out on purpose, to give him a fright.

'Mar . . .'

He was about to call her by name, forgetting that they did not speak to each other.

He opened the door . . . He put on the light. And there she was, on the rug, as he expected to find her . . .

The sight did not surprise him. What was curious was that she had turned back her bed and taken off her dress. Death had struck her in her slip . . .

Had she called out? Had she uttered his name in the emptiness of the house without an answering voice?

He was seized with panic, went down the stairs, left the house without thinking of closing the door, and walked quickly to the corner of boulevard Arago where Dr Burnier lived. Bouin had never seen him. The doctor did not come to the house, but one day when Emile was following Marguerite, he had seen her enter the building and he had read his name on the plaque.

He rang and rang . . .

'What is it? The doctor isn't . . .'

A dark-skinned servant with a heavy foreign accent. A discreetly lit marble entrance hall.

'My wife . . .'

'I told you that the doctor . . .'

'But . . . It's my wife . . .'

She tried to close the door, but, as she looked at him, she suddenly changed her mind.

'What's the matter with you?'

'Nothing . . . It's my . . .'

He staggered forward. At the left was a Louis XVI bench covered with faded pink velvet, like one of the dresses . . .

The fog enveloping him also was pink.

When he opened his eyes, he saw at first only whiteness. It seemed to him that there was sunlight. Turning his head slightly, he distinguished beds, faces.

'Don't move.'

He tried to look the other way and succeeded. A grey-haired nurse was holding his wrist in one hand and a watch in the other.

'Sh . . .'

She was counting, moving her lips, silently, the way Marguerite counted her stitches.

'My . . .'

'Sh . . .'

'Where . . .'

'Lie still. Don't be afraid. You're at the hospital, and we're taking care of you . . . The professor will be here shortly.'

The word 'professor' made him wonder where he was – at school? He didn't have all his wits about him. His body was so numb that the nurse laid his hand on the bed without his feeling it.

'My wife . . .'

'I know . . . It's been attended to . . .'

The professor . . . Attended to . . . Attended to what? . . .

He found the strength to say: 'But she's dead.'

He thought he was screaming, and his voice could hardly be heard.

'Be quiet . . . Here he comes.'

She stood up in relief and spoke in a low voice to a middle-aged man in a white coat. They were both looking at him.

'Do you feel like vomiting?'

He did not know. He felt nothing. It was as if his body no longer belonged to him.

No nausea or sharp pains . . .

His left hand felt his chest, and he was surprised to find a rigid bandage under his fingers.

'You underwent an emergency operation last night ... Above all, you mustn't move.'

'My wife ... '

'It's being attended to ... '

'She's ... '

'Yes ... '

'What about me?'

The doctor could not refrain from smiling.

'You'll live, but I won't hide from you the fact that you'll be here a long time ... You'll have to be patient ... '

He promised. He had always been patient. He would be patient as long as they liked, as long as they allowed him to be.

He was ... It was hard to think. The doctor's smile ... There was ... He tried to find the word ... He did not find it ... There was no longer anything ...

Epalinges, 5 October 1966

More about Penguins and Pelicans

Some of the Simenon crime fiction available in Penguins

Maigret Meets a Milord
Maigret and the Hundred Gibbets
Maigret and the Enigmatic Lett
Maigret Stonewalled
Maigret at the Crossroads
Maigret Mystified
Sixth Simenon Omnibus*
Eighth Simenon Omnibus*

Not for sale in the U.S.A.
*Not for sale in the U.S.A. or Canada

The Seventh Simenon Omnibus

Maigret and the Killer

'Haunting account of a cat-and-mouse
encounter with a sad psychopath' –
Matthew Coady in the *Guardian*

'A small masterpiece' –
Andrew Hope in the *Evening Standard*

The Confessional

André Bar's parents doted on their son,
but hated each other.
A poignant study of loneliness.

Maigret Takes the Waters

An elderly spinster is strangled in Vichy,
and Maigret's holiday is unfortunately
interrupted.

'A splendid array of well-observed
characters, an immaculate plot, and
Maigret in his best form; the book is a
cure in itself' – *Glasgow Herald*

Not for sale in the U.S.A. or Canada